"What a pity. Leslie will miss my unveiling of our surprise, but then she knows about it already." Dr. Durrell chuckled and sipped his sherry.

"Unveiling a surprise? Professor, what are you talking about?" Lewis suddenly looked alarmed.

"Surely we can share our secrets with our good friends here. After all, Lewis, these people are students of history, not criminals."

Lewis Hunter's brows beetled in anger. "Listen, Dr. Durrell, I think we should—"

"Hush, Lewis, it's all right. We'll just ask our friends to keep this information under their hats, so to speak." The tubby scholar walked over to the mantlepiece. "Besides, I'm too excited to keep quiet any longer. Ladies and gentlemen, we have done it! We've found the treasures of the Abbey of St. Oswald of Northumbria! Or part of them, anyway."

He lifted a cloth and revealed a gold chalice, studded with jewels. . . .

ST. OSWALD'S NICHE

Laura Frankos

IVY BOOKS • NEW YORK

Ivy Books
Published by Ballantine Books
Copyright © 1991 by Laura Frankos Turtledove

All rights reserved under International and Pan-American Copyright Conventions. Published in the United States by Ballantine Books, a division of Random House, Inc., New York, and simultaneously in Canada by Random House of Canada Limited, Toronto.

Library of Congress Catalog Card Number: 91-92212

ISBN 0-8041-0530-8

Manufactured in the United States of America

First Edition: January 1992

To the memory of my mom, for all the cuppas;
to Barbara Mertz, for *all* her books;
and especially to Harry, who always said I could do it.

Author's Note

The city of York, of course, is real and beautiful. The medieval Abbey of St. Oswald's and the later Church of St. Oswald's which I describe in this book are completely fictitious and bear no resemblance to any actual ecclesiastical establishments which may have the same name. The museum mentioned here is equally imaginary. Certain other landmarks, however, such as York Minster, Clifford's Tower, and the Shambles, do exist and are well worth visiting if your travels take you to York (and I hope they do).

The characters in this novel are also fictitious, with the exception of actual historical figures. Gerard was archbishop of York from 1100 to 1108, was accused of the crimes I described, and was buried under the porch. The events surrounding the appointment, deposition, reappointment and murder of St. William FitzHerbert are also real, and far more convoluted than my pared-down summary. The accounts of Hugh the Chanter, Hugh of Flavigny and William of Malmesbury exist, and it is the historian's task to ferret out the facts from the inaccuracies within them. The chronicle of the Abbey of St. Oswald, like the abbey itself, is invented.

No real archaeologists would behave as recklessly and unprofessionally as mine do, or operate with such small crews, but that is the liberty of the novelist. Actual excavations in York are undertaken by the York Archaeological Trust, 47 Aldwark, York, England, YO1 2BX. They do outstanding work and deserve support.

Finally, any errors are entirely my own, and I take full responsibility for them.

+ + + + + + + + + + + + + + + + +

I

MOST PEOPLE TRAVEL to Canterbury as tourists, twentieth-century versions of medieval pilgrims. Jennet Walker was there ostensibly as a sightseer, but her real reason was to escape the presence of her Ph.D. advisor, Samuel Thomas Preston. Jennet had traveled to England with Preston to participate in a conference on Anglo-Norman studies. Afterward, she planned to spend the summer backpacking around Great Britain. She had passed her doctoral exams at UCLA that spring and felt she deserved a bit of a vacation. She had spent spring quarter practically glued to Preston as the "Golden Shark" propelled her toward her exams and dragged her through his seminar on medieval manuscripts. He occupied the seat next to her on yesterday's long flight from Los Angeles to London and talked nearly the entire way because he couldn't sleep on planes. While Jennet looked forward to the conference, she was not happy about three more days in close proximity to her mentor. She liked and admired Preston, but she simply had to get away, if only for the day, so she flashed her BritRail pass and hopped a train to Canterbury.

She sat on a wooden bench in the Old Butter Market, just outside Christ Church Gate, and munched on an egg-salad sandwich. *It wouldn't do to have a Wimpy burger stand in the middle of the medieval marketplace,* she thought. The sandwich vendor was mercifully unobtrusive.

1

The bees, however, were not. They seemed extremely interested in her lemon-lime soda and hovered about noisily. "Shoo," Jennet muttered, waving her hand at them. It had no effect. She shifted the other way. The bees followed. "Begone, bees," Jennet said. They ignored her.

Her confrontation drew the interest of an old man who was seated on an opposite bench. "Just stay still, my dear," he said, "or you'll spill your sarsaparilla. That would truly give them something to buzz about. If you sit still, you'll discover the bees won't find you so appealing."

"Easy for you to say!" Jennet replied. "You've finished your lunch!"

The old man chuckled and removed his hat. He mopped at his head with a gaudy handkerchief. He was completely bald, and his scalp reflected the early summer sun.

"We're having quite a hot spell for you visitors to our fair land. It must be close to eighty-five!"

Jennet laughed. "I'm from Los Angeles. I know what hot weather really is."

"Ah, a Californian! I haven't visited there for almost a decade." The old man replaced his hat and looked appraisingly at her. "Tell me," he said with a glance toward Christ Church Gate, "do you know why Becket was murdered?"

Hohoho, old man, Jennet thought. *You think you've got some air-headed California bimbo who spends all her time on the beach. You're probably planning to give me a little history lesson. Just you wait . . .*

She took a deep breath. "Thomas Becket had been Henry II's chancellor, and served him well. He was an excellent administrator. After Archbishop Theobald died, Henry required a faithful man to succeed him. He chose Thomas. The church had grown strong during Stephen's reign, and Henry hoped Thomas would help him knock it back down, particularly in the area of ecclesiastical jurisdiction.

"But Thomas immediately opposed Henry. Even so, at a council in Clarendon in 1164, Henry required accused clergymen found guilty in an ecclesiastical court to be turned over to the king's justice for punishment. Becket argued, then reluctantly went along. But he soon changed his mind, and sought papal absolution.

"That enraged Henry. Becket fled to France. They quarreled for six years, and a fresh battle broke out when Henry had his son crowned as his successor in 1170. The archbishop of York, Canterbury's longtime rival, performed the ceremony. When Becket published some papal bulls which suspended the archbishop of York, Henry bellowed to his household that they were all traitors because they couldn't rid him of this one man. Four knights took him at his word, slipped off from Normandy to England, and murdered Thomas." Jennet slurped thirstily at her soda and noticed, somewhat to her surprise, that the bees had vanished during her lecture.

The bald gentleman was staring at her with rather a different look in his eyes. "My word! Are you just exceptionally well informed, or have California schools taken to producing geniuses?"

"The former," Jennet said. "You just happened to stumble onto my academic specialty. I'm a graduate student in medieval history, and my forte is the Anglo-Norman period. I'm here for a conference in London."

"Fascinating stuff, history; I've studied a lot of it. What will happen at this conference?"

"I get to give a paper; I'm counting on two years of teaching Western Civilization to help me get over my stage fright. My Ph.D. advisor is also pontificating. I have to sit in the audience and look impressed and applaud loudly. Then I get to run around and listen to lots of tenured profs giving other papers and hope they notice me. And drink awful sherry."

"It sounds like quite a time. I'm sure you'll do well, my dear—you gave a lovely lecture on Becket. And to think I planned to tell you a little bit so you'd enjoy your visit more! Well, you've certainly put me in my place today. My wife will tell me that's what I get for trying to impress charming young ladies." He rose, tipped his hat. "Good luck, my dear." He soon vanished into the crowd; he was hardly taller than Jennet, and she was only five-three.

She wondered how anybody could ever imagine the British as stuffy and reserved. Everyone she'd met on her travels was friendly and helpful. She finished the sandwich, tidied up, and went on a Canterbury pilgrimage of her own to the cathedral. Her visit was a little hurried; she had to return to London on a later afternoon train. *If I get back late enough*, she plotted, *I can avoid seeing Preston until morning, and by then all the festivities will be under way.*

She planned well, and got back to her hotel room unseen. She called room service for a late dinner, and pored over her notes for her paper. When her dinner arrived, she tipped the pimply-faced youth who brought it and settled down to eat. *Such luxury!* she thought. Ordinarily she stayed in youth hostels when she traveled, but she felt she had to bend her budget to stay in the hotel where the conference was held. Seeing her tromping in with her backpack every day would give the wrong impression to all those big-name medievalists. Besides, room service was far more enjoyable than heating a can of soup at a hostel.

She sipped a cup of tea and stared at her much-worn, Xeroxed pages of Roger of Howden's *Gesta Regis Henrici Secundi* until she found her eyelids drooping. "Good night, Roger," she said, and she went to bed.

The next morning looked as glorious as the previous day. Although Jennet was genuinely looking forward to hearing some of the speakers and, if fortunate, to meeting them, she still felt it a crime to waste a sunny English day indoors.

With a lingering look at the clear skies, she headed toward the conference room. Most of the people had gathered about the tables loaded with tea, coffee, and pastries. Jennet grabbed a cup of tea and soon found herself in a conversation with two Dutch medievalists. It was enjoyable talk, and they made plans to meet again after the morning panels ended.

Jennet was on her way to Room C, where she would give her paper, when she saw the bulky figure of Dr. Preston. "Jennet! I've been looking everywhere for you! You do know you're on this morning, don't you?" he bellowed.

"Yes, Dr. Preston, I'm on my way," Jennet said, thinking, *Oh, God, now he's going to get all possessive and start showing off.* Sure enough, Preston grabbed her arm. "Louis," he called to another portly man. "This is one of my students, Jennet Walker. Jennet, meet Professor Louis Bizet."

"I'm very pleased to meet you, sir. Perhaps we could talk later? Dr. Preston, I really have to get over to Room C."

Bizet smiled. "But of course! I understand you will be giving a paper? Come then, Samuel, we can all chat later. Let us find some seats and let Miss Walker prepare."

Bizet had some clout, obviously, for Preston was not usually shut up so effectively. He led the way to Room C, which was gradually filling. Jennet went up to the speakers' table and met her fellow panelists, a student from New York and a Japanese professor. The panel's topic was Richard's governorship of Aquitaine under his father Henry II's rule.

The girl from New York went first. Jennet had already read the other panelists' papers while preparing for the session, so she surveyed the crowd while the other girl talked. She doubted she'd recognize very many people; medievalists, unlike best-selling novelists, do not get their pictures plastered on the back covers of their books. Still, there was

Professor Staley from Michigan, Professor Willis from
Berkeley, and that charming Professor Benzinger from
Cambridge whom she'd met when he gave a guest seminar
at her university last year. . . .

Suddenly Jennet spotted another familiar face: the bald
gentleman from Canterbury. He caught her bewildered gaze
and grinned outrageously at her. What was he doing here?
Good God, maybe he was a Somebody. And all those things
she'd said yesterday! What must he think of her? He kept on
grinning. She had to smile back; the whole situation was
just too idiotic.

Soon it was her turn, and she bravely took the podium
and discussed Richard's capture of the castle of Arnold of
Bouteville at Castillon-sur-Dordogne. Jennet's contention
was that it had been a far more difficult task than the chroniclers (including Roger of Howden) described. When her
presentation and that of the Japanese medievalist ended, the
audience began to ask questions. Jennet, to her relief,
fielded hers with ease. She kept glancing over at the bald
man, but he was just quietly smiling.

Preston stuck his hand in the air and asked her a leading
question that let her show off a bit. He certainly could be
bombastic, but he was brilliant and he did look out for his
students' welfare, which was more than a lot of profs did
these days.

After the questions ended, the crowd broke up into
smaller groups. Some people hurried off to catch other panels, others stayed to chat. Preston hovered over Jennet like
a mother hen with a chick. "You did great," he whispered,
squeezing her shoulder. "That's doing the old man proud!"
Jennet nodded her thanks and allowed him to introduce her
to several more of his colleagues, but she had her eye on the
bald man. Finally Preston noticed him also.

"Edwin! So good to see you! I'm surprised you dragged
yourself away from St. Oswald's. Last I'd heard, you were

buried in work. I want you to meet one of my students, Jennet Walker. Jennet, this is Edwin Durrell.''

Jennet felt her stomach lurch, her throat tighten, and her jaw drop all at once. Edwin Durrell! She'd given a lecture on Thomas Becket to Edwin Durrell, one of the greatest living medievalists in the world? She wondered if there was a hole somewhere to dive into.

''I'm delighted,'' said Dr. Durrell, ''but then, we've already met. That was an excellent paper you gave, Miss Walker, though I almost prefer the irreverent tone of yesterday's talk.'' He grinned again. Jennet blushed, mumbled thanks. Preston looked confused.

''What do you mean, you've already met? Jennet, why didn't you tell me?'' Preston clearly felt that it was his duty to make connections for his grad students.

''It was a chance encounter, Samuel,'' Dr. Durrell said. ''Tell me, are you free for dinner? I'd love to take you and Miss Walker out to one of my favorite places. And Lillian also, if she's come with you.''

Preston nodded. ''Can't leave Lillian behind if I go to Europe. She uses it as an excuse to shop. If I can drag her out of Harrod's, we'd love to come. Right, Jennet?''

Jennet felt a momentary irritation at Preston's making all her decisions, but nothing on earth would stop her from going to dinner with Edwin Durrell. She suppressed an urge to rush out and join Mrs. Preston at Harrod's. What, she wondered, does one wear when dining with a legend?

She collected her wits. ''Of course. I can't think of anything I'd like better.''

Dr. Durrell grinned again. ''Shall we get you some tea, my dear? I know how dry one gets lecturing. And then there's a good panel at eleven on Stephen and the church.''

The rest of the day passed in a blur. Somehow Jennet found herself smack in the middle of an international ensemble of renowned medievalists. Various professors, rec-

ognizing Dr. Durrell, came up to greet him, and the cherubic
Englishman promptly introduced them all to Jennet.

She felt rather uncomfortable about the whole thing. Dr.
Durrell himself was a sweetheart, and all the medievalists
she was meeting were quite polite, but she kept having that
what-am-I-doing-here feeling. These men and women had
filled library shelves with their works; she'd had three articles published. She tried to slip away several times, but
Dr. Durrell caught her and dragged her back.

By the end of the afternoon, Jennet was annoyed. She
was used to Preston's methods. He occasionally monopo-
lized her, usually when some important person was in town.
She'd work as his flunky and be put on display as his prize
student. But Dr. Durrell, although he kept her constantly in
his presence, never once treated her as anything less than an
equal. Which was ridiculous, Jennet thought. What was the
old man up to?

Finally, the afternoon panels ended. By that time Dr.
Durrell had a group of around a dozen medievalists with
him. He addressed them all. "I've made reservations for
eight o'clock for a large table at the Mason's Arms for those
of you who would like to come. The address is 36 Fortnam
Street. Right now, though, I imagine we'd all like to freshen
up a bit. I'll see you there." He nodded to the group, then
walked toward the hotel elevators.

Jennet wanted to go up to her room also, but decided
she'd rather stay away from Dr. Durrell until she knew what
was going on. She hoped his interest in her was not of a
sexual nature. He seemed a courtly, polite gentleman, but
sometimes appearances were deceiving.

She thought she'd go to Charing Cross and poke around
in bookstores for a while, but as she headed out of the hotel
lobby she saw Lillian Preston, arms full of packages, trying
to open the door. Jennet's Girl Scout training surfaced, and
she ran to help.

"Thanks so much, Jennet," Mrs. Preston gasped. "I'm forever grateful. I'd be even more grateful if you'd carry me to my room."

"That's asking a bit much, Mrs. Preston, but I'll help with the bundles." They squeezed into the elevator.

Jennet glanced at her mentor's wife. Lillian Preston, for all her love of shopping, was no dummy. She was a highly respected scholar of Chinese history and had recently been named vice chair of the history department. She also was expert at caring for her husband, who frequently became so wrapped up in his work that he tuned out the real world. She had—and needed—real brains and plenty of common sense and patience. Jennet decided to chance a question.

"Mrs. Preston, how well do you know Edwin Durrell?"

"Edwin? I've known him for close to twenty years now. He's one of the loveliest people I know, and of course he's quite a genius. Why do you ask?"

The elevator door opened. Jennet hoped that the conversation would end before they reached the Prestons' room, or that Dr. Preston was still downstairs. She really didn't feel like having this discussion with him. Briefly, she explained how she'd met Dr. Durrell yesterday and his interest in her today. Mrs. Preston seemed more amused than anything but didn't answer until she unlocked her door and threw her bags on the bed. She sank into a chair.

"Oh, my feet! I should exercise more," she said. Jennet set down her load and waited. Then Mrs. Preston looked up at the grad student. "Jennet, I could tell you a lot of gossip about a lot of people at this conference. Samuel could probably tell you even more. But the only thing I can tell you about Edwin Durrell is that he's been happily married to a delightful lady for fifty-one years now. They have three grown children and a tribe of grandchildren. Probably great-grandchildren by now! Anyway, I think he's a dear, and I would eat my hat—or even my shoes—if he tried to make a move on you. I admit I don't know why he's kept you in his circle of buddies today, but my advice is just to enjoy the company. It certainly isn't lacking for brains. But then neither are you, Jennet. I don't think Samuel has ever been prouder of any student than you. Just feast yourself on good food, good drink, and good talk. Believe me, with that crowd there'll be plenty of everything."

"Thanks, Mrs. P. You've put my mind at rest," said Jennet. "I thought he was a love, but he kept hanging around me like a bodyguard. Also, I'm not used to being in such fast company, if you know what I mean."

"Have no fear, it won't be long before you're as fast as any of them. Then you'll have grad students trailing behind you!" Mrs. Preston sounded supremely confident. Jennet, all too aware of the job market for experts in Anglo-Saxon and Anglo-Norman military history, simply smiled and went to her room for a much-needed shower.

Clean and refreshed, she toweled and brushed her short, curly brown hair until it shone, then slipped into the one good dress she had brought from the States. It was dark green and played up the color of her hazel eyes.

She studied a map of London until she found the tiny side street where the Mason's Arms was located. It was in the old city, not too far from St. Paul's but some distance from the hotel. Jennet expected most of the party would go by taxi, but on her student's budget she tried to avoid unnecessary expenses. She was not adverse to taking the tube, however plebeian it might seem to her fellow guests.

She got off at Barbican Station and wandered about in the evening rush. She passed by the twelfth-century church of St. Bartholomew the Great, but it was locked for the evening. Jennet poked around the rather charming cemetery, reading Victorian tombstones until the light became too dim. Then she hurried over to find the Mason's Arms. She had no qualms about spirits of the dead haunting the grave sites; on the other hand, spirits of the living might find a solitary female in a poorly lit area tempting prey.

As she walked up the block, she saw Dr. Bizet and the Prestons emerge from a taxi. For a moment, silhouetted in the twilight, slender Lillian Preston looked like a bowling pin between two enormous balls. Jennet paused and let them enter the restaurant as a group. *I'm an individual*, she thought, *not just some adjunct to Sammy Boy*. She saw Dr. Takahashi arrive next, along with Professor Staley of Michigan. She waited several moments after they entered, then followed.

The Mason's Arms was an unassuming brick building, dark with decades of soot and dirt. The heavy oak door had a lovely stained-glass window in it, but that and the restaurant's sign were the only outside decoration. Inside was altogether different. It was far more brightly lit than most eating establishments, Greek music blared on a stereo, and the aroma of roasted lamb with plenty of garlic dominated everything. Over on one side of the room was a long bar, crowded with patrons being served by a gray-haired Greek woman. The rest of the room was filled with small tables, which obviously could be jammed together for large parties. Jennet saw a number of Dr. Durrell's party already seated at the largest group of them.

She was admiring the posters of Greek statues and reliefs that decorated the room when a short dark man approached her. It was hard not to stare at him. He had the most incredibly bushy mustache Jennet had ever seen.

He bowed slightly. "You are one of Edwin's people? Please come this way." He elegantly took her by the hand and led her to the assembled tables. Dr. Durrell was seated at their head. He rose to greet her.

"Jennet, my dear, I'm so glad you could come. Michael, this is Jennet Walker of California. You must be certain to keep her glass and her plate filled, so she will know how hospitable we English can be. Jennet, this is Michael Stephanos, now owner and manager of this establishment. And doing as excellent a job as his father before him, I might add.''

Stephanos smiled. ''If all our patrons were as devoted as you, Edwin, we'd be opening a second restaurant. Do let me know if I can get you anything, Miss Walker. Some wine, perhaps?''

His accent was as thoroughly English as Dr. Durrell's, with no hint of anything foreign. It seemed odd, coming out of a face that looked as Greek as Pericles's—with mustaches. ''Some wine would be lovely,'' she answered, ''and I must compliment you on your decor.''

''Papa always said that his grandfather was so enraged when Lord Elgin brought the Parthenon reliefs to Britain that he followed them there. Actually, his motives were purely economic, but it's a good story. Let me get you your wine.''

The rest of the guests soon arrived and were seated. Stephanos clearly had high regard for Dr. Durrell; although he left the actual serving to the waiters, he hovered about and several times pulled up a chair to chat with the old man.

Jennet found herself between Professor Bizet and Mrs. Preston, and opposite an attractive young professor from Durham, Miles Beckwith. The conversation was lively, ranging from shop talk to the inevitable gossip, much of which centered on scholars Jennet knew purely by reputation. Miles Beckwith, clearly only a few years removed from his own university days, regaled them all with a story of one obstinate don.

''He got a divorce from his wife, you see, and he won custody of their cat. Was more devoted to it than to her, if you know what I mean. Anyway, he kept bringing it with him to his office, brought the cat pan and all. Smelled up the entire building; one secretary threatened to quit. Everyone asked him politely to leave the cat at home, but he wouldn't. Finally, he approached his chairman because he wanted to have a kitty door cut into his office door so dear Willow could come and go at will.

"For those of you who don't know, the office doors at Durham are solid oak, and several hundred years old. The chair told him the doors had been there a good deal longer than he or his cat, and that they would stay there, intact. The don picked up his pussy and announced his resignation. Last I heard of him, he'd taken a job at a small college where the doors are plywood and not nearly so venerable."

Miles addressed the entire group as he spoke, but kept sending more glances over Jennet's way than common courtesy required. She began to have higher hopes for the weekend. Not too bad: she'd met a group of experts in her field, given a good paper, was feasting on good food (and at somebody else's expense!), and now she was chatting with a charming young Englishman. She hoped the rest of her vacation would go as pleasantly.

All too soon, the evening grew late. Dr. Bizet and Dr. Takahashi rose together. "My very dear friend," Bizet said to Dr. Durrell, "thank you for such a splendid dinner, but I must retire. Some of you may sleep in late tomorrow, but I must moderate the morning's first papers."

"I also shall return to my room," said Dr. Takahashi. "I find my spirit is willing to continue the party, but my body thinks it is still in Tokyo."

Soon others began approaching Dr. Durrell to make their farewells. Jennet noticed, as she moved down to the end of the table, that Miles Beckwith was lingering off to one side. *Well*, she thought, *what have we here?*

"Dr. Durrell," she began, "I'd like to thank you for inviting me . . ."

He never allowed her to finish. "Think nothing of it, my

dear. I specifically wanted to have you along. I do hope you can oblige me and stay a short while longer? I've a bit of business I'd like to discuss with you and Samuel.''

So much for slipping away with young Professor Beckwith. Jennet really couldn't see running out on Dr. Durrell, not after such a delightful meal. Also, if the Prestons were staying, she reasoned that her host's intentions were honorable. She sat down in the chair he indicated.

Somewhat to her dismay, she saw Miles give his thanks and then depart alone, no doubt assuming she preferred Dr. Durrell's company to his own.

Michael Stephanos poured fresh coffee for his four remaining guests. Dr. Preston jabbered a bit about some Greek restaurants he favored back in the States, but neither Jennet nor Dr. Durrell paid him much attention. Each, it seemed, was trying to read the other's defenses, as if they were opposing chess players. There was a brief silence after Preston finished his paean to moussaka, then Dr. Durrell plunged in.

''I've probably confused the very devil out of you, poor girl, and I can just imagine what you've been thinking of me. Here this silly old man meets you by chance, asks you a question of medieval history, and spends a few moments in pleasant conversation. The next thing you know, he shows up at your conference, listens to you give a paper (quite a good one, I might add), and drags you off to dinner. I shouldn't be surprised if you wished to check my reputation!''

Here Jennet felt herself flush slightly, remembering her discussion with Mrs. Preston. Fortunately, Dr. Durrell continued without pausing.

''I can assure you I have no etchings to show you! Instead, I'd like to show you some archives: the archives of the Abbey of St. Oswald of Northumbria, to be precise.''

He paused to drink some coffee. Professor Preston inhaled deeply, as though about to speak, but then he exhaled again. *Thank you, Shark,* thought Jennet, *for leaving the ball in my court.* As calmly as she could, she asked, "In what capacity would I be looking at them?"

Dr. Durrell answered, "I need someone who can do secretarial work and act as my editorial assistant. My regular assistant, bless her, has just had a baby. Naturally, I knew she'd take a maternity leave, so I hired a replacement. The thing is, although she's a very good secretary, she's a modernist."

He said it sadly, as if being a modernist were some disease. "I didn't bother searching out a medievalist to help me this summer because I didn't think I'd be needing anything more than help with letters and such. Suddenly, though, my publishers are showing signs of life instead of sleeping like the dead. They've rushed galleys of my next book to me, with demands that I send them back as quickly as possible. Meanwhile, I'm trying to finish an edition of the *Life of St. Oswald* and supervise a small-scale excavation of the medieval abbey underneath the church itself. Actually, I supervise in a very general sense. There are some very competent archaeologists doing the real work; my digging days are long past. I am, however, preparing the excavation records."

He paused, folded his napkin neatly and laid it on the table. He spoke in a low, intense voice, eyes directly on Jennet. "And there are some other surprises in store."

It struck Jennet as odd; a sudden undercurrent of excitement in the midst of the professor's rather matter-of-fact description of his need for an assistant. But it was just that one sentence, for Dr. Durrell was rambling on as before.

"So, as you can see, I have many kettles, all boiling at once. It's only the start of the summer, but it's clear that this girl can't do what needs doing. I had, of course, long planned to come to this conference. It occurred to me that I might find some student here who might be interested in such a summer job. Ah, this sort of thing never happened to me before I retired from teaching! I knew what all the department's students had planned for their summers, knew which ones were available at any time.

"There you have it. I came here hoping to find a student who was both trained in medieval history and free for the summer. When I met you yesterday and learned of your background, I felt the Fates had conspired to drop you in my path. Can you forgive me for my silly ways? You see, I believed that somehow you would disappear, and I didn't want that to happen, not until I could present my offer to you. What do you say, my dear?"

Jennet was flabbergasted. One part of her wanted to scream, "Yes! When do I start?" Another part recalled how exhausted she had been when she finished her doctoral exams. She desperately wanted a break from academic prose. True, attending this conference had perked her interest in things medieval again, but she was so looking forward to vacation. On the other hand, "assistant editor to Dr. Edwin Durrell" would look awfully good on her resume.

She suddenly realized that everyone was waiting for her to say something. "I'm sorry," she said. "I feel rather like Tevye the Milkman, pondering my choices. Maybe you could tell me a little more?"

"Certainly, certainly," Dr. Durrell pulled out a much-folded paper and read off the official job description and the salary. Admittedly, it was not much, but medieval studies would never pay as well as say, computer engineering. The clincher came, when Dr. Durrell said, "There's a technical college in York that is closed during the summer, and they've given us use of their dormitories for free. There's a nice little group staying there: the workers on the St. Oswald's excavation, some students and archaeologists from a nearby Viking dig, and a team from one of the Roman sites, which includes some Americans. My own house is within walking distance of the college and St. Oswald's. Oh, I beg your pardon; it's not entirely free. You do have to pay for utilities.''

That did it. "I'll do it," she said loudly.

Dr. Durrell's round face beamed. "I'd so hoped you would. I knew you were just the person for the job. I haven't even mentioned the position to any of my colleagues here. Heaven knows enough of them would have students to fit the bill, but I do like doing things on my own. And now I've found you!

"I suppose, to be official, I should check your references." He grinned at Dr. Preston, who was remaining quiet to Jennet's astonishment and delight. "Well, Samuel, how to you rate this young lady?"

"Edwin, I've known her work since she was an undergrad. She asked me for a letter of recommendation to graduate school. I told her I'd write a short letter. It read: 'Admit her.' And I haven't regretted doing so."

Lillian snorted. "Of course you could get away with writing that kind of letter. You were on the department's admission committee that year."

"True, true," Preston agreed, "but you know how much I hate writing letters." He looked at Jennet. "I know how much you wanted your vacation, but I think you'll get a lot out of working with this man. And when you get back, maybe you can apply it to your dissertation."

"Argghh. You promised not to mention that word, not until October."

"Tut tut, my dear," said Dr. Durrell. "If you wish, we shall avoid discussion of such topics all summer, but I'm happy to be of service in any way."

From the corner of her eye, Jennet saw her advisor mak-

ing ghastly faces. She had the horrible feeling that if she
didn't return to California with the first chapters of her diss
complete, and with encouraging notes from E. Durrell ap-
pended, Preston would disown her. Time to take a stand,
she decided. "To be honest, Dr. Durrell, I had planned this
to be a vacation from academics. Now that you've offered
me this job, I'll do whatever's required, but I'd like to leave
my own material dormant."

Preston coughed, gave her a look that clearly said, "You
fool! Think of the opportunity!" Dr. Durrell, however,
smiled knowingly. From under the table came a loud thump.
Preston's expression changed to one of pain. Jennet de-
duced from Lillian's beatific smile that she had stepped on
her husband's foot.

Dr. Durrell rose then, and offered them all a ride back to
the hotel. He brought his guests to a small sporty car parked
in Stephanos' back lot. But for the English scholar's steady
stream of talk, the ride back was silent. Preston sulked all
the way.

When she entered the lobby, Dr. Durrell whispered to
Jennet, "Don't worry about your mentor. I'll convince him
that you should be able to do what you want."

"That's nice of you, but I can fight my own battles; I've
been doing it for a number of years with him. He fumes and
fusses, but he has been known to back down. I've learned
to take it in stride. A friend of mine, who didn't, ended up
quitting and got an ulcer to boot. This time, Dr. Preston will
have forgotten everything by morning."

As it turned out, that was exactly what happened.

The final two days of the conference were a delight.
Jennet finally overcame her feelings of inferiority at being
one of the few graduate students there and enjoyed herself
thoroughly. She had lunch with the two Dutchmen and at
the dinner banquet sat between Miles Beckwith and a professor from Cornwall who had read and admired her arti-

cles. That immediately endeared him to Jennet, although he looked to be a hundred and four and smelled of Scotch and peppermint, the latter no doubt to cover the former.

After the conference concluded, she checked out of the overpriced hotel and boarded a northbound train to York, ready to start a new job with one of the finest medievalists in the world.

++++++++++++++++++

II

TWO YEARS BEFORE, on her first trip to England, Jennet had fallen madly in love with the city of York. She had trouble explaining the feeling to anybody else—York was just something special to her, unlike any other city. She spent four glorious days there, marching around the city walls, climbing York Minster's tower, and having the time of her life. A feeling of exhilaration crept over her when the train pulled into the station. She was back!

Dr. Durrell had called ahead to let the others at the dormitories know she would be joining them, but Jennet had declined their offer of a ride. York was a pleasant city to walk in, so she planned to explore a little before meeting her new dorm mates. She stowed her backpack at the station baggage check and set off for a little sight-seeing.

She first stopped at the nearby National Railway Museum, which offered an outstanding collection of historic locomotives. This visit was more of a concession to her father's interests than her own; Michael Walker was a confirmed railroad junkie. Jennet recalled how perplexed she was at the age of six when she discovered that some people actually parked cars in their garages, instead of housing several hundred model trains. She never inherited her father's passion, but she had learned enough from him over the years to be properly impressed by the museum's great hall, which featured two turntables and over twenty-five

20

classic locomotives. She scooped up a handful of postcards and books, which she knew her father would enjoy, then headed toward York's great cathedral, the Minster.

She never got there. On her way, she walked through the Shambles, the old butchers' quarter. The medieval streets there were barely three feet wide, and the upper stories of the old buildings leaned dangerously toward each other. The Shambles were crowded with tourists that day, so she had to elbow her way through. Suddenly the crowd parted slightly, and she wondered if she had stepped into a time machine. There, in the middle of the street, were two Vikings.

As Jennet peered at the smiling Vikings, she realized that only one of them looked like the traditional picture of a Norseman: blond, bearded, long-haired. The other, though he was dressed in costume like his friend, was built like a Viking, but the kind that plays football in Minnesota. His coloring was dark. He had thick black hair and was extremely tan. The more Jonnet watched the dark Viking, the more familiar he looked. She couldn't place him from a distance, but she was convinced she knew him from somewhere. She decided to approach them.

The Vikings were collaring tourists and giving them fliers. Jennet picked up a discarded one. It was an advertisement for the Viking excavation. Perhaps these costumed salesmen were part of the group staying at the dorms.

The blond Viking noticed her first. "Arr, miss, welcome to Jorvik! My name is Harald Greycloak, and this be my comrade in arms, Erik Iverson! Permit me to give you this treasure map, which will guide you to ancient Viking gold in this fair city!" He handed her another copy of the ad for the excavation site.

Jennet curtsied. "I thank you kindly, Master Greycloak, but would I be correct in identifying you and your mate as natives not of mighty Jorvik, but distant Vinland?"

"Aye, that be so," answered "Erik." "Vinland must be your home as well, if I be not mistaken. To be exact, the southern Californian part of distant Vinland, if my memory serves me well. You study in a famous enclave of scholars there, as I have done also. Is not your name Jennet Walker?"

Recognition dawned. "That's right!" she replied. "And you're Matthew Jonas, aren't you? We were in Dr. Henley's seminar on the fall of Rome together; must have been three or four years ago. I thought you were one of her students. Have you taken up the Vikings now?"

Matthew shook his head. "Odin forbid! I've had enough trouble with Latin and Greek to want to mess with those Scandinavian languages! No, I'm still with Henley, and so is Harald here, AKA Pete Sharp of Johns Hopkins. Henley, for the moment, is not with us. Two days ago, she fell at our Roman site and sprained her wrist. She's feeling lousy now, so we're all on vacation until she wants to get back to work. We're staying in dorms with another couple of archaeological crews, so the Viking boys asked us if we'd mind drumming up some business for them. Part of their site is open to the public and decorated with requests for donations, you see."

"I'm sorry about Dr. Henley. I did a minor field in Roman history, and I like her. I hope she's not hurt badly."

"Nope," Matthew said, "more her ego than anything else. She should be back to work soon."

"And so will we, unfortunately," Pete said.

"Are you just visiting York?" asked Matthew. "We can show you the sights as well as the sites, if you take my meaning."

"No thanks," Jennet grinned. "But I'll be grateful if you can get me a room with a view in your dorms."

The two Vikings looked somewhat taken aback. "Uh, Jennet," Matt began, "we have a special arrangement . . ."

"Yes, yes, I know. Only the crews can stay there. I'll

have you know that you're looking at Dr. Durrell's new assistant.''

They stared. Then Matt burst out laughing, and Pete yelled, ''Wahoo! Let's see if we can keep this one away from Olaf, Matt! We've got a fighting chance; she's our countrywoman and we saw her first!''

''Olaf?'' Jennet asked. ''Is this another pseudo-Scandinavian?''

''No.'' Matthew rolled his eyes heavenward. ''Olaf is the genuine article. Or close enough, anyway, he's from the Orkney Islands. I'll not say another word. You'll be meeting the teeming horde soon enough.''

''Do you want to have lunch with us?'' Pete asked. ''We're due for a break soon.''

Jennet declined, saying she had eaten on the train. By now her curiosity was piqued, and she wanted to meet the rest of her summer companions. ''I think I'll just get my gear and move in,'' she said.

''Okay,'' Matt said. ''We'll see you this evening, then.''

On her way back to the station, Jennet indulged in a little sight-seeing. One couldn't help it in York; practically every other block had something worth seeing. She strolled down Piccadilly past the Merchant Adventurers' Guildhall with its splendid fourteenth-century timbered roof. Clifford's Tower, build in the thirteenth century on top of a Norman mound, loomed on her right. Fishergate Tower, one of the fortified gates on the city walls, was ahead. She promised herself that she'd return soon and climb the mound, and perhaps poke around the nearby Castle Folk Museum with its reconstructions of life through the centuries. She recalled an especially delightful exhibit of antique veterinary tools that paid tribute to Yorkshire's most famous vet, James Herriot.

Soon, soon, she promised herself. She walked briskly along the city walls to the station, where she picked up her backpack. She strapped it on, gave fleeting thought to a taxi, but vowed to make the hike on foot. After all, she had originally planned to spend her whole summer that way. A couple of miles fully laden should be a piece of cake.

Still, she was sweating in the early summer sun as she made her way along the north side of the city. She stopped for a moment on Ogleforth Street, in the shadow of the Minster, to gaze at the rather dull eighteenth-century brick building that was the church of St. Oswald. Here, no doubt, she'd be working with Dr. Durrell, while he and his crew tried to unearth parts of the original Norman abbey below the Georgian structure.

The technical college that housed the various crews was not inside the old city itself, but was just outside the Monk Bar gate. Jennet wandered around the small campus for a while before she found the dormitory. She knocked at the main entrance but received no answer, so she opened the door.

She had only a moment to glance around the cramped foyer, which was littered with papers, books, sweaters, and an assortment of sports gear. Greasy smoke poured down the hallway, and Jennet could hear incoherent yells. She dropped her pack and ran toward the racket.

The hallway ended in a dormitory kitchen. Jennet took in the scene in a split second: a grease fire blazing in a pan on the stove, a stocky redheaded man holding his left hand against his chest while squirting the fire with a water bottle, and several other people running in shouting from other doorways. Jennet flung open a likely cabinet and grabbed a large lid, which she placed on top of the frying pan. The redhead stared at her. Jennet stared back. "Don't you know not to put out a grease fire with water? The best way is to smother it."

"And who the devil might you be?" he bellowed, sucking on his knuckles.

A short man with shaggy brown hair chuckled. "If I didn't know better, I'd say she was the fire marshal. Actually, Douglas, I suspect this is our new American colleague. If her Latin is half as good as her rescue techniques, she'll be a definite asset to our team. I'm Roger Barclay, of the St. O.'s crew," he told Jennet.

"I'm not the fire marshal," she said, "but I was in the Girl Scouts. I *am* Jennet Walker. I gather Dr. Durrell told you I was coming?"

"He told Roger," a slight blonde girl answered, "and telling Roger is almost as good as announcing it on the local news." Roger stuck out his tongue at the girl, who thumbed her nose at him.

"My wife Amy," he said. "Good thing we're married, or I'd complain to Dr. Durrell about insubordination."

"Insubordination?" Amy said. "Listen, Professor Barclay, you may have got your degree before I did, but I've been on a good many more digs and I can tell you . . ."

"Hush, hush, what will our new colleague think? She's sure to find out all our sins soon enough—this miserable dorm has us tripping over each other all day—but let's not tell everything in the first five minutes!"

The looks the Barclays exchanged convinced Jennet that their bickering was all in fun and that there was a tight bond between them. Roger had rather an unkempt look about him, very peasant-like. Amy, though, was a petite beauty with long blond hair that curled at the ends. Her short-sleeved shirt revealed well-muscled arms. Clearly, Amy did not let her stature keep her from the harsh work of archaeology. Jennet then noticed that everyone in the room had calluses, scrapes, and scars on their hands and arms, as Matthew and Pete had. She felt slightly embarrassed to have painted fingernails.

Roger began introducing some of the others in the cramped kitchen. "The redhead with the red knuckles, whose bacon you just saved, is Douglas MacNucator, working with Dr. Graham's Viking team. His brother Kenneth is also with that team, and Olaf Guthfrith, a student from the Orkney Islands."

"Good God, Roger, how can we warn her about Olaf?" Amy asked.

A statuesque woman with a deep tan and broad shoulders had been quietly taking in the whole scene. She suddenly spoke up, in an American accent: "There's no way in the world to prepare for Olaf, short of wearing a chastity belt at all times. Earplugs are also useful." She thrust a hardened, calloused hand at Jennet. "I'm Carleen Clark, formerly of California State University, San Diego, now moldering in third-century Roman dust. Roger mentioned that you're from UCLA. This place is turning into an enclave of Bruins. Our dig's director teaches there, and one of my teammates, Matthew Jonas, is a UCLA grad. Do you know them?"

"Yes, Matt and I were in one of Dr. Henley's seminars a few years back. I met him and Pete Sharp just a while ago in the Shambles."

Douglas suddenly stopped treating his burned hand and looked up. "Were they wearing the costumes? Did they say if business is guid? Was it crowded in the Shambles?"

"Douglas had the idea of distributing leaflets while wearing Viking dress, so he is rather concerned about two Americans messing up his idea," Roger explained. "Actually, the Viking team has been so busy that he hasn't had a chance to play dress-up himself."

"Well, I think they were doing a decent job. For a moment, I wondered what century I was in," Jennet said.

"Och, if only ye could see Olaf and me in the suits." Douglas sighed. "We'd pull so many tourists into our dig, the coffers would overflow."

"More likely the Yorkshiremen would flee to their houses

and lock up their women, the way they had to in the Middle Ages," Carleen said. "Jennet, can we get you anything? Tea? Coffee? Munchies?"

"Something cold would be fine. I've been sight-seeing in full kit."

Douglas beat Carleen to the refrigerator and presented Jennet with a Fanta, an overwhelmingly sweet, orange soda. He placed the can before her with a flourish. "I fear I was a bit short with ye before. It was the sight of all my lovely lunch burning up to a crisp that put me in an ill manner."

"Apologies accepted. Does anybody know when I should get in touch with Dr. Durrell? I don't know what I should be doing."

"As little as possible for as long as possible," suggested Amy, who was busy making sandwiches. "Dr. D. is a dear, but he works like a dog. And works us like dogs, too. You'll probably do most of your stuff in his office. You don't have any formal archaeological training, do you?"

"No, but I'd be grateful for anything you could teach me. I didn't even plan to work this summer until I had an encounter with Dr. Durrell at the Anglo-Norman conference. I just passed my exams a few weeks ago and had come to give a paper and take a vacation." The others nodded understandingly. "Dr. Durrell offered me this job in front of my Ph.D. advisor. Brilliant planning. If I were crazy enough to turn him down, Samuel Preston would work in nasty ways to change my mind. Cut my stipends, eliminate future research assistantships, steal my passport. . . ."

"The old man is a sly devil," Roger chuckled. "You know, your coming is really cause for celebration. First, we'll have somebody competent working on Dr. D.'s notes."

"Huzzah! Up with Latinists!" Amy shouted.

Roger continued as if she had not spoken. "And second, he's invited all the crews to his place—he's got this huge house, had lots of kids, you see—for a big dinner tonight!"

"And his cook is Julia Child and James Beard all rolled into one!" Amy patted her stomach with glee.

"But not quite that fat," Roger said.

"How many of us are here in the dorm?" Jennet asked. She was having trouble keeping track of names and specialties.

"You make it eleven," said Carleen. She began ticking off fingers. "Three Romanists—me, Pete and Matthew; three at the Viking dig—two MacNucators and Olaf; three medievalists—our happily married couple here, and the director, Lewis Hunter. Plus Leslie Stafford, Dr. Durrell's assistant. Plus you. That's eleven, right?"

"Aye," said Douglas. "Guid thing you went in for history, not math."

They chatted for a while, then Jennet asked help in picking out a room. Douglas offered to act as a guide. He scooped up her pack and headed for the stairs. "The ground floor is fairly simple to remember," he said. "Ye've seen the kitchen and the front hall; to the right is a living room with a bonny fireplace, for which we ha' nae need in June. To the left are a storage room and a laundry room. We've given the first floor to the women and the second to the men." He used the British method of counting stories. Jennet automatically translated it to second and third floors.

She harrumphed. "Did you think we females couldn't climb another flight of stairs?"

Douglas blushed. "Weel, ye see, there's but the one lavatory and shower on each floor."

"Oh. All right. Simpler this way, I suppose. So where do the Barclays sleep?"

"They have the third floor to themselves. They're still newlyweds, so we agreed to let them alone. This first room is Carleen's, the one opposite is Leslie Stafford's. She's the lassie who had been Dr. Durrell's assistant before he found you. I gather she'll still be workin' for him; seems he has a mess o' projects to finish. And now, which o' the remaining luxury suites will you have?''

Jennet looked down the long dark hallway. "I'll take number 27, two doors down from Leslie's. It isn't likely that we'll bother each other, there being only three of us on this floor, but we don't have to crowd together.''

"Och, we're not all that quiet. You Americans throw a fine party. And we're always after excuses for holidays or picnics.''

"Sounds like fun.''

"Aye. Who wants to work when ye could play? The Romanists are always good for a bash, especially if there's plenty o' beer, and so is most of the St. Oswald's crew.''

"I guess that's me, though I'm not actually with the dig. It sounds wonderful. I wish I'd brought my guitar.''

Douglas's eyes sparkled. "I brought mine. An' Matthew has one. We've a piano in that living room, too. An' Olaf has a guitar and an accordion!''

She laughed. "Who ever said academics were narrow-minded specialists? If we didn't make our fortunes studying the past, we could always go on the road!''

"A grand idea. I'll leave you to your unpacking an' such. Give a shout if you need anything.'' He took the key to number 27 from the master ring, handed it to her.

"Thank you, Douglas. You're an excellent guide.''

"Any time. And I'd be happy to show ye the next floor as weel. Och, but not now. My fool of a brother's up there.''

"We'll see.'' Douglas's offer was made with a carefree air, but Jennet didn't want to commit herself to anything—or anyone—before finding out more about her new colleagues. Any time you put a group of males and females together in the same living quarters for an extended period, chemical changes started happening. Even if they were all history majors.

After Douglas went downstairs, Jennet studied her summer home. Like all dorm rooms, it was bare and impersonal. There was a bed with a gray-green spread, a chipped and scuffed nightstand with an austere lamp on it, and a wooden wardrobe. She thought of Jerome K. Jerome's essay "On Furnished Apartments": how they looked so lifeless without one's personal belongings, household goods, and knickknacks scattered here and there. Jennet remedied the situation by unzipping her pack and putting a pile of books and papers on the nightstand. Even the worn Xerox of Roger of Howden made it look more like home. It took just a few minutes to hang up her clothes. Then she pulled out her travel alarm and decided to rest for a bit.

She had been asleep for almost an hour and a half when the sound of voices woke her. She couldn't make out the words, nor tell from which direction they came. Chalk one up for British craftsmanship, she thought. The American dorms in which she'd lived as an undergrad had walls thin as cardboard. Nobody could keep anything a secret there.

Curious, she wondered if the woman's voice was that of Leslie Stafford or if it was Carleen's. She couldn't make out any kind of accent. A man's voice rumbled in response. Then all was silent. A few minutes later, a door clicked shut somewhere down the hall. Jennet turned to the pressing problem of what from her limited selection to wear to dinner.

Some time later, she went back downstairs. She wandered into the living room, where she found Douglas working on some papers at a large table. Carleen was sprawled in an easy chair with a thick book. A woman with long black hair tied in a ponytail sat typing at a small desk. Douglas was the only one to look up when she came in.

"Excuse me, Douglas, but I was wondering what time we're expected at the Durrells'."

He rose from the table, and Jennet instantly knew something was wrong. There was something more deliberate, more restrained, in his movement. "You're not the first and you won't be the last to make that mistake. I'm Kenneth MacNucator, Douglas's brother."

"Oh. You're twins. I didn't realize . . ."

"And Douglas certainly wouldn't tell. He was probably plotting something devious, like convincing you he could be in two places at once. I take it you're Jennet Walker?"

"Yes. I'll be working with Dr. Durrell." She glanced over at the dark-haired girl, who continued to type, paying no attention to their conversation.

Carleen Clark, however, was watching. She waved a hand at Jennet, then decided to join in. "Hey, Leslie, the cavalry's here."

The typing stopped. "I beg your pardon?" The voice was cultured, cool.

Carleen tossed her head toward Jennet. "The cavalry. You know, reinforcements. Your savior. Somebody who can read all those dead languages." She put her nose back into her tome. "Jennet, this is Leslie Stafford. Leslie, Jennet Walker."

Kenneth shifted his big frame uneasily. Jennet had the distinct feeling something was going on here. Carleen clearly didn't like Leslie. She cleared her throat. "I'm glad to meet you at last. I understand you'll be staying on with Dr. Durrell? I'll be looking to you to show me the ropes."

Leslie did not look at her with anything like warmth. "Really, Miss Walker, I don't know how I can show you any 'ropes.' First of all, I have only been in this post for three weeks. Second, as Miss Clark points out, I am not a medievalist. You will be working on the professor's projects that involve your skills. I shall have other duties. I could give you the number of the professor's regular assistant, who would be better able to help you. That is, of course, assuming she hasn't had her baby yet.''

She stood up, whipped her paper out of the typewriter. ''I took this job as a favor to Dr. Durrell, who has known my family for years, and to Dr. Hunter, the head of the St. Oswald's excavation. If you'll excuse me, I have work to do.'' She pushed past them and stalked down the hall.

Kenneth, Jennet realized, had been holding his breath. Now he let it out. ''Whisht! That one has a temper.''

''Bitch,'' muttered Carleen.

Jennet felt uncomfortable. ''Look, is she angry with me because I can read Latin and Anglo-Saxon? I'm not taking her job, am I? I thought I was just brought in to help with the work load.''

''Don't get defensive,'' said Carleen. ''She's just got her nose out of joint because you're here at all. It's not that you're a medievalist and truly qualified for this job—which she certainly isn't—but she thinks she can run all three of the digs that operate out of here. Plus, she's buddy-buddy with Lewis Hunter now. I don't think she wants anybody moving onto her territory.''

''I don't mean to make any trouble. The only reason I'm here at all is a chance encounter.''

Kenneth MacNucator said, ''I wouldn't worry about it. Once you start doing what you were hired to do, she'll settle down to her own work. This isna the first display of temper we've seen from Leslie. As for the party, we'll be leaving in about fifteen minutes. It's only four blocks away and a very pleasant walk. That reminds me, I'd better write a note so Olaf won't think we've all left him alone. He's still at our dig.'' He sat down again and began scribbling.

Jennet noticed something. ''You're left-handed. Is Douglas also? He burned his left hand earlier.''

"Oh, is that what happened? I asked, he just snarled at me. Clumsy fool. No, I'm left-handed, he's right-handed. That's one way to tell us apart. There's the door—maybe it's Olaf."

The two Vikings, Matthew and Pete, charged into the living room, tossing pieces of their costumes everywhere. "Douglas stopped by the Shambles," said Matthew, "and said that Dr. D. was having a 'Welcome Jennet' dinner. So we stopped handing out Viking leaflets so we could fill up our stomachs in civilian clothes. C'mon, Pete, if we hurry we can grab a fast shower. See you soon, Jennet."

Kenneth looked at his note, shrugged, and threw it away. "Wasted effort, if Douglas was there." Then he asked Jennet, "You have met Matthew and Pete?"

"Well, I just met Pete earlier today, when I ran into the two of them in the Shambles, but Matt and I had a seminar together a few years ago."

"Ah, you're at UCLA. Do you know Professor Jacobssen, who teaches Old Norse there? I asked Matthew, but he said the only Vikings he liked were the ones who play American football."

"I can see that," Jennet said, remembering her own thoughts. "A Romanist doesn't have much need for knowing the *Elder Edda.* But yes, I took a survey course with Jacobssen on Viking literature two years ago. It was a lot of fun, and I learned some useful things." They chatted for a while about the sagas. Then the Americans returned, Pete with his long hair still wet.

"Shall we escort our guest of honor?" asked Matthew.

"Guest of honor!" snorted Jennet. "Starting tomorrow, I'm a working stiff just like you. Though I don't really consider standing around in a costume all day as work."

"Hey," complained Pete, "we drummed up a lot of business for the dig. Do we get any of it? No. Do the tourists ever wander over to *our* dig? No. Maybe we should dress up as Romans, Matt. Toga parties are always popular. Got any spare sheets?''

"Even if you did dress up, it wouldn't make that collection of postholes you call a dig any more interesting to the average tourist," said Kenneth. "Olaf and I have decorated our site with posters and pictures. We have even less to display than you, but we've made it more eye-appealing."

He opened the door and led them out onto the street. They argued along the way about the merits of letting the public into a dig. Both the Viking and the Roman crews permitted it, and tried to request "donations." The St. Oswald's dig, however, was restricted, as it took place under the later church.

The Durrells lived in a quiet neighborhood of stately houses dating from the twenties. Trees shaded the street and almost every yard boasted lovely gardens, some of them so bursting with summer flowers that the houses seemed to peep from behind, awkwardly taking up space which could have provided more blossoms. Roses were clearly the flower of choice, and the walkway to the Durrell home was lined with bushes of several varieties. Jennet and her group met most of the others by the prize of the garden, a huge specimen ablaze with white roses. The Barclays were talking with a slender man in his forties, presumably Lewis Hunter. Douglas stood beside a barrel-chested man who was conspicuous for two reasons. First, he was taller than Douglas, who checked in at over six feet. Next, his hair was so blond it was almost as white as the roses. This must be the mysterious Olaf, Jennet decided. Douglas poked his companion, who looked up and immediately headed in Jennet's direction, his walrus-like mustache twitching into a grin.

Suddenly the door opened and Dr. Durrell welcomed them. His scalp shone under the porch light. "Come in, come in, so good to see you all. We'll have introductions inside, I think. Here's Betsy, my wife." Mrs. Durrell was a diminutive woman with curly gray hair. She greeted Jennet cheerfully and hurried off to the kitchen, leaving her husband to tend bar.

"Well now," he said a few minutes later, "do you all have your poisons? I gather Jennet has already met some of you. Who needs introducing?"

The thin man began to rise, but the burly blond was faster. "I am Olaf Guthfrith of Orkney, and most pleased to meet you," he said, confirming Jennet's guess. He had a beautiful speaking voice, with a slight accent.

"And I'm Lewis Hunter. We'll be working together quite often this summer. I'm doing the actual digging at St. Oswald's, but the professor handles the paperwork, and that's where you come in."

"Tut, tut, Lewis," said Dr. Durrell. "Let's not start in on the poor girl till morning. That reminds me, where is Leslie?"

"I spoke with her just a while ago," said Lewis. "She's not feeling well, so she planned an early night."

Jennet, Kenneth, and Carleen exchanged glances, but said nothing.

"What a pity. I do hope she feels better. She'll miss my unveiling our surprise, but then she knows about it already." Dr. Durrell chuckled and sipped at his sherry.

"Unveiling a surprise? Professor, what are you talking about?" Lewis suddenly looked alarmed.

"You know, my boy. And Jennet will have to know, since she'll be typing our notes on it. I certainly don't mean to make it public yet, not until we know more, but surely we can share our secrets with our good friends here. After all, Lewis, these people here are students of history, not criminals."

Most of the students of history in the room looked puzzled. The Barclays appeared relieved. Lewis Hunter's brows beetled in anger. "Listen, Dr. Durrell, I think we should—"

"Hush, Lewis, it's all right. We'll just ask our friends to keep this information under their hats, so to speak." The tubby scholar walked over to the mantlepiece. "Besides, I'm too excited to keep quiet any longer. Ladies and gentlemen, we have done it! We've found the treasures of the Abbey of St. Oswald of Northumbria! Or part of them, anyway."

He lifted a cloth and revealed a gold chalice, studded with jewels.

III

Lewis stormed over to the fireplace. "Are you out of your mind? I thought we agreed not to go public with this discovery until we were more certain about just how much there is in the walls! Now I find you've been carting one of the chalices all over York and you're blabbing about it to everyone!" His skin, naturally dark, flushed deep red with rage.

For a moment, Dr. Durrell's expression was that of the little boy caught with his hand in the cookie jar. Then his smile dissolved into a frown. Jennet feared he would start shouting in return, but he just turned his back on his angry associate and contemplated the chalice.

"Beautiful, isn't it? And there are three more like it, too." He took a deep breath. "Lewis, listen to me. I still think we should wait another week or so before releasing our news to the press. But these are our friends, our colleagues. We can trust them." He turned to the others. "You see, St. Oswald's security system isn't that secure. Nobody thought we'd find anything here, but we've stumbled onto a chest sealed in a niche in the walls in the sixteenth century."

"Frightened monks hiding their goodies from Henry VIII's boys?" asked Matthew.

"Just so. One of the things I've been working on is a sixteenth-century edition of the *Life of St. Oswald*, which includes a summary of the abbey's chronicle—the high-lights, you could call it. Anyway, the final chapter mentions that before fleeing during the Dissolutions, the monks hid the abbey's treasury, relics, and a tapestry.''

"That happened often, I expect," said Kenneth. "But you found a stash that Henry missed."

"An' to think I was celebratin' last week when I found that buttonhook," muttered Douglas. "Just what all did ye find?"

"Roger found it," Amy said proudly.

"Could have been you or Lewis just as easily," her husband said. "I was in the right place, that's all. We found a silver casket with the arms of Oswald on it. It contained the four chalices, two boxes of coins, several small paint-ings depicting scenes from the life of St. Oswald, altar cloths and other church material, and a box of relics.''

"That's not all." Lewis suddenly returned to the conver-sation. He had been sulking in his chair, nursing a glass of beer. Jennet supposed he felt the damage was done, and he would have to put up with it. "We've found three more editions of the Abbey's chronicle, with substantially differ-ent accounts from the standard text in the Rolls Series.''

When Dr. Durrell uncovered the chalice, it excited the treasure hunter in the hearts of all those present. Everyone, and especially struggling archaeologists, dreams of finding shining relics of gold and silver. Lewis's revelation, how-ever, touched the historian in all of them. Lovely golden chalices please the eye and tell of an era's craftsmanship, but new editions of chronicles are even more welcome.

Jennet felt an adrenalin rush. Perhaps she'd get to help with those! Wait until Preston heard! He'd probably offer to take her place!

Everyone, even the Romanists, started asking questions at once. "What're the differences?" "When do they date from?" "Are they copies of each other?"

"All in good time," chuckled the professor. "They appear to be copies of each other, dating from the fourteenth to fifteen centuries, but incorporating earlier material."

Roger Barclay looked smug. "It's an incredible addition to the materials we already have on the Church in York. It discusses the abbey's founding, adds a few snippets on the legend of St. Oswald, chronicles the work of some of the archbishops. Splendid stuff!"

Jennet asked, "Does it mention the dispute with Canterbury over the primacy?" One of her minor fields was ecclesiastical history, and she was quite familiar with this controversy. The classicists present, however, were not, so she added a little detail for their benefit.

"During the Anglo-Norman period, the archbishops of York had a running feud with their counterparts in Canterbury over which was Primate of England. One of our best sources for the York side was Hugh, the chanter at the cathedral. He's hysterically prejudiced, a kind of medieval cheerleader. I was wondering, does the abbey chronicle match Hugh's account of the same events?"

The professor beamed. "Now you all see why I hired this young lady! That's exactly the kind of thing we'll do this summer. To answer your question, yes, it does match Hugh. But it offers a less raucous account. Those monks were a staid bunch compared to the secular canons at the cathedral."

Betsy Durrell poked her head into the room and said, "Dinner is ready."

"We can continue discussing it at the table," said Dr. Durrell. "Betsy doesn't mind the shop talk, do you, my dear? But we can't keep Matilda's dinner waiting. You all know the way, I think, except our guest of honor. Jennet?" He turned to find her in the crowd, which had risen at Mrs. Durrell's entrance.

If he had trouble spotting her at once, it was because Olaf

and Douglas had both pushed their way to her side to see who would escort her to the table. She smiled sweetly at them both and stepped forward to take Dr. Durrell's arm. Douglas bristled, Olaf's mustaches twitched, and Matthew Jonas, chuckling, hurried to accompany Betsy Durrell.

The dinner was exquisite—chicken breasts in a cream sauce liberally spiked with champagne—and the conversation was lively. Lewis, after his angry outburst, cheered up considerably and described how they had discovered the loot.

"All we've found lately has been postholes," Pete said glumly.

"Forgive my ignorance," Carleen said, "but just who was St. Oswald, anyway? Anything after 476 A.D. is Greek to me, except, of course, that I know Greek."

"That's Roger's specialty," Lewis said. "Amy and I are better at art history. Roger works with hagiography, the study of saints and saints' lives."

Roger nodded. "Let's see how well I can boil this down. The best account is in Bede; nearly everything we have after that seems derived from the Venerable One, with a few other miracles thrown in here and there.

"Oswald was born in the middle of the seventh century, smack in the middle of the Dark Ages. His father Aethelferth was king of Northumbria. The Welsh king Cadwallon conquered Northumbria when Oswald was a youth. He went into exile. In 633, he killed Cadwallon and regained the kingdom.

"He'd become a Christian while in exile: he'd visited the monastery on the Irish island Iona, one of the great centers of knowledge in that dark time. He became pals with St. Aidan and later acted as his interpreter, having learned Irish during his exile.

"He brought Aidan and other missionaries to Northumbria, and spread Christianity through the land. Bede tells a

lovely tale of a feast given by the king. Some poor folk
come, begging for scraps. Oswald gives them his own food
and breaks a silver dish, distributing the pieces among the
crowd. Aidan is so moved, he grabs the king's hand and
proclaims, 'May this hand never perish!' "

Roger delivered the tale with dramatic emphasis. He
paused now, and seemed to expect something. "Well?"
asked Matthew. "Did it?"

"Of course not," Roger said. "Oswald did, but the hand
didn't. He died in battle in 642, and his arm was severed
and did not decay. It was kept in a silver casket at Bam-
burgh."

"So what happened to the rest of him?" Jennet asked.

"His mortal remains, like those of so many saints, are
scattered all over England," said Dr. Durrell. "I believe
most went to Bardney Abbey, while his head went first to
Lindisfarne, then to Durham."

"What about the relics you've found?" asked Kenneth.
"Are they Oswald's?"

"They're really only pieces, wrapped in crumbling cloth.
It's hard to tell just what's there. There were scraps of
parchment in the cloths, listing several saints' names, Oswald's among them. I've sent all of them to some specialists
I know, Dean at the University of Edinburgh and Harrington
at Belfast." Dr. Durrell patted his stomach. "I'm for dessert. Is anyone else?"

The rest of the evening passed quickly. Jennet got to
know her colleagues a little better as they talked about their
backgrounds and specialties. Lewis Hunter was a graduate
of Cambridge who specialized in art history and archaeology. He had worked at a number of digs throughout England in the last two decades and, from his comments, at
almost as many universities. Jennet pondered what was
keeping him from finding a tenured spot someplace.

The MacNucators and Olaf Guthfrith were students at the

University of Edinburgh. The twins had their Ph.D. exams
scheduled for next winter, but Olaf had passed his last year
and was working on his dissertation.

"Of course, I've left it at home for the summer. Archie
Graham, my mentor, would rather have me slaving in a
tenth-century, wattle-lined pit than sitting comfortably in
my air-conditioned flat, producing a work of scholarly genius."

"Your home's in Orkney, isn't it, Olaf?" asked Dr. Durrell. "I don't get as many chances to travel as I used to, but
in my youth I enjoyed visiting the Scottish islands, Shetland
especially."

Olaf made a curious noise in his throat. Douglas laughed.
"Professor, ye've gone and insulted the man. Orkneymen
and Shetlanders consider themselves something other than
Scots. Didna ask me just what."

The big blonde shrugged his heavy shoulders. "We're an
independent lot. That's what comes of centuries of being
bounced between Norway and Scotland. But I'm unusual.
My mother's from Inverness, and I've spent most of my life
traveling with my father from London to Edinburgh to Canada to New York, then back home for a spell."

"Olaf's father's a stinking rich oil man," Amy remarked
cheerfully.

"No, no, no." Olaf sounded like he'd explained this
hundreds of times. "He *works* for an oil company, but
that's not where the money came from. You see, Father
inherited some from . . ."

"Spare us the explanations!" Roger rolled his eyes. "I
gather it was not procured through the vile, environmentally
nasty, oil industry."

"No."

Amy patted Olaf's brawny arm. "We love you anyway,
Olaf, and if you ever want to share some of the family
riches, there are plenty of poor folks in the dorm. Like

Roger and me, for example." She turned toward Jennet. "We're 'currently unaffiliated,' as the saying goes. Roger had a post at Marsden University, and I transferred from Kent to finish my degree in art history there, but we left last year. Not our kind of place."

Roger looked serious, as did the Durrells. "No, not the right place for us at all," Roger said. "But fortunately for our finances, we met up with Dr. Durrell again. Then came jolly old St. Oswald and his casket of goodies, and you know the rest."

Carleen was working on her dissertation also, Matthew and Pete had finished theirs recently. It was interesting to compare the youthful energy at the Durrells' dinner table with the comfortable stodginess of many of the older scholars Jennet had encountered at the conference. At what point, she wondered, did zeal turn into middle-aged complacency? Fortunately, not everyone wound up like that, or Jennet would not have chosen to enter academic life. There were always people like the Durrells who never seem to age, except in terms of how many birthdays they'd had.

At the party's end, they all thanked the Durrells and walked back to the dorms together. Olaf, who seemed to have a talent for languages, had entertained them with some folksongs during the evening. Now he tried bellowing an Irish love song to Jennet, but Douglas clapped his hand over the mustache.

"None o'that, me lad, ye'll wake the neighbors and they won't let the professor have any more parties."

Everyone agreed and, as if on cue, said, "Olaf, shut up!"

Olaf paid no heed, but he did lower the volume. "It's no good, Olaf," Jennet said. "I don't understand Erse."

"It's the thought that counts," he answered.

They walked into the dorms, laughing and joking. Jennet thought once more how lucky she was to have such a job fall into her lap. A delightful boss, exciting work, fabulous treasure, and her kind of folk as co-workers. She felt full of enthusiasm, ready to start at once.

"I'm for bed," Matthew announced. "It's hard work being a Viking all day."

The rest of the men agreed with his suggestion and began to march up the squeaky staircase. "Not me," said Carleen, "I'm going to wallow in some more scholarly prose."

"You do this every night," said Olaf. "Don't you ever relax? Or at least read it in bed?"

"I do so relax. Sometimes. And this tome is so turgid, if I tried reading it in bed, I'd be asleep before the second paragraph. My goal is a chapter a night. It's better than tranquilizers, and there's no chance of ever getting addicted."

"What is this classic piece of scholarship?" Jennet asked. She'd wallowed through her share of ghastly academic prose and could readily sympathize.

"Untersuchungen zur Geschichte des Kaisers Septimius Severus," Carleen rattled off the German with ease. *"Schlafen Sie wohl!"*

"Gute Nacht!" Lewis replied.

"She's dedicated, isn't she?" said Jennet as she joined the procession.

"She is that," said Kenneth, who was directly ahead of her. "Well, here's your floor. Good night, and welcome."

The hallway was dimly lit by two low-wattage bulbs, one by the stairwell, the other farther down the hall by the bathroom. As Jennet walked towards her room, humming snatches of Olaf's ballad, she saw something just outside her own doorway. She knelt and picked it up. It was a red cloth billfold of Oriental design, with kimono-clad ladies holding parasols. She was about to open it to see if she could learn who owned it when Leslie's door opened. She emerged in a flowing silk bathrobe. She stopped suddenly when she saw what Jennet held.

"That's mine!" she remarked in surprise. "What're you doing with it?"

"Nothing. I just found it outside my door. I didn't even know who . . ."

"Give it to me!" Leslie grabbed it, scratching Jennet's wrist in the process. "Perhaps Dr. Durrell should check into his assistants' backgrounds more closely, insteady of just hiring someone off the street."

Jennet was so struck by the unjust accusation that she couldn't come up with any response. She stared at the other woman for a moment, then Leslie turned and stalked back into her room.

The encounter itself was trivial and stupid, but what bothered Jennet the most was how it had spoiled her euphoric mood.

The next few weeks found Jennet settling into the routines of work and dorm life. The professor told her of his schedule for the summer: first, copyedit the galleys for his forthcoming book on medieval monasticism, which he wanted finished as quickly as possible. Then they could plunge into the intriguing mysteries of the newly found versions of the Abbey's chronicles. Dr. Durrell had already gone over the manuscripts once and was desperately eager to get back to them, but felt he had to get his previous obligations out of the way. On top of all that, there were the excavation notes. Jennet soon learned the academic habits of her colleagues on the St. Oswald crew. Lewis Hunter's work was as neat, precise, and well-ordered as his clothes. Amy Barclay's notes tended to sprawl over sheets and need editing. Her spouse, on the other hand, had a sparse, almost shorthand style, sometimes so abbreviated it became thoroughly illegible.

The crew met with Dr. Durrell and Jennet and Leslie every other afternoon to discuss their progress. This obviously was a concession to Dr. Durrell's age. As he had remarked, he wasn't physically able to work on the site itself, but he wanted to keep close tabs on its developments. Jennet soon found out about the hostile conditions underneath the church when Lewis took her on a tour of the dig itself early one morning.

Jennet's first impression was that it was no job for a claustrophobic. They descended the metal stairwell to the church's undercroft. There was virtually no natural light, and Lewis insisted that they wear hard hats. Steel girders were everywhere, making a strange contrast to the medieval masonry.

"What's all this hardware?" Jennet asked, pointing to the lattice of girders.

"That's both the boon and the bane of archaeology in Britain," he said. "St. Oswald's was undergoing some much needed reconstruction of its foundations when the engineers found the principal outer walls of the twelfth-century monastery below, which had been wrecked during Henry VIII's reign. Construction work destroys much of our past, but also is responsible for many discoveries. The best examples here in York are the enormous Viking dig on Coppergate Street during the late seventies and the incredible excavations underneath the Minster which revealed the original Norman cathedral. Our site has a lot in common with the Minster, but fortunately, we're not pressured by the engineers as they were."

"Why was the crew at the Minster pressured?"

"It wasn't just the crew. The Minster was in danger of collapsing, so the engineers and the archaeologists worked round the clock to save both the foundations and the historical past. It's quite a story."

Jennet adjusted her hard hat and nervously looked upward. "St. Oswald's won't collapse, will it?"

"Have no fear, it's several centuries younger and isn't so

waterlogged below. Our engineers have agreed to let us mess about for a while before getting back to their welding. It was sheer good fortune that led to their finding those walls, which, in turn, led us to those mysterious niches mentioned in the *Life of St. Oswald*. Here, look." He crouched down, pointing at the walls. "You can see the supports the medieval masons used here: three running timbers through the walls, which were around seven feet thick. That's what we call timber grillage. They used Roman stones in the wall and Roman rubble in the mortar."

"Stealing from the best, no doubt. This vault looks interesting—the way the stonework on it looks like herringbone." Jennet fingered the unusual pattern of the small, thin stones.

"That's exactly what we call that kind of counter-pitched facing: herringbone. Again, they're using Roman materials, just like in the original cathedral. And these are our two famous niches."

At first, Jennet didn't see anything to distinguish the excavated areas from the rest of the undercroft, but Lewis turned up the high intensity lamps, and she could just barely see where the mortar differed in color and texture in the second niche where the treasure was found.

"When the sixteenth-century monks filled in the niche to hide the stash, they were out of Roman rubble. Had to use lesser quality mortar. That's the difference," said Lewis.

Jennet shook her head in admiration. "Your eyesight is better than mine."

He laughed. "We had help. Photography, which happens to be one of my hobbies, reveals differences better than the naked eye. That's another hint we picked up from the Minster excavations. They learned so much from photographs, they set up a darkroom on the site. We're rather small potatoes compared to them, so I just use my dorm room for developing negatives."

"Small in size, yes, but that treasure will have historians and art lovers gasping for decades."

"Indeed. And who knows what else we'll uncover?" Lewis looked thoughtful. "We estimate the wall runs along another thirty feet, so there's room for two more niches."

There was a horrendous clanging behind them as the Barclays descended the stairs. Amy looked utterly inappropriate in her hard hat and coveralls, but homely Roger wore them well.

"Hullo, Jen," he called, his voice echoing in the undercroft. "Have you come to join us moles in our tunneling?"

"Could always use another pair of hands," suggested Amy.

"No, thanks," Jennet said. "I've only been here ten minutes, and I already feel like the walls are caving in. Besides, the professor needs this pair of hands to make sense of those galleys."

"Californians!" Roger snorted. "Can't work without the sun."

"Be fair," said Lewis. "Jennet doesn't get any sun inside the office, either."

"At least she has windows," Amy said longingly. "And she gets to go the post office, too!"

"Which reminds me," said Lewis. "Could you please mail the four envelopes I left on your desk, Jennet? They're rather urgent."

"Certainly." And with that, she left the three archaeologists to their digging.

Although she admired their diligence, Jennet knew she'd never make a good archaeologist. She was far better at a keyboard than with chisels and picks. She quickly learned the professor's filing system and office routines from Leslie Stafford, earning praise from the English girl. Leslie's initial coldness abruptly vanished in those early weeks, and she chatted pleasantly about her schooling, travels, and family during idle moments in the office. Strangely, she made no further mention of the episode of the billfold. In a way, Jennet regretted it: she had thought up some good retorts. Leslie's cheerfulness was almost overwhelming at times. Jennet wondered if it was genuine and, if not, why she was putting on such an act.

The others noticed it, too. One morning at breakfast, Douglas bellowed, "Quit lookin' so damn peppy all the time, especially at seven in the mornin'!"

"And would you like a second cup of coffee, Douglas?" She offered him the pot.

"Bah!" He scraped his chair back and left the kitchen.

Carleen was eating a bowl of cottage cheese. She suddenly looked up. "I've been meaning to ask everybody, but it keeps slipping my mind: has anyone seen my gold pen? It's a Cross fine point, black ink, with my initials on it. A graduation present. It's been missing about three days."

Nobody knew anything about it. Lewis said, "I'm missing my portable alarm clock. I brought it downstairs the other day when I was cooking something and now I can't find it.

"I didn't know you could cook, Lewis," said Pete. "But while we're on the subject of missing goodies, I've lost my Walkman. And it had a tape in it, too: *Hotel California.*"

"You're always bringing it to the dig," said Matthew, who was picking raisins out of his cereal and piling them on his spoon. "Maybe you left it there, or maybe the locals swiped it, hungry for American rock 'n' roll."

"This they can find at the local music shop," said Olaf. "I think we have a poltergeist among us."

Jennet said nothing, but she was remembering Leslie's billfold. Then she noticed the English girl staring at her, but when their eyes met, Leslie quickly turned away.

"Well, I'm heading over to the church, so I'll ask the Barclays if they know something about this," said Lewis. "Are you ladies ready?" he asked Leslie and Jennet.

"I am," said Leslie.

Jennet suddenly had no desire to go strolling with Leslie. "No thanks, Lewis, I think I need some more caffeine before I start work."

"Ah, we all have mornings like that sometimes. I'll see you later."

"Sometimes?" said Matthew. "I'm like that every morning."

"Remind me not to marry you," said Carleen dryly.

"I wasn't planning to ask you," replied Matthew, but he gave Jennet a sly glance and flicked a raisin at Carleen.

Jennet, to her dismay, felt herself blushing, so she got up and went to make a piece of toast that she didn't really want.

"C'mon, partners," drawled Pete. "The boss lady is coming back today. No more Viking about, leering at the beautiful tourists, handing out leaflets. It's noses to the grindstone time."

"Dr. Henley's back? Please tell her hello for me," said Jennet.

"Sure," said Matthew. "Hurry up, Carleen, and finish that disgusting stuff. Why can't you eat cold pizza for breakfast like normal people?"

"Huh! You wouldn't know healthy food if I hit you in the face with some yogurt."

They continued arguing out the door. The silence that followed their departure seemed vast.

"That's what I like about you Americans," said Kenneth, who had buried his nose in the paper throughout breakfast. "You're so lively. Let's get to work, Olaf. 'Bye, Jennet."

She waited until everyone had left the building, then gathered her things to take to Dr. Durrell's office. *Really, what's the matter with me?* she wondered. *A couple of people have misplaced some things, Leslie gives me funny*

*looks, and I'm feeling all jittery inside. I know I haven't
done anything. So why do I feel so strange, as if something's wrong? It's probably all in my head.*

The peculiar feeling continued for most of the morning.
Then Jennet got so absorbed in proofreading the galleys of
Dr. Durrell's book, she lost track of time. When a shadow
fell across her desk, she jumped and let out a startled,
"Gak!"

"Is that any way to greet somebody thoughtful enough to
bring you your lunch?" Matthew said reproachfully.
"You'd better like Indian food, and heaps of curry."

"Lunch? Will you look at the time! How'd you know I
haven't had lunch yet?"

"Easy. There's no phone in this office, but Dr. D. has
one. I called and asked him if he knew if you'd gone to
lunch yet. He said no, he didn't think so. So, I took a
chance and ran over to the Tandoori Inn. Okay?" He sat on
the floor and began spreading napkins. "You may remain
seated at your desk like the lady you are, but I have the dust
of countless centuries on my pants."

"Don't be silly. I'll join you. Mmm! It smells wonderful!"

Matthew opened cartons and extracted plastic forks from
a large bag. He then dished out chicken, rice, peas, mush-
rooms, and flat bread, all accompanied by tiny containers of
chutney. They ate in silence for a while. Then he asked,
"How's it going here?"

"Do you mean, here, at work, or here, in York in general?"

"At work, for starters."

"It's fascinating. The dig is amazing, though I'm glad
not to be stuck down there myself. I do the tidying up of the
notes, so it's like being on the spot without the sweat. As
for my other duties, it's more pleasure than work. Dr. Durrell writes lovely, readable prose, the kind you'd find in the

nineteenth century, not like so many scholars today. They think they have to sound imposing and obscure to be effective. I'm at a sticky part right now, though, because the chapter I'm proofing has a lot of references to the Greek New Testament. The Vulgate I can handle, but I don't know any Greek."

Matt gave her a long, hard look. "How long have you been a grad student? Don't you know about pooling resources?" He waved a chicken leg in the air. "If I need help in an area that's not my specialty, I go to an expert if one's handy. We *all* do it. My specialty's end of the Western Empire, Carleen does the third-century crisis, so we overlap a good deal. Pete's is Roman religion, primarily Mithraism and the Oriental cults. Lewis does medieval art history. Roger, when he's not digging things up, is a whiz at paleography and hagiography. The MacNucators do medieval social history. Olaf plays with some kind of Scandinavian prosopographical stuff; who was who in late thirteenth-century Iceland and that sort of thing."

"So? We all have different specialties."

"The point is, silly, when you need help, you ask somebody who may know. How in God's name did you ever get this far? Do you know everything yourself? No, you've admitted you don't know Greek." His tone was mocking, but his eyes twinkled at Jennet, who was getting slightly flustered.

"All right. I see what you mean. We did our share of pooling talents back home. But I didn't think of it here. I mean, all of us are busy working on different jobs. It's not like we're all in the same seminar, doing the same material."

"True. But it's smart to know what's available. I mean, I'm not likely to ever need to know about Thorstein the Staff-Struck, but one day I may need help translating an article from Norwegian. I can go to Olaf for help." He took a long swig of cola.

"Oh. Whom should I ask for help with these references, then?"

Matthew confidently tapped his chest with his forefinger, then gaped in dismay at the grease stain it left. "Have to wash this shirt anyway—look no farther, Bo-Peep. This sheep can read your Greek. If you want to get technical, though, Pete's Greek is better than mine, but New Testament Greek is baby Greek, and I've had plenty of contact with it, doing early Christian fathers and the like. Just show me what you need done this evening."

"That would be a big help, Matt. Thanks. I was going to ask the professor, but he's so busy I hated to bother. I've been saving up all the pages with Greek on them for one of his free moments."

"We'll play with them tonight, then. Now I've got to run to get back before Henley notices I'm taking a longer-than-usual lunch. Can I leave the mess for you to clean?"

"It's the least I can do. Thank you for bringing it, and for offering to give me a hand."

That evening they settled down with the galleys and Jennet's notebook at the kitchen table. Matthew reasoned that they'd do a lot of talking, and evening was quiet time in the living room. "This way, we won't bother anyone, and we can help ourselves to the refrigerator."

It occurred to Jennet that they could work on the galleys in the privacy of Matthew's room, but she was oddly relieved that he suggested the kitchen instead. She soon found out that Matt knew his Greek well—he quickly breezed through the text. She also noticed again his sharp, quirky sense of humor. To her chagrin, he spotted two typographical errors she had missed in the main text, though he pointed out that one of them was in German and thus harder to spot.

"That doesn't make me feel better," she said. "It's the ones in Latin and German that I'm paid to catch. That's why I'm doing these proofs and not Leslie."

Matthew began to say something in reply, but instead suddenly reached for another page of galleys. "Let's see . . . This is from St. Paul to the Romans . . ."

It took three nights to get through all the references, and Jennet found herself sorry that their translation sessions came to an end. She thanked Matthew again, but he assured her that she could pay him back later. "Now I have some articles I want to read," he said, and went up to his room.

Jennet worked a little longer on the galleys, made a cup of tea, and went upstairs herself. The tea, unfortunately, perked her up instead of relaxing her as it usually did. She tossed and turned, bothered by brain-fuzz, her name for the irritating little thoughts that clutter up the mind when one is trying to sleep. She found herself worrying about Leslie, about the galleys, about typing the excavation notes (her typing was good, but not great), about fending off Olaf's next amorous advance, about Preston, about her exams (two months past, but she still got nervous thinking about them), and a dozen other petty problems. She was still awake at one, and was contemplating turning on a light to read a book when she heard a noise at her door.

"Who is it? Who's there?" she called softly.

The noise stopped. Puzzled, Jennet put on her robe and got out of bed to investigate. She opened the door and looked up and down the dim hallway. There was no one in sight. She was wondering if she'd imagined it when she heard a muffled noise downstairs.

If I had any sense, I'd turn around and go to bed, she thought. But she was wide awake, and ever since she'd been a child, clutterbumphs in the night had bothered her. If she went back to her room, she'd only lie there wondering what it was. Better investigate and find it was nothing than to let imaginary fears stalk her sleep.

She began to go down the stair, trying to mask the noise of her descent. The old suitcase creaked dreadfully. Jennet thought she heard another noise from somewhere else in the building but wasn't sure. She reached the entry hall and looked around. Everything seemed perfectly normal. The moon was full, its light glowing eerily through the double windows of the hall.

She stood there for a moment, feeling like a fool. Then she noticed the door of the small closet built into the staircase was ajar. She began to move toward it when there was a sudden shadow at the window. She whirled about, but it was gone.

An instant later, she heard keys jingling, and the front door opened. It was Lewis, carrying his briefcase. He flipped on the entry-hall light and blinked in surprise at finding Jennet standing there.

"You're up late, aren't you?" he asked. "Can't sleep?"

"No, I couldn't," she replied. "And then I thought I heard a noise, so I came down to see what it was."

He laughed. "Brave girl! Why didn't you rouse one of those behemoths from the Viking dig to chase your ghoulies away?"

She sniffed indignantly. "Where I come from, women deal with problems face-to-face. With the possible exception of large bugs."

He put his briefcase by the stairs. "Well, if it's not an insult to your independent spirit, may I join you in searching for the noisemaker? I'm very good at cockroach bashing, I might add."

"Sure." Now that the lights were on and she wasn't alone, the entire escapade seemed foolish to Jennet. She was especially embarrassed it was Lewis who had discovered her prowling in her bathrobe. For one thing, he was one of her superiors at St. Oswald's. For another, he was easily the oldest of those living in the dorm. And for a third, like most of the men here, he was attractive and single. Nobody likes to look silly, but all that made it worse. Now if Olaf or Douglas had found her, they were such hams that they could have played "brave macho male" to her "helpless female in distress," but everyone would realize it was a game. Lewis seemed to take everything so seriously.

They poked around, but found nothing amiss. Lewis pointed to the kitchen window, which was slightly open. "Maybe you heard the curtains flapping."

"I've been to too many rock concerts for my ears to be that good. It was probably just my imagination working overtime. Speaking of overtime, aren't you working late?"

Lewis was rummaging in the refrigerator. He pulled out two bottles of beer. "Funny, I never liked my beer ice-cold until I spent time in the States where everyone drinks it that way. I've been cooling mine ever since." He pushed a bottle at her. "Go on, it'll help you sleep.

"To answer your question, I was working on a press release for the dig. Dr. Durrell wants it soon. He's of the opinion that we've found all there is to find. As you know, I disagree. But it's up to him when we go public, so I've put it all together for his discretion." He yawned. "And now I'm tucking myself in bed with my beer, and I suggest you do the same."

Suddenly Jennet felt extraordinarily tired. "You're right. I'll see you in the morning."

Jennet woke up to shouting from downstairs. "Shut up, Douglas," she muttered. She felt grumpy and fuzzy from lack of sleep. She pulled on her jeans, a T-shirt, and slippers, and started for the bathroom. Then the words Douglas was bellowing filtered through her foggy brain.

". . . telling ye what happened. I coom downstairs and find the closet door open. I go to shut it, an' I see it willna shut 'cause the earplug wire from this tape recorder's stickin' oot!"

"And everything that's been missing is in there?" asked Matthew.

"Aye, it looks that way. Here's Pete's name on the recorder, an' a gold pen with C.A.C. on it, an' a clock, to say nothing of all these other odds an' ends."

"Some of them still have the original wrapping and price labels," Kenneth said, his voice like and yet unlike his brother's.

In full cry, Douglas could rival a foghorn, so it was only moments before everyone came clattering downstairs to see. Douglas held up each object and began his tale of discovery again, but Carleen cut him short.

"I've got my pen back, that's all I care about." She snatched it from his fingers. "And I don't intend to have it disappear again." She began to stomp upstairs.

Matthew said, "Hold it, Carleen. I think we should face an unpleasant fact: it looks like one of us is a kleptomaniac."

"A thief," Leslie muttered. She tugged at the cuffs of her robe and tightened the belt in a defensive manner.

"Thief, shoplifter, whatever," said Pete. "We can't have this kind of thing going on. Pretty soon we'll all start suspecting each other of all kinds of things. Not a healthy atmosphere to live in."

"I agree," said Lewis. "Let's make an announcement, as long as we're all assembled. To the culprit: stop these pranks instantly."

"Or face eternal damnation," added Pete. "Especially if

my Walkman vanishes again. Let's have breakfast.'' He clipped the device to his belt, popped on the headphones, and sauntered off to the kitchen, blond ponytail swinging. Carleen continued upstairs. The others wandered off except Lewis, who continued to stand in front of the small closet.

His black eyebrows beetled as he frowned. Jennet suddenly thought he seemed much older than his actual age. He rubbed his chin. ''Do you know anything about this, Jennet?'' he asked quietly.

''About the thefts? Just what we all know: that some things were stolen from Carleen, Pete, and you.''

''I'm afraid Leslie told me she saw you making off with her wallet, and I found you alone in the entry hall late last night. It does seem a little peculiar.''

''I don't know anything about these stolen things. As for Leslie's wallet, it was lying right in front of my door the other evening. I had no idea who owned it. She overreacted when she saw me holding it.''

Lewis shrugged. ''She can be high-strung. Well, maybe we'll talk about it later.'' He sounded almost paternal. The tone irritated her immensely.

''No, we won't. I'm not a thief, Lewis, and I'm dead serious about my innocence. I've never touched any of those things. Maybe we could take fingerprints or something. Call the police or keep quiet.''

Lewis looked offended. ''Let's not get carried away! I was just curious about the whole problem. Don't fret about it, and I apologize for my comments. I didn't mean to get you so upset.'' He began to walk toward the kitchen.

Jennet stamped up the creaky stairs, relishing each groan. When she reached the landing Matthew called softly from the men's floor:

''What was that all about?''

''A mere difference of opinion,'' she replied and headed for the bathroom.

She was in a foul mood all day, but fortunately Lewis and Leslie were both busy with other projects, and she didn't see them at all. She did snap at Dr. Durrell once, causing him to blink in surprise. She apologized instantly, pleading a bad headache. He offered an aspirin, but she declined.

Lewis wasn't at dinner either, which was a strange but tasty concoction of Kenneth's called "Chiddingly Hot Pot." Afterward, Jennet saw Leslie working at one of the desks in the living room, so she went back in the kitchen to look over the pantry in preparation for her next turn as chef. She found Olaf and Douglas at the table, translating Beatles songs into Old Norse.

"In heaven's name, why?" asked Carleen.

"It's good practice," said Roger, who was making tea.

"That's true," Jennet said. "I once translated 'Jabberwocky' into Anglo-Saxon."

"But why the Beatles?" Carleen persisted.

"We all know the words," said Olaf, "and some of the ballads translate quite nicely."

"But not 'Why Don't We Do It in the Road'?" asked Roger.

They all laughed, and Jennet joined in the translating, though her Norse was not that good. Then she scribbled a shopping list and went to bed, feeling much better. She decided that if Lewis ever bought up the subject of the stolen goods again, she would go to the police. Being the object of suspicion was no fun.

But it was not Lewis who next mentioned theft. It was Dr. Durrell. The group, almost in its entirety (Pete was in the shower), was having breakfast the next morning when the doorbell rang again and again. Amy answered it and found Dr. Durrell outside, ashen-faced.

"Amy, have you or Roger done something with the treasure?" he asked.

"Of course not, Professor. Come in, don't just stand

there.'' She guided him to a kitchen chair, put a cup in his hand. ''Whatever is the matter?''

The elderly man gulped at his tea. ''Leslie, Lewis, did either of you take the treasure? Of course you didn't, I'm forgetting the window.''

Lewis stood up. ''What are you talking about, Dr. Durrell?''

''The relics, my boy. They've been stolen from St. Oswald's. Everything gone, except the chronicles and the chalice that was at my house.''

++++++++++++++++++

IV

THAT DAY WENT by in a fuzzy blur. One minute, they were all eating scrambled eggs in domestic yet academic coziness. The next, or so it seemed, saw the St. Oswald's crew wandering around the church offices and assisting Detective Inspector Dennistoun and his assistant, Sergeant Corbett, in their investigations, much to the discomfiture of the small ecclesiastical staff.

The staff of the church had always looked on the archaeologists with a certain disdain. They tracked dust everywhere, they blocked parts of the church from use while they tunneled underneath; perhaps worst of all, they had appropriated two rooms from the office space for their own use. Now something of theirs was stolen, and this Inspector Dennistoun was poking his pointy nose into everything. *Really*, one could almost hear the dignified ladies think, *why on earth was it ever arranged that these people could come digging under our church?*

Inspector Dennistoun rather perfunctorily examined the broken window the thief used for entry. He then herded the crew into the larger office for questioning. Dr. Durrell was too shaken to be of much help; he sat in the room's one easy chair, his chubby face pale. Amy Barclay perched on the arm of the chair, looking like a mother hen keeping watch on a chick. Leslie Stafford seemed annoyed when told she could not yet return to her work, but found the young sergeant's good looks worth watching.

And Lewis Hunter, the dig's director, who was senior to everyone but Dr. Durrell, sat staring into space in a black rage. So Roger, his peasant features solemn and washed-out, brown hair characteristically mussed, acted as their spokesman.

Dennistoun whistled when he saw the photographs of the treasures. "Incredible! And all this is gone now? Everything you've dug up?"

"Well, no, not quite," said Roger. "Everything that was in the silver casket is gone, except for the three editions of the Abbey's chronicle and the one remaining gold chalice at Dr. Durrell's house."

Jennet heaved a huge sigh of relief, one the inspector quickly noticed. He directed his question at her: "These chronicles valuable, too? Like those fancy painted ones?"

"To a historian like me, they're priceless sources of information, but I imagine they wouldn't be as valuable on the black market as the art and religious items. But they aren't illuminated, like books of hours. That probably explains why they weren't taken." She felt uncomfortable under his intense stare, and then realized everyone else was watching her closely as well.

"Probably," Dennistoun said dryly. "So this is quite a haul you folks have found, isn't it?"

Roger said, "It's one of the finest of the century, certainly. The casket and most of the coins are from the sixteenth century, but the paintings are from the early 1300s, and the chalices are even older."

"Probably early twelfth century," muttered Amy, the art historian.

"So why is it that uneducated sods like me haven't heard all about it on the telly? Like Sutton Hoo and King Tut and that bunch digging up Camelot and the big Viking excavations here in the seventies. Why, I live on Castlegate, right near this place where they've been finding Viking remains this summer. Every time they find a pin or a buttonhook, they've got posters and pictures up all over.''

Olaf and the MacNucator twins looked slightly embarrassed at being praised for their efforts while their colleagues had suffered such a staggering loss.

Jennet said, ''They have a talented artist on their staff, Inspector. In their case, it pays to advertise. Our excavation is not able to accommodate tourists. There's barely enough room for the crew itself down there.''

The policeman hardly noticed her comment. He pressed on. ''I put it to you: why hasn't this great discovery been on the evening news yet? You've said you found it several weeks ago, I believe.''

Lewis snorted angrily and Roger cleared his throat, but Dr. Durrell answered. ''I fear it was my decision to keep the news from the media for a time. Ironically, I did it for reasons of security. I won't bore you with the details, but if you examine this diagram that shows our reconstruction of the original abbey, you'll find there aren't many places the monks could have hidden their valuables securely. And that silver casket was secure for over four hundred years.''

He rose heavily from the chair, gently pushing Amy aside. Dennistoun remained behind the professor's own desk, peering uncomprehendingly at the diagram. The decades-long habit of lecturing overcame Dr. Durrell, and he put aside his personal worries to instruct the policeman.

''We found nothing in this first niche, but then, of course, no archaeologist expects to find a fabulous treasure clearly labeled 'X marks the spot.' We then worked our way over to *this* niche, where we found the silver casket.'' He paused, perhaps remembering the thrilling moment when Roger discovered the hoard. He pulled out his handkerchief and mopped at his forehead, although the morning was cool.

"Leslie, dear, could you get me a glass of water, please? That's a love.

"Where was I? Oh, yes, we found the treasure here." He pointed to the diagram.

Dennistoun studied it, then remarked, "So you guess there're two more niches to explore?"

From small nods and thoughtful expressions, the speed with which he figured that out impressed the crew. Dennistoun's face was long and craggy, with a sharp nose and a cleft chin. It seemed composed of nothing but angles, like one of Picasso's paintings, but a long curved scar on his cheek disturbed the geometric symmetry.

"Very good, Inspector," said the professor. "We have estimated that there are two more niches to explore. We hope to get to the third one within the month."

"You still haven't explained why you've kept this secret," Dennistoun persisted.

"Oh, haven't I? Well, as you've seen, security at St. Oswald's isn't very good, I'm afraid. And it would be very easy for someone to break into the church and break through to the third and fourth niches. We feared that if the general public knew, someone might try what I just suggested."

"So you were the only ones to know?"

"Not the only ones," Dr. Durrell said. Lewis snorted again, and the elderly scholar turned toward him. "I'm sorry, Lewis, you may have been right in wishing to keep a total silence, but I still can't believe that any of those young scholars could have anything to do with this. It's too impossible."

Dennistoun pursed his lips in annoyance. "What young scholars? Give it to me in plain English, if you please. Who knew about the discovery?"

Roger said, "Until six weeks ago, only those of us on the dig knew. Some samples of the relics were sent to Edinburgh, but those specialists don't know the details of the find. It was at a party celebrating Jennet's arrival that Dr. Durrell broke the news to the rest of our dormmates, all of whom are historians and archaeologists themselves.''

The inspector's pointed nose swung around toward Jennet again. ''So she's the newest member of your team?''

''Yes, she is,'' Roger said softly.

''But only by a few weeks,'' added Dr. Durrell. ''You see, Inspector, unlike full-time specialists, most of us are employed at universities and can devote only the summer term to archaeology. So we began this summer's work on the abbey about six weeks before Jennet came. I hired her at a conference last month in London. Ah, thank you, my dear.'' This last was to Leslie, who had returned with his water.

''I've put a pot of tea on,'' she announced. ''Would anyone like a cup?''

''Not for me,'' Dennistoun said as he rose from the desk. ''Do you mind if I take these photos and papers for copying? No? Right. Well, then, I'll get to work on this, and either the sergeant here or I will come by to take statements from the others.'' The two policemen began to walk down the hall.

Lewis followed them, and Jennet heard him saying, ''Could I speak with you in private, Inspector?''

She realized, with a sinking feeling, that he was going to tell the whole story of the stolen objects in the dorm. Preoccupied, she lost track of the conversation until Amy all but echoed her thoughts.

''He doesn't believe anything we say!'' she said, slamming the teapot Leslie handed her down on the table. ''I swear, he thinks we've made all this up!''

''Who, the inspector?'' asked Leslie. ''Well, why not? Doesn't it look strange, in this era of electronic media and instant publicity for everything from channelers for past incarnations to people claiming they were abducted by

UFOs, that we find a genuine treasure, but keep it a secret? I know why we did it, and I agree, but look at it from an outsider's point of view. We come up a right bunch of idiots.''

Jennet was so convinced she was about to be dragged off in handcuffs that Leslie's comments took a moment took a moment to sink in. She had to admit, the St. Oswald's team did look rather stupid.

''I suspect you may be right, Leslie,'' said Dr. Durrell. He sighed deeply. ''At least we've got the archives, and the possibility that there may be more hidden in the other niches. So I suggest we get back to work.''

Amy, Roger, and Leslie all broke in at once, telling the professor to go home and rest. Only Jennet agreed with the old man, and he used her support to convince the others that his place was at his desk. After they left him in his office, Amy rounded on Jennet. ''How could you encourage him to work, after he's had such a shock? He's not a young man, you know.''

''No, he's not,'' Jennet replied. ''But he is a very proud one, and he thinks he can help best here instead of being coddled at home. Besides, I've discovered something else about him. Come here.'' She walked back to the professor's office, where the door was slightly ajar. They heard a faint snoring from within.

''He can fall asleep faster than anyone I've ever met. The other day he asked me to check a reference in a book in the other office, and when I came back one minute later, he was snoozing away. If I thought he was going to overwork himself, I would have told him to go home, too. But I suspect he'll sleep better here.'' She waited for their reaction.

''I hadn't thought of that, but now that you mention it, I have walked in on his naps a number of times,'' said Roger.

''It's happened to me, too,'' said Leslie. ''Well, I have a

lot of errands to run today, including the post office, so I'm getting to work right now.''

Amy was trying to peek into Dr. Durrell's office, and when she turned around, Jennet could tell she was still upset. ''Keep an eye on him, Jennet,'' she said. ''You know where we'll be.''

Everyone left. The professor snored for over two hours, while Jennet painstakingly worked on the index for his new book. After his nap he tried to help her, but soon realized that she had her own method of organization and his efforts were only slowing her down.

She felt quite sad for him then: he suddenly looked his real age. His eyes lacked their usual blue twinkle, his plump cheeks seemed to sag. Nevertheless, he announced that he would see how the excavation crew was getting on, then go home for lunch. Jennet was not surprised when Betsy called an hour later to say he would not return that afternoon.

Jennet grabbed a quick lunch at a nearby pub, then went back to the index until she felt an uncontrollable urge to fling three-by-five cards all around the office. It was then that she remembered it was her turn to cook dinner for the dorm that night. Deciding she'd done enough work on the index for one day, she quit an hour early and walked over to the market to get what she needed for a chicken casserole. She was wandering around looking for smoked ham when she heard someone calling her name. Waving at her from the far side of the side of the store and drawing the disapproving glances of Yorkshire housewives—was Olaf.

''Hi, Jennet! What's all this Douglas tells me about you folks and a robbery?'' He began muscling his way through the shoppers, leaving dusty footprints behind. She gestured at him to keep his voice down. ''Then it's true? The treasure's stolen?'' he asked.

He was standing in the middle of the aisle, which was

none too wide, and his six-foot-seven frame effectively blocked it. An elderly woman first tried to push her cart around him to the left, then to the right, and finally rammed it into his backside. "You may have nowt to do all but but stand there blathering, but Oi've me shopping to do, and Oi mean to finish it today!" She glared fiercely at Olaf. He bowed with as much dignity as he could muster, then drew Jennet alongside the canned goods.

"Well? Tell me all. We've been fretting about it all day at the site. I just popped out to get some ice for the cooler, and now I can tell the latest to the twins when I get back. Give forth!"

"It's all gone. Everything that was in the casket except, thank God, the archives and the chalice at the Durrells'. The thief got in through a broken window some time during the night. That's all we know. An Inspector Dennistoun is handling the case and will come to take statements from all of you."

"Don't they having anything to go on, any leads?"

"Yes and no. We're all suspects, you see, because we were the only ones who knew about the theft—or the treasure. On the other hand, we're not even sure the police are taking us seriously about this."

"In heaven's name, why? The value of those chalices alone is mind-boggling, and those miniature paintings of the saint . . ." He broke off, mustaches drooping. "You mean he doesn't believe the treasure was real."

She nodded. "The Professor's reasons for keeping it secret seem silly now." She threw up her hands. "All those relics had been safe for so long, and now they're gone. It makes me sick."

"I know, I know. Here, let me help you with your shopping. You sound like you've had a rough time." He took her basket.

"Don't you have to get back to work?" she asked.

"Ja, sure, but the twins will understand, and Dr. Graham will just have to put up with it. Let's see that list . . . Hmm. The ham is over that way; the rice is back on the second aisle."

He strode through the market, plucking things from the shelves and singing a silly folk song about a girl who tries to murder her old father but gets the tables turned on her:

"Oh, take ye sixteen marrowbones, and make him eat them all.
And when he's finished he'll be so blind, he won't see you at all."

He stopped singing. "Say, Jennet. No one saw me at all, at all."

"What are you talking about?"

"Last night. I had to drive up to Edinburgh for Dr. Graham, and on the way back I thought it was such a lovely night that I stopped at some farm, unrolled my sleeping bag, and slept under the stars." I came back at dawn. He looked almost gleeful, and Jennet began to get annoyed. "I've got no alibi for the theft," he said.

The chicken casserole was a success, but the dinner itself was gloomy. Lewis, us was often the case, did not attend, but everyone else was there. They all stared intently at the rice on their plates. Douglas tried to clown in his usual manner but gave it up when he saw he had no audience. They all scattered in silence to their own projects after dinner. Jennet was beginning to clear the table when Matthew came back into the kitchen.

"Want some help?" he asked.

"I thought you were allergic to kitchen chores."

"Hey, I do my fair share. Didn't you love my chili the other night?"

"I did. My insides didn't. If you're really offering, though, I'll take you up on it. Do you want to wash or dry?"

"Wash," he said immediately. "I hate drying, and I can never remember where anything goes. Then all the neat freaks around here like Carleen and Kenneth scream when they can't find their cereal bowls or steak knives. But at least I know where Pete's *hashi* go."

Pete had a passion for Oriental food, and insisted on eating it with a lovely pair of finished cedar chopsticks. When they disappeared one day, he was frantic until Amy admitted she'd thrown them out, thinking they were disposable. He and she went excavating in the garbage for half an hour before they found them.

Remembering the chaos brought a smile to Jennet's face, but she still didn't feel very pleased with the world. She and Matt worked in silence for a while, until he asked, "Want to talk about it?"

"About what?"

"Anything. Everything. The robbery. I can tell you're upset, so I wanted to let you know I'm willing to listen or sympathize or whatever."

Jennet stopped wiping plates and looked over at him. As usual, he sounded flippant, and he was up to his elbows in soapsuds, but his dark eyes were serious. Still. . .

"Of course I'm upset. We're *all* upset. A priceless treasure from the Middle Ages has vanished, and we all know damn well that one of us is the most likely suspect because nobody else knew about it. Yes, I'm upset, but. Aren't you upset?"

"Well, sure I'm upset, but . . ."

Kenneth poked his head into the kitchen. "Let's all be upset together, shall we? The police inspector is here and would like a chat with us."

Everyone gathered in the living room. Inspector Dennistoun and his assistant Sergeant Corbett were there, as were

Lewis and Dr. Durrell. The detective thanked them for "assisting the investigation" and carefully noted the names and addresses of the members of the Roman and Viking teams.

He seemed only mildly interested—to Olaf's evident disappointment—to learn that Olaf had spent the night on a Yorkshire farm. Douglas hissed at his colleague: "It's nae guid for an alibi, but none o' us has any better, saving the professor. Could ye nae find a willing lassie for the night, Olaf?"

Dennistoun set his notebook down and thoughtfully rubbed at the scar on his cheek. "You six who work on these other projects, tell me, when did you first see this treasure from St. Oswald's?" he asked.

"The night Jennet came," said Pete, "at the dinner at Dr. Durrell's house."

"And that's where you first saw it?"

"Yes," Pete said, and Carleen and Olaf nodded, but Jennet knew what the inspector was thinking, and judging from their faces, so did Matthew and the MacNucators.

"Let's be precise for the inspector, Petey," said Douglas. "We first *learned* about the treasure that night an' saw that bonny chalice."

His brother continued. "But we only saw photos of the rest."

"These photos?" Dennistoun held up a handful. They nodded. The inspector made a noise that sounded like "uh-huh" and neatly tucked the pictures into his case.

"Very well, then," Dennistoun said. "You'll all be staying in town while we conduct our inquiries?"

"Aye," Kenneth said gloomily. "We all have jobs to do."

Lewis coughed suddenly. "Um, Inspector, there was that little matter we discussed this morning." He looked uncomfortable.

"Oh, that." Dennistoun smiled. "We're looking into that. I think that's all for now. Come along, Sergeant." The policemen left, and the group visibly relaxed.

Pete, whose face seemed pale under his usual peeling layer of sunburn, rose and went to the hallway. "I don't know about the rest of you, but I need a drink. There's something about figures of authority that rattles my nerves. I keep seeing them giving my hair suspicious glances. If they come back, remind me to tuck my ponytail into my shirt and wear a ski cap."

"In July?" asked Kenneth.

"Hell, yes. C'mon, Kenneth, and we'll fix everybody up with something."

They soon returned with beers, wine, and Scotch, which were the group's favorite potables. Everyone sat quietly for a few minutes. Then Dr. Durrell, who had been uncharacteristically silent, said, "Lewis, would you please explain what this little matter is that you discussed with Inspector Dennistoun? If it's something to do with this theft, I think we all should know about it."

For a moment, Lewis looked startled. Since the theft, he had been dejected and sullen, but that was not uncommon behavior for him. He often was moody and withdrawn, and could snap when provoked. The Barclays had taken to alerting others when Lewis was in a temper by humming "In the Mood." Just as quickly, though, he could shift out of it and be as carefree as his younger colleagues. He sipped his beer, marshaling his thoughts.

"It may not have anything to do with the theft, but it's strange enough that I thought the Inspector should know about it. You see, Professor, last month some things began disappearing around here: small, valuable objects. We came to the conclusion that one of us was, er, a thief."

He pulled at his beer again, and Jennet thought, *Uh-oh, here we come.*

"The other week," Lewis went on, "I came home late from the dig and found Jennet wandering around downstairs. She says she heard a noise and went to investigate."

The professor said nothing, but his bushy, white eyebrows rose a little. Olaf, however, flushed angrily, and volatile Douglas jumped to his feet, shouting, "Ye canna believe Jennet first filched those things from us and the store and then the treasure from St. Oswald's! It's ridiculous."

"Hear, hear!" said Olaf.

"Why not let Jennet have a say?" said Matthew, who had been intently watching the scene.

"Oh, I have plenty to say, but I'd rather say it after Lewis is finished."

"Please, Jennet." Lewis looked pained. "I don't like doing this, and please don't think I'm accusing you of anything. But we're all academics here. We have to work with the facts we have, and unfortunately, these are the facts.

"To conclude, Professor, the next morning we found that the stairway closet was ajar, and the missing items, along with some things we believe were stolen from a local store, were there in a box."

Dr. Durrell poured himself another glass of wine, a bemused expression on his rotund face. "Come now, Lewis. *This* is your case against Jennet? Some things may have been stolen, you find her walking around late one night, and she's your culprit when they're found the next morning? And on the basis of that, you suspect her of stealing the treasure? Tut tut, Lewis, you're arguing on very flimsy evidence. I won't accept it." He put down his wine glass with a definite thump.

"Thank you, Dr. Durrell," Jennet said. "I was going to point that out, and I've already told Lewis I'm willing to be fingerprinted. I'm sure there would be fingerprints on those stolen things, and I guarantee mine aren't on any of them."

Olaf cleared his throat uncomfortably. "I'm afraid we

can't check your prints on the things from the store. I returned them. I'm sorry. If I'd known they'd be important, I wouldn't have done it, but I thought the store should have its property back.'' He glared at Lewis.

"Calm down," Lewis said, "and keep in mind that I never said Jennet took the treasure or those other things. It just seemed strange enough to mention to the police.''

"And there's another thing; I found her rummaging in my pocketbook one night after I'd misplaced it.'' Leslie's voice, unlike Lewis's, was harsh and bitter, and her cheeks were flushed.

Jennet willed herself to remain composed. "You 'misplaced it' outside my bedroom door the first night I arrived. I had no intention of stealing it. I only meant to find out who was its owner.''

The others watched the exchange with interest. Even Carleen, who had vanished into her weighty tome, lifted her head. She gave a small disappointed sigh when a free-for-all did not break out. Leslie crossed her legs and turned the other way.

The Barclays glanced uneasily at each other. Roger spoke: "I admit it's weak evidence, Professor, and I don't want to accuse Jennet outright, but we have to admit that we're the only suspects. We should keep a few other things in mind as well. The thefts in the dorm began after Jennet joined the staff, she knew the layout of the church well, and we know little about her background. Right now, we're *all* suspects, but I agree with Lewis; there's a number of strange coincidences that involve Jennet, and I suggest we look thoroughly into everything.''

His wife nodded her agreement. "I don't like anything that's happened, and we've got to check everything out.''

Dr. Durrell had clearly had enough. "I want these ridiculous accusations to stop right now. We're historians, not detectives. I say we should leave it to the police. It's their

job, not ours. Do you understand me?'' His wrinkled hands
trembled slightly, but his voice was firm. ''Come, Lewis,
there're some things I'd like to go over with you.''

Roger said he had left some papers back at the church, so
he left with them. Amy mumbled something about not feeling well and went upstairs. Leslie simply melted away without a word. The others stayed behind in the living room,
keeping mostly quiet.

Jennet was glad of the professor's words of support, but
she knew the strange events had planted suspicion in the
minds of most of her colleagues; however much Dr. Durrell
yelled at them, it wouldn't be enough to prove her innocence. She was rattled by everything that had happened,
and it seemed she wasn't the only one. She noticed Pete
helping himself to a third—or was it a fourth?—Scotch and
soda.

What Pete's troubles were, Jennet did not know. She did
know his solution was not for her. Too much liquor just
made her sick, and she did not want to add a queasy stomach and hangover to her already pounding headache. Food,
on the other hand, was much more comforting.

She rose from the couch and headed for the kitchen. She
instantly knew she was being followed; the sound of the
footsteps gave away their makers' identities. The heavy
steps thumped, and there were two sets, not one. Four of
her dormmates topped six feet, but Matthew moved like a
cat, and Kenneth, despite his stocky build, had a litheness
his brother did not possess. On the other hand Olaf, the
biggest of them all, made even Douglas seem graceful.

They were only a few paces behind her, yet she caught
them completely by surprise when she whirled around to
face them just after she entered the kitchen. They looked
like an old Warner Brothers cartoon as they got stuck trying
to squeeze through the door at the same time—a door which
could barely accommodate either one of them. Douglas had

the advantage; he did not need to duck. He pushed past Olaf, who dipped his head and followed. They both stood and looked at Jennet. She folded her arms and stared back.

"Can I help you gentlemen?" She didn't mean to sound quite so rude, but she was momentarily exasperated by these overgrown puppy dogs.

Olaf spoke first, his beautifully accented voice ringing. "I don't know if you can help us, but I want you to know that I'll help you, in any way, whatever you need. Truly I will."

"And I also," said Douglas. "I know ye've nowt to do with this crime, and I'll stand by ye to the end."

They both looked so completely sincere that Jennet's resentment evaporated. It was good to have somebody behind her. She gave them each a hug. "Do you know, that's the first time I've ever seen you two agree about anything?"

"Aye, weel, there's a first time for everything," said Douglas.

"We're staunch believers in worthy causes," added Olaf. "Now, you must have come in here for something. Can we help you get anything?"

"As a matter of fact, I decided it's banana-split Saturday night, even if it is only Thursday. It may be fattening as hell, but right now I couldn't care less."

"Say no more. Your wish is our command. Douglas, you get the ice cream. I'll get the fixings."

She sat at the table and watched them step on each other's toes as they created a frozen masterpiece suitable for four Jennets. "I can't eat all this! It's too much!" she said and ordered them to help finish. They were scraping the last of the fudge sauce from the bottoms of their bowls when Kenneth called from the living room.

"Hey, are you laggards going to stuff yourselves in there all night, or am I going to get some help with these papers? Dr. Graham will have our heads if this isn't finished."

"Bloody slave driver," Douglas muttered.

Olaf shook his head. "No, he's right. Graham's in a right snit about getting behind in the paperwork. We'd better go help him. Are you all right, Jennet?"

"Fine. Really. You're wonderful cheerer-uppers. I'll have some tea, I think, then work on some notes myself. As Kenneth said earlier, we all have jobs to do, and I'll be damned if anybody's suspicions are going to stop me now." She tossed her curly head and mugged a defiant look. Her friends laughed.

Douglas said, "That's the ticket!" Olaf began to sing "You've Got a Friend" in a resounding baritone, so loud that Carleen and Kenneth simultaneously yelled at him to shut up.

Their support encouraged Jennet, but she knew things were going to be difficult to bear at St. Oswald's until the theft was solved, if indeed it ever was. She made tea and wandered out to the living room to proofread some more of the professor's notes. The Viking team was studiously working; the MacNucators' red heads were close together, but Olaf gave her a quick grin. Carleen, as ever, kept to her book.

Jennet felt briefly annoyed, then depressed, that Matthew was nowhere to be seen. Olaf and Douglas clearly showed their concern for her, even to the extent of ignoring their work for part of the evening. (That, though, was not saying much in Douglas's case; he was notoriously lazy.) Matt, who had been attentive before and helped her out when she was having trouble with the Greek footnotes, had just vanished when she really needed support. And whatever he was doing diverged from his usual habit of the evening, which he spent either in the kitchen—his favorite workplace—or seated on the tweedy, sagging couch.

She spent more time fretting about his sudden disappearance than proofing, and when she realized she had read the first paragraph on page 211 four times, she knew it was time for bed. An upsetting, exhausting, awful day.

Carleen had silently vanished some time before, but the "Vikes" were still going at it hammer and tongs, or perhaps battle-ax and shield, when she said good-night.

She went up the creaky stairs and down the dimly lit hall. Leslie's room was dark, but Carleen's light was on, and the door was ajar. Faint gurgling and clunking sounds came from the bathroom. Then Jennet noticed her bedroom light was on. She thought she'd turned it off after she dressed that morning, but she couldn't be sure of anything that had happened that day except for the Professor's horrifying announcement that the treasure was gone. She wearily turned the handle and pushed the door open.

And there on her bed, reclining in a pose reminiscent of the effigy on the tome of Archbishop Bowet in York Minster, was Matthew.

+ + + + + + + + + + + + + + + +

V

MATTHEW SUDDENLY OPENED his eyes and stretched, looking considerably less like a corpse. He glanced at his watch.

"Eleven o'clock! What were you doing in the kitchen with those two galoots, having a party? I've been waiting up here for ages!"

A multitude of responses went through her mind, but all she could manage was, "What are you doing in my room?"

"We've got a problem, right? Let's start working on it. God knows the police aren't going to do anything in a hurry." He hopped off the bed, pulled the room's only chair over to the nightstand and threw himself into it. "C'mon, sit down, we haven't got all night."

Jennet continued to stand by the doorway. "What you mean *we*, keemosabe? *I'm* the great medieval casket robber, not you. And where do you get off barging into my room?"

Matthew looked slightly sheepish. "Well, I admit it was a bit rude and crude, and an invasion of your privacy, and all that, but I couldn't see any other way. Not with Olaf and Douglas playing bodyguard. I could see you were upset tonight, and I wanted to help. I figured I could do something more constructive than making hot-fudge sundaes."

"What can you do that's more constructive? Olaf and Douglas have said they'll back me, no matter what."

"Well, good for them. But while they were chopping up

79

bananas and nuts, 'I've trodden the garden threadbare, completing a way to save you.' ''

"Don't you start quoting Christopher Fry at me! I was named for the lead character in *The Lady's Not For Burning*." She stomped over to the bed and collapsed. Then she lifted her head up again. "What way to save me?"

He folded his arms confidently. "Why, we'll just have to figure out who really stole the goods."

"Ha. You and who else, Holmes? I already told you, I'm the great med . . ."

"Horse puckey," he said politely. "You couldn't be the casket robber."

"Why not? I know the layout of the church, I'm the newcomer to the gang, I'm broke and I could sell the stuff, I know the period better than . . ."

He waved his hands, interrupting once more. "Spare me the details. Everyone's overlooking one thing, and it's easy to overlook. I do it every day."

"What?"

"You're five foot two, right? And the only muscles you own are in your writing hand. How did you lift that casket?"

"Oh." She thought it over carefully. "Now why didn't I think . . . no, wait, I could have had an accomplice. There's plenty of people here with muscles. Besides, I'm five three."

"You could have had an accomplice, but you didn't. Or are you better friends with those Vikes than I thought?"

She brushed that aside. "Maybe I took the items out piece by piece. I certainly could carry the paintings, chalices, and other things singly."

"But the casket's gone, too. Do you think you could maneuver it, even if it was empty?"

She shrugged. "I don't know. Probably not. But all this speculation doesn't put me in the clear. The police will say

I had an accomplice or access to a wheelbarrow or something. Look, Matt, you're being very sweet, but right now my head is splitting open. If I don't get some sleep, I'll be a wreck tomorrow.'' She flopped back on her pillow, rubbed her temple.

Matthew stood up slowly and walked over to the door. "That's me all over, barging in recklessly . . . I'm sorry. Take two aspirins and call me in the morning.'' He reached for the door.

Jennet peeked out from under her arm. "Matthew?"

"Hmm?"

"I won't call you in the morning, but maybe we could meet for lunch?"

The grin returned to his face, and he nodded as he left. Jennet was sure she wouldn't be able to sleep, but when her head hit the pillow, she dropped instantly into a dreamless slumber.

The morning was ghastly. She spent part of it working on the index, a dreary task at any time, but especially awful when one's mind is occupied with other matters. She heartily wished that Professor Durrell had a computer, which would eliminate much of the drudgery. Then she had to help Leslie with the latest batch of excavation notes. The English girl was dressed impeccably, as usual, and chattered merrily as she worked. She acted as though nothing were amiss, as though she hadn't all but denounced Jennet to the police the night before. It disturbed Jennet, because she saw no pattern in Leslie's attitude. She gritted her teeth and kept on typing.

Jennet had discovered that Leslie enjoyed talking about her family, which was quite large. She had one older brother and four younger sisters.

"My father was the eighth baron of Rivington, but he renounced his title a few years ago. It scandalized my grandmother. He said it was because he didn't think the system of nobility was destined to last beyond the twentieth century. Just between ourselves, I think he didn't want to pass it on to my brother, a rather shiftless chap! A pity I wasn't born the eldest! Still, I'll get what I want most: Daddy has a shooting box in Scotland, a lovely little lodge in the Spey Valley. Fine hunting, and wonderful skiing in winter. They've done so much development there in the last few decades that I'm rather glad our place is away from the crowds.'' She sounded wistful, yet Jennet found the words more revealing than the tone of voice. Leslie often tried to join in the group's leisurely, nonacademic plans, but always with a certain aloofness. At first, Jennet attributed it to their different training. Leslie was a modernist, and while she could follow the in-jokes and jargon of her friends with fields in ancient and medieval history better than the average person, much of their conversation held little interest for her. Jennet now suspected that at least part of Leslie's reserve came from her family background. And considering how aggressive the slim English girl could be at times, she was not at all surprised to learn Leslie enjoyed hunting.

Still, she was being pleasant, which is more than the Barclays were that morning. Jennet had been eating a fried egg at breakfast when the couple entered. Amy glared at her as though she were the cause of the world's woes, muttered, ''I'm not hungry,'' grabbed a piece of toast from the basket and left. Her husband stood indecisively for a moment, then followed her. Jennet ordinarily did not see much of them during a workday, which they usually spent in (actually, under) the church. The one time Roger did come in the office, he said not a word to the two women, but spoke only with Dr. Durrell. Jennet decided to take advantage of Leslie's good humor.

''Where's the ancestral home?'' she asked.

''About twelve miles northeast of Buxton. That's in Derbyshire. It's a nice enough place, though I much prefer living in London.''

"Peveril Castle," said Jennet, somewhat abstractedly.

"What!" Leslie looked astonished. "Don't tell me you've been there! It's a moldy old ruin on top of a limestone cliff.''

"Nope, never been there. But my specialty is warfare, so I plotted every known castle site in Britain before my first trip here to squeeze in as many as I could.''

"You did well to miss that one. It's small, and the only good thing about it is a splendid view. You had me frightened for a moment. I've seen the Spey Valley overrun with tourists. Maybe Buxton is next!" She chuckled.

The door of the professor's office opened, and he emerged, clamping his straw hat on his bald head. "I'm heading home for lunch, ladies, so anyone who needs me can ring there.'' He nodded to them and left.

"He's not taking this well," Jennet said, more to herself than to Leslie.

"I can't say that I blame him," Leslie said. "We had a serious robbery three years ago. They practically emptied the house while we were at the lodge. All the family silver, everything. Mum still hasn't recovered. Well, I simply must run, I've got a date for lunch. See you this afternoon.'' She grabbed her purse and dashed out.

Jennet finished the page she was working on, then followed. She planned to meet Matthew in a pub on Peasholme Green. She walked down the street, thinking about the theft, when she saw Leslie's familiar profile in the window of a restaurant. Her date looked like someone she'd seen before, yet Jennet couldn't remember Leslie ever bringing anyone to the dorm. Then it hit her, like a slap in the face. That handsome Yorkshire face, with its strong chin and well-defined cheekbones, belonged to Inspector Dennistoun's assistant, Sergeant Corbett. He wasn't in uniform, but the fact that he was dining alone with Leslie bothered Jennet. She hurried by, head down, and hoped they didn't notice her noticing them. She wondered what Matthew would make of *this* development.

"Ver-r-ry interesting," was his only comment. "But I want to know more about the Baron of Buxton, or whatever he was."

"Why? Do you think Leslie stole the treasure to regain her family title? The monks of St. Oswald's Abbey may have been notoriously lax in observing the rules of celibacy, but there's no evidence linking them to minor nobility in Derbyshire. Besides, from what she said the barony doesn't date back to the Middle Ages. And Stafford is a fairly common name. If you want to talk about the *earls* of Stafford, that's another matter."

"No, no, no. Daddy was a baron, right? He's got a shooting box in Scotland, right? Leslie dresses better than any of us, right?"

"Right. So what?"

Matthew had ordered a ploughman's lunch, and now began waving his pickle like a baton, punctuating every word with a gherkin exclamation point.

"So why is she studying modern English history—what a depressing field!—and working for peanuts as a secretary to our good professor? And, mind you," he flourished the pickle once more, "why was she so upset that she might lose this peanut-paying job? She was, you know. Before you came, she was in a real state about getting canned, on and on. She wouldn't be so upset if the ex-baron of Rivington were rolling in dough, would she?"

"If you wave that pickle in my face one more time, I swear I'll bite it."

"Go ahead. English pickles remind me of most English

cooking: soggy and flavorless. The only good pickles are kosher dills.'' He took a hefty swig of beer. ''So. You haven't answered my question.''

''Questions, plural. First of all, we have no idea what her financial situation is, either personal or family. Maybe she's on an allowance, and needs this job to maintain her wardrobe in the state it's grown accustomed to.

''Second, you can't assume her father is filthy rich. Plenty of minor nobles have titles and nothing else to go with them. Anyway, the Staffords don't even have the title anymore: her daddy gave it up. Not only that, but she mentioned this morning that the family had suffered a serious robbery a few years ago.''

''Hmmm.'' Matthew frowned in concentration. ''What about the hunting lodge in the Highlands?''

''It could even be a liability to the family, especially if it's isolated from all the tourist development in the valley.''

''We'll have to check into that.'' He pulled a small notebook from his pocket and began scribbling.

She watched him for a moment. ''Matt, this is just too crazy. How do you expect to find out any of this stuff? And how can any of it help?''

He stopped writing and looked up. ''We're historians. We're pros at research. Finding things out will be a piece of cake. And as for what will help, which of your medieval scholars said, 'Learn everything. Afterward, you will see that nothing was superfluous'?''

''Hugh of St. Victor.''

''Hugh, meet St. Oswald. We'll get to the bottom of this.''

''It still bothers me, prying into people's backgrounds like this. I can't be detatched about it the way you seem to be.''

''Oh, it bothers me all right. But it bothers me even more to think they suspect you, when we know you didn't do it, but one of them most likely did." He doodled on his napkin.

"You certainly seem convinced of my innocence." It was a statement, but it had the ring of a question. She watched Matthew doodling a row of curly coated sheep, his dark hair obscuring his face.

"Just call it . . . intūition," he replied, without looking up.

They didn't get much done in the remaining lunchtime, so Matthew suggested they pack a picnic for Saturday. Dr. Henley had her Romanists work a half day, while the St. Oswald's crew theoretically had the day off, though Lewis and the Barclays usually put in some time at the dig. As Lewis remarked, there wasn't a lot to do around town, once you'd seen the sights.

Jennet however, lived in California, where art deco buildings from the twenties were historic landmarks and eighteenth-century missions were considered positively ancient. She couldn't get enough of the sights of York.

She had packed ham sandwiches and was washing the dishes while the brownies baked, when Douglas came into the kitchen. For a moment, she mistook him for Kenneth, for he entered rather quietly. But Kenneth's face habitually wore a studious expression, while his twin tended to slyness. The red hair only increased the resemblance to a fox.

"I knew I'd find something good in the kitchen, a sweetie baking sweets!" He sniffed dramatically. "Fudge cookies?"

"We call them brownies. Aren't you working today?"

"Aye. The heid bummer—that would be Dr. Archibald A. Graham—has nae mercy in his soul. I've come for some papers Kenneth left. Could I gorble a few o' those brownies afore I go?"

"Certainly. They'll be done in a few more minutes."

"I'll find those bally papers first." He dashed upstairs,

clattering and clunking all the way. Jennet squeezed out the sponge, rinsed the last bowl, and took the pan out of the oven. The big Scot barged back in, throwing a folder on the table. He looked expectantly at the pan.

"I really should wait for them to cool a bit, but if you have to get back to work, I'll cut a few for you now," Jennet said.

"Dinna remind me," he said mournfully. "I suppose you'll be flitting aboot the city today." He munched on his cookie. "Mmmmm. Will ye be going alane, or is that a picnic for two?"

"I'm meeting Matthew."

Douglas flushed red. "It's nae fair! Why won't he wait till ye both return to California? He'll see ye plenty then."

Jennet was learning how to handle Douglas. Distracting him often worked well. "Would you like me to pack some brownies for Kenneth and Olaf?"

"Let Carleen bake brownies for Kenneth!" That would have been impossible. Carleen's cooking was so bad that Pete accused her of being unable to boil water; she could make one dish, an ordinary beef Stroganoff.

"What about Olaf?"

"He can bake his own bluidy brownies!" Douglas grabbed another handful, then stormed out.

As he left, he bellowed, "May ye picnic hae eemoks!"

Jennet wondered idly whether eemoks were bugs or those fuzzy aliens in the Star Wars movie, but she decided not to look it up. By dinner, Douglas' steam would evaporate, and he would forget the whole thing. She finished packing the picnic and headed out into the sunny street.

The city seemed so vibrant, so full of crowds of tourists out for a stroll in the summer warmth, that all Jennet could think was *what a great day for a picnic*! She sobered only slightly when she remembered the purpose of the picnic was to discuss the theft.

The Roman dig was a few blocks south of the medieval Shambles, tucked away on a sidestreet called Straker's Pass. Jennet walked past the narrow opening without even noticing it and had to double back. The dig itself was situated in a tiny vacant lot, sandwiched between a shoe-repair store and a pharmacy. A small white trailer was parked on the street nearby. It bore a sign which proclaimed, HELP US UNEARTH ROMAN YORK! Underneath was a box labeled Donations, and a stack of pamphlets. Jennet saw Pete and Carleen under a canvas tarp in the fenced-in lot, but they were too busy to notice her. She walked toward the trailer, where she could hear Matthew's voice raised in argument.

"Does he at least admit the *possibility* that it may be Serapis?"

A smooth contralto with a Southern accent answered. "He's considering it. He doesn't want to eliminate Jupiter-Helios either."

"What about the inscription of Claudius Hieronymianus?"

"He won't forget it. Don't get so het up, Matt. I told him what we—why, look who's here! Come on in, Jennet, and tell this fella to simmer down. Everything gets taken care of in its own sweet time, and in academia, time is both sweet and slow."

Dr. Mary-Lou Henley was seated at a desk wedged into the corner of the crowded trailer. She was a small, plump black woman with iron gray curls, the daughter of a Georgia minister and respected scholar. Reverend Henley had had no sons, but fortunately didn't believe that education was wasted on girls. He began teaching Greek and Latin to Mary-Lou when she was five, and a half-century later, she was an established scholar. Her easygoing nature made her one of Jennet's favorite professors, always willing to listen to her students.

She look as unruffled as ever, though Matthew was clearly annoyed. "It's good to see you again," Jennet said. "Is there something going on right now? I could wait outside."

"For heaven's sake, no! Matt's just disappointed that the one prize of our dig hasn't netted blazing results yet. I tried to tell him it just plain doesn't work that way, not unless you get spectacular luck. It has to do with this particular goodie."

She handed Jennet a small jet bust about four inches tall. The head was of a man with long flowing hair and a thick curly beard. It was vaguely familiar to Jennet, who had done a minor field in Roman history, but whose expertise in art history was sketchy.

"Very pretty. Who is it?"

"That's what we'd like to know," Matthew said. "We know from an inscription that somewhere in York there was a temple of Serapis, a Greco-Egyptian sun god. I think our little guy is Serapis, but the experts haven't consented to give an opinion yet."

"Do you think you've found the temple here?" Jennet knew enough to realize what a triumph that would be.

"No," Matthew said gloomily. "One bust does not a temple make. This is just part of the legion's fortress. Maybe it's part of the hospital. Carleen found something weird that might be a surgical forceps, and we've found fibulae, the safety pins used for sutures." He sighed. "Damn! I was hoping that Wallingham would give an identity to Fuzzy Face. Let's call it a day, boss." And he headed out of the trailer, muttering things like "syncretization of solar deities . . . looks just like the one in the Walbrook Mithraeum . . ."

"Get some chow into him before he chokes on his theories," Dr. Henley laughed. "I told him it would be a while. Now how about you, honey? I heard what happened at the church. It's a shame, a damned shame. How's Edwin holding up?''

''As well as can be expected, I guess. Everybody's making him take it easy. We still have no leads to follow.'' She thought briefly about confiding in the older woman, but feared that Henley, too, might start suspecting her.

''You tell him to call me if he needs a hand. I still have one good one, anyway.'' She held up her left wrist, still bandaged from her accident. ''Get on with you, then, before Matthew starts bellerin' for his lunch. Stop by some morning when it's not so frantic, and I'll give you a tour.''

''Thanks, I will. 'Bye.'' Jennet blinked when she emerged from the dark trailer into bright sunlight. The diggers, she saw, had stopped their work. They were drinking sodas by the low brick wall that marked the end of the lot. Something small and furry sat on the wall: a fluffy black kitten. Matthew scratched its head while he talked with his co-workers.

''I can't believe Wallingham is unwilling to identify the bust yet. I know it's Serapis, Henley knows it's Serapis, you,''—this was to Pete—''our resident expert on religion, know it's Serapis, but the man whose vote counts just hems and haws. Burns me up.'' He scratched the kitten vigorously. It purred in ecstasy.

''What I don't understand,'' Matthew continued, ''is how calmly you're taking this, Pete. When we found the damn thing, you were literally dancing in Straker's Pass.''

''The shoe-shop owner came out and told him to stop because he was scaring away customers,'' said Carleen.

''And now you're either as cool as a cucumber or you don't care anymore. What gives, buddy?''

Pete stared at the ground. His long blond hair was tucked into a blue and white, checkered bandana to keep it out of his eyes. It was one of the few times Jennet had seen him with his hair pulled away from his face; she was surprised how boyish it made him look. "Oh, I don't know. I'm disappointed that Wallingham didn't come right out and agree with us, but it's not the end of the world." He shrugged. "I'm going to get some lunch." He walked away slowly.

"I don't get it," Matthew said. "Pete's been dying to hear what Wallingham had to say. I figured he'd go through the roof about this. He's been so quiet lately."

"Maybe he's gaining maturity," Carleen said. "Unlike some people I could name, not everyone is into primal screaming." Matthew made a face at her.

A nasty thought began tugging at the back of Jennet's mind. She pushed it away. "Whose cat is this?" she asked.

"The dig's. His name is Hadrian." Hadrian blinked at Matthew but refused to respond in any other way.

"I figured you'd give a pet a classical name, but why Hadrian?"

"We're in Britain, and this is the cat's favorite place for sunning, the wall. Therefore . . ."

Jennet groaned. "It's Hadrian's wall. That's not funny, Matthew, it's convoluted. Is Hadrian coming to lunch, too, or does he dine at home?"

Carleen picked up the kitten. "Dr. Henley keeps threatening to take him to a shelter, but guess who bought him his own dish and feeds him gourmet cat food every day? This is going to be the fattest kitten in all Yorkshire by summer's end. I'll check what she has for him today, seafood delight or chicken elegant. See you folks later."

Matthew watched her go, with Hadrian peering over her shoulder like a second head. He rubbed his hands on his pants and turned to Jennet. "Shall we do it? I know a good picnic spot."

She nodded, letting him lead the way. Her feelings perplexed her. She was glad that they were trying to do something, instead of just leaving the theft to the police, whose enthusiasm on their behalf was not noticeable. But she wished she could duplicate Matthew's confidence.

They walked through central York in silence, heading west. "Where are we going?" she finally asked.

"You'll see." They passed through the lovely gardens of the York Museum, Matthew pausing briefly to point out the fine Roman tower. They stopped near there, in a shady nook by the ruins of St. Mary's Abbey. Jennet found something majestic about the ruins. They appeared almost artistically arranged on the green grass, rather than as victims of destruction and time. The clear sunlight bathed them in a golden glow, as birds hopped around searching for insects in the broken masonry. Although no people were in sight, the area seemed curiously alive.

Jennet sighed with pleasure. "If I ever find people who think ruins are depressing, I'll take them here."

"I thought you might like it." Matthew munched on his sandwich. "Shall we get back to business?" He opened his notebook.

"I wish it would just go away and leave me alone."

Matthew stopped, pen in midair. He gave Jennet a questioning look.

She shrugged her shoulders. "But I guess it's not going to, so we may as well give it a shot. What have we got so far?"

"Interesting speculations about Leslie's family background and the state of her finances, which may or may not be healthy. How about the Barclays? They certainly would know their way around the church, and Amy's an art historian, so she'd probably be able to make necessary contacts to market the goods. And, although neither one of them is very big, we can assume they'd be in it together. What do you think?"

"Maybe. I do know they're hard up for cash, but really, I think we can say that about everybody except Olaf, with his Volvo and his father in the oil business. We aren't historians because we want to make fortunes."

"Unless we steal them," Matthew pointed out. He grabbed a handful of brownies.

"True. I do know one other thing about the Barclays that I found strange. The first night I was here, at Dr. Durrell's party, Amy briefly mentioned that Roger had worked at Marsden, a very good small university in Sussex."

"I remember. Amy said she packed up her dissertation-in-progress and came with him. They left because it wasn't their kind of place or something like that. Do you know any more details?"

"Not too much, which is weird in itself. I mean, all of us jabber constantly about work conditions at our own universities all the time. The way Pete goes on, I feel like I personally know half the department at Johns Hopkins. But have you ever noticed how closemouthed the Barclays are about that time at Marsden? Amy talks about Kent, Roger remarks about his student days at Oxford, but nothing about Marsden. They haven't been very explicit about this, but I gather that he ended up leaving that post abruptly. And it wasn't just a lecturer's gig, either; it was an assistant professorship. There might be something in that affair."

"That *is* weird. If I got an assistant professorship at Marsden—or anywhere else!—I'd do just about anything necessary to keep it short of human sacrifice. I wonder what happened and how we could find out more." He reached for another brownie.

"You're getting crumbs on your notebook," Jennet remarked. "It's not going to be easy checking up on that. Personnel records, which would tell us if he was canned or just quit, are confidential. We'd have to get the information from some other source. The way Amy talked about it, it seemed like something she didn't want to talk about, if you take my meaning."

"Uh-huh. Well, there may not be anything in it. Maybe he mortally offended the department chair, or they decided it wasn't where they wanted to settle. It might be anything. The question is, was it anything serious enough that could corrupt them into stealing the treasure? Or did the move hurt them financially, so they felt forced to do it?"

"That leaves Lewis. All I can tell you about him is that while he's the director of the dig, everybody recognizes that Dr. Durrell is the one in charge. He's just not up to the same amount of physical activity. And I'd say that pretty much sums up Lewis' career."

"What do you mean?" Matthew asked. "That he's always toiling unnoticed?"

"Not exactly. If it were only that, I'd eliminate him completely from our list of suspects because the St. Oswald's find would certainly make his name well-known.

"It's something harder to define. Look at most of us here: we're all young, either brand new Ph.D.s or in the process of finishing our degrees. Lewis is a little older, but though I admit he has talent, he hasn't displayed much of it in print where it counts. He's had just three articles in the last ten years. They're good pieces, but that's not much production."

"Publish or perish," Matthew intoned solemnly. "Go on; this is interesting."

"As far as positions go, I don't know too much about his background, except that he's a Cambridge product. He's worked at about a half-dozen digs, but none of them had anything extraordinary happen. No fabulous discovery or mysterious thefts. I'd say Lewis is your average academic mercenary, going from one short-term contract to the next. It's a little puzzling that he hasn't gotten tenure after all this time." She shrugged, and twisted open a bottle of lemonade. "I mean, I've known folks that don't mind living that way, and it's much easier to handle if you don't have a family, but ugh! I'm insecure enough to know that if I haven't found a post when I'm his age, I'll simply get out of the field. I couldn't live knowing my contract might evaporate at every meeting of the board of directors."

"Me, too." He leaned back against the tree under which they were picnicing and stretched impressively. Then he laughed quietly and turned toward her. "You old naysayer. You sounded so dubious the other night when I proposed that we try a little detective work on our own, and here you are, a veritable font of information! You've really been giving this some thought, haven't you?"

"I guess I have." The idea surprised her. The events of the last few days had upset her so much that she hadn't thought that they could accomplish anything with their investigation. Now she felt more energetic, as if the simple act of talking out some of the questions in her mind had jump-started her brain. Maybe they could do something!

She had been lost in thought for a few moments, and suddenly felt his intense gaze upon her. Their eyes met, briefly, and Jennet couldn't say which one of them had looked away first. She fiddled absentmindedly with the wax paper wrappers from the sandwiches, folding them over and over.

"So that does it for Lewis." Matthew's voice was a touch huskier than usual. "He's been in the field for years without making a name for himself, hasn't published much tsk, tsk!—and, like the Barclays, knows the church better than anyone else."

"Also, like Amy, this period is his forte. He wouldn't have much trouble marketing the finds. I wonder what would mean more to him, the raw cash value of the treasure or the boost that finding it has given to his reputation?"

"There's a way he could have both," Matthew remarked. "If he markets them secretly, he'll still go down in academic circles as 'the finder of the St. Oswald treasure, which was so tragically stolen.' ''

Jennet looked aghast. "I hadn't thought of that! I assumed that whoever stole it would just vanish into the criminal underworld or something. Oh, that's an awful thing to think, that the thief could have his cake and eat it, too.''

"How about the Vikings, now? Or don't you want to think of those musclemen as sneak thieves?''

"I don't like thinking that any of the people I know is a thief." She was annoyed. "You said it before; we've got to consider everything. And everybody. I can't give you any specific suspicions about the MacNucators or Olaf simply because I don't have any. I can point out the obvious things, though—can you?''

"Whoa, whoa. I apologize for the earlier remark. Definitely tacky on my part. I will take a shot at playing detective now. It was my idea, after all. I've even scrawled a few notions down. See if you have anything to add.'' He brought out his notebook again. "I think we can agree that money is the key motive here. Why else would you steal a treasure trove? As you pointed out before, most of us need money. I will assume that Kenneth and Douglas are in the same boat. How badly do they need money? Badly enough to steal the treasure? I don't know. Do you?''

Jennet shook her head, so Matthew continued. "Okay, that's something we can ponder. You mentioned that Olaf comes from a wealthy family. I also know he's never been to St. Oswald's, at least not to anyone's knowledge. A few weeks before you came, we gave each other tours of our sites. Olaf was running some errand and missed the visit to the church. That, I think, is a point in his favor. Kenneth and Douglas, however, did come, so they at least know the layout of the place. And, of course, all three of them are strong enough to carry the casket with no difficulty.''

Matthew started rummaging in the pockets of his windbreaker, so Jennet interrupted his discourse. "You're forgetting one thing: Olaf's alibi is the weakest of anyone's. The rest of us were all asleep in the dorm when the theft happened. That means that the thief had to take a chance on sneaking out quietly. Unless Olaf did it. He had driven to Edinburgh for Dr. Graham and says he slept in a field on the way back. And he's the only one of us with a car, too."

"Good point." Matthew found what he was looking for, a dark green rubber ball. Jennet had seen him exercising with it several times. He squeezed it while he continued: "That's it for the Norsemen, I guess. We'll have to see if we can find out anything about the twins' finances, learn if they're desperate enough to try increasing their wealth illegally.

"Now for my gang, the twentieth-century triumvirate. You'll just have to take my word that I'm innocent, because God knows I could use the money. Still, apart from my student loan, I'm not as bad off as some. Pete's in hock up to his eyebrows, poor turkey, and I loaned him two hundred dollars so he could fly out here for this summer. And you know we're not getting rich here on this teeny-weeny stipend."

The thought that had nagged at Jennet before returned. "Matthew," she said slowly, "when we were at the dig you mentioned something about Pete acting strange. Do you think it's his money troubles, or is he hiding something?"

Matthew's face was long and lean; when he frowned, it looked even longer and leaner. He frowned now. "I'd really hate that. We've gotten to be good friends. You're right; it's hard to be objective about this. But I can't deny that something's bothering him. I hope it's not a guilty conscience. I'll try working on him." He squeezed the rubber ball even harder, as if expressing his determination in physical action.

"And didn't Pete once tell me he did a minor field in

Western medieval history?'' she asked. ''Or was it Byzantine history?''

''Both. With concentration on religion and theology. Pete started out in a Jesuit seminary and got a degree in Christian theology. I don't know what caused the switch from Christians to pagans, but it was pretty dramatic. He's a bit of a rebel now, is Pete.''

''With all that knowledge, he'd also be better at disposing of the goods, too, I would think. Does Carleen have that kind of background?''

Matthew snorted. ''No, she's a true classical scholar. Greeks, and especially Romans, are her first and only love. She agrees with Gibbon that everything after them is degenerate. She'd have a harder time selling the goodies than most, but she's very smart. She could probably find a way. Now that I think about it, she asked an awful lot of questions when we went on our tour of the church. I assumed that was just typical Carleen Clark thoroughness, but maybe she's put that knowledge to bad use. She's a big girl, too, not pint-sized like you.''

''Oh, this is so depressing! Let's put that stupid notebook away and go for a walk. I can't see that we've accomplished much except realize that any or all of our friends could have done it, and we knew that before.'' Jennet began gathering up the remains of their picnic and crumpling the wrappings violently.

''You know that's not true. We've got some things that we can check out, we've aired a lot of thoughts, and we've had a lovely picnic in England in the summertime. Not a bad day's work.''

He helped her clean up, and they took a lesiurely stroll along the city walls. They discussed classes they had taken, the hideous experience of their Ph.D. exams, their favorite music, and a host of other things that had nothing to do with

missing medieval art treasures. Matthew was disappointed
to learn Jennet was not a baseball fan.

"I do like football," she said.

"That's great, but baseball is a real historian's game."
He flipped the green ball up and down.

"Why? Because they keep records of everything from
double plays to sacrifice flies to how many times they spit
tobacco before they bat?"

"Exactly!" He spoke with the fervor of an addict. "I like
to think I stood a chance of making it to the big leagues
before I tore up my arm. I was scouted by three teams when
I was in high school." His eyes had a faraway look. "Good
thing I realized it was gone when I got hurt. Some guys
never admit they've lost it. So I turned to history instead.
That's what I get for playing war games when I was little."

They walked in silence for a while until Jennet murmured, "I wonder where it is now." There was no need to
mention what "it" was.

"I've been thinking about that. I'd bet it's around some
where near. After all, he or she or they can't have had any
time to hunt for prospective black-market buyers. Maybe
we should look around." He led the way through the campus gate and up the walk to the quad.

"Where? The dorm? Are you nuts? Why would the thief
keep the treasure where anybody could find it?"

"Who'd find it? That's a big building. Remember how
long it took to find those stolen radios and things? And all
those empty rooms? You could hide a horse in there and
nobody'd notice. I think I'll go snooping tonight. Treasure
hunting, me hearties!"

"I think you're out of your tree. Besides, if the thief is
from the St. Oswald's crew, then he could have set up a sale
long before the theft itself."

Matthew's enthusiasm did not diminish. "I doubt it. I'd

imagine these things take some time to prepare, and if I were a private collector, I'd want to see the goods before forking out the money for them. I'm betting the treasure is still nearby."

They returned to the dorm, where Carleen was preparing yet another boring beef Stroganoff. Dinner was fairly quiet, but afterward Olaf brought down his accordion and began playing Orkney sea chanteys. While most of the group treated Jennet with a certain coolness, there was more of a return to normal routine than in the last two days. She went to bed early, feeling virtuous after plowing through a turgid article on lordship and feudal settlement in Northumbria.

She was awakened in the night by a tapping at the door. "Who's there?" she whispered.

"Matthew," came the hoarse reply.

She opened the door, ready to chew him out for rousing her. What she saw made her gasp. He was clinging to the door frame for support with one hand, while the other pressed a towel against a bleeding scalp wound.

"If I am out of my tree," he muttered, "it's because I was pushed."

+ + + + + + + + + + + + + + + + +

VI

"**W**HAT HAPPENED?" JENNET gasped. She put one arm around Matthew and guided him to a chair. He sat down cautiously.

"I don't know, exactly. Take a peek at my head, tell me if it's still attached, and then I'll give you the gory details."

The phrase was to be taken literally—the terry cloth towel was damp with blood. Matthew flinched as she gently lifted it to see the wound. His thick dark hair made examination difficult. She grabbed the high-intensity light from her desk and tried to estimate how serious it was. She gave up. "I want to be a doctor of philosophy, not medicine. It looks like a two-inch gash, and it's bleeding a lot."

"Scalp wounds always bleed," said Matthew, somewhat stoically

"So? When do they stop? I think this one needs some stitches. Here, let me get you another towel." She went over to her closet, noticing that her hands were shaking. He pressed the clean towel to his head.

"Ouch. I tell you what: let's go visit the local ER, and I'll tell you what I remember on the way." He stood up, wobbling slightly.

"Let me get somebody to help you, Olaf or Douglas or . . ."

"No." His tone was firm. "I'll be fine with just you. Let's

keep this between you, me, and whoever conked my noggin.''

Jennet dressed in a flash and saw that Matthew was not injured seriously enough to keep him from watching this procedure with appreciation. They made it down the stairs relatively quietly. The stairs, as usual, creaked, and Matthew kept murmuring curses under his breath. The night was cool. She wished she had put on her sweater. Matthew, however, felt warm and clearly needed some physical support (or so she told herself), so she snuggled closer to him as they walked to the nearby hospital.

"So I was right: somebody *had* the stuff here, at least!" He sounded jubilant.

"What? The treasure? You found it—really saw it?"

"Well, no. I didn't *see* it. I poked around all over downstairs, then started on all the empty rooms on each floor. I didn't find a thing. But when I got to the fourth floor—the Barclays' floor—I found a locked door. All the other rooms, except the occupied ones, were unlocked. I tried the handle, jiggled it a bit. Then I remembered there were some keys down in the kitchen cabinet. I went downstairs, found the ring of keys, went back up. I tried around a half dozen keys before finding the right one. I opened the door, then boom! everything went black. I woke up a few minutes later in an empty room. At least I don't think anything was there, but I admit I didn't look very closely."

"So whoever it was likes sleeping with medieval relics and didn't want you finding out. Well, I can see why he'd do that; sleeping with them keeps them safe, and he probably felt that his own room wasn't secure enough. But where could the thief have moved the treasure so quickly? Into his room? Someplace else? That's taking a big chance. How could he know how long you'd be out?"

"Not that big. My guess is that he moved it to another room nearby, and plans to put it somewhere more secure very soon. Maybe even now, while my head's getting screwed back on. Unfortunately, I'm not up to hunting for him just this minute.''

"Hang in there, the hospital is right around the corner.'' Jennet tried to sound cheerful. She didn't like the haggard look on Matthew's face.

St. Bartholomew's Hospital was not large by American standards. It was a dingy gray structure dating from the postwar period, but it was full of well-trained, sympathetic personnel. Jennet tried to help by filling out the various forms, but she kept finding too many things about Matthew that she didn't know. Birthday, middle name, address—did that mean here in York or back in the States?—all those little vital statistics that make up a person on paper. She gave up and left it for him to finish. The nurse clipped Matthew's hair, teasing him about his new punk appearance, but warning him not to bonk the other side of his head, even though it was fashionable to be symmetrically shaved. The emergency room doctor then neatly put a few stitches in Matthew's scalp and gave a standard lecture on concussions.

"It's not my first, doctor. I played football—American football, that is—and have been hit harder than this. There's just not so much blood when you're wearing a helmet. I know the routine. I'll try not be so clumsy next time.'' He chatted with the doctor, telling how he slipped on the stairs.

That perked Jennet's ears right up. Why wasn't Matthew explaining about the theft and the assault? What was he up to?

Her questions had to wait until everything was finished, however. Matthew clearly did not want to discuss the matter with the doctor. Once they were outside, though, she almost pounced on him.

"What's with you? We finally have something concrete to take to the police, namely, your head, and you tell the doctor you've just had a bit of a nasty fall? I assumed we'd go to Inspector Dennistoun as soon as we got you patched.''

Matthew smiled smugly. He had more spring in his step; the painkillers were obviously at work. The white bandage slanted rakishly through his black hair. He grabbed her hand and squeezed it.

''Don't you see? We're doing great on our own!''

''Oh, yeah, just great. You get your head split open, come to my door looking like something out of *Night of the Living Dead*, and you wipe out the one lead we had by saying it was all an accident! We're doing just peachy keen.'' She walked along without looking at him.

''No, I mean it, Jennet. I don't want to bother the police with this.'' He pointed to the bandages. ''They'll probably say you hit me on purpose to clear yourself.''

''That's ridiculous.''

''Sure it is. Anyway, it's my head, and if I want to keep what happened to it a secret, that's my business. Personally, I think we've done a lot today, in spite of the headache it's given me.''

Then, to her surprise, he turned right at the next intersection and headed south. She trotted after him. ''Where are you going? The dorm is the other way.'' Maybe the blow addled his sense of direction. She was convinced it had addled his common sense.

''I want to go to the trailer at our site. It has a spare pillow, and I think I'll need it tonight. Besides, aren't you in the mood for a moonlight stroll?'' He grinned.

''No, I'm freezing. Look, you're in no shape to trot all over York. Why don't you wait here, and I'll run and get it?''

''Unescorted young ladies should not wander the city at night, even as lovely a city as this.''

She sighed. *Some escort*, she thought, *if we were mugged, he'd be no help at all.*

Matthew laughed. "I know exactly what you're thinking: that I'm acting like a dumb macho male, and couldn't fend off an attacking four-year-old, let alone a mugger. You're right, but maybe my size alone will deter any baddies. Besides, I know a short cut."

With that, he threaded his way through a few sidestreets to the Roman dig. He suddenly stopped in surprise. The lights were on in the trailer.

"Could it be Dr. Henley?" asked Jennet.

"Not a chance. Mary-Lou is country-bred and -born. She likes to rise with the sun, but goes to bed at nine-thirty every night. We threw a farewell party for her three years ago, when she went on sabbatical to Zurich, and she was the first one to leave. Maybe it's Carleen . . ."

The mystery was solved when the lights shut off, and Pete opened the door. Matthew started forward, but Jennet grabbed him, pushed him into a nearby doorway, and proceeded to kiss him. He seemed astonished at first, but quickly responded. After a few moments, she broke off the embrace and tried to peek around his shoulder.

"Well!" Matthew whispered. "What was all that about? Did you suddenly decide my charm was irresistible?"

"No, dummy. I didn't want him to see us. Couples making out in dark alcoves don't draw a lot of attention." She peered into the dark street, following Pete's dim figure.

"Oh." Matthew sounded disappointed. "I thought it would be something like that. What now? Shall we follow my colleague?"

"As discreetly as possible."

This, as things turned out, was not difficult. Pete stormed along, his hands jammed deep into his grubby windbreaker. He moved like a blond bulldozer, oblivious to everything in his path.

"He's definitely upset about something, isn't he?" Jennet observed.

"Maybe Dr. Wallingham's opinion of our bust of Serapis is getting to him at last."

"Be serious."

"I am, I am. Pete is a dedicated scholar of Roman religion." Matthew tried to sound convincing. "That, of course, is the only innocent explanation for his behavior that I can concoct."

"But lots of not-so-innocent ones," Jennet murmured.

They turned the corner and reached the campus of the Miller Technical College where the dormitory was. They ducked behind a hedge and watched Pete enter the building. He clearly did not care that it was nearly three in the morning and his friends were asleep. He slammed the door.

Jennet and Matthew hurried after him. "Look up there," Jennet pointed to the dorm windows. "Pete's not the only night owl."

"Whose windows are those?" he asked. "I can't remember where everybody rooms."

"That's the Barclays', remember? They're the only ones on the fourth floor."

Matthew stopped in his tracks. "Are you *sure* that's their bedroom? Maybe it's the room that had the treasure in it."

"No, that's their bedroom. It's the first window past that little one over the stairwell. And that light down there is their bathroom."

As they watched, another light came on, this time on the third floor: Pete's room.

"Let's run around the building and see who else is prowling," said Jennet.

The other side revealed lights in what Jennet thought was her room ("I must have left them on.") and in what was either Kenneth's or Lewis' room. Matthew couldn't remember exactly where his dormmates slept.

"Funny, you sure knew where my room was," Jennet said, deadpan.

"I had incentive. Why should I care where the guys sleep? Ladies and gentlemen, this concludes our sound-and-light spectacular for this evening. We hope you enjoyed the performance . . . How about I show you where *my* room is?" He leered at her, but she saw how tired he was.

"Of course. You've done much too much tonight for a man with a concussion. Let's go in."

They entered quietly, but immediately heard noises from above. They hustled up to Matthew's room, from which they could tell that Pete was responsible for the commotion. He clattered about for a bit, then thumped his way to the bathroom for a shower.

"A shower in the middle of the night?" Jennet asked incredulously.

"Out, damned spot! out, I say!" Matthew declaimed. "I hope he's not washing my blood from his hands. What a night! I think those pills are wearing off, too. My head is thumping like I'm at a Stones' concert." He eased his way onto his bed. "Care to tuck me in and kiss me good-night?"

Jennet didn't rise to this bait. She pulled the bedclothes up from the foot of the bed where he had shoved them before beginning his prowling and covered him gently. He tilted his head up, and she bent down to kiss him. It was a quiet kiss, not like the one in the doorway near the dig. Jennet could tell from Matthew's expression that he was hoping for a little more, but she reminded him that the doctor told him to take it easy.

"You're not supposed to overexert yourself, you know," she remarked as she stepped lightly out of his grasp.

"Who said anything about exerting?" He tried to look lecherous, but even as he spoke, he was snuggling down into the pillow.

"Sleep tight." She started back to her own room, feeling cheerful despite the night's events. Pete had finished showering, and was now running his blow-dryer, its high-pitched whine echoing through the halls. Jennet was tiptoeing down the stairs to her floor when a door was flung open and Douglas bellowed down the hall: "Let a body sleep! Can ye nae wait till morning to get clean?" He thundered his way to the bathroom and began yelling at Pete, who screeched back.

Jennet couldn't make out the words as she slipped back into her room, but she was convinced that everybody in the dorm would wake up now. As she drifted off to sleep, she wondered if Carleen had remembered to buy more coffee. They were all going to need it in the morning.

The mornings began with a disaster: Carleen *had* forgotten to buy more coffee, annoying everyone but Amy, who only drank tea, and Matthew, who didn't like coffee anyway and had yet to make an appearance that morning. Everyone was reading the Sunday papers, muttering about the lack of coffee, so much so that Jennet felt as if she were in some academic version of "The Coffee Break" song from the musical *How to Succeed in Business*. Finally, Carleen gave up. She beat her chest dramatically, crying "Mea culpa, mea maxima culpa! If I get some coffee, will you all shut up? It wasn't *my* idea to wake everybody up last night."

She grabbed her purse and ran out the door, almost crashing into Dr. Durrell, who had taken to spending Sunday mornings at the dorm while his wife was busy with her church group.

We certainly don't look like respectable scholars, do we? thought Jennet, and from the frown on Dr. Durrell's face, he clearly thought the same. Of all of them, the only one who looked as if he'd had a good night's rest was Olaf, who was whistling as he studied the soccer scores. Everyone else looked like hell. Douglas sprawled on the couch, his red hair rumpled into dozens of cowlicks. Amy was paler than usual, and Pete's eyes were spectacularly red. Lewis clutched his tea cup with both hands, lost in what some call "the thousand yard stare." Even Leslie, generally the best dressed of the group, was not in her customary fine attire. Her short-sleeved sweat shirt was clearly a designer label, but Jennet noted maliciously that it needed ironing.

Dr. Durrell took all of this in and, with an audible sniff, puttered into the kitchen for tea. Matthew's dramatic entrance moments later brought him hurrying out, a canister of Earl Grey still in his hands.

Blood smudged the edge of Matthew's bandage, his eyes were blackened with lack of sleep, but he smiled without concern. "Hiya, folks. What's new?" His companions stared for a moment before bursting with questions.

"What in God's name happened to you?" Kenneth asked. "Did you run into a truck?"

"I ken what it was," Douglas said. "Ye had a set-to with Pete, and that's why he was barging around in the shower in the dead of the night, a-washing off the bluid and waking up us hard-working souls. For shame, Matthew, a big hulk like ye should be able to handle a pipsqueak Pete's size wi' one hand behind your back. Or did he belt ye from behind?"

Jennet had been watching Pete's face since Matthew appeared, and it registered an amazing array of emotions from surprise to concern to horror and finally, confusion at hearing Douglas's proposed explanation. Matthew saw Pete's distress, too, and jumped in with his explanation.

"I can't say why Pete was up late, but I got up around one and took a spill on the stairs leading into the storage room. I split my head open, like a dummy, and imposed upon Jennet to help me to the ER for some stitches. And that's it. It's really no big deal." He tried to sound nonchalant, but his appearance belied his voice.

"So that's what all the ruckus was last night? With all the banging and clattering, it's a wonder we got any sleep at all!" Roger said.

His wife yawned. "And I'm exhausted all the time lately, terminally tired. I'm glad you're not badly hurt, Matthew, but really, is this late-night activity necessary? Whatever were you doing up at that hour?"

"I was, ah, looking for something that was misplaced," Matthew said truthfully. "I didn't find it."

"And what were you doing up so late, Pete?" asked Lewis. "Was that you slamming the door around three? I did hear your confrontation with Douglas, and I must confess, I felt like joining in."

Olaf emerged from the soccer scores. "I guess sometimes it pays to be a sound sleeper. I didn't hear any of this. Care to explain, Pete?"

Pete had gone from looking merely confused to outright bewildered. Now he was white-faced. He pushed his chair back, scraping the well-worn dormitory linoleum. "It's none of your business," he said curtly, and left the room.

"Well!" said Leslie. "Unusual to see him so tense, isn't it?"

Dr. Durrell had taken in the whole scene in utter silence, but he was getting more and more irate. Finally, he exploded.

"What's the matter with you people? Are you scholars or little children who need a nursemaid? What do I have to do to establish some orderly behavior here, set a curfew? I'm ashamed of you all, and have no intentions of spending my Sunday listening to these petty squabbles." He was pale, and breathing hard. "Jennet, if you have a chance today, I hope you can finish the captions for the book's photographs. Then we can at last start going over the chronicles. I'll be at my office if you need me." With that, he stalked out of the room, still carrying the tin of tea.

The dormmates looked at one another. "Who stuck a pin in him?" Olaf asked.

"Shut up, Olaf," said Lewis. "He's upset about a lot of things." He took his tea cup into the kitchen for a refill.

Amy came over to Jennet. "I don't like to ask this of you," she began, sounding slightly embarrassed.

Jennet mentally translated, *I don't want to ask you because I suspect you.*

"But I'm worried about the Professor. Since it appears he'll be working with you later today, could I ask you to keep an eye on him? I don't like seeing him so upset; he has a heart condition, you know. I'd feel so much better if I knew you'd check on him. Roger and I owe him so much."

Jennet murmured that she certainly would and followed Carleen and her precious cargo of coffee into the kitchen. Sometime later, when she went upstairs to get her briefcase from her room, Matthew followed her.

"Hoo hoo!" he chortled. "And what do you think of today's developments?"

"What developments? All I could see was a bunch of people who had a bad night's sleep." She flipped open her briefcase and rummaged through the papers.

"No, no. I meant Dr. Durrell and what Amy said about him." He sounded disgustingly chipper for someone who'd had a concussion the night before.

"What about it? He's in his seventies; at that age, it's very common to have heart ailments, to say nothing of a host of other problems."

Uninvited, he stretched out on her bed. "Not that. The part where Amy said she and Roger owe him so much. What if Roger was in some criminal trouble before, and that's why he lost his professorship, and they're grateful because he gave them this job?"

"They may suspect me, but I'll be the first to vouch for their credentials. They're good scholars, both of them. I don't see what you're trying to get at." Jennet still couldn't find the missing Xeroxed article, and that, plus Matthew's insatiable curiosity, contributed to her annoyance. She felt a sudden sympathy for the relatives of the Elephant's Child.

"Well, maybe that's not it, or maybe that's just part of it. It does strike me as odd. Why should she be so concerned for his health? What exactly do they owe him? It's intriguing."

"It's irritating." Jennet snapped. "Whatever their background may be, they're working for him now, they're glad they have this job, and they're concerned about the old man's health. I think you're barking up the wrong tree."

"And, as you pointed out, they still suspect you. Don't you think we should investigate everything, however distasteful it may seem?"

"I fail to see how Amy's comment can shed any light on this mystery." Where was that stupid article? Under the bed?

Matthew closed his bloodshot eyes, but relentlessly pressed on. "Maybe there's even more to it than simply hiring Roger after a bad rap. Maybe the three of them are in this together."

Jennet was on her hands and knees, searching among the dust bunnies under her bed. She looked up at Matthew, whose eyes were still blissfully closed.

"What are you saying?" she asked, making her voice as cold and still as possible.

He blinked, and was surprised to see her glaring at him from the floor. "Well, I was just wondering if we shouldn't include Dr. D. on our list of suspects. I know he couldn't move the treasures alone, but if he worked in cahoots with the Barclays . . ."

"Out."

"Hmmm?"

"Out," Jennet repeated. "I'm glad you're on my side, Matthew, but I think you're taking your role as chief inspector too damn far. There's not a shred of evidence linking the professor to this business. The next thing I expect to hear you say is that you suspect his wife as well.''

He sat up on the bed, tried to spread his hands in supplication. "Now, wait, Jennet, I only meant to say that we shouldn't exclude anyone, and—''

"Out." She pushed him, and he slid off the bed, revealing the missing article. She snatched it. "I have work to do. If you come up with any more brilliant speculations, Sherlock, keep them to yourself.''

Matthew took a step toward the door, paused as if he meant to say something, then tossed his hands in the air and left. Jennet slogged through the crumpled pages of the article, then decided to clear her mind with a walk through town.

It was too late for Sunday services at the Minster, but that was just as well with Jennet, who disliked crowds. Perhaps it was because of her training, but she had a particular passion for medieval stained-glass windows, and the Minster boasted the finest stained and painted glass in all England. She wandered around the cathedral, admiring glass from the twelfth to the twentieth centuries and trying to decide which was her favorite. The splendid Five Sisters Window was a dazzling gray-and-green geometric mosaic, but the delightful details of the Pilgrimage Window—such as a rooster reading a lesson and a monkey's funeral—never failed to make her smile, just as they'd made people smile since the fourteenth century.

After her tour, Jennet felt a little better, but was still outraged at Matthew's suggestion that Dr. Durrell could be a suspect. She told herself he was only trying to be objective about the theft, but the notion offended her so much that she knew she couldn't be rational about it. Moreover, it made her start wondering about Matthew's own motives. Why was he so interested in clearing her name? Did he really care about her? Was he simply using this for . . . for what? Some kind of ulterior motive? And how dare he accuse the Professor!

These thoughts ran around and around in Jennet's mind while she went around and around the two hundred and eighty steps leading to the top of the cathedral tower. There is nothing like winding one's way up a narrow spiral staircase for focusing one's thoughts. By the time she reached the top, she was ready to consign everyone—Matthew, the Barclays, Leslie, Pete, Inspector Dennistoun, the thief, the slow-moving unwashed tourist just ahead—to a one-way trip to Hades.

The breath-taking view of York, however, swept everything from her mind. She simply stood there and absorbed it all. Even the unwashed tourist seemed to appreciate it and merely whispered reverently, ''Willya lookit that?'' Jennet did. The breeze was brisk and had blown the clouds from the sky. York stretched out below, its many architectural treasures gleaming like jewels in the sun. The tourist clicked away with his camera, wondering what this or that building was. Because Jennet had all the answers to his questions, he became convinced she was a tour guide on leave. She assured him she wasn't, pointed out some nice spots for sightseeing, and refused to give him her phone number. He soon left, no doubt to check out Micklegate Bar and Clifford's Tower. Jennet remained for another twenty minutes or so, until her stomach told her it was lunchtime, and her common sense told her she couldn't hide from her problems on the top of the tower, however pleasant the view might be.

Her mental rumblings were noisier than her tummy rumbling, so by the time she reached the bottom, her ill temper had returned. She left the Minster and headed for the Shambles, contemplating suitable places for lunch. Smack in the middle of the tiny medieval street was a redheaded Viking, hawking pamphlets. She could now tell the MacNucator

twins apart fairly well, and this was Kenneth. Or was it?
The Viking had put on an exaggerated Scandinavian accent,
was flourishing his wooden sword with gusto, and was
squeezing the waist of a young female student, whose companion was trying to take her picture but was laughing too
hard. Could that be quiet, studious Kenneth?

"Arrrggh, I t'ink I keep this one meself, and I'll ransack
her duffle bag later!" He squeezed a little tighter.

The girl giggled, and clutched at her backpack. "Hurry
up and take the picture, Sandy! I think he means it!" She
giggled more.

Kenneth put on a ferocious scowl and declared, "We
Vikings are known for ravishing fair maidens, but pillaging
is more profitable!"

The camera finally clicked, and after Kenneth released
his prisoner, he gave her one of the Viking site's pamphlets
and showed her a pegboard of miniature paintings. The two
girls made admiring noises but decided against buying any.
Viking Kenneth appeared disappointed but kept on with his
work. Jennet came up to him.

"What's this? When I saw Pete and Matthew playing
Vikings on my first day here, they didn't have any paintings. By the way, you look quite magnificent in your fin-
ery." Kenneth was wearing the silver-gray cloak Pete had
worn. It set off his red hair nicely.

"Oh, hullo, Jennet. These are just some of my own
works. They're medieval in theme, so when I'm out here
drumming up business, Dr. Graham doesn't mind if I bring
them along. I tell the folk I've plundered them from monasteries." He smiled, but he clearly was proud of his creations. And, when Jennet looked more closely, she decided
he had good reason. The paintings were all small, no larger
than six inches on each side, but they shimmered with vibrant colors and were bordered in gold. They depicted kings
(Charlemagne, Henry II, several of Richard III), common-

ers (peasants with scythes, wagons, and farm animals), and saints (Sts. Martin, Peter, George, Andrew, and a few more she didn't recognize). They were gorgeous. Jennet felt herself salivating.

"They're lovely! I can't believe you haven't shown them to the gang. Don't you think we're the right audience? The Charlemagne looks just like the one on that manuscript of Einhard's *Life of Charlemagne*, and the St. Nicholas is modeled on the window in the Minster, isn't it?"

Kenneth smiled broadly; she had recognized some of his sources. The more closely she looked, however, the more she realized that his models weren't all medieval. She snickered, for in one of the peasant paintings, leaning idly against a cart while others worked, was Douglas. And was that Carleen in the guise of fair Rosamund? And here was Dr. Durrell, as a rotund Franciscan friar, and Olaf, appropriately dressed as a Viking. Suddenly, Jennet wanted to examine all the paintings to see if she could find any other recognizable faces. But Kenneth began shuffling his feet.

"I'm sorry, you probably think I'm taking up space and driving away potential customers. But, honestly, Kenneth, please consider me one! I'd love to have a picture. How much are they? Are there any more back at the dorm?"

The big Scot's impression changed from slightly impatient to thoroughly businesslike. "Weel, I hope you won't be put off by the price, but the thing is that each one takes a long time—I'm following actual medieval painter's guides, even using real gold—so they average, um, two hundred dollars apiece. Of course, I'd knock a wee bit off that for you."

The price was steep, but the vibrant colors captivated her. "I think I can manage it. After all, I'm earning money this summer when I didn't plan to. I guess I'm entitled to splurge a little, don't you?"

"By all means," he replied, "and if you want to splurge

it all on my paintings, my bank account would appreciate it. We MacNucators may be brilliant and talented, but we're not yet rich. I'd have to sell a dozen of these to get our funds in shape after the beating they've taken recently. Speaking of money, I did get a decent donation for the dig this morning. Could I ask you to drop it off there? Dr. Graham plans to dash up to Edinburgh this afternoon, and he'll be wanting to make a deposit tomorrow. I'm sure he'd like to take this one along, and if I keep it in my pocket much longer, it might tempt my scruples."

"Of course. I'd be glad to." He handed her thirty pounds, and said he'd show her his complete collection that evening, if she really was interested. She insisted that she was and left him to his pamphlet-pushing.

As she walked along, the images of Kenneth's paintings remained in her memory. Strange how he didn't want to show them to the others. Was it because he didn't want them to see his little characterizations? No, artists' egos were generally tough enough to deal with the kind of crit icism that caricatures produced. Maybe he didn't want them to see his idealized version of Carleen. The serious, studious Carleen as the Middle Ages' top temptress struck Jennet as extremely unlikely, but obviously Kenneth thought differently.

She was musing over what other goodies Kenneth might have when something he said reminded her of the theft and all its attendant unpleasantries. She and Matthew had wondered what the twins' finances were like. Now she knew they were in debt and, if Kenneth's comment was accurate, to the tune of some two thousand dollars or more. She supposed she'd have to pass that unfortunate piece of news onto Matthew, assuming he still wanted to be the great detective. Well, let him figure it out. Right now she'd drop the donation off and see about lunch.

Inspector Dennistoun had commented on how cleverly

decorated the Viking dig was. Upon seeing it herself, Jennet had to agree. Where the Roman dig had only a modest sign and a few simple explanations of the finds on a bulletin board, the Viking site sported a boldly colored poster of two life-size, leering Norsemen. The one on the left beckoned tourists to take a closer look, while his companion gazed in astonishment at a bulletin board of photographs, drawings and short articles. A balloon above his head declared, "By Odin! Look what they've found now!" The center of the board read THIS WEEK'S FINDS, which included a small silver clasp and several bone and antler needles. Dr. Graham's gang might not have had that much to work with, but they certainly made what they had look good. A small group of tourists evidently thought so, also. Several stood admiring the board, and one elderly couple engaged Olaf in a discussion of a Norse saga. The big blond winked at Jennet as she walked by, searching for Dr. Graham.

There was a small shed to the right of the dig itself. Jennet peeked in and saw a mousy-looking man studying some papers with Douglas. He had pale blue eyes set in a face full of freckles and sandy blond hair, which stuck up in little wisps around his ears. "Dr. Graham?" she asked.

He glanced up, an inquiring look on his face. Douglas' reaction to Jennet's sudden appearance was not so mild. With a cry of "Jennet!" he leaped to his feet, knocking over his metal folding chair. He appraised the damage, which was minimal, then began making introductions. Dr. Graham, meanwhile, rescued the chair, stood, and presented his hand.

"So you're another of this summer's flock of diggers. I'm Archie Graham. What can I do for you?" His voice was unexpectedly rich and mellow and seemed not to fit his body.

She took the chair that Douglas offered her. "Well, to begin, I'm not an archaeologist, but my specialty is medieval history. I'm working for Dr. Durrell. I stopped by today because I ran into Kenneth, and he asked if I'd drop this off. It seems he got a nice donation today.''

The two men's faces were a study in opposites. Dr. Graham's lit up with pecuniary pleasure when he saw the amount. Douglas, however, was evidently under the impression that Jennet had come to see him, and visibly drooped at learning the truth. He did not wait long, though, to try to alter the situation.

''Now that's a lovely bit for the bank,'' he remarked. He made a show of looking at his watch. ''Would ye look at the time, Professor? Are ye sure of the time of your train? We wouldna want ye to be late. Maybe we should call it a day's work. What do you think?''

''Douglas MacNucator, you know perfectly well my train won't leave until three-thirty. Howbeit, I suspect there's more to this than your usual lazy, shiftless behavior.'' He turned to Jennet, who was watching the scene with mild amusement. ''Have you had your lunch, lassie? No? Well then! Douglas, since you're in such a flaming hurry to leave, why don't you take Miss Walker to lunch, to repay her for her kindness.''

Douglas smiled broadly. ''I always follow orders, sir.'' He paused. ''Would this be considered a business lunch, sir?''

Graham's eyes flashed. ''There's a limit, son, to my patience, and . . .''

''Och, can ye no take a joke? We're off, we're off. Have a guid trip, and I'll see ye Tuesday.'' He grabbed Jennet's hand and led her out.

''*Were* you joking about lunch?'' she asked.

''O' course not. I didna think he'd pay, but I thought it worth a chance. Come, I ken a fine little pub down the street.''

Olaf was still the senior citizens' captive. He gave Douglas a dirty look. His voice increased substantially in volume. "The story is that two dwarfs first stabbed him, then drained his blood into a cauldron and two tubs, and then mixed honey with it, making mead." Olaf looked so positively bloodthirsty that the elderly gentleman instinctively wrapped his arm around his wife.

The wife was not dismayed by his ferocious demeanor. "Oh? Then what did they do?"

Olaf mournfully returned to his narrative as Douglas escorted Jennet down the block. The tall Scot chuckled.

"Honestly, you two act like little children sometimes," said Jennet. "I am not a prize up for the taking, you know."

"No, no," Douglas agreed. "But time spent in your bonny company is precious indeed, and ye must forgive us if we do tend to squabble o'er it. Especially as ye seem to prefer to spend it wi' Matt."

Jennet made a small noise, but Douglas noticed it. "Oho! Is that the way the land lies, then? One night ye help him get his heid patched, the next ye'd liefer break it open. Care to tell me about it?"

"No." She sniffed. "Where is this pub? I'm starved."

"Whatever ye say, lass. And the pub's right here." He opened the door of the Goose and the Gander pub for her, guided her to a booth in the gloomy interior. The proprietor, a swarthy Magyar, nodded to them.

"I know what you're having, Douglas, but what would your guest like? I can recommend the goulash."

"Och, Gus, ye always recommend the goulash." Douglas rolled his eyes heavenward." Bring us two bowls and two pints. Unless Jennet would prefer something else?"

She shook her head. Her nose caught the sweet smell of paprika as soon as they entered. In general, she had found exotic food in England to be rather hit-or-miss prospects. Sometimes, as at the Greek tavern in London, it could be exceptionally fine. Other times—a "Mexican" restaurant in

Canterbury came to mind—it could be ghastly. She hoped Gus knew what he was doing.

Douglas chatted about recent finds at their site until the steaming bowls arrived. Hers was delicious, and she ate every bit, scraping the bowl clean with a piece of bread. Douglas looked on admiringly, though whether he was admiring Jennet in general or merely her appetite she did not know.

"I climbed the Minster tower this morning," she said. "I was famished. Thanks for bringing me here, Douglas."

"My pleasure, surely." He gazed at her over his mug.

Something had bothered Jennet for weeks about the twins. She decided to find the answer. "Could you answer a question for me?"

"Anything ye desire, my dear, anything at all." He edged slightly closer to her.

"It's clear you and Kenneth are twins, but why do you speak with a much broader accent than he does?" she asked bluntly.

Douglas threw back his head and howled with laughter. "And here I was hoping ye'd ask me something more personal and special! That's easily explained, love. When we were wee tots, our faither died, and Ma just didna have the siller to raise two strapping lads. So I stayed with Ma in Inverness, and Kenneth went to live with Faither's brother in London. Uncle Jamie was a true Scotsman, but Aunt Bea is from Essex, and I guess Kenneth lost a bit of his Scots under her influence." His blue eyes had a faraway look. "We missed each other like the very deil, even though we wrote letters and got together for holidays. I guess that's why we went into the same field: we couldna play in sandboxes together as lads, so now we can dig at the same site as men. Does that explain the mystery?"

"Of course. It makes sense. I've known friends from New York whose accents faded after living in California for years, but if you put them in a room full of New Yorkers, the accent comes back rather quickly. I've noticed that when Kenneth is upset, his accent gets more noticeable.''

Jennet sipped at her drink, which was properly room temperature. While she wished it was refrigerated, Douglas continued his stealthy slither along the booth's bench. He completed it by wrapping his left arm around her and drawing her close to him. Then a huge grin spread across his broad Scots face, and he bent his head down to kiss her.

Jennet didn't like the idea of making out in public; on the other hand, it was dark in the pub, and Gus didn't seem to be paying attention. What about Matt—who cares about Matt—and *now* what was Douglas doing?

There are limits to what one can do, romantically speaking, in a public house, and Jennet felt that Douglas had just overstepped them. Yes, she had to admit, she was rather enjoying his attentions, but she realized she'd better cool his ardor before he got too carried away. She broke off the latest in a series of long kisses and swatted at his hand, which had crept under her blouse. It was like telling an elephant ''shoo''!

''Come on, Douglas! Knock it off!'' she hissed. Douglas's reply was unintelligible, as he had his mouth buried in the nape of Jennet's neck. It went something to the effect of ''ma bonny, sweetie, angel, darling'' so she knew she wasn't getting through. She tried shoving him. She'd met boulders that moved more easily. Her efforts only succeeded in relocating his caresses to her thighs.

''Stop it, Douglas!'' she snapped. Whether he would have heeded her or not suddenly became supremely irrelevant, for a vast darkness fell over the booth. At first, Jennet thought the lights had been shut off. Then she worried that Gus was purposely turning them down as a favor to Douglas. A moment later she realized it was Olaf standing by their table, his face red with anger.

"Ja, stop it, Douglas. Can you not see the lady does not appreciate your attentions?" he bellowed. He reached in, grabbing the startled Douglas by his shirt, which promptly tore. Olaf got a firmer hold on the Scot's arm and, for an instant, looked as though he hoped it would find the same fate as his shirt. He soon came to realize, as Jennet had, that six-foot-four of fighting MacNucator was not readily budged.

Douglas knocked Olaf's hand away with a meaty thwack. "And by what right do ye come barging in here, unwanted? And I'll have ye know, I'll be wanting ye to replace this shirt."

"Unwanted? Why not ask Jennet if I'm unwanted here? I heard her telling you to keep your filthy hands to yourself!"

Olaf was breathing rapidly, clearly grinding his gears in preparation for a brawl. From the looks of things, Douglas seemed to have fallen into the same mode. Jennet could feel it in the air. She didn't know whether to laugh or cry. Fortunately, Gus could sense the change in temperature as well. He remained behind the bar, but shouted, "Keep it clean, gentlemen. My establishment has a reputation to uphold."

The two men paid no attention to him, but continued to glare at each other. Jennet decided to take action. "If I were a Provençal poet, I'd have you two fight this out bloodily and to the death. Then I'd write it up in lyric song. However, there are laws against that these days, and unlike Queen Guenevere, I don't like being fought over anyway.

"You"—this to Douglas—"had better learn the meaning of cease and desist when a lady tells you to. Otherwise, you're going to be slapped not with a hand, but with some nasty lawsuits."

Douglas looked thoroughly shocked. "Och, ye canna think that I would . . . without even asking . . . and in a pub . . ."

She turned on Olaf. "And I didn't ask you to come in here playing macho hero, either. What were you doing, following us?" Actually, Jennet was glad Olaf had intervened; she wasn't sure she could have held Douglas off unaided. But she wasn't about to give him the satisfaction of knowing that.

"And what if I was? It's a public house, isn't it?" Olaf sounded disappointed that Jennet wasn't prepared to swoon into his arms in gratitude for his gallant rescue.

"Now, I want you both to leave, vamoose, scram. In opposite directions, if necessary."

The steam of their anger slowly fizzled under her assault. "Humph," Olaf said. "I've got better things to do than waste my time pasting this worm to the wall."

"Is that so?" Douglas retorted. "Ye may have a lang reach, Guthfrith, but I ken a thing or twa. But I'll not fight ye, since Jennet doesna wish it."

They both stood, then Olaf turned smartly and stalked out the door. Douglas followed a a moment later, Jennet and Gus the proprietor heaved a mutual sigh of relief.

Then Jennet realized Douglas had stuck her with the bill.

+ + + + + + + + + + + + + + + +

VII

JENNET PAID THE tab, ruefully realizing that the price of two drinks and two servings of goulash was worth keeping two friends out of trouble—even if they were acting like utter chowderheads.

Remembering that she had promised herself to do more sight-seeing in this part of the city, she headed for the Castle Folk Museum. She wandered about until late afternoon, admiring Victorian fashions. Feather boas, bustles, pinched waists—they were gorgeous, but Jennet was grateful she didn't have to cope with such trappings. She enjoyed wearing dressy clothes at times, but favored comfort more. Her backpack was a scaled-down version of her wardrobe at home: casual sportswear, jeans, cotton camp shirts, sweaters, some moderately priced dresses. A graduate student's budget did not allow for high-priced fashions. That thought reminded her of Leslie's exquisite clothing, and she felt a stab of envy. The slim English girl was one of those lucky women who looked well no matter what they wore. That Leslie's family money allowed her to patronize the best names only increased the effect. Jennet wondered what Leslie would have looked like in a bustle. Probably as stunning as ever, she concluded. She then tried imagining herself in Victorian garb. She peered over her shoulder at her rear, unconsciously imitating the model opposite her. When another tourist entered the

125

room and stared at her, she stifled a snort and hurried on
to the next exhibit.

After exhausting the museum's finds, she climbed the
high Norman motte of nearby Clifford's Tower. Since her
academic specialty was medieval warfare, she had visited
this thirteenth-century castle on her last trip to York. She
remembered that morning's outing: she and some other students from the local youth hostel tramped over to the tower,
where she displayed her expertise in describing its unusual
quatrefoil design and how its walls still stood at their original height, though the interior was long gutted.

The tower looked subtly different now, the late afternoon
sun glowing through the balistraria, the arrow loops. Long
shadows stretched from the stonework. Suddenly Jennet
found herself thinking less about the design of the shell keep
and more about its grisly history. On this same Norman
mound, an earlier wooden castle burned to the ground in
1190, killing 150 Jews who sought refuge there during anti-
Semitic riots. Jennet shivered, though the weather was not
chilly. She decided to return to the campus.

She arrived at the dormitory near six, just in time for
dinner. It was Roger's turn to cook, and he had shown
himself to be a dab hand in the kitchen. She hoped he had
something scrumptious prepared; museum-trotting had
worked up her appetite.

Everyone was at the dining room table, waiting for Roger
to emerge with his latest creation. The conversation was
limited to Lewis's and Amy's raving over how close they
were coming to the next niche, which might contain more
finds. Kenneth and Carleen congratulated them, but everyone else—Matthew, Jennet, Olaf, and Douglas—sat in
stony silence.

"When do you think you'll get there?" asked Leslie.
"And will this one be kept a secret also?"

"Ho no!" replied Lewis. "I think the good professor has

decided to take this one to the media in full force. We should break through in another week, unless the monks tampered with the building's structure, and there's no niche there at all.''

"Or else there is, and it's empty," said Kenneth.

"Sure, just like Al Capone's vault," Carleen said. The British didn't know what she was talking about, so she told them the story of the opening of the famed criminal's secret vaults, which took place on nationwide, live TV and revealed absolutely nothing.

"Well, I hope we won't be that embarrassed. Still, I expect Dr. Durrell will ask you to let the news networks and such know when we get close to opening the next one.'' Lewis sniffed the air. "Hurry up, Roger, we're dying of hunger.''

Jennet sniffed, too. It couldn't be. No, it just wasn't fair. But it was.

Roger shoved the kitchen door open with his foot and staggered out bearing a steaming pot of goulash. "I though we'd have something exotic tonight, just for a change.''

Almost everyone murmured appreciatively, but Douglas scraped his chair back. "I'm nae hungry tonight." He left the room abruptly.

Kenneth stared in fascination. "My brother not hungry? He must be sick.''

"I wish," muttered Olaf.

Jennet ate her goulash slowly, wondering if one could die of a surfeit of paprika. She didn't feel much better after dinner, not with Olaf hanging around like a hurt puppy and Matt making his presence felt less obtrusively. She spent the evening ignoring them both and working on page layouts for the illustrations that would accompany the professor's book, an analysis of the differing relationships between church and state in Western Europe during the ninth through eleventh centuries. Somewhat to her surprise,

Lewis sat by her and offered to help. He had never shown much interest in the work she did on the new book, though he naturally discussed the work she produced that dealt with the St. Oswald's dig. It was especially astonishing, considering his remarks to the police the other week. Nevertheless, she soon found he was an outstanding art historian.

He picked up one of the pictures, looked at her caption for it. "Hmmm. This one's that splendid ivory plaque in the Museo del Castello Sforzesco in Milan, isn't it? I like the way it illustrates the religious view of kingship in the tenth century: all the angels floating neatly overhead and Jesus standing right by Otto II's side. That's an excellent caption you've done, by the way."

She appreciated the compliment. The Professor had left the captions and layout to her, since he had so much other work to do. She was deathly afraid of writing something that would jar with his elegant prose.

"Thanks. My favorite part of that plaque is the carving of baby Otto III at Jesus's feet. Only he wasn't Otto III then, just a squirming toddler. It's nice to remember that even stuffy medieval monarchs were babies once."

"True. That's one aspect of Dr. Durrell's writing that I especially admire. He makes the part come to life. His people aren't just dry figures with crowns or miters, they're real. I wish I had that ability. Unfortunately, I'm one of those folks who can store lots upstairs, but I have trouble turning it out on paper in a coherent fashion. I have to rely on the help of the verbally gifted. And from the looks of these, I'd say you belong in that category. Maybe I'll send you my next monograph to edit!"

Jennet smiled. "I now I'm not bad, but I think you're overrating my abilities. Besides, writing captions for photos is peanuts compared to doing articles and essays. You forget, I haven't even started my dissertation yet, much to Dr. Samuel Preston's dismay."

Lewis's dark eyebrows arched in surprise. "You're right, I had forgotten that. It's just you're more competent than people with much more experience. And I believe I read an article of yours in *Historische Zeitschrift* last spring that was quite good. So I am not overrating your abilities."

"You'd better stop, or I'll end up with a swelled head," she said. Out of the corner of her eye, she saw Olaf glaring at Lewis, as though fearing that a new contestant for her favors had emerged. The tall Orkneyman suddenly slammed his binder down on the floor. The noise made everyone jump except Jennet, who saw him do it.

"I've had enough," he boomed.

Enough of what?, Jennet wondered. Was he going to take on Lewis now?

"Matthew, put away your notebook and come for a drive with me. I know a health club where we can go and work off some of this . . . energy." Olaf flexed his muscles dramatically.

Matthew was up like a shot. "You're on. Do they have a basketball court?"

"Everything."

"Then let's go." They ran upstairs and down like a pair of pregnant rhinos and slammed the door so loudly the dormitory seemed to shake. The silence that followed was incredible. Carleon sighed with pleasure and reached for her German-English dictionary to puzzle out another phrase in the everpresent *Untersuchungen zur Geschichte des Kaisers Septimius Severus*.

Lewis cleared his throat, as if he felt he had to make a noise before speaking. "I wish I had their energy. After a day under the church, I'm too tired to do much of anything."

"I imagine it takes a lot to wear out Olaf, and I know that Matthew is a fine athlete. I'm with you, though. Exercise is something you ought to do, I suppose, but I'm not crazy about it." Jennet picked up another photograph. "Here, this one's been giving me fits. Can you lend a hand?"

They discussed the captions for an hour, then Lewis went upstairs early, as was his habit. Jennet worked a while longer, wondering idly when and if Matthew and Olaf would get back, then went to bed. She had long since fallen asleep by the time they got back.

The next few days went by in much the same fashion. Jennet, still annoyed at Matthew's suspicions about Dr. Durrell, continued to avoid him, and he made no serious attempt to resolve their differences. He did try humor, however, which suited him better than the sour face he had worn before. Olaf and Douglas, on the other hand, were another matter. Since their lunch at the pub, Douglas had been in a black mood. She did not know if it was simply because she had spurned his advances, if he thought he missed an opportunity because he had pushed things too far, or more likely, he was embarrassed because Olaf had seen her reject him. Olaf himself seemed to think *he* was the injured party, since she did not appreciate his heroic intervention.

The whole situation would have been unbearable had it not been for the thrill of working at last on the abbey's chronicles with Dr. Durrell. Jennet found herself increasingly thankful that she had survived UCLA's two-quarter killer course on paleography. The course on old manuscripts included an infamous two-day, sixteen-hour final exam, which often made or broke aspiring medievalists. Jennet weathered it, showing a fair talent for the subject, and here it served her well. When the professor first brought out the precious manuscripts, she was able to follow the crabbed hands without much difficulty, and her intensive study of medieval Latin let her translate them readily. Of course, Dr. Durrell had decades of experiences, so she wasn't up to his speed, but he was clearly impressed with her skill.

"You know, my dear, I'm beginning to think we were fated to meet on that bench in Canterbury. What a godsend you are! I never could have managed this with Leslie, though I understand she is quite competent in her own field." He gently pushed the manuscript aside. "Now, let's go over what we have so far."

She shuffled her papers. "There are two hands, one mid-fourteenth century, the other early fifteenth, but they seem to have copied older materials, some dating back to the foundation of the monastery in 1107 by six Norman monks from the Benedictine abbey of St. Benigne in Dijon. That abbey, as we know, was affiliated with the powerful abbey of Cluny. The oldest section of the chronicle states that the six men came to England under the patronage of Archbishop Gerard. Thirteen English monks joined them, and that was the start of St. Oswald's."

"That's interesting in itself. There already were two Benedictine houses in York—St. Mary's and Holy Trinity, founded in 1088 and 1093, respectively—and they also had ties to Cluny. Later archbishops favored St. Mary's, which grew to command thirty five daughter-houses throughout England. I wonder what prompted Gerard to establish another?"

"Isn't 1107 rather late for a Cluniac house? Weren't the trends in monastic reform shifting in the early twelfth century, moving away from the Cluniac tradition?" said Jennet.

"I must remember your specialty is military, not ecclesiastical history," chuckled the professor. "In a sense, you're correct: there were many remarkable developments in monasticism at this time, many of which directly challenged Cluny and ultimately weakened it, but not until much later in the century. We also know, from many sources, that the archbishops of York were always at the forefront of the new movements. For example, the chronicle of Hugh the Chanter at York Minster discusses how Archbishop

Thomas I introduced Norman-style secular canons in the 1070s in York, when he rebuilt the see after the Norman conquest. Then came the Cluniac Benedictines like St. Mary's and St. Oswald's. Next, the archbishops helped the Augustinian canons spread in the early twelfth century. That was led, interestingly enough, by the priory of St. Oswald's in Nostell. No relation to our abbey of the same name.''

"And then came the white monks of the Cistercian order, who tried to reform what they thought were Cluniac abuses of the monastic rule of St. Benedictine. I know their abbeys covered the north of England during the twelfth century. Wasn't there a Cistercian who became an archbishop of York?'' Jennet asked.

Dr. Durrell beamed. "Very good! Henry Murdac, who was the protege of the Cistercian leader, St. Bernard of Clairvaux, became archbishop in 1147. But he had a devil of a time getting there! It was during Stephen's chaotic reign, and there was terrible infighting over the see. It began when Stephen named his half-nephew, William FitzHerbert, as archbishop in January of 1141. Bernard and the monastic leaders in England protested about secular interference in an episcopal election.''

"When did that ever stop an Anglo-Norman king from naming his own candidate to a see?''

"Not very often, as you know. But when Stephen was captured at the Battle of Lincoln in February 1141, the Cistercians brought their case to the pope, charging FitzHerbert with various ecclesiastical misdemeanors. The pope was in a bad position: he didn't want to judge the case because whichever way he ruled, he would alienate somebody, either the monastic reformers or the royalist clergy.''

"So what did he do?'' Jennet asked.

"He booted the case back to England, of course, where two judge-delegates would decide it. One of those judges was Henry of Winchester. . . .''

Jennet hooted. "Who just happened to be King Stephen's brother and William FitzHerbert's half-uncle! So FitzHerbert's case was pretty solid, then."

"Give the pope a little more credit, Jennet. He included a catch: if the dean of York Minster, who supervised the election, testified that FitzHerbert's trial was canonical, all the other charges would be dropped. The reformers were pleased, since the dean was on their side and would certainly testify against FitzHerbert."

"The plot thickens," said Jennet. "What next?"

"After everybody returned to England in May 1143, FitzHerbert suddenly produced a papal document permitting witnesses other than the dean to testify." Dr. Durrell began pacing, caught up in the rhythm of his lecture. "There is no such document in the papal register. David Knowles suggests it was either a forgery or an informal letter, because it is unlikely that Henry of Winchester would have acted without some type of authorization.

"Our abbey chronicle is valuable here, though you haven't read that far yet, Jennet. It mentions this letter and calls it 'a complete fabrication.' "

Jennet chewed on that for a moment. "Hmm. So despite its original ties to a Cluniac daughter-house, by the middle of the century the monks of St. Oswald's had allied with the Cistercians over ecclesiastical reform."

The professor waggled a finger. "Don't forget the climate of the 1140s— England was smack in the middle of a civil war. Our monks of St. Oswald's, though not Cistercians themselves, clearly felt there was altogether too much royal interference in episcopal elections, a frequent conflict of church and state in this era."

She nodded. "I see. What happened then?"

"Much conniving on the part of Henry and Stephen to keep FitzHerbert as archbishop, and a series of popes dying like flies. Between 1143 and 1145, the papacy changed hands four times, alternating between popes who favored the reformers and those who favored King Stephen. The last one was a pupil of Bernard's. He finally brought FitzHerbert to trial and deprived him of his see in 1147.''

"Whew! Is that it?"

"Oh no. Now we get to the violence and the murder." He grinned at her, tapping the Xeroxes of the abbey chronicles. "Though our monastic scribe is a tad skeptical about the events."

"Murder! This is turning into a soap opera, Professor," said Jennet.

"While FitzHerbert was on trial in Rome, his followers vandalized the Cistercian abbey of Fountains and attacked the archdeacon of York. Amid the chaos, the canons held yet another election and named Henry Murdac, Bernard's follower, as archbishop. By this point, the two sides were so embittered that Murdac's five-year archepiscopate was a nightmare of destruction and confiscations.

"William FitzHerbert, meanwhile, vacationed in Sicily and then studied at his uncle Henry's cathedral in Winchester. When the three men responsible for his deprivation— the pope, Bernard and Murdac—all died within four months of each other in 1153, he went back to Rome."

"Let me guess—that would be just in time to meet the new pope, Anastasius IV, who was anti-Cistercian. Oh, what a mess!" She groaned.

Dr. Durrell shuffled papers. "Here's where our chronicle is quite important. We have many other sources for what happened next, but most are pro-FitzHerbert. The St. Oswald scribe is refreshingly doubtful in tone."

Jennet smacked her head. "What a dimwit I am! FitzHerbert is St. William of York, isn't he? The history of Roger of Howden drones endlessly about him. I never made the connection between the names."

"Jolly good. Naturally, the canons protested FitzHerbert's reappointment when he returned in 1154, and a group of them, led by Archdeacon Osbert, went to complain to the archbishop of Canterbury. But FitzHerbert suddenly died, apparently poison in his chalice during Mass. Miracles soon occurred at his tomb, and he was canonized in 1226.''

"What an unlikely candidate for sainthood! A royal pawn caught between sides. I seem to recall Roger of Howden accusing one of the canons of his murder. Does the Oswald chronicle tell more?''

Dr. Durrell leafed through the pages. "Not really. Archdeacon Osbert, who led the opposition, was accused, but the pope acquitted him, and he returned to York. Here's what the abbey chronicle says . . . you puzzle it out.''

Jennet studied the tiny squiggles. " 'Archdeacon Osbert was blameless in this sorrowful matter, and grieved at the sudden death, though he held FitzHerbert his enemy.' It would be more useful if it provided Osbert with an alibi.'' She handed the papers back.

"I think that's enough for now, don't you?'' Dr. Durrell stifled a yawn. Jennet suspected he was ready for a nap. She scooped up her papers and left the office, still pondering the tumultuous events of the twelfth century. Truth was often stranger than fiction, which was one of the many reasons she decided to study history.

While Jennet was closeted with Dr. Durrell, rehashing the chronicles, there was growing excitement in the St. Oswald camp as Lewis and the Barclays came closer to what they hoped was another niche. Their enthusiasm infected the others, even bringing Jennet's grumpy suitors out of their ill tempers. They all wanted to know if they could get ringside seats for the big day, which Lewis estimated would be the following Monday. They were discussing this prospect when the old problem of the theft rose again in an unpleasant manner.

Kenneth was trying to convince Lewis that he'd twist himself pretzel-shaped if that's what it took to get a spot in the undercroft.

The dark-haired scholar threw his hands up in surrender. "I give up! From this very moment, I'm putting the problem in Dr. Durrell's hands. He's the one dealing with the media and planning to have BBC cameras looming over our shoulders. If there's any room for you, ask him about it. I am but a humble digger of dirt."

"Ha," snickered Roger, "you just don't want the responsibility."

His wife chimed in. "You're wrong, Roger, he doesn't want them to blame him because he has to live with them for the rest of the summer."

They were having a good laugh when the doorbell rang. Leslie answered it, and the others heard her talking in a low voice with whoever it was. A moment later, the tall, uniformed figure of Sergeant Corbett entered the room. His attractive face was deadly serious, so Jennet knew he was not just visiting Leslie.

"I do apologize for interrupting your evening. Mr. Barclay, I'd like you to come with me to the station for some questions."

Roger's face registered surprise for a mere instant, then settled into its ordinary peasantlike stoicism. He stood, then turned to his wife, who was beside him on the couch. Whatever he meant to say never left his lips, for he suddenly gasped in alarm.

Amy had fainted.

Roger immediately went to support her, with Corbett by his side. Everyone else crowded around trying to see what had happened. She revived within moments, but looked deathly ill. She clutched at Roger's shirt, and cringed at the sergeant's nearness, as though she feared he would whisk her husband away. Corbett recognized this, and tactfully moved off. Olaf and Lewis brought a pillow and some blankets, while Carleen fetched cool cloths and some water.

After it became clear that Amy had merely fainted, and was not in serious danger, Sergeant Corbett edged back into the spotlight. He was polite, but insistent. "I'm sure your friends will stay with you, Mrs. Barclay, and I promise we won't detain your husband for long. It's just a matter of clearing things up."

"You don't mean to say that you suspect him of the theft, do you?" Amy's voice was fierce in her defense of her spouse.

"I'm not at liberty to say, Mrs. Barclay," the policeman said in the time-honored fashion.

Holding Amy's hand tightly, Roger bent over to kiss her cheek. "It's probably not anything to worry about. I'll be back in a while. I love you." He rose and began to follow Corbett.

"Wait!" Amy cried. "Help me up to our room first. Do you think you can wait as long as that?" The last was directed at the sergeant, who nodded.

"Let me," Olaf shoved his way past Roger and scooped up the petite Amy in one smooth motion. "It's no trouble."

Roger laughed weakly. "I won't argue, not when I know damn well what all those stairs would do to my back." They marched upstairs noisily.

While they were gone, the rest of the group looked around anxiously at each other then descended on the outsider.

"Do you have any more leads?" asked Matthew, following a quick glance at Jennet.

"I'm not at liberty to say, sir," repeated Corbett.

"Do ye ken if Jennet's name has been cleared?" Douglas said sharply.

"I'm not . . ."

"Och, aye, not at liberty," Douglas muttered. "What I'd give tae find that scoundrel and put him 'not at liberty.' "

Lewis, perhaps because of all those present he was most
closely associated with the treasure itself, remained impersonal. "Can you tell us if they've had any leads on the black
market? Any new interest in Anglo-Saxon and Anglo-
Norman art objects?"

The sergeant shook his head and began his litany again.
"I'm terribly afraid I can't tell you anything right now,
other than that we're working on everything. We hope that
Mr. Barclay can assist us. When we make some progress,
we'll let you know."

Jennet knew that however many questions they fired at
Sergeant Corbett, he wouldn't give them a shred of information. As a result, she paid little attention to the conversation. She was more intrigued by Leslie's face. Her
features softened, the elegant British girl was unabashedly
gazing at the young detective. Then Leslie realized that she
was being observed, so she suddenly appeared as serious as
everyone else. Her body language interested Jennet. Leslie
always seemed such a hard-edged person; could it be she
had fallen for the handsome sergeant? Heavens, what would
the former baron and baroness of Rivington say? Or was she
merely using affection to gain information about the case, as
Jennet had feared when she saw them dining together the
other day? If that was true, she hoped that Sergeant Corbett
had the moral fiber to keep business from pleasure.

Roger didn't bother saying good-bye to his friends; when
he reached the entryway, he shouted to Corbett, "Well,
come on, I'm yours for the taking," at which the policeman
left. Olaf came in the living room moments later and announced that Amy was resting.

They spent a most uncomfortable evening, trying to work
on their own projects, but all the while wondering what was
happening to Roger.

*   *   *

Roger returned late, and although they all pestered him for details, he would say nothing more about his experience than that they asked him "a good many questions." The following day, he told Dr. Durrell that he had been brought in for questioning. The little scholar frowned deeply, then asked Roger and Amy into his office, shutting the door after them. Leslie and Jennet, working in the outer office, could not hear a word. When the Barclays emerged later, it was evident that Amy had been crying. Dr. Durrell squeezed her shoulder and walked with them to the dig, leaving Jennet (and, presumably, Leslie) to wonder if Dr. Durrell had had the whole story from Roger. She thought sourly, *That would fit nicely in Matthew's theory that the three of them are working together, wouldn't it?* The case against the Barclays, she admitted, was stronger now that the police had taken an interest in Roger, but she still could not accept the professor's involvement.

She kept working on her rough translation of the chronicle. The oldest section, dealing with the abbey's first thirty years, was written in a rather erudite style. She suspected the unnamed scribe had a better-than-average monastic education and wondered where he was schooled. Lost in thought, she jumped in surprise when Dr. Durrell stuck his head in the office doorway,

"Jennet, my dear, I've made an afternoon appointment with a Miss Selena Embry. Remind me at lunch so I don't go wandering off, would you?" And with that, he disappeared again.

"Do you know who that is?" asked Leslie.

"Never heard of her. Do you?"

Leslie shook her head. They both went back to work. Jennet dutifully reminded the professor, who made a point to eat lunch in his office, not at home. Although the old man was fond of exotic and gourmet cooking, he also had a passion for Wimpyburgers, a passion that he tried concealing from his wife and live-in cook. Jennet had discovered one of her duties, not listed in the job description, was the removal of greasy wrappers and limp fries from the inner office waste basket, so Betsy wouldn't see them. Dr. Durrell obviously enjoyed his occasional cholesterol binges, and his assistant did not mind disposing of the evidence.

An hour later, both Jennet and Leslie were astonished to see a woman, wearing a flowing cotton sarong dyed in a riotous blend of reds and oranges, step into the office. Her long brown hair was done in cornrow braids, and at the end of each braid was a set of tiny brass bells. She wore an incredible assortment of jewelry, mostly bronze and copper, and gold necklaces, though her left hand and wrist bore only silver rings and bracelets. Jennet tried to imagine how much all of those necklaces weighed and what they must feel like around her neck, but gave up. At first, she thought the woman was a college student, but as she moved closer— jingling musically all the time—Jennet realized she was close to forty. However fancifully bedecked she was, her eyes were those of a mature woman, not some kid playing dress-up. Her face, while attractive, was marked with laugh lines and faint shadows under the eyes. She smiled pleasantly. "I'm Selena Embry. I'm here to see the professor."

"Yes, of course. Right this way." Jennet bounded up, rapped on the inner door. "Dr. Durrell, Miss Embry is here."

Dr. Durrell threw open the door and enthusiastically welcomed his visitor. "My dear Miss Embry, I'm delighted to meet you at last! Won't you come in? Jennet, could I trouble you for a fresh pot of tea for my guest?" He then quietly closed the door.

Jennet began to heat water and measure out tea. Leslie stopped typing and stared at the inner door. "This makes the second time today that I wish I could eavesdrop. I wonder why on earth he's invited her over? She doesn't look like an academic, she looks like a holdover from a sixties movie.''

Jennet chuckled. ''I agree with you, though I've met my share of academics who looked like sixties holdovers, including a few who *were* sixties holdovers. Can you imagine typing with all that on? Or even turning pages in a book? If I wore those bells to the university library, they'd throw me out for making too much noise.''

''Still, it does make an effect, doesn't it? I'd have loved to see the looks on the old ladies' faces in the church office when she walked in.'' They both laughed at the thought.

Miss Selena Embry, chains, bracelets, bells and all, did not stay long. Shortly after they finished their tea, the professor came out, leading her by the arm. He nodded politely to his workers. ''Ladies, Miss Embry and I will be going out for the rest of the afternoon. If you want to get in touch with me, we'll be at my house.''

And with that remarkable statement, they left. Leslie and Jennet looked at each other. Leslie said slowly, ''You don't suppose they're going there to . . .''

''Don't be ridiculous. In the first place, he's devoted to Betsy. In the second, why would he make an assignation and then broadcast the news to us? Besides, you heard him say he'd never met her before.''

''Maybe she's a call girl,'' said Leslie in mysterious tones.

''To quote Douglas, 'Pish!' I simply can't see it. There's got to be some other reason.''

That evening, the group was amused to hear of Dr. Durrell's surprise visitor, and they played guessing games about her identity. Pete's suggestion that she was a movie agent hoping to put ''The St. Oswald Story'' on screen topped all others. Much to Jennet's relief, Roger joined in as cheerfully as ever. Amy was more subdued, and Jennet wondered again if she was well. The only one who stayed out of the fun was Matthew, who looked concerned when he heard about Miss Selena Embry.

Jennet knew that there could be a host of hidden motives behind Miss Embry's visit that the gang did not suggest in their game. She also knew they were methodically filed in Matthew's suspicious mind. Perhaps the woman was a fence for the treasure. Judging from the amount of jewelry she was wearing, she certainly was familiar with the subject. Or maybe she was there to put the professor in touch with someone who knew the black market. Other suspicions came to mind.

Suddenly she looked up, feeling Matthew's gaze. His bright brown eyes were thoughtful. *Damn him, damn him anyway, for making me think things like this! I won't accept it! I won't!* But she knew, once again, that there was a certain appalling logic to it.

The rest of the group was busy planning their midsummer picnic, which was scheduled for that Sunday. They had talked about canceling it after the theft, but their spirits were high again as they moved closer to yet another niche. Lewis asked Roger if he felt up to a picnic.

"Sure I am! It'll take more than Inspector Dennistoun to keep me away from a picnic. Especially since Dr. Durrell's packing the food!" He grabbed a bunch of grapes from the table and began munching.

"All you can think of is your stomach. Anyway, you mean Dr. D.'s cook is packing the food. You know perfectly well that the professor can't boil water." Amy affectionately patted her husband's midriff.

"Well, Carleen, at least you can do that," said Pete. She threw a pillow at him.

The rest of the evening was spent devising the other aspects of the picnic menu, which seemed to consist largely of beer, beer, and more beer. Finally, it got to the point where they had discussed the merits and disadvantages of several dozen brands; they started inventing brand names. Matthew began chanting, "Lagers and pilsners and beers, oh my! Lagers and pilsners and beers, oh my!" Whereupon everybody threw couch pillows at him.

Sunday morning was bright and clear, perfect picnic weather. On the whole, it had been clear for most of Jennet's stay in England. Either it was an extraordinary run of good luck or she was just breaking even, for her first visit several years earlier had met with almost continual downpours. As a Californian, Jennet took sunshine for granted and didn't like real weather at all.

Roger, Kenneth, and Olaf were busy fixing last-minute goodies in the kitchen. Carleen was packing paper plates and plastic cutlery. Jennet looked around, realized she couldn't be of immediate assistance, and decided to have a continental breakfast. Kenneth was teasing Roger over Amy's recent slothfulness.

"She used to be the first one up, every morning. I'd become spoiled by it, Roger. By the time I'd get downstairs, she'd already have a pot of tea brewing and toast on the table. Such service!"

Roger shrugged. He knew Kenneth was kidding but didn't respond with his usual quips. "I don't exactly understand it. The only think I can guess is that she's too worked up over, um, everything that's happened." His eyes flicked briefly toward Jennet. He continued. "And, of course, we're quite busy, now that we're moving closer to the next niche. I'd say it's overwork and worry. This picnic will be a welcome break from the routine."

Olaf was slicing onions and snuffling loudly. "You are spoiled, Kenneth, if you can't make your own tea and toast—Akk! These onions are fighting back!— Maybe you should get your own wife, and stop taking advantage of Roger's.'' He inelegantly wiped his eyes on his sleeve.

"I didn't say I couldn't make my own tea, I just said I had become used to Amy's early rising!'' His face was red, as was Carleen's.

"Ta, Kenneth, don't get so upset. Join me in a chorus, 'I've Grown Accustomed to Her Toast.' '' He began humming and chopping in rhythm.

"You look more like Sweeney Todd than Prof. Henry Higgins,'' Jennet told him.

"How about 'Lang Lankin'? Do you know that one?'' He wickedly brandished the knife.

Beware the moss, beware the moor, beware of Lang Lankin,
Make sure the doors are bolted well, lest Lankin should creep in.
There was blood all in the kitchen, there was blood all in the hall;
There was blood all in the parlor, where my lady she did fall.

"That's disgusting,'' said Roger.

"Isn't it just?'' said Olaf cheerfully. He began sauteing the onions in butter.

Matthew and Pete came in. "What's all this about blood? Smells like onions to me,'' said Matt. "Can we help, or is this picnic solely prepared by bloodthirsty killers?''

Olaf tossed Pete his car keys. "Start loading the boot. We're almost done here. And be careful not to scratch anything!'' Jennet snickered. She knew mothers who never lavished such care on their children as Olaf did on his Volvo.

Some time later, everyone assembled in front of the campus gate. They all piled into the Volvo and Dr. Durrell's minivan. By consensus, the taller members of the party went in the van. Jennet, Amy, and Roger squeezed into the back of the Volvo. Pete and Dr. Henley sat in front.

"I thought these were roomy cars," Jennet complained as her knees bonked against the front seat.

"I think there's plenty of room," said Olaf. "At least, there is now that I had the driver's seat moved back. And I'll remind you, it's my opinion that counts: I'm the driver. Shall we race the others?"

"There's no point," Pete remarked. "The van has most of the food. All we have are paper plates and such."

Olaf obviously wished to show he was the Orkneys' version of Mario Andretti, but Dr. Durrell maintained a sedate pace with the van as he led the way through North Yorkshire.

Dr. Henley in particular enjoyed the scenery. "I've been working here for so long, but I hardly get a chance to see anything. This is so beautifully green. I expect to see James Herriot pop up at any minute, treating some of those sheep." She all but pressed her nose against the glass in excitement.

"Actually, Herriot's territory was a little farther north of Ripon," Roger said.

"Who cares? It's the right atmosphere," she replied happily.

It wasn't long before they reached the spectacular ruins of Fountains Abbey. Jennet found herself wondering where Henry Murdac's feet once trod before he became archbishop. They chose a likely field slightly northeast of the abbey, and brought out the baskets of goodies. There were cold chickens, obscenely thick ham sandwiches, pickles, sausages with Olaf's onions on freshly baked rolls, coleslaw and green salad, fresh fruits, with brandied apricot tarts and an almond fudge torte for dessert. And, of course, the carefully selected beers and wines.

"I'm so glad you didn't cancel the picnic, my dear," Betsy Durrell said to her husband. "You look more relaxed than you have in weeks."

The professor himself, nattily attired in a light blue checked shirt, a straw hat, and no tie, leaned casually against a tree. He smiled at Betsy, took her hand in his. "Dear heart, everything is going splendidly, and I can guarantee that it shall continue to do so. I've even taken steps to make sure." His eyes twinkled with an eagerness Jennet had not seen since that night when he told the group about the St. Oswald treasure.

The food, although plentiful, disappeared with astonishing speed. Lewis suggested that they finish their drinks, and then take a tour of the abbey.

"While we wait, though, why don't we have some entertainment?" asked Douglas. "Olaf, I'm forever telling ye tae shut up. Now ye hae the whole of Yorkshire to shriek in, and I'll complain not a bit. Gie us a song!"

The huge blond smacked his hand into his fist. "Damn, I knew we should have brought my concertina and the guitars! Well, no matter. What would you like?"

The requests ranged from drinking songs (Douglas' suggestion) to "anything Scottish" (Carleen) to traditional folk (Jennet) to "something right for the season" (Dr. Henley). But it was Dr. Durrell who requested a love song, and Olaf promptly obliged.

Since e'er I was a laddie, and toilin' at the plough,
I have wrestled sair wi' fortune, this weary world
    through,
But what lightens a' my toil is that happy hour at e'en,
When I meet my bonny lassie 'neath the gloamin' star
    at e'en.

Olaf continued in his fine baritone for several verses. Jennet noted that he cut an impressive figure in a dark blue polo shirt, his wavy blond hair framing a well-defined tan face. Yet as dashing as Olaf looked while he sang of the laddie's love for his bonny lassie, Jennet found she was subtly aware of Matthew's every move as he sat nearby. He certainly lacked Olaf's flair, and most of the men present were wearing better clothes than his patched jeans, red T-shirt, and baseball cap. He had a Bass ale in one hand, the dark green exercise ball in the other. She watched the muscles of his arm and wondered . . .

> Why should I seek for riches when toilin' at the
>   plough?
> There's flooers intae the peasant's path a king could
>   stoop to pu'
> For yonder comes my lassie in beauty like a queen,
> And I'll clasp her to my bosom 'neath the gloamin' star
>   at e'en.

"Bravo!" shouted Dr. Durrell.

"It was lovely, Olaf, but maybe it would be better when the gloamin' star appears in the evening sky," said Leslie.

Huh! thought Jennet. *Either she's a barbarian or she's making a move on Olaf.*

But Olaf paid no attention and launched into something far more cynical entitled, "Gie me a lass wi' a lump o' land," that, surprisingly enough, Dr. Graham also knew and joined. Then they made their way down to the abbey for a tour. Dr. Durrell was a good friend of the caretakers, and arranged for a special tour of their own. Most of the medievalists had been there before, but the Romanists were fascinated.

"I wish we had more sites like this," Matthew sighed.

"You aren't the only one," Dr. Henley replied.

They wandered through the chapter house and undercroft of the monks' dorter, following a sequence that presented aspects of the monks' daily life. Dr. Durrell was giving a lecture on the Cistercian order that under the circumstances Jennet would have paid money to hear, yet when Matthew gently touched her arm and drew her aside, she followed him immediately. They both spoke at the same moment.

"Look, I've been meaning to say something . . ."

"I'm really sorry that . . ."

They broke into laughter. Matthew took her by the shoulders and kissed her quickly. He glanced around. "Maybe the old monks wouldn't approve, but I had to do that. This past week has been driving me crazy. I've decided I don't like it when you're mad at me. You're right; I'm every kind of dummy to have even considered that that sweet old man could have anything to do with the theft, and furthermore . . ."

She put her finger on his lips. "Shhh. It's okay; your intentions were honorable. There have been a few things going on that have perplexed me about Dr. D., although I'm confident he's innocent. Just some funny things, like Selena Embry. Maybe we could talk about them later?"

"Maybe we could." He put his arm around her waist. "Let's rejoin the group now."

"Do we have to?" He sounded like a little kid. "I mean, Kenneth and Carleen are probably out finding love among the ruins, if you hadn't already noticed."

"Yes, but neither one of them is doing a doctoral dissertation on Anglo-Norman England. I'm glad we're not tearing each other's throats out anymore, Matthew, but where else can I get an opportunity like this? C'mon, you'd do the same if Theodor Mommsen was lecturing on Roman legions while walking along Hadrian's Wall." She grabbed his hand, led the way back to the group. He followed, laughing.

"You're right. And that would really be something to

see, considering that he's been dead for eighty-odd years."

"You know what I mean."

The remaining tour was delightful, and everyone went home tired and happy. Jennet felt more relieved than she had for days, and the excitement of the Oswald team was at a fever pitch. They all had a very light supper and sat in the living room, rubbing their hands in anticipation for next day's work. The contents of the next niche would soon be known.

As things turned out, it took slightly longer to break through the masonry the monks used to seal the niche than Lewis had anticipated. By nine o'clock, television and radio news teams had assembled in the church, with their colleagues from newspapers and magazines squeezed under the lights, wires, and cameras. A slightly less raucous group, comprised of visiting medievalists from Oxford, Cambridge, Edinburgh, Paris, and other universities, gathered in the nave.

Lewis had originally estimated the work would take three hours, but as noon came and there was no word from the undercroft, some of the reporters packed up and left in search of faster-breaking stories. The others wandered around, flattering the church's office staff, interviewing the vicar, and pumping Jennet and Leslie.

Jennet idly wondered if any of her words would wind up in the *Los Angeles Times*. If so, she hoped her family would notice. Then she cringed, and prayed that Dr. Samuel Preston would *not*. He'd probably accuse her of wasting time with the media while serious work was at hand. Not that there was anything for her to do just then, except act as Dr. Durrell's gofer. The elderly scholar was down below, and Jennet, as his aide, was one of the privileged few permitted to descend to where the archaeologists were chipping away at the centuries. Kenneth's wishes went unheeded: none of the dormmates were allowed below, and they had trudged off to work at their own sites.

Jennet hovered around the entrance to the cavernlike stairwell, one ear turned to a freckle-faced reporter from some disreputable tabloid who was trying to get one of the guest scholars to connect the dig with King Arthur.

Dr. Durrell called softly, "Jennet, my dear, we've done it. Come down here; I'll brief you on our strategy."

And so she hurried down once more, to join in the discovery. The four crew members were covered with dust from head to toe and grinning like idiots. On the floor, conspicuous among the modern impedimenta of their trade, was a sumptuous decorated chest. It was about three feet by two feet and covered with silver filigree, now blackened with age and broken in many places. It stood on four stout legs, carved like eagle's talons. An enamel border, featuring cheerful ecclesiastics and menacing soldiers, covered the bottom three inches.

She gulped. Her first instinct was to scream, "Open it! Open it now!" like a kid with a long-awaited birthday present, but she knew the contents might be damaged by the dust-filled air.

As though reading her mind, the professor said, "We're all anxious to open it, of course. Could you address our friends upstairs, Jennet? Tell them we've found a chest, similar to the stolen one, and that we'd like them to clear a path to the north porch of the church where we set up that table. Then we'll see what we have, and make the arrangements with the museum staff."

Jennet hurried to carry out the orders, but before she left she saw Lewis's dark head nod briskly. She wondered if he was wishing that they had taken these precautions with the first chest of treasures.

Having already set up their equipment near the stairwell, the reporters reluctantly moved back. Eventually the way was cleared for the three younger archaeologists and their precious burden. Jennet had to chuckle: the chest wasn't even open yet and the academic disputes had begun. Lewis and Amy, as they carefully sidestepped through the church, were arguing over the age of the chest itself.

"The border is similar to the one done in 1128 for Geoffrey of Anjou," muttered Lewis.

"Possibly," replied Amy, the group's other art historian. "But if this is local work, don't you think that similarity would argue for a later date, say, the thirteenth century, especially considering that silverwork?"

"Quit sniping over dates!" huffed Roger. "Let's set the blamed thing down!"

They did, gently. Then they all stood aside and let the professor do the honors. He had removed his hard hat and his bald head dripped with sweat in the packed church. When he had mopped it with his handkerchief it only worsened matters; the dust from the excavation made muddy streaks on his scalp. Yet despite his messy appearance, he was clearly in charge. His eyes sparkled, he all but bounced with excitement.

"Ladies and gentlemen, shall we see what's waiting for us?" He rubbed his hands and opened the simple catch. The hinges creaked but worked well considering their age. He peered inside, smiling broadly, then motioned for his crew to come near.

"Well, well, well, well," Roger said weakly.

Within the chest, neatly folded, was a bundle of stitched linen squares. They were exquisitely embroidered in vibrant colors and in a style reminiscent of that of the Bayeux Tapestry. They had found the tapestry mentioned in the abbey's chronicle.

+ + + + + + + + + + + + + + +

VIII

"**S**O SPEAK! TALK! Give forth! Lecture, for heaven's sake! And don't crowd those pictures, laddie; we all want to see!" The dormmates of the St. Oswald's crew had waited for their triumphant colleagues to return home, and now they were bellowing for insiders' details. Douglas, of course, bellowed the loudest.

"I gather you've found some kind of spectacular tapestry?" asked Matthew.

"We were watching on the telly, but after Dr. D. opened the chest, they didn't show much more than a peek inside it. Too fragile to remove quickly, I suppose?" said Kenneth.

"What's on it? Are those pictures?" asked Carleen, pointing to a pile of photographs.

Jennet, Leslie, the Barclays and Lewis had collapsed on the couch. They wearily looked at each other, then at their enthusiastic friends. Jennet leaned forward, elbows on knees, chin supported in her hands. "Let's make a deal. We need food, drink, and rest. It's obvious we won't get any rest until we satisfy your curiosity, so why don't you ply us with liquor and leftovers and maybe we'll work up the energy to explain what's happened."

"Say no more!" Instantly, the others charged into the kitchen and returned with beers, sodas, pretzels, and cold chicken from the picnic. They dug into the food with a vengeance, but their excitement was such that not even hunger and weariness could keep the story held back.

Roger chewed on a drumstick and began the tale. "You're right, Kenneth. It was too fragile to just lift it out of the chest. We did it at the museum, with the help of their technicians. It's frayed badly in a few spots, but otherwise it's in good shape." He took another mouthful, and Amy resumed the narrative.

"It must have been used in the same way the Bayeux Tapestry was used: for holidays and special occasions, and that's what kept it in good condition. It wouldn't be so vibrant if it had been hanging up all these years."

"You're keeping us in suspense! What's on the damned thing?" asked Olaf. His beer sloshed on his shirt. He ignored it.

"I'd guess it was directly inspired by the Bayeux work," said Lewis. "It not only resembles it in style, though the colors are more varied, but it even has the same theme: a tremendous battle that solidified a kingdom. In this case, the battle of Tinchebray."

Olaf and the twins showed immediate interest. Their specialty demanded a thorough knowledge of English medieval history. The Romanists, however, looked blank.

"Gee, could you enlighten us poor ignorant slobs who think history ends in the fifth or sixth century?" Matthew shrugged helplessly "It sounds neat. Who won? Who fought?"

Lewis gestured towards Jennet, who was working on her second bottle of Watney's and her third piece of chicken. "Here's our resident expert on medieval military matters; ask her."

She took a long swig, gazed at her expectant audience. "Okay, I'll try to keep it short, but believe me, that tapestry will have scholars arguing and squealing for the next decade. It looks like our tapestry was done in honor of Henry I, William the Conqueror's youngest son, just as the Bayeux work celebrated his father's victory at Hastings.''

''It opens with this scene in the New Forest. The date is August 2, 1100.'' She grabbed the stack of photos. ''This guy here, with the arrow in him, is William Rufus, the Conqueror's second son and his successor to the English throne. He's just died in a hunting accident, unless it wasn't an accident at all. They were on a stag hunt—see the deer in the background?''

She picked up the next photo. ''Here's the third son, Henry, riding off to Winchester. The tapestry doesn't show what he did once he got there: he secured the treasury, being no fool. It does show him being anointed, issuing a coronation charter, and marrying the Scottish king's daughter. These next panels are fascinating, because they indicate how he solidified his claim to the throne, but let's move on to the juicy conflict in Normandy.

''You all probably know that William the Conqueror was Duke of Normandy before he crossed the Channel in 1066 and conquered England. His eldest son Robert inherited the Norman duchy when William died in 1087, and William Rufus got England. The two brothers didn't get along. They both schemed and plotted, sponsoring rebellion in each other's territory. Finally they made an agreement in which Rufus loaned Robert money to go on the First Crusade, and Robert pledged Normandy in repayment. During the years Robert was away, Rufus restored order in the duchy.'' She paused for some refreshments.

''Where was young Henry during all this?'' asked Matthew.

''I'm glad you asked,'' said Jennet. ''Henry had dabbled a little in intrigue, too. He got in hot water with both his big brothers, but still remained their heir presumptive, since neither had offspring. From all accounts, Rufus may have been gay and didn't plan to have kids anyway. We're not sure. In any event, he was around forty, unmarried and without issue, as they say. So Henry was next in line for *both* the kingdom and duchy. He was part of Rufus's retinue when the king was killed in the New Forest.''

"And where was brother Bob? Still crusading?'' asked Pete, who had perched on the arm of the couch and was intently studying the photos.

"No, he was just returning to Normandy with a pretty new wife. He had his duchy back and began scheming to take England, too. That's this panel here: Robert put together a fleet and landed at Portsmouth in July 1101; he was rather surprised at the size of the army Henry had, so instead of a battle, they made an agreement. Henry got England, Robert kept Normandy. Naturally, nobody had any intentions of honoring any of it.''

"I suppose this snaky-looking chap is Robert?'' asked Carleen. "What's all this here, bodies on the ground and women weeping?''

"We haven't had much chance to analyze the whole tapestry yet,'' said Lewis with a tired smile. "My guess is it's showing the anarchy in Normandy under Robert, giving Henry an excuse to intervene.''

"Was Robert that bad? We have plenty of Roman emperors who got bad press, but really were not bad administrators,'' said Matthew, helping himself to a piece of pie.

Jennet made a rude noise. "Robert Curthose was a mighty fine soldier, and that was it, folks. Henry had the most brains in that clan. Robert got into more and more administrative and ecclesiastical messes, while Henry systematically wiped out the duke's supporters in England and planned an invasion of Normandy.''

Douglas laughed. "You could call it *The Norman Conquest II* and make it a sequel.''

They had come to a series of photos depicting battle

scenes, crowded with cavalry and foot soldiers in colorful armor, and castles under siege. Matthew whistled through his teeth. "You people are going to be busy with this for a long, long time. I'll bet this will give you all kinds of new information on armor, weapons, battle order, the works."

"You'd win your bet," yawned Jennet. "Dr. Durrell's already putting together a tapestry task force. Uff. I'm falling asleep right here."

"Don't do that!" begged Carleen. "Finish the battle first."

"Okay, okay. Here's Henry in Normandy, taking castles left and right in 1105 and 1106, ending with the siege at Tinchebray itself. Tinchebray belonged to Robert's chief supporter, William of Mortain. That's him with the crooked nose, leading the Norman charge. They pushed back Henry's men, who then dismounted. Plenty of hand-to-hand melee followed. Then Henry's reserve squad rushed in from the left flank. They squashed the Normans, and Robert was captured. The end."

"That's truly a remarkable record," said Olaf. "The prosopographical value alone will be incredible, knowing just who was in the battle and on whose side and how that matches the written records." He shook his head in amazement.

"Come on, everyone," said Kenneth. "Let's put our conquering heroes to bed—look, Amy's out already. I'm sure we'll all be experts on the Battle of Tinchebray by the summer's end."

Jennet was so exhausted, she felt sure that she would fall asleep brushing her teeth. Yet she woke up after several hours' sleep because the room was too warm. She staggered over to the window, stubbing her toe on the nightstand, and pushed the curtains aside to open it. A moving figure caught her eye. It was striding purposefully toward the campus gates. As the figure passed under a light, she noticed the blond hair. It lacked Olaf's size, so there was no question as to who it was. She and Matthew had seen that hurried gait before. It was Pete.

Jennet briefly toyed with the idea of playing detective and following him, or at least of staying up until he came back, but her bed was too inviting. She decided to tell Matthew about it in the morning.

The next week was so hectic that Jennet sometimes wondered when any of them found time to breathe or eat. Her own schedule was so demanding that she had found no chance to talk with Matthew. The professor gave several news conferences on the discovery, and jokingly admitted to the media that he himself knew nothing about preserving permanent press, much less ancient linen, so he was leaving that to the museum staff. The reporters adored him.

All the attention brought back another familiar face: Inspector Dennistoun. He and Sergeant Corbett invited themselves to the dorm one evening, no doubt curious about the latest discovery. The inspector sat down on the couch, chewing on the end of his pen, which he rarely used for its intended purpose. Taking notes was left to the sergeant.

"Well, this time you're in all the papers and on the Beeb as well. A lovely bit of work, that tapestry. Locked up safely, I hope?"

No one answered for a moment. "Yes, Inspector," said Lewis in a toneless voice. "We're taking proper care this time."

Dennistoun turned to Jennet. "Tell me a little about it, then. This case is offering me more lessons in history than I ever had at school."

She briefly recounted the events depicted in the tapestry, but she noticed that Corbett was not bothering to jot notes while she talked. She concluded that Dennistoun was merely trying to soften them up by expressing an interest in the dig.

"Thank you, Miss Walker. Isn't it astonishing how many marvelous artworks from long ago survive to our era, only to disappear in the hands of thieves?"

Such a question had no real answer, so again, no one said anything of substance. Olaf grunted, "Yes, astonishing."

Dennistoun flipped open his notebook. "For example, there was the theft of some medieval illuminated manuscripts from Chichester two years ago; some Greek pots from a private collection in Glasgow in 1986; a couple of thirteenth-century ivories from a church in Senlis, France. The list goes on and on."

He closed the notebook and pointed his angular face at Amy. "Mrs. Barclay, you have a cousin in Chichester, don't you?"

Amy had been sitting rigid with fury since Dennistoun's arrival. Even Roger's comforting arm draped over her shoulder could not calm her. She snapped at the inspector. "Why do you bother to ask questions when you obviously know the answers? Yes, of course I do: Mrs. Emily Mac-Ready. What of it?"

"And you both visited there during the summer those manuscripts were stolen from the university?"

"Yes. But if you'll check your records, Inspector," Amy replied with scorn, "you'll find that we visited in July and the theft was in September. We were back at the University of Kent by then. Have you been wasting your time on that instead of working on this case?"

Dennistoun was unperturbed. "Surely you historians appreciate the value of research. Another thing I've discovered while investigating this case is how often crimes occur at archaeological sites."

His gaze was on the trio of Romanists as he spoke, and it seemed to Jennet that Pete blanched further under his sunburn. She wondered if his late night business was legal and if Dennistoun knew about it.

Matthew, however, had nothing to hide except his mysterious confrontation of the other evening and a sneaking desire to solve the crime himself. He replied, "That's not surprising, really. Most sites are open places, hard to keep secure. People always associate archaeology with treasure hunting, but most digs—St. Oswald's is a grand exception—produce very ordinary objects."

"Oh, I was thinking of some other crimes. For example, Mr. Sharp—" Pete jumped at his name. "You once worked at a site in Oklahoma which was attacked by a group of Indians, allegedly claiming that the diggers were disturbing their ancestors' resting places. They destroyed the shed which housed the crew's finds, stole their money and supplies, and confiscated the discoveries. Care to elaborate on those events, Mr. Sharp?"

Whatever line of questioning Pete had expected, it wasn't that one. He appeared relieved, somehow. "I can't see what this has to do with St. Oswald's. It was an open site, far from the nearest city. A gang of ten or twelve Indians, who had earlier protested the dig at the state capitol, drove up to the camp at night, tied us all up, and trashed the place. I had absolutely nothing to do with it. It was only my second dig, so I was a very junior member."

"Oh, of course, it's obvious you were a victim in this case, Mr. Sharp. It is curious, however, to note that within a few months of that incident, during which the Indians greatly publicized the issue of religious belief against the archaeological studies, you dropped out of the seminary and enrolled in Johns Hopkins."

Pete flared up. "My decisions were personal. Do y'hear me? Personal. They had nothing to do with those Indians. In fact, I had already chosen to leave the seminary before I joined the dig. You can ask any of my friends from back then; ask Father Spacarelli at the seminary. Not that it's any of your goddamn business."

The inspector was as cool as ever. "Rest easy, Mr. Sharp. We're merely checking into everything which might have a bearing on this very serious theft."

"Well, my personal beliefs aren't concerned with it at all."

"Just so, just so. Of course, in these violent times who of us isn't personally acquainted with crime? Miss Stafford knows it well, or so I've heard from the Buxton police. Could you elaborate on the burglary at your family's home a few years ago?"

Leslie shrugged. Her tight dress made this a process worth watching, at least to male eyes. Sergeant Corbett waited to jot down her response, his pencil hovering over the notepad.

"The local police have all the details. We were away at our lodge in Scotland. Two men in masks overpowered our house sitter and took everything that wasn't nailed down."

"Were some of the items art objects or antiques?"

"Certainly. The family silver, some of Mum's and my jewelry, one decent painting . . . but, Inspector, the electronics and other modern items probably equaled them in value. We weren't burglarized because of an extensive art collection, if that's what you mean."

"We are presently investigating all possible angles," said Dennistoun soothingly.

"Weel, the lot of us must get back to our work. Is there an end to your investigating?" asked Douglas.

"Presently. Just a few more questions: mostly for Mr. Hunter."

Lewis, perched on a stool from the kitchen, had been silently watching the confrontations. He now looked up in surprise. "I assure you, Inspector, that I have never been the victim of a burglary, nor has anything unusual ever happened at any site I've worked. Until this one."

"We're aware of that, Mr. Hunter. My questions concern your finances. Would you rather we discuss this in private?''

''These are my friends, my colleagues. They're familiar with the ups and downs of an academic's finances. Mine are perhaps a little more irregular than most; my father was a stock broker, and I still dabble in investments when I can manage it. What did you want to know?''

''Are they going well?''

He waved his hand from side to side. ''Some yes, some no. I admit to being badly hurt in the recent Wall Street crashes, but I've mostly recovered that, thanks in part to a small inheritance from a cousin. My accountant is Louis N. Short; he has all the details. Right now he's annoyed with me for investing in a Japanese firm, Yatusga Electronics, that's sadly floundered. Are you looking for a money motive, Inspector? I rather think we all could use more money, this being a very poor-paying field, but finding the St. Oswald treasure is probably worth more to my career than its cash value would be to my bank account.''

''I see. That brings us to the problem of those missing, presumably stolen, objects which you brought to my attention the day of the theft.'' The group of scholars shuffled in their seats, wondering if Dennistoun had some kind of revelation in store. Some of the dormmates cast sidewise glances at Jennet.

''We checked the shops which were involved. Each one reported that the items were stolen during the week of June 17th, and were returned by Mr. Olaf Guthfrith, who claimed he had found them on the campus.''

Olaf said, ''I didn't want to go into the whole nasty story. They were so pleased at having the merchandise returned intact that they never mentioned trying to press charges against me, in case any of them thought I was responsible.''

Dennistoun smiled for almost the first time. It cracked across his angular face. ''Mr. Guthfrith, I spoke to the shop managers. They were too afraid of what you might do if they accused you of shoplifting.

"In any event, we dusted the items for prints. We found three sets on each: the respective store managers and two others. I assume one set is yours, Mr. Guthfrith. The other is most likely a man's hand, very large with a significant scar on the left thumb."

Douglas held up his thumb. "Och, that's me. I found the stash in the stairway closet and brought them out. But I dinna steal them."

"Could you gentlemen stop by the station this week so we can verify the prints? We'd just like to be on the conservative side." He nodded briskly at them, and rose to leave. "Thank you for your cooperation, and we shall contact you regarding future developments."

The group relaxed after the policemen left. Pete thundered upstairs as soon as the door shut. Carleen shuddered. "Ugh. That Dennistoun makes my skin creep. Mind you, I'm a law-abiding citizen back home, and I have nothing but respect for the police, but there's something fishy about his looks and voice. It's as if he thinks we're a pack of loonies or liars or worse."

Kenneth was sketching a broken bracelet that Douglas had found that morning. He never stopped his work during the policeman's visit; he'd seemed to pay no attention to them at all. But he said, "I don't know about that. He's on to something; he just won't let us know that he knows anything. I'd hate to play cards with him."

Lewis had been working with Leslie on some materials the professor would send to other medievalists, asking them if they were interested in joining the tapestry team. He gave a rueful laugh. "I think the inspector is only just starting to take us seriously. Before, we told him about a stolen treasure that nobody but us knew about. Naturally, he thought we were concocting the whole story out of thin air. Now we're on the evening news with a spectacular discovery. Ho ho, he thinks, maybe there *was* a treasure. So he's suddenly taking a new interest in the case.''

Amy muttered something so coarse that Jennet wasn't sure she heard it properly, but Roger grinned and told her, "Shhhhh."

Later that night, Matthew followed Jennet into the kitchen. "What do you think about all that?" he asked. "We haven't seen the great detective for a while, then *boom!* he's on our doorstep."

She was wrestling with the lid of a jar of apple juice. It opened with a *pop* that provided a sound effect for Matthew's comment. She poured two glasses, then motioned towards the door. "Let's take these outside. It's a beautiful night, and we can talk by ourselves."

Their colleagues in the living room hardly noticed their going. Lewis and Leslie were still addressing envelopes; Olaf and the twins sat at the big table, arguing over something (Olaf and Douglas on opposite sides, as usual); Carleen continued plodding through her turgid tome, with some three hundred pages to go; and Pete, Walkman in place, worked on excavation notes. The Barclays were absent.

Matthew and Jennet walked across the dormitory lawn to the campus quad, which was lined with benches. They sat down and admired the night sky.

"Do you realize if we did this at home at this hour, we'd probably get mugged?" asked Matthew as he casually slid his arm around Jennet's waist.

"There is a night watchman here, you know. Or haven't you met him?"

"Oh, sure. He's that fragile-looking guy who could pass for Dr. Durrell's father. He must provide lots of protection. Too bad he wasn't around the night of the theft." He began kissing the nape of her neck.

"He's not here for protection, he's here to notice if anything funny happens. And you should cool it, Matt, or he'll call the bobbies if he sees you."

"Why? Do you think he'd regard this as 'funny'? I regard it as 'fun.' '' He kissed her thoroughly, knocking her glass of juice over in the process.

He jumped up, cursing mildly. She laughed and tried to wipe the mess. "Now that's 'funny.' Come on, Matthew, this isn't the right time. Anyway, I've got something I wanted to tell you. Do you remember that night when you went snooping for stolen relics and got your head bonked?"

He ineffectually dabbed her skirt with his handkerchief. "I'm not likely to forget it, barring a fit of amnesia. What about it?"

"Do you remember we saw Pete sneaking out of the trailer at your dig? I spotted him making another solitary jaunt around two in the morning."

He arched one of his eyebrows in a splendid imitation of Mr. Spock. "Fascinating. What day was that?"

"The day we unearthed the tapestry. I thought about staying up until he got back, but I was too sleepy. What do you think he's up to?"

"Beats me. I can't imagine anything good, either. Maybe he's trying to make some contacts so he can unload the treasures if, of course, he has them. What on earth would he be doing at the trailer? He couldn't be plotting to snatch the tapestry; it's in the museum." He sighed heavily. "Do you have any more good news?"

"Yes, I do. You know it's been a zoo here since tapestry day. The professor is budgeting every minute of the day, meeting scholars, reporters, members of Parliament, you name it. We may even have royalty dropping in! Prince Charles visited the huge Viking dig here in the late seventies; he's known for supporting archaeology. We're establishing contacts with his staff. And in the midst of all this,

Dr. Durrell wanders into the office and asks Leslie to make an appointment for Miss Selena Embry on Friday.''

"Hmm. Lady Bojangles. Wish I could do something sneaky like bugging his office. That's certainly interesting, but I don't know if it helps us. What about the return of the fuzz?"

Jennet reached over, helped herself to Matthew's still-full glass. "I refuse to think of Inspector Dennistoun as the fuzz. He's decidedly unfuzzlike. At least he's not looming over me with his pointy nose anymore. I agree with Lewis: that he felt he had to make an appearance since we've had so much press lately. Amy certainly dislikes him."

"Amy hates anything that threatens Roger, and Dennistoun did just that. I wonder if there's any way to find out what that was about? Sergeant Corbett wasn't very helpful the other evening. Hey, you finished my juice." He tried to sound indignant, but his smile betrayed him.

"Next time don't spill mine. Do you want to hear something else strange? With all of the excitement surrounding the tapestry, the theft of the first treasure just doesn't seem very important right now. I know it is, of course, but I wasn't here for the first discovery. It's as though it all happened in another time, to another person. I don't even feel that I'm the center of suspicion anymore, not with Roger getting hauled in for questioning." She stood up and wrung her skirt again and smoothed out the wrinkles.

"Do you really think the others still don't suspect you?"

"It's hard to say. I don't think they *actively* suspect me the way they did before. But it may just be that they're all so busy they don't have time to worry about it. The Barclays still do, but everyone else has quieted down. And Olaf and Douglas think I'm pure as the driven snow."

Matthew smiled broadly. "Those two will start suspecting you of *something* if you stay out here much longer with me." He rose to stand by her side.

"Oh?" she replied softly. "Maybe we could think of something guilty to do." She put her arms around him, tilted her head up to kiss him.

Several minutes later, a querulous voice interrupted them: "Now then, young sir, young miss, this isn't the place for that sort of thing."

The next morning everyone gathered at the table for breakfast. Matthew drew Pete out of his silence by speculating wildly on the status of the baseball pennant races back in the States. He slurped his cola and made disparaging remarks about the Phillies. "No bullpen, nobody that hits for power, nobody gets on base . . . what a load of stiffs! The Cubs will clean their clocks."

Pete's eyes flashed, and he stabbed an egg viciously. "Izzatso? What about your favorites, the Angels? That's not a team, it's a bunch of also-rans. Why, they couldn't win the big one if . . ."

Olaf snapped his newspaper imperiously. "Children, please. Some of us are trying to dine in peace."

Leslie spooned some more yogurt into a bowl. She remarked, "Go easy on them, Olaf. They can only fantasize about what their teams are doing because the papers here don't cover most American sports. Besides, you and Douglas were going hammer and tongs over the latest football scores last week." She smiled at the Americans. "That's soccer to you. Of course, your brand of football has become quite popular here. It's all the rage."

Kenneth came in with the mail and began distributing it. "Letter for Leslie, official-looking junk for Lewis, *two* letters for Carleen, a bill for my darling brother, and some kind of overnight delivery for Jennet."

"What on earth could that be?" she wondered, ripping it open. She read it quickly, eyes widening.

"I do hope it's not bad news," Douglas said.

Jennet began laughing weakly. "It depends on how you look at it. My advisor is joining the tapestry team for the rest of the summer. He wants to stay here."

Preston's letter was as forthright as the man himself. It mentioned the importance of the discovery, how he hoped (read: demanded) she would make the most of the opportunity, and that he planned to stay at the dorm with them, assuming there was room (and he knew perfectly well there was). He planned to arrive in two days. The implicit message requested a ride from Manchester airport, although Jennet knew Preston could find transportation himself if he needed to. She decided to ask Dr. Durrell about it.

When she entered his office that morning, she met with the second of the day's surprises. Seated opposite the professor was the charming young scholar from Durham, Miles Beckwith, with whom she had dined in London. He rose politely when she came in and warmly shook her hand.

"If I remember correctly, Ms. Walker, you came to England to deliver a paper and travel. The next thing I know, you've a summer job that just happens to include finding one of the most splendid archaeological discoveries of the century! Not bad for a few months' work, I'd say. Are you enjoying it?"

"Yes, very much. The tapestry is a true work of art, and it offers such wonderful information for my own area of specialization—armor and weaponry—that I'm tempted to take up Dr. Durrell's suggestion and change my dissertation topic."

"Why not?" Miles said. "What other graduate student is right on the cutting edge of the tapestry's history? You have an unbelievable advantage, and I'd wager you'd have no problems publishing it afterward."

Jennet sat down, took a cup of tea from Dr. Durrell.

"Please! Don't you start in, too. I'm going to get it from both ends in a few more days. Dr. D., my boss wants to join the tapestry team."

The elderly scholar clapped his hands enthusiastically. "In case you don't recall, Miles, her boss is Samuel Preston. How delightful! I thought he and Lillian were traveling this summer. I do hope he's not cutting their vacation short. Lillian will be so annoyed."

"No, they were staying home. They were both working on books, and if I had to guess, I'd say Lillian's will see print first. The boss is prone to writer's blocks. He looks for excuses to quit and let the mental juices simmer. Not that the tapestry is an excuse, mind you. It simply gives him added incentive to join us."

"We'd love to have him. Where will he be staying?"

She squirmed slightly. "He wants to stay at the dormitory." She still couldn't reconcile the image of the Shark roughing it in student rooms with a rowdy group considerably younger than he was. Actually, the rowdy part wasn't so bad. She'd seen Preston dancing to rock music at some of the postseminar bashes he'd given. He also was good with students, if bombastic at times. It was the picture of him in those tiny, sparse rooms, sharing bathroom facilities with Olaf and Douglas, taking his turn cooking (cooking!), that set her mind reeling. Not to mention having him constantly underfoot, nagging her about her dissertation. . . .

She was so lost in thought that she missed the professor's reply. Something about Miles? Then it sank in.

"Perhaps he and Miles can have adjoining suites, though I don't suppose you could exactly call them suites, eh, Jennet? Would you be a dear and settle Miles in with your colleagues? He's going to be an important part of our team. Have you read his book on the Norman nobility? It's quite good. He'll be an enormous help identifying Henry's and Robert's supporters."

"I thought the section on the late eleventh century was especially well done." She tactfully did not mention that it was the only part of the book she'd read. It had come out just before she took her exams, and she was down to reading bare essentials by then.

Miles nodded modestly. He slipped on a light leather jacket, hefted his suitcase. "Dr. Durrell has said he'll take me over to the museum this afternoon. If you like, I'll take you to lunch after you show me where I'll be staying."

Dr. Durrell beamed with avuncular delight. "That's a marvelous idea, Miles! Jennet deserves a leisurely lunch. She works like a slave around here."

Something within Jennet tugged disconcertingly. She couldn't put her finger on it. It wasn't the prospect of lunching with Miles. She'd enjoy that; he was good company and they had plenty to discuss about what they'd be doing. It wasn't that Miles planned to stay at the dorm. He wasn't far removed from his student days, so he'd fit in well. She could even imagine him fixing dinner on his assigned evening. So what was it?

Whatever it was, it would surface eventually. "I'd be delighted to help. By the way, Professor, there's another stack of mail for you. Nothing urgent, but you may want to reply to Drs. Bizot and Staley before you crawl through the rest."

"Oh bother!" muttered Dr. Durrell. "See to it later, would you? Just give them the standard answer that I'll get back to them in greater detail later. Say, next year. Now be off with you. I'll see you later."

As they left the inner office, Jennet saw that Leslie had taken her place at the other desk. She saw Miles, and gave him a dazzling smile, which he returned. The young professor might not be able to compete with Sergeant Corbett for striking good looks, but he was definitely worth noticing, with close-cut, light brown hair and a well-defined

chin. Jennet introduced them, and mentioned that Miles
would join them at the dorm.

"Leslie is Dr. D's other slave. We may not do heavy
work like the crew, but we push papers for hours on end."

"I'm sure you do," Miles said. "What's your field, Ms.
Stafford?"

"Late nineteenth-century economic history." A brief
chill descended.

"Oh." The word was no doubt meant to be noncommi-
tal, but everyone in the room knew better. To Leslie, it
meant another bloody medievalist who didn't care how
much she knew about colonialism and trade in India. To
Miles Beckwith, it classified Leslie as a pretty secretary
who couldn't read Latin and was therefore of limited value.
To Jennet, it meant tightening the tension in the dorm by
another few notches.

They soon left. Jennet guided Miles to the campus and
showed him the dormitory. He accepted the Spartan sur-
roundings with equanimity, remarking that he was pleased
to have rent-free accommodations. "I couldn't sublet my
flat in Durham on such short notice and didn't think I could
afford this escapade until Edwin told me about this place. I
look forward to meeting your friends tonight. Shall we have
lunch now?"

He chose a pleasant seafood restaurant in the center of
town. The conversation was stimulating, though the wait-
ress did give them curious looks when Jennet began sketching the battle order at Tinchebray on her napkin. She found
herself having a wonderful time until that nagging thought
came back. She finally pinned it down while they walked
back to St. Oswald's.

Miles Beckwith had written a scathing review of Preston's last book in the *English Historical Review*, and the
Shark had had screaming fits about it. The confrontation
would be interesting.

* * *

The dormitory crowd accepted Miles politely. Olaf and Douglas, though, watched him like a pair of hawks that first night, and Matthew seemed annoyed that Jennet spent the entire evening chatting about the count of Brittany with the newcomer. The Barclays knew him by reputation, and Lewis had met him several times at conferences. He had an unassuming nature and a quiet sense of humor, so Jennet was confident that he'd fit in well, given a little time.

She was not so sure about the impending arrival of Preston. Fretting about it, however, wouldn't help matters. Olaf had offered to drive her in his cherished Volvo to Manchester airport; Jennet did not know whether he viewed that as a chance to spend some time alone with her or merely as an excuse to leave work. He was not notoriously lazy, as Douglas was, but the Viking crew had been plagued with bad luck lately, and Dr. Graham was acting "positively menopausal," as Kenneth rudely put it.

They left in the morning after breakfast. Jennet discovered that the front seat of the Volvo was far roomier than the rear, owing to the adjustments made for Olaf's height. The big blonde was in a peppy mood, and spent the first twenty minutes of the drive singing bawdy ballads. Jennet didn't recognize most of them, but she enjoyed them all. She joined in when he began "The Two Magicians" about a blacksmith's relentless pursuit of his beloved, a stubborn witch.

She became a trout, a trout all in the brook,
And he became a feathered fly and catched her with his
    hook
She became a rose, a rose all in the wood,
And he became a bumblebee and kissed her where she
    stood.
Hello, hello, hello, hello you coal black smith, you

have done me no harm.
You never shall have me maidenhead that I have kept
    so long.
I'd rather die a maid, she said, and be buried all in me
    grave
Than to have such a dusty, musty, crusty, fusty coal
    black smith.
A maiden I will die.

They ended the song, and Olaf thumped his hands on the steering wheel. Jennet jumped nervously. She knew her singing wasn't in a class with Olaf's, but she was good enough to sing solos in her high-school musical productions. But it wasn't how well she carried a tune that bothered Olaf.

"We sing well together, don't we?" he asked. His accent was a bit thicker than usual; 'we' sounded more like 've.'

"You sing like a professional. I'm just adequate," she replied.

He remained silent for a few moments, intent on squeezing past a slow-moving truck.

"Truly, Jennet, I find you a great deal more than adequate in more ways than I could ever say, but it's little use even trying to tell you. It's that American fellow, isn't it?"

She wondered how to put it delicately, then gave up. "Yes. At least I think so."

He sighed. "Well, he's a damn sight better than Douglas. That Scottish lout lured away a girlfriend of mine two years ago, only to dump her three months later. She vowed never to date an archaeologist again. I told her archaeologists were only interested in dates."

Jennet began laughing in spite of herself. She now saw where the famous rivalry had begun. While she chuckled, Olaf asked her with great seriousness, "Did I place second?"

"I really hadn't created a contest here, you know. I'm

beginning to realize how Paris must have felt with the three goddesses looming over him, waiting for his choice. Matthew and I . . . just happened. I don't know how or why, we just did. But if it's any consolation, Olaf, I do understand that your feelings are sincere. I've never been quite sure about Douglas.''

Olaf said something Norwegian that sounded nasty. ''I had to ask, anyway. I'm starting to get paranoid where he's concerned. I even hoped that the new chappie from Durham would outdistance Douglas.''

''Miles?'' Jennet sounded surprised. ''For heaven's sake, he just got here!''

''True, but you knew him already and worked in the same field. I reasoned that gave him some distinct advantages.''

''That's ridiculous.'' Then she wondered if Matthew thought the same thing. Miles was pleasant and attractive, and they did have a lot in common, but she certainly wasn't planning to make a conquest out of him. And he behaved like a gentleman, not some lovelorn adolescent.

Olaf sighed again. ''You know how I feel, Jennet dear. Don't forget it, and I'll keep on hoping you'll change your mind.'' With that, he broke into a resounding Alfred Drake imitation and crooned, ''So In Love.''

There is something mesmerizing about hearing a love ballad rendered with utter sincerity. Jennet had to shake herself mentally. She was glad they were on the road, because she had the feeling that she was melting. Better to move to a different topic, quickly. She applauded. ''Why on earth don't you go professional? It'd be far more profitable than digging up Vikings.''

''Why don't you abandon your field? It doesn't have any more career opportunities than mine. We stay because we love it. Besides, the kind of music I like is too strange a blend to make money. It's a mix of folk, rock, and Broadway musicals. And you forget, my dear, I come from a feelthy rich family. I'm digging up Erik Bloodaxe because that's what I want to do. And I sing what I want to sing. I yam what I yam, and that's all what I yam." His tone was defiant, which Jennet thought was a good sign. She liked Olaf and didn't want to see him glum.

"Good heavens, do they have Popeye the Sailor in the Orkneys? Such culture. What do they call you people, anyway—Orcs?"

He sniffed. "Orcadians. We bear no relation to nasty Tolkien monsters. Or else Orkneymen."

"Do all Orcadians sing like you?"

"Oh no. I'm not very typical. I'm much too loud. I favor my mum, who was from Edinburgh and sings like an angel and makes more noise than any three people you could name. Including Douglas. I had to speak up to get a word in edgewise at home.

"Most Orcadians are silent types—my dad is one. We tell a story about two brothers. One suddenly left home without a word, went to Canada and became a trapper. Twelve years later, he returns home. His brother looks up, says 'Where are thu been all this time?' The trapper replies, 'Oot.' Now *those* are true Orcadians.

"My family's more of a North Sea amalgamation: relatives from Scotland, Orkney, Shetland, Norway. My grandfather, who married a pretty Norwegian lass, has a good-sized cattle ranch near Kirkwall, the largest town in Orkney. My father didn't want to be tied down to it. There's sailor's blood in the Guthfriths, and it popped up in him. He traveled around the world, spent a lot of time in Canada with Grandmother's brother, who had emigrated and ran a successful auto-parts factory. He died childless, leaving Father with a fortune. Father had learned about business from the inside out, but now he felt it was time to get some formal training. He enrolled at the University of Edinburgh, where he met Ma, an engineering major. They made a great team. They went into manufacturing—transistors at first, but now they've diversified, gone into computers. In the meantime, they produced me and my older brother Tirval, who runs the family's Ontario branch.''

Jennet remembered something the others had said. "But I thought your father was an oil man.''

He shook his head. ''Not in the strictest sense. He's on an oil development advisory council, and there's not much money in that, really. My family are not major stockholders in Mobil Oil or anything like that. Actually, Father got involved more for defensive reasons than anything else. You see, when major oil and gas basins were found in the North Sea back in the early seventies, it meant a lot of changes for communities as small and vulnerable as Shetland and Orkney.''

"You mean it was you folks versus the oil industry?''

"Yes. Everything had to be done from scratch—terminals, air strips, rigs, housing for the construction crews and the new oil workers, schooling for their children. There were a lot of hard decisions that had to be made quickly, and believe me, the oil companies were in no mood to wait. We established the council to maintain as much local control over these matters as we could and to help divert some of the revenues toward developing traditional Orcadian industries like crofting, cattle raising, fishing, and knitting.''

"Has it worked?''

"Yes and no. In many cases, we're still at odds with the oil companies over certain issues, but at least we didn't let them run roughshod over us.'' He sighed. ''I sometimes wonder if the changes were worth it. On the one hand, it's brought new jobs and new blood, but unlike the rest of Britain, we were fairly stable before the boom. I watched them turn the little island of Flotta into a huge oil terminal, saw them blast the hillside of Mavis Grind in Shetland to build new roads. And o'course, there are spills, some of which were deliberate dumps. I know the modern world runs on fossil fuel, but I wish they didn't have to get it in my backyard.''

"I feel the same way about offshore rigs in L.A.,'' said Jennet.

"We'll be at the airport soon. Care to clue me in on this professor of yours?''

Jennet did, giving a brief rundown of Preston's specialties and his recent publications. She also mentioned certain of his personality traits. "He loathes flying, so he'll be in an awful mood.''

"He could be a two-headed ogre, and he'd be more polite than Graham's been this week. If we don't find something soon, he may strangle Douglas and bury him just so he can find some bones. Come to think of it, that's not a bad idea. I'll handle your man.''

The plane was nearly an hour late, and it took forever to clear customs. When they did find Preston, he was almost visibly steaming. His silver hair stuck up in unruly cowlicks, his suit bore dozens of wrinkles. He began to tell his tale of woe when Olaf smoothly interrupted. "Dr. Preston! It's a grand pleasure to meet you. Jennet's told us so much about you. Here, let me take those bags.'' He hefted them easily. "I believe I read a monograph you did on the Danegeld several years ago with Gregory Andersen. Marvelous bit of work. I know you'll be most welcome at the dorm. Not that it's the Hilton, of course, but we're a right jolly bunch. This tapestry is rather incredible, isn't it? Wish we'd get something like that in our field. Oh. Right. I'm Olaf Guthfrith, currently working with Archie Graham.''

Jennet didn't know how he did it, but Olaf kept up a running stream of patter that held Preston still until the suitcases were loaded. Then he took them to a restaurant for lunch, which Jennet regarded as a brilliant move: once

Preston was fed, he'd feel much more agreeable about things. It worked. Olaf left the table during lunch, and Preston said eagerly, "What a delightful young man! You know, I was a little uneasy about moving in with all of you. Now I'm convinced it will be tremendous fun!"

Jennet groaned inwardly.

Her worrying was needless, as things turned out. Preston was so excited over the York Tapestry that he was at his most convivial. The modest accommodations produced no complaints, and it was then that Jennet remembered the Prestons often traveled in the Orient under much more primitive settings than a college dorm.

When Amy brought up the problem of the dinner schedules, he eagerly offered to join in. He also made a trip to the grocery and stocked up the refrigerator with piles of expensive food and drinks, which he offered to all. He also urged them to call him Sam. Jennet had the feeling he'd start bellowing "Hail, fellow! Well met!" if given the chance. Good ol' Sammy, just one of the guys.

This notion lasted until the after-dinner work session began. The Dr. Durrell came over, bringing the very latest of the work on the tapestry. Then the professors were separated from the grads and recent grads. Preston plunged into the material, ignoring any sign of jet lag. He made suggestions, he asked questions, he devoured tiny details. For a while, Miles Beckwith kept up with him, but it was only because he was slightly more familiar with the panels. After two hours—during which Jennet was taking frantic notes— they quit.

Preston rubbed his eyes. "Damn, this is fun! But we'd better call it a night or a day or whatever. I'm beginning to see little embroidered soldiers where there aren't any."

"You should get some rest, Dr. Prest . . . uh . . . Sam," said Roger. "Tomorrow you'll see the real thing in the museum. And we'll be back at work underneath St. Os-wald's."

"How are things going? I'm not an archaeologist myself, so speak in layman's terms."

Lewis, the dig's leader, answered. "We've found a strange indentation in the floor of the niche where the tapestry was. It has a covering of that sixteenth-century mortar. We may have more to study in a few more days."

"And we *had* even more," grumbled Amy.

"The treasure that was stolen? Terrible, just terrible. And I suppose nobody has a clue where it is?" He began folding papers into origami birds, a practice he'd developed while traveling with Lillian.

There was a brief silence, then Dr. Durrell replied, "No, we have no leads." Jennet was glad he did not elaborate. Her mind wandered; then Dr. Durrell was asking her a question.

"My dear, I know we have so much to do here, but would you object to a little overtime, starting tomorrow?" He smiled at her, knowing the answer already. What could she say but yes, especially with the Shark sitting there, nodding contentedly?

She said it, and the professor outlined what he wanted her to do: keep on with the paperwork for the new developments at the dig and continue to assist him with the newly found editions of the chronicles, but now she was also to be the official amanuensis for the tapestry team. She would be Dr. Durrell's right hand as he coordinated the efforts of the international team of scholars now invading York. It was a splendid professional opportunity. The best part about it, she realized, was that she'd be able to work even more closely with the elderly scholar than before.

"Some days I'll need you to come to the museum with me, some nights we'll have to stay up late putting together the day's results. On those nights, I suggest you bring a bag and use our spare room. We old folks don't sleep much, you know!'' He chuckled. So did his crew, thinking of times they'd found him napping.

"I really don't think that's necessary, Professor. It's such a short walk to the dorm from your house."

"Nonsense! I can't have you walking around the city at night. It's settled. You'll be no trouble at all. Betsy agrees with me, it's much the best plan."

Jennet felt a mild twinge of regret: she'd miss her evening visits with Matthew and the others, but the prospect was so inviting, she accepted with delight.

The work was thrilling, as she expected, but it was not so overwhelming that she became a permanent houseguest of the Durrells. She found she was spending every third night there, and along with the joys of working closely with one of the world's experts in her field, she reveled in enormous breakfasts the Durrells' cook made. When she ignored the Indian take-out he brought, Matthew complained she didn't eat lunch anymore.

"No, honestly, Matthew, I couldn't eat a thing," she protested. "You can't believe what the Durrells eat for breakfast—heavenly crepes, omlettes stuffed with all kinds of goodies, pastries—I'm going to have to go on a diet just to compensate."

Matthew looked glumly at the little packets of curry. "I suppose I could take it back to the dorm's refrigerator, but Douglas will probably scarf it down when I'm not watching. You're really wallowing in this stuff. And I don't mean the hearty breakfasts, either. Is it the tapestry?"

"Yes, partly, but I'm not enough of an art historian to go after that angle. I'm happier dealing with its historical relevance. But that chronicle! We're plunging into a text that's never been seen before. I admit, it's not earthshaking material; it's not going to drastically alter our views on medieval England, but still, there's all kinds of tasty goodies in every sentence. How would you feel if you found the missing books of Livy stashed away in some desert hideaway in Egypt?''

He gnawed on a chicken leg and pondered the question. ''I'd read them secretly, then bury them again. Do you have any idea how much extra *work* that would mean for struggling grad students in ancient history?''

''Be serious!''

''Okay, okay. So enlighten this barbarian. What tidbits did the old monks of St. Ozzie's have tucked away?''

''Plenty. There's some additional background to a serious conflict over the archepiscopate in the 1140s, nifty descriptions of the daily life in the monastery which we can compare with the accounts of Jocelin of Brakelond, even early textual criticism.'' In her enthusiasm, Jennet began nibbling at pita bread. Matthew affected not to notice.

She continued. ''The unnamed earliest chronicler apparently got his hands on the *Chronicon* of Abbot Hugh of Flavigny, which is in France. Abbot Hugh came to England as papal legate in 1096 and had some very rude things to say about the country, its king, its clergymen. Our monk takes notable exception to Hugh's descriptions, denying them as products of a 'misguided soul.' It's fairly biting.''

''Sounds like it. I wish we had a tenth of the material you do.'' He cleared up the mess, placing the bag of leftovers on the ground. He looked around cautiously, but the office was empty. Leslie, as usual, was dining out, and the professor was at home. He gathered Jennet into his arms, kissing her gently.

''I miss you, you know that? I miss seeing you hunched over those stupid three-by-five cards, miss talking with you at breakfast. Having Preston sitting in what I regard as *your* chair just isn't the same.''

She smoothed the hair out of his eyes. ''I miss you, too . . .''

He interrupted. ''No, you don't. You've got the good luck to be on the cutting edge of academic history, and you're making the most of it. That's what you should do. Though I confess I'll be happy when things settle down a bit.''

She tried to think of something to say, but couldn't. He was right, and she knew it. She'd hardly given a thought to anything in the twentieth century for days. She gave a tiny shrug.

He laughed. ''Some men might be offended to realize their lady loves find greater fascination in musty manuscripts than in their amorous ambitions. Fortunately, I'm another academic.'' He bowed in his best courtly fashion, kissed her hand. For some reason, she found it tremendously erotic and wished he didn't have to leave.

''When things settle down,'' he repeated as he headed out the door.

Whatever Matthew and Jennet may have hoped for, developments at St. Oswald's only grew more complex. Lewis and the Barclays worked at the mysterious indentation in the niche and revealed some badly carved letters under the layer of mortar: ARCHIEPISCOPUS GIRARDUS. The tapestry team, Jennet among them, hurried over when they heard the news. The medievalists were dredging up what they remembered of the career of Gerard, Archbishop of York, while Lewis and Roger carefully cut away the carved segment of stone. It lifted easily. Amy peered into the crevice and gave an involuntary shriek. Lewis leaned over. He cleared his throat, shouted up to the waiting scholars:

''There's a body in here.''

+ + + + + + + + + + + + + + + + +

IX

To be precise, there were pieces of a body in the crevice. But when Jennet's turn for a glimpse came, she understood why Amy was so startled: part of the skull grinned eerily at its observers. At the time, she thought it would have made a terrific lead photo for the tabloids, but as matters turned out, the Fleet Street scribes had plenty to keep their readers entertained.

A trio of experts from the museum carefully removed the bones for further study. The excited crowd of medievalists followed them back for more of what Preston called "tapestry tales." Amy, Roger and Lewis looked on forlornly, perhaps wishing they'd kept all the news to themselves.

That evening was Pete's turn as chef. He had prepared a magnificent seafood salad, and while he was concocting it, he banned everyone from the kitchen. All the others were already seated and chattering about the day's discovery, when Pete kicked open the door and displayed his creation in a huge glass bowl.

"That's lovely, Petey dear," said Douglas, "and I'm sure we're all delighted that ye've worked so hard fixing it. But ye've no heard the news: our Oswaldians hae found a body in the church."

Pete almost dropped the heavy bowl. Lewis, seated nearest the door, took it from him. "It looks too good to spill, Pete. Come, sit down and hear what's been going on."

"Yeah, sure," said Pete. "A body, huh? How old? What I wouldn't give to have even a piece of a Roman!"

"We're not certain yet," said Miles. "If the engraved letters on the stone are correct, then what we have are the remains of Archbishop Gerard, who died in late 1108."

Carleen whistled in an unladylike manner. "Almost nine hundred years old."

"Wait a minute." Matthew speared a shrimp, crunched it, and looked puzzled. "This was an archbishop of York? So why isn't he buried with all the rest of them in York Minster?"

Preston smiled. "He was waiting for us to find him. No, seriously, that's a good question. Who wants to answer? Jennet?"

Jennet silently cursed her advisor for his habit of turning even dinner discussions into study sessions, but the material was so fascinating, she jumped in. "Gerard was archbishop from 1100 to his death. Before that, he was bishop of Hereford and a chancellor. He was one of the few prelates around when Henry seized power after Rufus's death. It's been argued that he helped crown Henry, and if the tapestry is accurate, he did. Some chroniclers say he only did it on the condition that Henry give him the next vacant archbishopric. I don't know if that's true, but he did get York a few months later; Henry certainly needed support early in his reign and often gave followers church offices."

Matthew shrugged. "So, he snuck his way into office. Big deal. I imagine lots of bishops did, and they're buried decently in cathedrals. Did Gerald molest nuns or something?"

"He may have, in what some chroniclers called 'his depraved youth,' but while he was archbishop, he reacted the opposite way in matters of sex. He tried to enforce clerical celibacy on the canons of York. Celibacy was important in the late eleventh-century reform movement, but it was just finding its way to England. The canons didn't like it, and they found a loophole in the counciliar reform plans which stated that they couldn't entertain women in their homes. They gleefully pointed out that there was no clause which forbid the entertainment of women in their *neighbors'* homes.''

The scholars howled with laughter. "What did Gerard do?" asked Kenneth.

"He complained to the archbishop of Canterbury, who had the luck to work with nice, dependable, celibate monks," said Jennet. "But the canons got their revenge. The chronicles say that after Gerard died, they accused him of necromancy and wouldn't let him be buried in the Minster—they put his body outside the front porch instead.''

"Nasty bunch," said Roger.

"How'd you like to be told you have to be celibate after years of thinking sex on the job was permitted?" asked Amy.

"You'd better know the answer to that one," he said, squeezing her hand.

"Necromancy," murmured Lewis. "Which chronicles accuse him of that? Anybody reputable?"

Preston said, "William of Malmesbury, some forty years after the fact, says Gerard read Julius Firmicus in the morning.''

Matthew and Pete sat upright in their chairs. "Firmicus! How'd he get a copy of Firmicus?" said Pete.

"Who's Firmicus?" asked Leslie, who, as usual, was having trouble keeping up with her more classically trained colleagues.

Matthew answered, "Julius Firmicus was a fourth-century Sicilian philosopher and a late convert to Christianity. He's best known for a textbook on astrology.''

"Ho ho!" roared Olaf. "So the archbishop was busy casting horoscopes? Very suspicious."

Roger picked up the tale. "Oh, Gerard is really weird. He also owned a Hebrew psalter, in an era of rife anti-Semitism, when the Cabala was forbidden and Hebrew script—itself not widely known—was used in magic."

Jennet drained a bottle of beer. She was still thirsty and felt as if she'd been talking nonstop since they uncovered the grave. "To get back to Lewis' question, there is a more contemporary source which accuses him of sorcery in rather explicit language."

Preston rubbed his hands together gleefully. "Oh, yes, this is good! This is great!"

Jennet said, "Hugh, the abbot of Flavigny, was papal legate to England in the late 1090s. He says that soon after being named archbishop, Gerard intended to make his servants and friends communicants of the devil. He commanded that his aide bring him a pig in his rooms. The servant was suspicious, so he hid and secretly watched Gerard. He was conversing with an unseen demon in unspeakable words, which ordered him to carry the pig through the privies, 'worshiping it.' After Gerard did this, he called the aide back, telling him to invite guests to a feast and to make appetizers from the pig, so that everybody would be certain to eat some. The servant buried the pig and cooked another, but the demon warned Gerard, who sent men to arrest the servant. The chamberlain fought the men off with his sword and fled to Henry's court on horseback, where he revealed everything."

Her companions gazed at her in disbelief. Kenneth shook his head solemnly. "Give over, Jennet, not even the tabs could come up with something so juicy."

"To quote Anna Russell, 'I'm not making this up, you know.' Hugh of Flavigny has an even nastier story about Gerard's brother, Peter."

"Go on," urged Carleen. "This is better than the soaps."

Jennet continued. "Peter was also a royal chaplain. He admitted having sex with another man, who impregnated him. The hideous growth eventually killed him. Hugh says Peter was refused Christian burial, and was buried outside the cemetery 'like an ass.' "

Douglas frowned. "And the canons buried Gerard, the sorcerer-astrologer, under the front porch of the cathedral. So how and why did he wind up under the Abbey of St. Oswald?"

Lewis said, "Remember, Gerard helped found the monastery, using a core group of monks from France. Church reform was better established there, so the monks would approve of an archbishop who tried to enforce celibacy, unlike the canons."

"That's what we concluded," Preston said. "The monks owed a lot to Gerard; Jennet even made a case for Gerard being the patron of the tapestry, which was obviously the abbey's greatest treasure in its early years. No, those monks would not have liked the way the canons treated Gerard."

"So they crept out one night and transferred his body from the porch to their abbey, hiding it in the niche where their tapestry was stored. What a plan!" crowed Olaf. "Even if the canons did notice the missing body, they could chalk it up to the necromancy charge."

They chatted about the find throughout dinner, speculating wildly about Gerard's career. Jennet was sorry she had to leave for the professor's house afterward. Still, she reasoned, she'd get an up-to-date report during this session with Dr. Durrell. When she arrived, Betsy answered the door. The diminutive woman took her overnight bag and guided her to the study. "I'm so glad you can help my dear. Edwin's putting himself under too much strain lately. See if you can get him to bed by one. Tell him *you* need your sleep, even if he thinks he doesn't."

The chubby professor was at his desk, scribbling hurriedly on a note pad. "Jennet, Jennet, try to read this and type it up. I've got a news conference at nine tomorrow to tell the world about Gerard. Ah!" He slapped his forehead. "First, though, could you shuffle through those issues of the *English Historical Review*? I'm looking for a short article by Galbraith on Gerard's career as chancellor under the two Williams. It should be in the 1931 or '32 issue."

She marveled at how Dr. Durrell could remember not just that there was such an article, but also the correct journal and years of publication. Then she realized he had been going over the same material for half a century. If she studied the field that long, maybe one day she could cite scholarly chapter and verse with the same ease. She found the article and set to typing the notes for the conference. The professor's conclusions (drawn with the assistance of the tapestry team) echoed the discussion at dinner, though liberally sprinkled with references. It was typical of him to put footnotes in anything he wrote, even a simple speech for laymen. She got an idea.

"Professor, you have all these beautiful notes here which no one will ever see. Why don't we make copies of your speech itself to present at the press conference? That way, nobody can misquote you, and the better papers might even print the references."

He glanced up in surprise. "That's a lovely idea! Perhaps the *Times* would do that. Most of the papers, I fear, will merely harp on the bones and not care that these are probably the remains of an important figure in Anglo-Norman ecclesiastical and administrative history. Tsk tsk."

His words were prophetic. By the afternoon, the tabloids were screaming about the "murdered archbishop" (the skull was not intact; therefore, it had been smashed while the victim was alive); the "magician of York Minster" (the necromancy story caught their fancy); and the "haunted church.'' This last paper creatively decided that Gerard had been keeping ghostly custody over St. Oswald's and that he had stolen the first treasure and buried it again. He was coming for the tapestry as soon as he gathered enough ectoplasmic energy. The story featured two interviews with women who claimed to have seen a figure in white, wearing a miter, walking down Tower Street.

The dormitory crowd knew nothing of these fabulous stories until that evening, just before dinner. Most of them were reading. Jennet was at the table proofing papers with Matthew. The Barclays were upstairs resting. Preston was making a hideous racket in the kitchen, aided by Kenneth, who volunteered to show the older man where everything was. Douglas slammed the front door in his usual violent way and entered the living room with a stack of newspapers balanced on his thick red hair. "I am the ghoooost of Arrrchbishop Gerrrrarrrrd!" he boomed.

"Whatever are you babbling about, Douglas?" said Leslie. She noticed the garish papers. "I can't speak highly of your reading matter, either. What happened to our scholarly Scot?"

"Wait til ye hear! Wait til ye hear! Ye'd nae believe me, so I had to buy 'em all, just to show. Yon papers are claiming that Gerard is a spook, a-haunting the church and stealing back its treasures!" He flung the papers every which way, hunting for a certain article.

"What?" The crowd descended upon him en masse. When Preston emerged ten minutes later to announce proudly that dinner was served, he was greeted with uproarious laughter as the historians read the mangled accounts in the tabloids.

"Oh my," Roger wheezed. "How will we ever show our faces in academic circles again, now that we've turned a medieval ghost loose in York?"

"But wait! There's more!" Lewis picked up another paper and continued. "This one picked up on the references to Gerard's early career as chancellor and says he was practicing magic even then. It suggests he was a reincarnation of Merlin, assisting William Rufus as he once did King Arthur."

"These chaps should write for the telly, they really should," Miles said.

"My favorite is still the little old ladies on Tower Street. What did they say? 'The ghostly figure raised its hand in benediction then departed in the direction of the museum, vowing to reclaim its treasure.' " Kenneth wiped his eyes.

Preston had been flipping through the papers with his customary speed. He tossed them aside in disgust. "That's all thoroughly ridiculous. I thought the British had more sense."

"Come, come, Samuel," said Matthew. "This is the nation that brought the world the 'Goon Show,' Benny Hill, Monty Python, and a host of other sillies."

"Humph," said Preston. "And I am the man who brought you pepper steak. And it's getting cold, damn it!"

That evening, Jennet brought the newspapers over to the Durrells'. She thought the professor should have some advance warning about the ghost of Archbishop Gerard, in case a pack of psychics camped outside the church in the morning. Dr. Durrell, however, was not impressed.

"I fully expected this sort of thing; happens all the time. I was only a tot when Howard Carter dug up Tutankhamen, but I remember my parents—and much of the Western world—turning into Egyptomaniacs and avidly discussing the curse of the pharaohs. Mind you, my parents were not stupid people, either. They simply were caught up in the excitement. That's just what's happening here. I suspect we'll see a good many more stories like these before the fussing over Gerard ends, especially since he's such an interesting figure. It's a pity, though, that they're making such a deal about a few bones, when the York Tapestry is one of the most significant discoveries of the century.'' He shook his head in dismay.

"It might not be a total loss, Professor,'' said Jennet. "Maybe it will spark new interest in medieval history. I know that when the Tut exhibit traveled across the States in the seventies, colleges that hadn't offered Egyptian history for years suddenly found their classrooms packed to the rafters.''

"That's a grand idea! And where there's a demand for classes, there's a demand for teachers. How delightful! If Gerard's bones bring even one unemployed medievalist back into the fold, I'll forgive them for these foolish tales about his ghost. Now, my dear, shall we get to today's conference notes?''

The stories about the ghost of Gerard continued to spread. A man saw the ghost "shambling through the Shambles'' at dusk. A tourist from South Carolina claimed Gerard helped her when she grew dizzy after climbing to the top of the Minster Tower. Another woman, who had read Dr. Durrell's account of the canons' ill treatment of Gerard's corpse, said she saw the ghost floating around the Minster, wailing for entry.

The dormmates began collecting ghost stories from the tabloids, when they weren't making up ones of their own. When Leslie complained that someone had used the last of the coffee, Olaf proclaimed, "I went into the kitchen early this morning, and even before I turned on the light, I saw a faint glowing from near the cupboard. There he was, pallium and all! Gerard stole the coffee as a part of his revenge on us!''

"Nice try, Olaf,'' said Matthew. "But they didn't have coffee in England in 1100. Or tea.''

"So? he's been out wandering for nearly a week. How do you know what tastes he might have developed?"

Jennet regarded the ghost stories as her colleagues did: silly tales invented by silly people trying to get attention. Perhaps it was because the British were more imaginative than their American counterparts, but she felt the stories themselves, while outlandishly ridiculous, were more entertaining than ones with similar themes she had read at home. She recalled one that bleated ALIEN WITH ELVIS'S FACE STOLE MY DOG AND GAVE HIM CURE FOR CANCER. It wasn't until late one night at the Durrells' that she gave any serious thought to the ghost of Gerard.

She had typed the last batch of notes from the tapestry team, noting with a rather perverse pride an exceptionally insightful comment from Preston. Having finished, she went to bed in the pleasant spare room, which no doubt once belonged to one of the Durrells' offspring. The room was next to the dining room, and it was a sudden noise from there that woke her from her sleep.

Her first thought was that it was one of the Durrells, unable to sleep and wandering the house. But she soon realized that the tread was much too quiet. She could barely hear it, but Betsy wore slippers that scuffed the floor as she walked and Dr. D. tended to plod noisily. Then Jennet remembered that the remaining chalice was on the mantle in the dining room. Thinking only to preserve it from whatever sneak thief might be lurking in there, she burst out of her room, making as much noise as possible. She charged into the dining room and stopped in her tracks.

Silhouetted against the moonlit curtains of the French windows was a figure wearing a miter and bearing a crosier.

Her first thought, she was embarrassed to admit later, was that it was a real ghost. She realized in an instant, however, that it wasn't glowing or shimmering in translu-

cent ectoplasm; it was an ordinary, shadowy figure—
dressed as a bishop. Upon her unexpected arrival, the figure
hastily moved back toward the windows. Its face was shiny
white in the moonlight, the features were frozen, expres-
sionless. Jennet suspected its intentions were not good, so
she gave several shouts for help as she ran toward the window. The bishop-intruder whacked her with his staff and
fled.

When the Durrells and their cook charged into the room
moments later, they found Jennet sitting on the floor, nursing a goose egg.

"My dear, what on earth happened?" asked Dr. Durrell,
concern deepening the wrinkles on his face.

She looked up. "You probably won't believe me, but
I've just been coshed by the ghost of Gerard, whose crosier,
I might add, is unquestionably real wood."

They helped her to her feet and brought her into the
kitchen for an ice pack. The cook and Dr. Durrell argued
briefly over whether to give her tea or brandy and wound up
serving both, while Jennet explained what had happened.
"I woke up, heard the noise, and went to investigate." She
cautiously shifted the ice pack.

Betsy was shocked. "Gracious! You should have come
for Edwin. A young girl like you has no business tangling
with burglars!" Jennet did not point out that the professor
was three times her age and, had he been flattened by the
staff, very likely would have broken a hip or worse.

"I was only thinking of the last chalice, you see, and I
thought that the noise would drive the burglar away. It was
rather horrifying to see a bishop-shaped shadow standing
there."

"You're certain it was dressed as a bishop? I'm not
doubting you; it's merely that we all have bishops on our
minds lately." The professor poured himself a generous
helping of brandy.

"No, he was definitely a bishop. The miter and the crosier were easy to see in the shadows, and he was wearing robes, though I didn't get a close look. And I think he was wearing a mask—his face looked like white ice."

"Drink your brandy, my dear. We must discuss this further. Betsy, why don't you and Mrs. Harrington go back to bed? I doubt our ecclesiastical thief will return."

"Edwin, don't you think we should ring the police? I'm sure Inspector Dennistoun will want to know about this."

"Yes, yes, yes, I quite agree. But there's nothing anyone can do now. I'll let him know in the morning. If he came over at this hour, we'd never see our beds before daylight. Do get your rest. I'll see to Jennet's needs."

Betsy hesitated a moment, but then turned toward the hall. Before she left, she scooped up the brandy bottle, and they soon heard the click of the liquor cabinet.

The professor pondered his glass. "She knows me too well. As long as I sat here, I'd keep filling this up and have a beastly headache tomorrow. Hence, she removes the temptation for me. Such a thoughtful woman!" He drained the glass. "Now about tonight's adventure . . ."

"You *do* believe me, don't you?" Suddenly Jennet feared that all of the old suspicions associated with the theft of the first treasure would come flooding back.

"Of course I do. There are two possibilities, as I see it. First, we are not a stupid nation, and I would venture to say that even some of our criminal element have a modicum of intelligence, wit, and imagination. It is possible that some thief has decided to dress as Gerard in the hopes of evading pursuit. A victim sees the figure of the archbishop, then thinks it's the ghost, not a real thief."

"That's giving an awful lot of credit to a burglar, Professor, but I agree, it might be possible. I still think that's too coincidental, though: a thief dressed as the Archbishop

Gerard just happens to break into the house of the man responsible for the dig at St. Oswald's.''

"Perhaps not. He could easily find out where I live. He may have thought I'd be an easy target. Afterward, everyone would say that Gerard was having his revenge on me for disturbing his bones and taking his tapestry.''

She set the ice pack down, fingered the lump. It was still rising. "Ouch! I'm lucky I have such thick hair. Gerard didn't count on your assistant being a light sleeper.'' She sipped her tea and replaced the ice pack. "Okay, the ordinary thief with an overactive imagination is one possibility. What's the other?'' Somehow, she knew, but she wanted to hear it straight from the professor himself.

"That the person dressed as Gerard is the same person responsible for the theft of the treasure.''

Jennet found she had been holding her breath. She let it out slowly. "Do you really think so?''

The old man's eyes sparkled. "Dear girl, I've been expecting him or her or them. I've even taken steps to prepare for that eventuality.''

She had heard him say something like that before. Where? The picnic, not long after he had met with Ms. Selena Embry. Maybe now she'd find out something about that.

He continued. "I'm going to tell you something. Not even Betsy knows about it.''

"Wait a minute, Dr. D., Should you be telling me this? How do you know that I didn't steal the treasure? Some of my dormmates think I did. There was even that outbreak of petty thefts at the dorm, and a bag of things stolen from a store were found, all beginning shortly after I arrived.''

He waved his hand airily. "Oh, that. I knew all about that, don't ask how. I do think the culprit is one of your colleagues, but I certainly don't think it's you. How could you lift that heavy chest by yourself?''

She tried the same argument that failed with Matthew several weeks ago. "I could have had help, you know."

"Rubbish! You'd only just arrived, clear out of the blue, plucked fresh from a conference on Anglo-Norman history. Even if you had decided to steal the treasure, I can't believe you could have convinced any of your colleagues to conspire on such short notice. You didn't know them, they didn't know you. Would an intelligent criminal trust someone she had barely met with her nefarious plot? Of course not. Such partnerships take time to develop."

Jennet almost pointed out that she and Matthew had met before, albeit only in a seminar, but decided not to tax the professor's trust. Especially considering that she and Matthew had, well, developed a kind of partnership on their own. She wondered if she should tell Dr. D. about Matthew's encounter with a noggin-bashing night prowler. Better hold that in reserve until he reveals what "steps" he had taken.

"Could you identify the intruder, our pseudo-Gerard? That would make things much easier."

She shook her head. "I'm fairly confident that it wasn't either of the twins or Olaf; they're too broad-shouldered to hide easily in robes, and Olaf's much too tall, but beyond that, I couldn't even tell you if it was male or female. Impressions in the dark are funny things: all shadows and humps."

"Pity. Well, I have baited my trap. The fish has taken a nibble, and I shall patiently await his return to hook him." He began poking around the pantry shelves. His upper body vanished from sight, and loud rustling noises ensued. Jennet tried waiting as patiently as the professor's metaphoric angler, but found she could not.

"Professor! What trap? What bait?" Her head throbbed and she was positive it was not only the bump that was responsible.

He peeked around the pantry door, a cellophane bag of gingersnaps in his hand. "That's not the real chalice in there, it's a forgery. I've taken the real one to the museum, where I should have put the treasure immediately. Ah, hindsight."

"A forgery?"

"A clever imitation created by Selena Embry, who can do amazing things with metal." He crunched as he talked.

"I can see why you'd put the real chalice in safekeeping, but why replace it with an imitation here? Oh, no, you don't meant that you *want* Gerard to come back? You do. Oh, God, you do. Professor Durrell, you are stone out of your mind!" The throbbing in her head had taken on enormous proportions. The mischievous look on the old man's face did not help matters.

"Perhaps we can catch him. If not, he may make some kind of mistake. Thieves always do, you know. No such thing as the perfect crime. I'm sure our culprit—let's call him Gerard for brevity's sake—wants to complete his set of medieval chalices. Naturally, he'll try for the one in my dining room. Only he doesn't know it isn't the real one—and even if he does get away, he'll be in for a nasty surprise. Imagine Gerard taking the set to some black market expert and being told the terrible news." He chuckled evilly.

Jennet could not believe her ears. Here was one of the wisest, most respected scholars in the world, wanting to play cops and robbers. "Does Inspector Dennistoun know about this?"

"Of course not. He'd never permit it. There are times when regulations bind the forces of law too tightly. We must take action ourselves. I will, however, let him know about our visitor."

"Promise me something, Professor. Get better locks put on those windows tomorrow and don't try anything stupid if

Gerard does try again. Take it from one who knows; that crosier hurts, and Betsy would never forgive you if you had your skull split over a phony chalice.''

"Oh, it will be fine, Jennet. He won't be coming back for a while now, anyway. I think this was just a scouting mission. He could have snatched the chalice and escaped easily, even with your unexpected arrival. The real theft will probably come after we find out what's in the last niche in the church. If there is anything, that is. We've been so spectacularly fortunate in finding the treasure, the tapestry and the remains of Gerard, it would be almost greedy to expect that those sixteenth-century monks tucked anything else away." He crinkled up the bag of gingersnaps and tossed them into the cupboard. Jennet wished she could toss the entire evening's events into some mental cabinet, where she could easily forget about them. She gratefully accepted the aspirin that the professor offered and returned to bed.

The most annoying thing about the entire episode was Dr. Durrell's utter nonchalance. Betsy continued to fret during breakfast, but her husband kept tut-tutting his way through the morning paper, insisting that he'd call the inspector as soon as he reached his office. Jennet found she had no appetite, so she left early, hoping to catch Matthew before he vanished into the dirt of Roman York. She was too late. The dorm was all but deserted. All the archaeologists — Roman, Viking, and medieval—had departed, with the exception of Lewis, who greeted Jennet as she entered.

"Hallo, Jennet. You're looking as though the head man is keeping you up late. Tell him quite plainly, 'It's bedtime,' if he insists on working until the wee small hours. We all know he can take naps during the day, but that's a luxury we're not allowed."

Jennet grimaced. She knew she hadn't had enough sleep last night, and what little she did have was punctuated by nightmarish revisitations by Anglo-Norman ghosts: Gerard brandishing his crosier at a group of canons wearing Groucho Marx masks; William Rufus, with an arrow stuck in him, dancing a tango with his brother Robert; Henry I on his charger, galloping to battle, the hooves keeping time with her pounding head. Still, no woman appreciates being told she looks like hell, which is what Lewis had meant, though he couched it in more polite terms. Irritated, she found herself studying the excavator. Could he have been Gerard? It was possible.

She made herself answer cheerfully before setting off the explosion. "Oh, yes, we've been burning the midnight oil lately. There is a great deal of work to do, as you know well. But we have to blame Gerard for last night."

"Gerard?"

"Yes. I may have to report it to the *Daily Yell*. An intruder dressed like a bishop tried to break into the house last night." There! Bombs away!

His dark eyebrows rose. "Surely you jest. You don't. That's astonishing. I do hope the police are investigating this."

"I expect they will. Dr. D is handling it."

"Handling what?" Preston poked his head into the entry hall. "Come into the kitchen, Jennet; you look like you could use a cup of coffee, and Miles and I just brewed some."

"Jennet's been telling me the most remarkable story," said Lewis.

"Let's hear it," said Preston. "We don't have to be at the museum until ten." The medievalists of the tapestry team, unlike their younger counterparts in the field, were a slow-rising group.

Miles, who had been washing dishes, wiped his hands and found a mug for Jennet. It was Carleen's, decorated with killer whales from her native San Diego. Jennet didn't care: it was the biggest cup in the kitchen, and she needed plenty of coffee.

She repeated her story, omitting her personal encounter with the archbishop's staff. Preston snorted and wanted to know if she'd been reading more science fiction. Miles Beckwith's expression, however, showed concern.

"You're fortunate he ran away when he heard you. Burglars can be dangerous."

"Ha! No burglar, just some kid trying to get into the papers. Too much in the news about our boy Gerard."

Preston spooned more sugar into his coffee. Jennet momentarily thought of scolding him about it—Lillian kept putting him on diets to no avail.

Lewis changed the subject. "I have to hurry over to St. Oswald's or the Barclays will think I've abandoned them. I was wondering, Dr. Preston, er, Samuel, if you'd take a look at this monograph of mine. It's an area of interest to you, I believe." He handed Preston a folder.

"Hmmm! 'The Impact of the Normans on Northern Society, 1066–1135.' Yes, this is right up my alley. I didn't think it was your field, though. Don't you usually do art history? What made you decide to mess about with Domesday Book statistics?"

The dark-haired Englishman spread his hands. "We all know what the job situation is. I felt it was time to branch out into other areas. I did some social history while at university, so it's not completely new territory for me. I've become tired of playing the academic mercenary. Maybe I can get a better chance at a job if I show I'm more versatile. I know the Oswald work will be a credit to me, though not as much as it would have been if we still had the casket. The tapestry is a tremendous acquisition, and I'm glad I was a part of finding it, but I'm missing out on the work you're doing on it because I'm still underground looking for more." He sighed, turned to Miles Beckwith. "You can't know how I envy you, Miles."

Miles made a neutral noise with his throat and offered Jennet more coffee. She felt embarrassed for him; what could he possibly say to Lewis? *"Gosh, I'm sorry that I'm ten years your junior, and I've already got a tenure-track job at a good university and two books to my name."* That was ridiculous.

Lewis launched into another of his lightning-fast mood shifts. He hopped from his chair, gathering belongings in one easy motion, smiling all the while. "I simply must dash off. The Barclays will love hearing about your ghost, Jennet."

Miles and Jennet said good-bye, but Preston merely grunted. He was already deep into Lewis's manuscript, flagging paragraphs with a little green pencil.

After the door slammed, Miles said, "I do feel awfully for the fellow. He's held almost a dozen jobs in around fifteen years' time, none of them with any kind of future. Yet he's quite likable, an excellent excavator according to Dr. Durrell, and his published work seems competent. Just can't seem to find a permanent place."

Preston's pencil rolled off the table with a *plink*! After he recovered it, he said, "That's a good word to describe the little he has published until now: competent. Not great, but not bad either. This is different." He pounded the folder with the eraser. "This will get published."

"We have a distinguished group here at St. Oswald's," said Jennet. "Roger will have an article published in the next year's *Cambridge Historical Journal*. It's on St. Erkenwald of Canterbury."

Miles laughed. "I don't think Roger is interested in anything unless it's been canonized."

"Well, there's always Amy."

"True. Roger's a sharp one. Amy is, too, though her work seems to be strictly in art history, so I can't judge it as well. I do know she had some well-respected names on her committee."

"Dr. Durrell's recommendation alone is significant," Jennet said.

"Oh, yes," Miles agreed. "Edwin Durrell doesn't miss much. Why, just look at what he found wandering around with the tourists at Christ Church, Canterbury! The very best editorial assistant he's ever had. He told me so. You've done marvels preparing the abbey chronicles and transforming the gibberish at our tapestry team meetings into readable English." He raised his coffee cup in a toast.

"Hear, hear," mumbled Preston, who was listening to their conversation, reading Lewis's work, and chewing on his pencil at the same time.

Jennet blushed. "Did he tell you the story of how we met? It was the Old Butter Market, not the church."

"My dear girl, he's told every medievalist in York," Miles said. "The ones who haven't heard it from him have learned of it from Samuel here."

Preston gave what his students called the "shark's grin." It looked particularly idiotic with the pencil sticking out of his mouth. *I'll kill you later, Sammy Boy,* thought Jennet.

Miles began tidying up. It was almost time to go. He kept talking as he washed the cups. "What I can't understand is how or why Roger left his last job. Marsden is an excellent university; Amy had transferred there and was doing well. What happened?"

Jennet and Matthew had already considered this problem, but had found no way to get an answer. Employment records were not public matters.

Preston popped his pencil out. "I can tell you the how, but not the why. He got canned."

Miles looked blank. "Canned?"

"Fired. Ousted. Given the heave ho. Apparently he did something they didn't like. Don't know what." He tossed the folder on the counter. "Remind me I left this here. I want to get back to it as soon as I can."

They began the long walk to the museum in a light rain. The two men discussed recent developments on the tapestry. Jennet could only wonder about Roger's firing. Mild-mannered Roger? What on earth could he have done that would have led to his dismissal? Drugs? Sex? Violence? Departmental politics (which could involve all three of the others)? Is that why the police were questioning him? Or why Amy said they were so grateful to Dr. Durrell? Could Roger have been Gerard last night?

By the time they reached the museum, her headache was back in full force.

The day did not go well. The room assigned to the tapestry team for its discussions was small and stuffy. The three French medievalists smoked, which made the air worse. Jennet was glad whenever they checked the actual tapestry instead of the photographs they usually used, because that was the only time the French stopped puffing. Even Preston's incessant remarks about pollutants had no effect.

A nasty argument broke out over the panels which depicted the siege of Tinchebray Castle in the summer months before the final battle in late September 1106. The majority of the team felt that one panel, which lacked any identifying labels for its embroidered characters, depicted William of Mortain, the lord of the castle, collecting his forces and supplies for the defense. Preston, a woman scholar from Nice, and two Englishmen disagreed, arguing that it showed one of Henry's men in the counterfortress they erected to oppose Tinchebray.

"It's Thomas de St. Jean," Preston snapped. "Look at panel twenty-three: it labels him there in the fighting."

"Of course," said Miles, "but you'll notice that figure is done entirely in greens, while the chap with the soldiers nearby is in red and brown."

"So?" The Frenchwoman exhaled and vanished into a cloud of smoke. "The Bayeux Tapestry shows no consistency whatsoever in these matters."

Dr. Durrell said, "Ah, but these were different artists, my dear. They tried to keep the same characters in the same colors. Almost like embroidered armory. Jennet, have you those cards on the colors?"

She flipped through a growing pile of index cards and began reading. "Alan Fergant is always in tan and olive, except in panels eighteen and twenty-four; Ranulf of Bayeux is olive and red, except in panels seventeen and twenty-eight; Robert of Bellême is black and brown—no doubt because he's a bad guy—except in . . ."

Preston interrupted. "We did all that ten days ago. They're more consistent than the Bayeux figures, but everybody still has a few exceptions. Why couldn't this be Thomas? I want a real reason, not just mixed-up thread colors! Jennet, you've done a lot of work on siege warfare. What do you think?"

She gulped. Most of the group ignored her, unless it needed some information in her records. Preston, Miles, and Dr. Durrell had occasionally pressed her for an opinion, but never before on a topic of heated academic debate. *Into the fray*, she thought.

"It can't be Thomas. I think this is Thomas with the king in panel thirteen, setting up the counterfortress. There are the knights and foot soldiers."

"We don't have any evidence that Henry was near Tinchebray then! The chronicle of Henry of Huntington . . ."

The team dissolved into a mass of shouting. When Dr. Durrell finally restored order, Jennet resumed her position and won over most of the group. She had the feeling that even Preston was convinced, though he obviously did not enjoy losing a battle to his student, even if he set up the situation himself.

The scholars accomplished so little that day Jennet did not need to work late at the Durrells'. Splendid news, as far as she was concerned; she had excavation reports to do with Lewis, it was her turn to cook dinner, and she wanted a long talk with Matthew about the ghost of Gerard, among other things.

She splashed off to the market in the pouring rain, only to find herself accompanied by Miles Beckwith.

"I saw you were scheduled to cook tonight. I thought I might give you a hand. It isn't easy to carry bundles and an umbrella at the same time."

"Thank you. I really don't mind the rain very much, though. Where I come from, it's treated with great mystique: when it rains in Los Angeles, everyone who can stay at home, does. They stare at the heavens, awaiting the Biblical flood."

"Surely it's not so bad?"

"I'm exaggerating, but only a little. We do know how to cope with earthquakes, brushfires, and mud slides fairly well." They talked about their homes while Jennet gathered the makings for a minestrone soup. After they returned to the dorm, he followed her into the kitchen and began chopping celery.

Matthew pounded into the dorm, dripping everywhere. "What's this about you and a burglar?" he shouted. The sight of Miles, domestically dicing at the counter, seemed to unnerve him slightly.

"Shh, shh," she said. "I'll tell you, but I'd just as soon save it for the table so I don't have to repeat the story a half dozen times.'' She gave him a bunch of carrots and a peeler, then told the tale again, still omitting the attack with the crosier.

He sat with the peeler, but didn't start work until the story was ended. He caught her eye, glanced uneasily at Miles. It annoyed her. Of course they needed to discuss this matter in private. But he needn't be so hostile about Miles. If anyone was innocent, he was the one. He and Preston were the only dormmates who hadn't known about the treasure, and therefore couldn't have stolen it. Sometimes Matthew acted so paranoid, you'd think they really were after him.

The crowd at dinner loved the soup and enjoyed her ghost story even more, with the exception of Preston, who was still sulking over Thomas de St. Jean. Carleen accused Jennet of making the whole thing up for a slow news day. The MacNucators were in tearing spirits, the result of a day's rest; their dig was too damp to accomplish much.

''Jennet, describe him to me in detail. I'll paint his picture for you,'' Kenneth said.

''We already have his picture. He's in the tapestry,'' Amy pointed out.

''Och! Your tapestry may be splendid for hauberks and spears, but all the wee faces look the same.'' As a scholar, he realized the immense value of the tapestry. As an artist with a love for portraiture, he disliked the stylized faces which the twelfth-century embroiderers created.

Douglas went into his ghost routine again. ''Fiiiiind meeee a nooooos-paper reporterrr! I must let the worrrld know of these dastardly scholars!''

Olaf alone showed concern. ''Why on earth did you go in there? Wouldn't yelling from your bedroom scare him off?''

''I didn't think of that. All I could think of was that last chalice, and I wanted to save it.''

The table talk came to a stop, broken only by the slurping

of soup. The memory of the lost treasures took all the humor out of the story of Gerard's ghost.

After dinner, she worked with Lewis and Leslie on some paperwork, but kept nodding off. Finally, Lewis ordered her "as your superior" to go to bed. She was aware that Matthew was irritated at losing another chance for a quiet talk, yet she simply could not stay awake.

As matters turned out, she was lucky she retired early. Late that night, the entire dormitory was awakened by someone banging frantically on the front door. Everyone—or so it seemed, though nobody thought to take a head count—gathered at the stairwell and peeked over. No one moved to answer the pounding for a moment, then Olaf lumbered downstairs, followed by Douglas and Matthew. The big Orcadian threw open the door, his companions flanking him.

Pete stood there, hand clapped to his nose, which was bleeding profusely. His clothes were torn in a number of places.

"Whad took you so lonb?" he mumbled. "I'b been attacked by Gerard."

+ + + + + + + + + + + + + + + +

X

THE MOB OF historians converged on Pete, dragging him into the kitchen for medical treatment and pelting him with questions. Pete, however, wouldn't talk until his nosebleed stopped. Then he addressed his pajama-clad friends, while Carleen dabbed medicine on his scratches.

"I was out for a walk," he began.

"At one in the morning?" several people roared simultaneously.

He shrugged, then winced as a scratch on his shoulder pained him. "I like the night air."

"Bull," said Carleen. "You've been drinking. I can smell it on your breath."

"So what if I have? What business is it of yours?"

"Plenty," she snapped back. "Matt and I have to work with you, and if you start drinking and your work goes to hell, it's going to hurt all of us. If Dr. Henley knew, she'd thrash you worse than any twelfth-century ghosts."

"The next time you see me drinking on the job will be the first!" He glared at her, shaking his long blond hair like a lion's mane.

Preston and Matthew both moved to get Pete's story back on track, but Matthew's quiet "What happened and where?" was more effective than Preston's bellow, "Get to the point!" Carleen tossed the first-aid supplies aside and took a seat near Kenneth, who had already filled her killer-

207

whale mug from the teapot Amy prepared. Pete took a deep breath to calm himself, then went on.

"It was a cloudy night but not, thank God, a dark and stormy one. I was heading back to the dorm . . ."

"Back from where?" asked Jennet, though she had her suspicions.

"Just walking about. I mailed a letter to my mom, for one thing. I was in the quad when I saw him: Gerard, or the clown dressed as him. He was wearing a miter, and he had a big crosier, too, just like Jennet said. He wasn't transparent, either. I know that. I said something like, 'Hey, you! Stop!' and he vanished around the corner of the South Hall. I followed, and just as I turned the corner, he hit me with something and threw me into the rose bushes."

It was extremely unfair to Pete, who did look quite pathetic with his bloodied shirt, his swollen nose, and blackened eyes, but everyone began to snicker. The chuckles soon turned to guffaws. Pete sat stoically until his comrades finished wiping their eyes.

"Damn me if it isna the best ghoostie tale I've heard in many a day," said Douglas. "And which paper is buying the rights to it?"

"Or did you maybe have a drop too much? We all have Gerard on our minds," said Leslie consolingly, as though it could have happened to any of them.

"You don't believe me, do you?" said Pete. "Why, I'll take you there. It's been raining lately; maybe there's footprints or something. Clues."

Olaf shook his head. "On the quad, near the rose bushes? Petey, the walk is paved. Unless Gerard waltzed in the flower bed with you, there won't be any footprints. Even if he escaped across the grass, they keep it rather thick here. You'd have trouble picking them out."

"We believe you, Pete," said Jennet. "I do, anyway; I've seen old Gerard myself." Yet even as she said that, she knew she didn't mean it. She was busy wondering if Pete's late night prowls had somehow led to mischief, and he concocted the story of meeting Gerard as a cover, or if Pete was Gerard himself and had an accident in his ghostly guise. She tried to measure Pete against the shadowy figure in the Durrells' house but couldn't be certain of anything.

The others made similar reassuring comments, except for Carleen, who was clearly dismayed to find that her co-worker had been out drinking in the wee small hours, and Dr. Preston, who was already bemoaning his lost sleep as he climbed the stairs. Matthew and Kenneth helped Pete get to bed. Most of the others followed. Jennet decided to wait a while longer in the kitchen in the hopes of seeing Matthew. Somewhat to her surprise, Lewis and Leslie stayed for another cup of tea. They sat in silence, yawning at times. Leslie had the fortunate talent of looking well whatever the circumstances, but Lewis appeared ready to fall asleep where he sat.

As she expected, Matthew returned moments later. He nodded to the others, then went to the refrigerator for a soda.

Finally, Lewis asked, "Do you think he's telling the truth? We may live with him, but we don't really know him well."

Matthew ran his hand through his black curls, mussing them even worse. "Well, I've worked with him a while, and I've never know him to screw up a job. He is a bit of a free spirit, I guess, and acts as rebellious as he can, but I'd say he's law-abiding on the whole."

"On the whole?" repeated Leslie. "Do you mean you think he's done something before this?" Her dark eyes widened dramatically. Jennet maliciously wondered if she slept in her mascara, and just how much that negligee had cost.

"He never came right out and said it, but I think he was busted for pot a few years back."

Lewis laughed. "Oh, is that all? you made it sound as though the poor lad was a hardened criminal. Now if he'd been arrested for antiquities smuggling or some such! That would be a matter of concern." His face grew somber. "And, considering the events of this summer, a matter for the police."

"I really think Pete's innocent of that affair," said Matthew. "He has been troubled about something, though. I don't like the fact that he's been drinking, either. As for tonight, who knows? Maybe you're right, Leslie, and he saw archbishops instead of pink elephants."

"Who knows indeed?" Leslie yawned. "I'm for bed. This is just too much excitement for one night." She waved to the two Americans as she left. Lewis followed.

No sooner were they gone than Matthew swept Jennet into his arms. "You've got a helluva lot of nerve, spending your nights first with that old man and now with a ghost!"

When she recovered her breath, she said, "It wasn't my idea, and believe me, I'd just as soon not meet Gerard again."

"Do you think Pete was telling the truth?"

"Yes; Gerard can be vicious if provoked. He conked me with his staff. No, stop fussing, I'm fine. Besides, whatever Pete's been doing has been down at your site. I can't make a connection between that and the theft of the treasure. My guess is that he met Gerard coming back by accident. What *are* you doing?"

"Looking for bruises," he mumbled. "Can I kiss it and make it better?"

"Only if the top of my scalp turns you on. Listen, there's more to Gerard's visit than my wee noggin, as Douglas would say." She extracted herself from his grasp and peeked out into the hallway. Everything was silent. She shut the door.

"The Professor's gone bonkers." She gave him the full

report, not sparing any detail of the old man's scheme for the phony chalice. Matthew sank into a chair, smacked himself on the head with his palm.

"Eeeee! He *is* out of his mind! Maybe I should break in and steal it first. Or you could do it the next time you stay there."

"That won't work. Somebody will get hurt, or we'll get caught, and they'll think we did it. Or he'll have Selena Embry make a new one. There's no stopping him."

"If Gerard does come back on some night when you're there, promise me you won't try tangling with him again," Matthew said as he reached for her hand.

"I assure you, I didn't mean to mess with him the first time. It was my outraged sensibilities taking over. You know, there's something fishy about tonight's ghostly visitation."

"What? I thought you believed Pete's story?"

"I do, I do." She rubbed her eyes, trying to concentrate. "Listen, I can see why Gerard would wear his episcopal gear while burglarizing the Durrells'. If anybody—like me, for instance—saw him, we'd think it's the ghost. It's very convenient for our thief that the papers are concocting Gerard's revenge stories, because the theft of the last chalice would fit that plot perfectly."

"Oh, I see," he said slowly. "What possible reason could he have for wandering around the campus in the dead of night dressed as an archbishop? You would think he wouldn't want to draw attention to himself if he was up to his dirty tricks."

"Maybe he did. What if he wanted to draw Pete's attention in particular?"

"Why?"

She threw up her hands. "How should I know? Maybe we aren't the only ones who know about Pete's late night jaunts. Maybe Gerard wants to discredit Pete or set him up

for something. Maybe he wants to drive him nuts. He must
have had some reason for appearing before Pete.''

"Hmm. We'll have to work on that. Right now, as much
as I'd love to sit here and tell you that you look gorgeous in
striped pajamas, I think we'd all better get to sleep.''

He kissed her twice, once in the kitchen and once on the
landing. They were soft, tender kisses, not the intense,
passion-inducing kind. She liked to think they helped her
get back to sleep quickly.

The next day dragged like molasses. Everyone moved
like zombies at breakfast. Pete's nose was swollen, his eyes
puffy. He couldn't even wear his sunglasses to protect them:
his nose was too sore. Matthew urged him to stay in bed,
but he refused. He even made a feeble attempt at a joke,
remarking, "I'll tell Dr. Henley that we got in an argument
over those pendants we found. And you won."

Jennet found the quarrels of the tapestry team altogether
childlike. Preston and Miles, perhaps because of their lack
of sleep, were especially quiet. With Preston's dominating
nature toned down, some of the less vocal scholars took
over the session. Dr. Durrell took everything in stride, even
when obnoxious Dr. Bertel bickered endlessly over an aspect of the Normans' armor they had discussed at an earlier
meeting. Jennet was overjoyed when Dr. Durrell called it a
day in midafternoon. She wasn't so happy when Preston
collared her and dragged her over to tell Dr. Durrell about
Pete's adventure.

The tubby professor shook his head in dismay. "This is
simply terrible! Do the police know yet? I'm meeting Inspector Dennistoun at four, so I'll tell him. Terrible, just
terrible! I do hope the poor lad isn't hurt badly. No? Thank
heavens for that! I can't believe the things that happen!" He
gathered his papers, making tsk-tsk noises, and hurried to
his meeting.

Jennet, Miles, and Preston trudged back to the dorm to catch up on their sleep. Jennet napped for an hour and a half. She woke feeling extremely grumpy, as often happened after a nap. She wondered if she would have been better off without it.

She found the typewriter downstairs unoccupied and began working on some excavation notes. Mysterious clanking, Scottish oaths, and the smell of lamb proclaimed Douglas's presence in the kitchen. Jennet dutifully pecked away for a while. Douglas, drawn by the noise, poked his head out and called a cheery, "Hello, lass!" but the cooking needed constant attention. Jennet worked uninterrupted for close to an hour. Then Miles hopped into the living room. At first she wondered if he was trying some strange exercise, but then she noticed his right foot was bleeding.

"I say, Jennet, do you have any sort of medical kit about you, the sort of thing Carleen had last night? I stepped on something sharp in my room and everything's a bloody mess. Pun intended." He eased himself on the couch.

"Of course. I'll be right back." She dashed upstairs and found the first-aid supplies. Miles's foot was slashed, but fortunately the cut was not very deep. She squirted antiseptic on it and was cutting strips of tape to hold the gauze pads in place when Douglas popped out of the kitchen.

"Jennet, my sweet, would ye tell me if this needs a wee bit more salt?" He came around the corner of the couch and stopped in his tracks at the sight of Jennet on the floor holding Miles's bare foot while Miles himself stretched out lazily.

The burly Scot turned almost as red as his hair. He whirled about, still carrying a small bowl of his stew. Miles burst out laughing.

"Come back, Douglas, it's not what you think, unless I develop a sudden interest in sadomasochism. I cut my foot open, and Jennet's patching it up."

Douglas slowly turned around. Jennet waved to him, adhesive tape stuck to one finger. Douglas still looked redfaced, but he grinned at himself and brought his bowl over to her. "Ye gave me a turn, there. Give this a taste for me, if ye don't mind."

Still seated on the floor, she tested the stew. "Delicious! But it does need a little more salt."

"It always does." The cook returned to his domain, quite relieved that the lady whose attentions he sought was not indulging the newcomer's foot fetishes.

Jennet finished bandaging the cut. "There! That ought to hold you for a while. Dr. Walker advises that you keep it dry and change the bandage tomorrow. Here's a supply. How on earth did you do so much damage to yourself?"

He reached into his pocket. "On this. It was just under my bed, where I couldn't see it, but my foot could find it. I can't imagine what it's from or what it was doing there."

He handed her a blackened piece of metal, cut in several curls. At first, she had no idea what it could be. Then she remembered seeing those curls repeated over and over, in a filigree pattern. There could be no doubt. Miles had cut his foot on a piece of the silver decoration from the St. Oswald casket. But what was it doing in his room?

Think, think, think. On the night that Matthew went prowling and got hit on the head (Gerard does like to cosh people, it seemed), in which room did he meet the criminal? Was it the one Miles had now? In any case, here was proof the casket had spent some time in the dormitory after its theft. She twisted the piece in her hands and was suddenly aware Miles was watching her intently.

"Something wrong?" he asked.

"Uh, no. It's a peculiar-looking thing, isn't it? Do you mind if I hang onto it for a while?" She wished she could think of some brilliant reason to give for her interest.

Miles didn't seem to mind. "By all means. Just don't

leave it where you can step on it. It's quite jagged. I think I'll hop upstairs and try to get clean without wetting my foot. Thanks ever so much for the nursing.''

"My Girl Scout training," she said weakly. After he left, she tucked the piece into her purse and went back to the notes, but her heart wasn't in the work anymore. She kept wondering about the broken piece of filigree and how it got in Miles's room.

Douglas's stew was a success, for which he received many compliments, yet it did not put everyone in a good mood. The atmosphere in the living room after dinner was decidedly varied. From the tone of their complaints, the St. Oswald's crew had had a difficult day, and both Amy and Lewis announced that they intended to retire early, after they caught up on the day's paperwork. Olaf and the twins doggedly waded through sacks of bulk finds: common discoveries such as oyster shells, animal bones, tiles, and pottery fragments. They washed them, marked the level where each tiny piece was found, then stored nearly everything for the specialists. The thousand-year-old oyster shells, however, were only counted and thrown away, though the dorm mates had each claimed a few for souvenirs.

Dr. Durrell joined the group after dinner to attack an enormous pile of correspondence with Leslie's assistance. Leslie had been trying to keep up with Dr. Durrell's other papers, while Jennet worked with the tapestry team, but her modernist's training failed her at times. As a consequence, she had a pile of notes that required Jennet's "expert" attention. This meant Jennet looked forward to an evening of translating Latin and German, when all she wanted to do was tell Matthew about the silver piece in Miles's room.

From the looks of things, however, Matthew was too busy. The three Romanists were engaged in a hot debate. They had unearthed a small cache of studs and roundels—

pieces of metal used in cavalry gear—and wanted to compare them to ones in the British Museum, but Dr. Henley had said she could only spare one of them for the trip to London. Naturally, they all wanted to go. It was not just a chance to get away for a few days, but it was also a wonderful opportunity to meet some museum higher-ups.

"Look at it this way," said Pete, tossing his hair out of his still bloodshot eyes. "You two both work in the Late Empire. These roundels are most likely first century, like the Fremington Hagg hoard, and that's my period. So I should go."

Carleen thumped the table with the flat of her hand. "Ha! Your period! They're military gear, and if my memory serves me, your area of expertise is religious history. If they were crosses or votive stelae or figurines of Isis, I'd agree: you should go. But they're not, so either Matt or I should go. Besides, considering what's been going with you lately, I really don't think that . . ."

"Watch what you say, Carleen, or you may say too much one day," Pete snapped.

"Please, please," said Matthew, "this isn't getting us anywhere. One of us has to go and there's no obvious choice. Why don't we do it in the time-honored, classical way and draw lots? Or straws or toothpicks. It is how the noble Greeks would have decided the issue." He sounded so overwhelmingly righteous that the room filled with laughter. Historians are people, too, and nothing is as fascinating as overhearing other people's arguments.

"Huh! The Greeks would have held an ostracism, and I can tell you who the leading vote-getter would be," Carleen said, glaring at Pete. He flushed red, as red as his perpetually sunburned face could get, but he kept silent.

Olaf hurried to the kitchen for toothpicks, eager to abandon the tedious task of labeling ancient mutton bones. When he returned, three stubs of toothpicks stuck out of his huge fist. "All right, short stick wins." They all chose, and Carleen won. Jennet wondered, but wasn't sure, if she saw a look of disappointment on Olaf's face after Matthew picked a long stick. Could he still have hopes for her? He'd been quiet since Preston's arrival, and she'd hoped he had forgotten the whole thing.

To everyone's relief, Pete seemed to make light of his loss. He picked up one of the roundels and pointed as he said, "You'll want to compare the patterns on this one with some at the museum. Webster catalogued that hoard a few years ago . . ." The conversation became technical once again, with "loops, terminals, tangs, and toggle ends" filling the air.

Jennet was surprised to see Preston taking so little interest in the Romanists' contest. Usually he reveled in that sort of thing, being given to extravagant displays himself. Instead, he had settled into the most comfortable chair, and was paging through Lewis's monograph. His salt-and-pepper brow was furrowed in concentration, his pen skipped up and down the page, making notes in his nearly illegible scrawl. He did not look happy, but Jennet couldn't tell if it was the quality of Lewis's material or something else bothering him. She hoped he'd brought his ulcer medication.

The room was so quiet that nearly everyone jumped when the doorbell rang. Leslie answered it, and her colleagues heard her exclaim, "Why, Sergeant Corbett, so nice to see you!" and then, in a subtly different voice, "And Inspector Dennistoun, won't you come in?" She led the two policemen into the living room and introduced them to Dr. Preston and Miles, whom they had not met.

Roger shuffled his papers noisily, then waved a hand at the room. "We're all here, Inspector; which of us are you going to arrest this time? If it's my wife or Lewis here, you'd best hurry. They both planned an early night, you see."

Dennistoun's dour face seemed to lengthen as a thin smile stretched across it. "We're not here to arrest anyone, Mr. Barclay. We hoped to tell you how our investigation is progressing, and we wanted to hear about these midnight encounters with, um, the ghost of this bishop."

"Archbishop," chorused the medievalists.

"Archbishop," said Dennistoun. He stuck out his hand, and Corbett plopped a notebook into it as neatly as a nurse handing a surgeon a scalpel. "Let's see. I can tell you that our sources have not noticed any unusual medieval art objects suddenly appearing on the black market."

"Wait a minute," said Preston. This was worth putting Lewis's monograph aside. "Why are you assuming that the thief took the goods to the black market? Isn't it true that in many cases of stolen art, the objects go to private collectors? I mean, when you have a one-of-a-kind art item, it would get noticed on the black market, unlike most modern jewelry or VCRs or computers. Wouldn't you expect the thief to have lined up some greedy private collector, who wants to salivate over the treasure of St. Oswald in his own secret vault?"

"Yes, Professor, in most art thefts, that is exactly what happens, especially in thefts from museums, such as the Isabella Stewart Gardner Museum theft. But you must remember that most objects in museums have been there for years, while the St. Oswald treasure was discovered only a short while before it was stolen. Nor was its existence publicized. Our culprit would have had to work very fast to find a prospective buyer, and quite frankly, we don't believe one has been found yet."

Preston grunted noncommittally; Dr. Durrell looked thoughtful. Jennet knew he was adding this bit of insight to his own theory that the thief would not act until it was certain that no more treasures remained in the underground ruins of the Abbey.

Dennistoun flipped open his notebook, which had grown fatter since his last visit. He began asking Pete about his experience with Gerard. Pete spoke steadily, though his hands shook. His overall appearance was thoroughly disreputable. He had not done his laundry for several days and was down to his last pair of pants, which were far beyond the classification of "grubbies." His long hair was matted, and the injuries to his face made him look more like a street thug than a promising young scholar. He told his story succinctly, without any changes from the one he'd told the night before.

Pete answered the inspector's questions completely, except for the ones that dealt with his reasons for being out in the midnight hours. Pete flushed angrily, "I told you. I wanted to take a walk and mail a letter to my mom. There's a mailbox up on the quad."

Dennistoun nodded slowly. "So there is. But that's a fair distance from here. Correct me if I am wrong, but isn't there a mailbox across the street from your excavation site?"

There was a moment of silence, during which Matthew sank into his chair as though he hoped it would swallow him. Carleen's eyes widened, and she stared at her colleague with renewed suspicion.

Pete was not throwing in the towel yet. "So what? There are mailboxes all over York. I'm entitled to use whichever one I want, whenever I want. Or is there something illegal about that?"

"Not at all, not at all, Mr. Sharp. We simply wanted to ascertain your reasons for wandering so late at night. Our city may not equal some of your American cities for violent crimes, but it can be dangerous."

"You're telling me!" Pete pointed to his swollen nose. "Just look at that!"

"Precisely what I meant, Mr. Sharp." Dennistoun sounded satisfied, like someone who has given a warning, seen it ignored, and now could crow *I told you so!* "Do restrict your walking to daylight hours in future. It's much safer." He turned a page in the notebook, then pointed his angular face at Jennet.

"Ms. Walker, I believe you also have met this ghost?"

Jennet retold her story, this time including the part about Gerard striking her. She did not know how detailed an account Dr. Durrell may have given the police, and she did not want to contradict it. Matthew, who had heard that part before, sank deeper in his chair. The reaction of the others was interesting. Most looked astonished, and shouted "You didn't tell us about that!" Preston was loudest among them. Olaf and Douglas, as though wishing to prove that their affection for her was still strong, rushed to her side, bashing elbows furiously.

"It's all right. I'm fine, really. It was just a bump." She tried to laugh, but it was hard with Dennistoun watching everything intently, especially her brawny defendants. "He must have been practicing with me, so his aim would be better with Pete."

"Ha ha," said Pete flatly from the corner of the room. He was pouring a stiff drink.

She concluded her story; the inspector asked a number of questions, most of which seemed designed to bring out more details. He seemed to know—or did he?—that she was holding back information, if not about her meeting with Archbishop Gerard, if . . . but about other aspects of this insane affair. The truth about Pete, Matthew's own encounter with a skull-bashing prowler, and the professor's mad plans screamed inside her head for release. The piece of silver carving from Miles's room remained in her purse, though it seemed to her that it was burning its way through the cheap leather in an effort to reveal itself.

Dennistoun concluded his questions, tossed the notebook to Corbett and rose to leave.

Douglas MacNucator bristled. "Ye claimed ye'd tell us aboot yer investigations. How soon will ye find this lunatic?"

The policeman shrugged. "It depends on the information we receive. When we know more, we'll be able to do more. Thank you all for your help."

Only Dr. Durrell rose to see the policemen out. Dennistoun strode to the front hall without another word. Corbett was silent, also, but no one could miss the look he gave Leslie Stafford.

"Leslie, what was that all about?" asked Amy. "Are you consorting with the enemy?"

Leslie smiled enigmatically. "At least the sergeant is a live, breathing human, unlike that cold fish, his boss."

Dr. Durrell returned from the hall in time to hear Amy's remark. He clucked like a broody hen. "Why is it your generation has this instinctive distrust of the authorities? I know for a fact that the inspector is working hard on this case. We discussed it in detail this afternoon. The recent proliferation of archepiscopal ghosts in town—apologies to you, Jennet and Pete—can't have made his job any easier."

Roger tucked his arm around his wife. "Oh, you know, Professor. Amy doesn't 'instinctively mistrust' the police; she's just still upset about my tangle with the forces of law and order."

Jennet's ears pricked at that. Amy snuggled closer to her husband, as if remembering something worse than a single evening deprived of his presence. Dr. Durrell nodded knowingly, as though he also remembered.

He rubbed his hands together and searched for a change of topic. "Well, I think they're doing as fine a job as can be expected under such difficult circumstances. I say, Samuel, what's that you've been studying so intently? Don't tell me: it's Herr Doktor Josef Wackenroder's latest book, and you're planning to tear it to pieces!'' Years ago, the celebrated German had published a translation of a minor chronicle just as Preston was finishing his own translation of the same work. He never forgave Wackenroder or himself, for delaying his work for so long. University legend had it that this led to the most inspired period of productivity in Preston's life, but that a few years later he slipped back into his slothful ways.

"Grrr. Don't mention that name around me. No, this is the work of your boy there, Lewis. Fine piece of scholarship.''

Lewis looked pained at being classified "a boy", but obviously appreciated the compliment. Dr. Durrell remedied matters. "No, no, Lewis isn't my student; he's had his degree a number of years now. He studied with Wyndham and Murray.''

"Oh. Sorry.'' Preston could be as diplomatic as a UN ambassador when he wanted to, but when it came to discussing scholarship, he left tact by the wayside. "Damned fine piece of work,'' he repeated.

Dr. Durrell beamed. "There, Lewis, I told you it was quite good. Once we're finished with the abbey excavations, you polish it up a bit and get it in print.''

"Uh-huh. I agree, it's definitely worth publishing.'' Preston twiddled his pen between his fingers, then returned to the manuscript.

Dr. Durrell said good-bye soon after, and gradually the others began to drift upstairs to bed. Jennet wondered what was bothering Preston. He could be overwhelmingly enthusiastic about a work he thought deserved publishing. He all but dragged one of her more reserved colleagues to the post office to mail her manuscript, swearing it would be a success, even though the girl hadn't yet finished her dissertation. He was right, as it turned out.

He had been much more excited about Lewis's work several mornings ago, when he first examined it. She gave a mental shrug. Preston could be tired, just like everyone else after their interrupted sleep. Or he might have found some flaw in the later chapters that he wanted to discuss privately with Lewis. That was one thing she wasn't going to worry about, though it would be interesting to see how Lewis held up under Preston's often devastating criticism.

The edged silver carving in her purse was another matter altogether. She was still pondering what to do about it when Preston startled the remaining late workers—Matthew, Olaf, Carleen, and Kenneth—by booming across the room, "Carleen! When are you traveling to the British Museum? Day after tomorrow? Wonderful. I'll come with you, if you don't mind. Where are you staying? Ugh. We can do better than that. I'll call an old friend of mine who lives in London; I'm sure she can put us up for the night. She has a huge house."

"Of course I don't mind if you come, Dr. Preston, though I'm not going first class or anything. But I really wouldn't want to impose on your friend. I just couldn't do that."

"What? You'd pass up a chance to meet Catherine Burkes-Power? I thought you were a student of Roman history." He scooped up Lewis's papers and marched to the door, then turned to survey the effect. Only Olaf didn't recognize the name of the prominent Romanist.

Matthew's mouth hung open for an instant. He snapped it shut, then muttered, "It's a good thing Pete's gone to bed, or we'd insist on picking straws again."

Carleen stared at Preston and stammered, "Really? I, uh, you mean you know her? You're sure we wouldn't, uh, impose or anything? When you said a friend, I just assumed, well, you know . . ."

Preston drew himself up to his full height. The effect was marred by his pot belly, but the face was magnificent in action. "You mean you assumed it would be another doddering old medievalist? My dear girl, not all my friends are medievalists." He paused for effect. "Just all my enemies." Having delivered his parting shot, he vanished.

Kenneth turned to Jennet. "How on earth do you study with that man? I never know what he'll do next."

Jennet replied, "After a while, you can start predicting certain things. That doesn't mean he can't still surprise you. I'm convinced he knows everyone living who's published anything significant on any aspect of European history before 1700. You'd do well to go with him, Carleen. He may be brusque and overbearing, but he does think students are important to the academic profession, instead of just being legs or gofers or nuisances. He enjoys making contacts between the old and new, so he'll like introducing you to Burkes-Power."

"Yes, didn't you tell us he had been planning to introduce you to Dr. Durrell at that conference and then discovered you had already met?" asked Olaf.

"That's right. It only rocked him for a minute, though. There were plenty of other people on his scorecard for that conference."

Carleen had let her fat book slide off her lap. She looked like a rock groupie about to meet her favorite singer. Jennet knew just how she felt, remembering meeting the men and women whose work had influenced her choice of careers and drawn her admiration, Dr. Durrell among them.

"Wow . . . I'm really going to meet her!"

"Now, now, Carleen, don't drool. You'll spoil your lovely book." Matthew sounded rude, but clearly was pleased for his friend. "Say hi for all us hard-working stiffs back in the quarry."

His comrade paid him no attention. ''I'm for bed. Though how I can sleep now is beyond me.''

As she headed for the hallway, Olaf serenaded her with the opening lines from ''I Could Have Danced All Night.'' Kenneth tossed the obligatory pillow at him, then followed Carleen.

Somewhat to Matthew and Jennet's dismay, Olaf showed no signs of going to sleep. He reduced his singing to a mere hum, wandering through Lerner and Loewe scores. Finally, Matthew caught her attention and motioned to the hallway with his eyes. She packed up her notebooks and followed him, saying good-night to the tuneful Orcadian.

''I'll be along in a moment myself, just going to get some juice from the kitchen.'' Olaf wriggled out of his chair and headed for the refrigerator.

Matthew grabbed Jennet in the front hallway and quickly kissed her. ''Now what's with you? You look like you were ready to jump through the roof tonight at everything Dennistoun said.''

''Really? I thought I was keeping my cool pretty well. Here, check this out before Olaf gets back.'' She rummaged in her purse, handed him the carved silver.

''What is it? Oh, no, it's part of that first casket, isn't it? Where did you find it?'' He broke off suddenly as Olaf thumped around the corner.

''Don't dally too long, boys and girls. We must all be bright and cheerful in the morning.'' He climbed the stairs, singing ''Follow Me'' from *Camelot*.

Jennet resumed the thread of conversation. ''Miles's room. He cut his foot on it, but he doesn't know what it is.''

''Bother, said Pooh. That's not the room I got my skull smashed in. I bet our thief—let's call him Gerard just for the hell of it—moved it there after I poked my nose around. I wonder if it would do any good to search the place again.'' He looked thoughtful.

"I doubt it," said Jennet. "This is a big dorm, but it's often empty. Gerard can't take a chance on somebody stumbling across it. It's probably long gone."

"Where? Everybody's staying here, our real homes are miles away. And nobody has a car, except for Olaf."

"Somebody calling me?" Olaf yelled from above.

"Aye, shut yer mouth!" Douglas hollered back.

Matthew shook his head. "What we need is a place to hash all this out in private. Too many snoopy ears around here, especially those attached to a big blonde."

"Not to mention finding any free time."

"Not to mention. Well, let's hit the hay. We can't do anything about it now. Maybe we should gather up what we know and go to the cops with it." He yawned. "I just pray for a night with no ghosties and ghoulies and long-legged beasties going bump in the night." He kissed her, then sped up the stairs with an athlete's grace.

It may have been his parting words that keyed her senses to noises in the night, or it may have been that her body was falling into the habit of waking in the wee small hours. Whatever it was, her clock said 1:47 A.M. and her body said, "I'm awake!" She tossed and turned a while, then sat up as she heard footsteps in the hallway. For a moment, she ignored them. Then she decided she was too damn fed up with Gerard to let his games continue. What could happen? He couldn't pounce on her without advance warning, and she could scream bloody murder and bring plenty of help running. But what if it was simply one of her friends out visiting the bathroom or some such innocent thing? The hell with it, she concluded, and she opened the door slowly. She peered into the dim light.

She cursed herself for a fool. There was Carleen heading back to her room from the direction of the bathroom. However, as Jennet watched, Carleen didn't stop at her room, but quietly crept *up* the stairs.

Jennet hesitated, then tiptoed down to the landing. She peeked upward, but saw no sign of Carleen. If the tall American girl had stopped on the men's floor, she could guess whose room she was visiting.

She headed back toward her room, wishing she'd worn her slippers. As she curled under the covers, trying to warm her toes, she wondered if her guess was right. She had nothing against sex between consenting adults, and they were being discreet about it. She tried to imagine what Matthew's reaction would be if she hopped into his bed in the middle of the night. He'd probably scream at the touch of her Popsicle toes or hit her with his baseball bat, thinking she was Gerard.

Gerard . . . that was her first thought when she heard Carleen in the hallway. She sat up in bed, punched her pillow. But what if Carleen wasn't on her way to a romantic rendezvous? What if she and Kenneth— or somebody else— were working together as Gerard? Carleen was a muscular woman; she could easily thrash a drunken Pete or carry the St. Oswald's treasure. Also, Matthew had said she'd asked many questions during the tour of the excavation site. It may have been merely professional interest at first, but after learning of the treasure's existence, she might have turned that knowledge into criminal gain.

It would be even simpler if she had an assistant. Suppose there was something brewing between her and Kenneth? Could it involve the theft and the assaults? *Arrgh*, she thought, *I won't worry about it anymore! Let's just go to sleep!*

Of course, sleep was impossible by then. She tossed and turned, contemplating various awful scenarios, including one in which she ventured upstairs to peep at keyholes to decide if Carleen's nocturnal wanderings were immoral or illegal.

When Jennet finally drifted back to sleep, it was late. She

had no idea when or if Carleen ever returned. Her alarm clock beeped, but she didn't hear it. An hour later, Matthew knocked on her door and woke her up. She threw on her bathrobe and flung open the door, glaring at him.

"Are you okay?" he asked cautiously. "You were late, so I got worried."

She tried to clear her throat and found she couldn't. The repeated nights of interrupted sleep had given her a cold. "No, I'm getting sick. Carleen was out and about last night, and I spent hours wondering if she was getting it on with Kenneth or planning to steal the crown jewels of England."

"Uh, could you give me that in English?"

She felt like unscrewing her head and tossing it out the window, but tried to explain. "I heard a noise in the night. Again. As always. I'm going to start sleeping with earplugs if this keeps up. It was Carleen. She disappeared upstairs. At first, I just assumed she and Kenneth were having a 2:00 A.M. tryst, but then I started wondering if they could be responsible for all this."

He had been tossing his green exercise ball, but stopped as she explained. "Kenneth and Carleen? That is something to think about! You don't suppose . . ."

"I don't suppose anything right now," she croaked. "I'm going to crawl under the nearest rock. Tell one of the medievalists that I'm out sick."

"Sure. Want me to bring you some tea with honey?"

"That would be lovely. Positively saintly of you."

"No, no," he said, "I have no desire to be canonized. Mr. Nice Guy of the Week will do fine. Leave sainthood to Oswald and Gerard."

She wanted to argue that Gerard was just an archbishop, not a saint, but she felt too fuzzy, so she returned to bed while Matthew went downstairs. He returned a little later with a steaming pot, a mug, a full toast rack, a jar of marmalade, and the newspaper.

"The marmalade is Douglas's. He sends it with his best wishes, but hopes you don't sneeze in it." Matthew shoved papers onto the floor and put the tray on her nightstand. "Everyone else has left, but I told Roger you had a cold. He says there may be something going around; Amy hasn't been feeling well either. Rest, get better soon. Want me to bring you something for lunch?"

"You're sweet, but I think there's some canned soup in the pantry. I'll survive."

He looked fondly at her and kissed her forehead. "No fever. That's how my mother always could tell. I'll give you another checkup tonight."

After he left, she drank the hot tea and went back to sleep for a few hours. When she woke, she could tell this wasn't a serious cold, just a minor nuisance. A few decongestants should get her back to a functional level. For the moment, she reveled the luxury of doing nothing. She munched on a few slices of toast, read the paper, then took a shower. The steam cleared her stuffy nose, and she felt well enough to get dressed.

She found it odd, being alone in the big dormitory. She tried to be diligent and read a chapter of a book Dr. Durroll had loaned her, but her head didn't appreciate the academic prose. Nor was she up to the rigors of the medieval Latin chronicle. A mystery story wasn't appealing, either, not after being personally involved in a puzzling theft. Her mind turned to the St. Oswald affair.

She remembered something Matthew had said last night, something about searching the dorm again. The prospect made her simultaneously nervous and eager; if she were caught in the act, she'd have a lot of explaining to do, especially considering the earlier thefts at the dorm. Still, she decided her opportunity was too good to miss. She doubted she would discover anything because she lacked Matthew's master key, and most of her friends locked their doors. Douglas's was the only one open, and his room was such a ghastly mess, she wondered how he ever found anything. If the treasure was in there, it was buried under a huge pile of dirty laundry.

She went on, methodically poking into closets and peering under beds of the unlocked, empty rooms. On the top floor, she discovered that two rooms had small balconies. She was musing over the privileged students who used these rooms when she noticed something else that was curious. A metal light fixture with a high intensity bulb was attached to the frame of the balcony door. Perhaps some student from last year had left it? It was the only explanation.

Then she opened the closet door of that room and found a small stack of miniature paintings. She assumed she had stumbled onto more of Kenneth's creations. But these were not original works, subtly characterizing her friends into medieval roles, as were the ones she had seen before. She recognized these, even without the identifying high resolution photographs that were neatly piled on the closet shelf. Kenneth was making copies of the miniatures from the St. Oswald's treasure.

+ + + + + + + + + + + + + + + +

XI

JENNET DID NOT know how long she stood there, staring at the exquisite paintings. When she finally came out of her reverie, she began looking around guiltily, as though she expected Kenneth to charge through the door at any moment, ready to plunge a paint brush into her heart. She hadn't felt particularly nervous while searching the other unoccupied rooms; she figured she would tell anyone who found her poking around that her mattress was too lumpy and she was looking for another. Now, however, with Kenneth's copies in her hands, she felt horribly vulnerable. She gave them another quick study, then neatly replaced them.

There were five completed pictures. One showed young Oswald in exile, visiting Iona and meeting St. Aidan. Jennet especially liked that one for Oswald's earnest face and Aidan's gentle, knowing eyes. Another depicted Oswald in battle, regaining his father's kingdom. The third and fourth were of the famous feast given by the king, at which he shared his food and silver with the poor. Jennet enjoyed the details on those pictures, in particular the food on the table and the king's hounds underneath. Oswald's death in battle was the theme of the last painting.

Jennet's work with Dr. Durrell and the St. Oswald's team had given her a great familiarity with the contents of the stolen treasure. She knew there was a sixth picture, of the opening of the saint's casket many years later and the discovery of his miraculously undecayed arm. Presumably, Kenneth had not yet finished that one, for there was no sign of it in the closet and no accompanying photograph.

She went downstairs, feeling oddly dismayed. Her first fear had been that Kenneth was making forgeries, yet as soon as she picked up the paintings, she knew that was wrong. The original paintings, which probably dated from the late thirteenth century, were on wood. Kenneth's reproductions were on stretched canvas, just like his other works. An art expert would take one look at them and immediately recognize that, while they imitated the medieval style, they were done with twentieth-century paint on twentieth-century canvas.

No, Kenneth could not possibly hope to pass these off as forgeries. Jennet knew little about the world of art forgeries, but she did know that it took expertise to reproduce the proper aged look and correct media. Also, due to the sensational recent history of the St. Oswald's treasure, experts would probably examine very closely any "recovered" paintings to establish their authenticity. Kenneth might have been an artist, but he was not a forger . . . at least, Jennet hoped he wasn't. She liked the quiet, intense Scot.

She heated some soup and made more tea. As she ate her meal, she puzzled over the significance of the paintings. Two questions were prominent in her mind. First, why did Kenneth make them? And second and more serious, was he copying from the originals or from the photographs? If he was working with the photographs as his model, where did he get them? The answer had to be one of the St. Oswald's team, who were all prime suspects in Jennet's mind. Again, why?

Or could this be another of Dr. Durrell's shenanigans, like the imitation chalice Selena Embry had made? For all she knew, the tubby professor was making recreations of the entire hoard and plotting to strew them all through the city of York in an attempt to trap the criminal.

She mournfully slurped her soup. What would Matthew think of this latest development?

The sudden slam of the front door made her jump in surprise. With his customary grace, Douglas came crashing through the hall and into the kitchen.

"Weel, up an' aboot, I see! Feeling a mite better? Good. Can I get ye something? I've got to find some papers my fool of a brother forgot, but I can spare time for ye." His blue eyes were solicitous, and his smile was sweet. Jennet found she liked that much more than his usual semilecherous leer. She felt guilty that she had been suspecting his twin of such awful crimes only minutes before.

"No, thank you, Douglas. This isn't too bad. I probably could even go to the museum later today and take coherent notes, but the French profs would destroy what's left of my nasal passages with their smoke."

He patted her on the shoulder. "Rest, lassie, rest. The old foofs can get along wi'out ye for a day or two. 'Twould do them good."

He thumped upstairs and began ransacking one of the rooms. Jennet had the feeling that Douglas, not Kenneth, was the forgetful twin this morning and that whatever was missing was lurking in the morass of his bedroom.

While he searched upstairs, she tidied the kitchen. She wasn't feeling industrious; she reasoned that the steam from the tap would help her head. She was nearly finished when Douglas returned. He had collected the day's mail, which he began sorting in piles.

"Here's a special delivery for Lewis marked 'urgent,' " he noted. "What do you suppose that could be?"

Jennet was mildly shocked to see Douglas holding the telegram up to the light in an attempt to read it. "Douglas! That's private correspondence."

He didn't look disturbed at all. "Nae sich luck. It's too

thick. Have ye nae noticed that Lewis gets twice as much mail as the rest of us, excepting Leslie, who must have a boyfriend in every city in the kingdom? If Mum writes us once a month, it's cause for celebration.'' The lascivious grin returned. ''An' ye know I've nae sweetie a-pining for me.''

''How do you know that Lewis doesn't have a bevy of girlfriends? He's attractive, and he's taught at many different places. Why shouldn't he get mail from his friends?'' She couldn't tell if she was truly defending Lewis and his right to receive mail or if she just wanted to change the subject before Douglas began ''a-pining'' for her.

He chuckled, then stuffed the telegram into his backpack. ''Lewis doesna ha' girlfriends all over the country. Not unless they all work at banks and investment firms. That's what our Lewis gets: quarterly statements, every two weeks. Maybe this will tell him that he's struck it rich in the exchange. Still, it is marked urgent, so I'll drop it off at the church.''

With a cheery wave, he hurried out the door, leaving Jennet to her cold and her suspicions.

As it turned out, the telegram brought bad news. Lewis's mother, who was in a nursing home in Stirling, had taken a turn for the worse. Lewis was agitated all evening, calling on the telephone several times for more information.

Dr. Durrell visited after dinner and graciously offered the use of his van: ''My dear Lewis, don't bother with trains and having people pick you up. Just take my machine. That way, you can leave whenever you like and return when things are settled.'' Perhaps it was because he himself was an old man, but Dr. Durrell didn't believe in creating false hopes in what was clearly a terminal case. He put his arm around Lewis. ''Don't worry, my boy.

You do what is needed, and we'll keep everything running smoothly here."

"Righto!" Roger said. "We promise not to break into the last niche until you get back."

"We'll peck around it oh-so-gingerly waiting for you," said Amy as she squeezed Lewis's arm.

Lewis smiled tiredly, "Thank you all so much, especially you, Professor, for the use of the car. It will make things easier. I'll try to get back as soon as I can. I'll leave in the morning."

Everyone wished him well, and expressed their hopes for his mother's recovery. The chaotic evening, combined with her stuffy head, meant Jennet didn't have a chance to speak with Matthew about the reproductions. She began to feel like Scarlett O'Hara, always putting things off until tomorrow.

When Jennet came downstairs for breakfast, the table was missing a few people. Lewis had left before dawn, Carleen and Dr. Preston were on their way to the British Museum, and the Barclays had gone to work early to compensate for the loss of Lewis's labor. Jennet took a seat by Matthew, poured a huge glass of grapefruit juice. He shuddered as he watched her.

"How can you drink that stuff? It turns my tongue inside out."

"It's good for you."

"Oh, yeah? If it's so good, why do you have a cold when you drink it every morning?"

She took a big swig. "I didn't say it was infallible. Besides, think of it this way, I'm probably pickling those germs right now."

"You certainly sound better," said Kenneth, who was flipping pancakes. "Would you like some hotcakes?"

Jennet accepted readily. Still, she couldn't help wondering if the charming red-haired cook was in reality Gerard.

She continued to think that the figure she saw in the Durrells' house was shorter than the twins or Olaf. Yet it was dark . . .

She ate the pancakes, then turned to Matthew. "I can't face the museum cafeteria today. It's likely to make me worse. Can you meet me for lunch?"

He frowned. "With Carleen gone for a few days, it'll be a little rough, but I'll try."

Pete looked up from his plate of raspberry danishes. "Don't worry, pal. We'll take care of Henley. Just explain that Jennet is already sick and needs you to save her from food poisoning. Our boss lady has eaten at that cafeteria often enough. She'll understand."

"Good idea," said Matthew. "I'll meet you at noon—where?"

"How about the Blue Fox? It's midway between the museum and your dig."

Feeling pleased that she'd finally have a chance to talk with Matthew in private, Jennet dosed herself with decongestants and walked to the museum with Miles. The thin Englishman had taken to waiting for her each morning, unless Dr. Preston buttonholed him first.

Miles told her what happened the day before. "It really wasn't very much. More arguing over identifications and some comparisons with the Bayeux Tapestry. Today Dr. Bertel has threatened us with a discussion of the significance of Henry's seizing the treasury."

Jennet gave an exasperated sigh, or she tried to. It turned into a gagging cough. Miles waited until she finished hacking, then remarked, "Yes, I feel the same way about Dr. Bertel." That made Jennet laugh. She was glad to know she wasn't the only one bored with that particular prof's habit of overstating the obvious.

"Too bad Preston will miss it. He's good at gouging holes in Bertel's arguments."

Miles grinned rather savagely. "I'll see what I can do."

The session was a lively one. Dr. Bertel did bore everyone with his analysis, but Miles plunged in, noting that almost everything the older man said had been discussed already. Jennet was pleased to see how useful her daily notes were. Miles referred to them constantly. At the end of the morning session, Dr. Bertel was thoroughly cowed, and Miles had gained significant respect in the group. The success of his attack must have given him some inner spirit as well, for he walked briskly over to Jennet and asked her to lunch.

She was somewhat surprised. He had appeared interested in her that first night they met at Dr. Durrell's dinner in London, yet since moving into the dormitory he had been friendly but distant. His face fell when she told him she already had a date.

"Oh yes, I did hear you discussing that with Matthew. Perhaps tomorrow? Well, I'll see you this afternoon." He abruptly left, leaving Jennet to wonder what that was all about.

Matthew was late. Jennet had expected that, so she ordered for them both, hoping Matthew wouldn't fault her selection. He arrived at a quarter after, and was glad to see the smoked haddock arrive soon after him.

"Mary Lou wasn't happy about my leaving for lunch, so I can't stay long. I gather yet another mysterious incident has occurred? You saw Leslie making out with the ghost of Gerard?"

"She's got her eye on that sergeant, though Douglas, who monitors the mail service, says she has boyfriends all over the nation. And, no, I haven't seen Gerard lately, at least not in costume. It's more complicated than that. I was hunting around yesterday, and I found five reproductions of the miniatures from the St. Oswald's treasure in a closet on the top floor."

He stopped shoveling fish into his mouth, swallowed, then asked, "Forgeries?"

"No, but it has to be Kenneth's work." She explained about the canvas and the photographs.

Matthew's eyebrows beetled. "Curiouser and curiouser. First we have Carleen paying late-night visits to Kenneth; now you find reproductions of the paintings, also involving Kenneth."

"We can't be certain Carleen went to see Kenneth that night; that's just a guess," Jennet pointed out. "Also, we don't know that he's the only artist among us. Maybe Roger or Amy are closet painters. They'd have easy access to those photos."

"Hey, I thought you said the paintings were in the closet, not that the closet was painted! Sorry, sorry. It was too good a line to ignore. Still, we do know that Kenneth paints. That does point the finger at him. Do you really think he is too tall to be Gerard?"

"I don't know. I don't know anything about that night any more. Anybody could have been Gerard except possibly Billy Barty and Kareem Abdul-Jabbar. What a mess." She blew her nose.

"Hang in there, Jennet. Cheer up. At least this way we're gaining more suspects." He seemed delighted by the idea.

"I don't like it," she sniffled. "I don't like suspecting my friends."

"How about this? Could Carleen and Kenneth be in this together? Maybe she was Gerard, and he's in love with her, so he's helping with the plot?"

"I already thought of that. It kept me up all that night. And now I'm sick, probably because of it."

Matthew refused to be dismayed by anything. "I'll leap on any clue that points suspicion away from you. I think I'll take a quick peek at these paintings myself." He glanced at his watch. "Can't make it now; I'll try early in the morning. We'll get to the bottom of this yet."

He hastily finished his meal, kissed her on the forehead, paid the bill, and dashed back to work. Jennet picked at her plate. She was hoping a talk with Matthew might have answered some of her questions. Instead, she felt more muddled than ever. She trudged back to the museum, wondering what Miles had for lunch.

That evening, Matthew told her that he intended to examine the paintings the following morning at five-thirty. Jennet, whose sleep had been interrupted too often by various late-night escapades, found that an appalling time to get up. Matt agreed, but it seemed to be the only time they could creep to the top floor unobserved.

He met her at the landing in the early morning darkness. "Anybody awake on your floor?" he asked quietly.

"There's just Leslie, and she probably won't come out without her acrylic nails."

"Meow, meow," he whispered.

"C'mon, let's finish this. I need coffee desperately." Her cold had all but vanished, but her need for caffeine was intense.

They tiptoed to the top floor, then went down the hall to the room with the balcony. Jennet led the way, pointing to the lamps in the metal brackets.

"He probably uses them for extra light. This balcony would provide some, but summer days in York aren't always sunny. So, where are these masterpieces?"

Jennet opened the closet door. The shelves were empty.

Matthew came over and peeked over her shoulder. "What's the matter? They're gone? Are you sure we're in the right room? You did say there were two with balconies."

"Of course we're in the right room! I wouldn't do something so stupid. He must have taken them. But where? And why?" She continued to peer into the closet, as though she could somehow make the paintings materialize.

"London, maybe, with Carleen as the transport. We have decided they're thick as thieves, if you'll excuse the expression."

"Good heavens, and Preston is traveling with her!"

"Samuel Preston is a big boy. He can take care of himself. I mean, it's not as though we're talking about ax murderers here." Matthew began looking around the rest of the room. His last comments emerged from under the bed.

Jennet sat on the utilitarian desk chair. "I'm not worried about his safety, silly. If we knew Carleen was taking the paintings someplace, we could have asked the Shark to watch her. He'd love that—he was Sherlock Holmes once at a faculty Halloween party."

"I remember hearing about that. Mary-Lou went as Messalina and kept calling Professor Danbury 'Claudius,' because the old geezer came dressed in a toga like a generic Roman."

"Maybe that's why he retired." She rubbed her eyes, then blew her nose. "Well, this isn't getting us anywhere. The paintings are gone. Short of asking Kenneth what they were for, which would put him on his guard, I can't think of what to do next. Any suggestions?"

"I might have a few," said a voice from the doorway.

Jennet whirled around to see Olaf standing there, arms folded. In his light blue shorts and skin-tight tank top, he looked like an advertisement for a health club. Matthew popped up from under the bed, dust bunnies clinging to his dark curls. He was not happy to see the brawny Orcadian.

"We're not interested in your suggestions, Guthfrith," he said, brushing ineffectually at his hair.

"Oh? I rather think you might be. You know, you're not the only one checking into this stolen treasure business. I

gather that's what you were doing, unless crawling under
the bed is some kind of bizarre foreplay." His tone was
cool. "Frankly, I can think of better places for a tryst than
Kenneth's studio, but some people like doing it in dormitories."

Matthew had reached his feet and looked as if he wanted
to paw the ground and run at Olaf. Jennet shoved him onto
the bed. "Let's hear what he has to say. For a start, Olaf,
how much of what we were saying did you overhear?"

"Enough. I understand you're looking for some paintings
which you suspect Carleen of taking to London. Mind if I
join you?" He indicated the bed.

"Oh, hell, why not?" muttered Matthew. "Jennet's
claimed all along that your intentions are good. Besides, she
thinks you're too tall to be Gerard. Join the party. What was
that you said about Kenneth's studio?"

Olaf sat on the bed and stretched. Although he was fair,
he had taken the care to tan gradually while working at the
site, unlike Pete, whose pale skin seemed to burn in suc-
cessive layers. Jennet couldn't help admiring his well-built
body, though his confident smirk annoyed her.

"We—that is, the twins and I—arrived before you Romanists and medievalists did. In fact, there were still some
students here. We had a week to waste, as Archie was
delayed up north. So Kenneth made this room into a studio
because he said it had the best light. I found that some
previous student had set up the attic doorway for exercise
bars. I had my mother send mine. It's not the same as a
gym, but it's nice. In fact, that's where I was going when I
heard you two jabbering away in here. And, I might warn
you, it's not the first time I've overheard you. You're not
the world's most discreet detectives."

"It's not exactly easy to discuss things in private when
you share a dorm with a dozen people," Jennet admitted.
"Did you know what Kenneth was doing here?"

"No," Olaf said. "He also liked this room because it was on the top floor, where no one would bother him. How is it you found it, and what has my colleague been doing?"

Jennet glanced at Matthew, who seemed resigned to Olaf's presence. "I found the room by accident, and you won't believe what was in the closet." She explained about the copies of the St. Oswald miniatures.

The big blonde thoughtfully chewed on his mustache. "That's not a bad idea, about Carleen taking them. I room next to Kenneth, and the other night somebody was sharing his bed, and not for the first time, either. I figured it was Carleen. But there's another possibility."

Matthew snorted. "Leslie? Kenneth can't stand her."

"No, no. I meant as possible transport for those paintings. Who else has suddenly vanished from our midst?"

"Dr. Preston?" asked Matthew. Olaf shook his head.

"Lewis?" Jennet asked in amazement. "But what about his mother?"

He shrugged his broad shoulders. "Surely a clever thief would have an accomplice willing to send messages and make phone calls. Do you happen to remember if there was a return address on that urgent message?"

"Douglas might know. He was ready to steam it open," Jennet said.

"That's our Dougie," sighed Olaf. "The world's biggest snoop. I wouldn't be surprised if he's the one to unmask Gerard . . . all because he pokes his nose where it isn't wanted."

"Unless his brother is the culprit," Matthew remarked dryly.

"True, O king," said Olaf. "Still, we should check out Lewis's story to see if he actually is visiting his poor ailing mum in Stirling. I hope Douglas remembers the name of the nursing home. I'll ask him today." He glanced at his watch. "I'd like to get in a little exercise before breakfast. Why don't we meet after dinner and discuss this some more?"

"Where and when?" asked Jennet. "That's always our trouble."

Olaf thought. "Hmmm. It's Douglas's turn to clear up after the meal. I'll offer to take his place. He'll say yes; he's a lazy sod. Come help me in the kitchen. If I bang pots and pans, we shouldn't be overheard by others. Ta." He slid smoothly off the bed and headed for the attic door. Jennet thought she heard a faint voice crooning "Till There Was You," but she wasn't sure.

Meanwhile, her remaining companion sprawled across the bed. His face was pressed into the mattress, so she couldn't guess his mood. "Matthew?" she ventured cautiously. Who knew how he felt, having someone else barging into their investigation? And one with a definite interest in her as well!

Finally, he lifted his head. There were still bits of dust in his hair, but his smile was as broad as ever. "Well, Jennet, my love, I'll just have to find out who Gerard is before Olaf does, so I can prove my heart is true."

"Don't be a dummy. This isn't a popularity contest. I want to find that treasure, and I don't care who does it." She paused for a moment. "Unless it's Preston. He'd be impossible for months. I say we should take whatever help Olaf can give us. Remember, he's filthy rich. Maybe we can use his money to answer some of these questions."

"Huh. Money." He looked disgusted. "And he sings, too."

She slammed the door so violently he looked up in alarm. "What do I have to do to convince you that Olaf's assistance has nothing to do with our relationship?"

"Try me." She noted with pleasure the return of the sparkle in his eyes.

Some time later, she asked him, "Are you convinced yet?"

"I'm convinced."

*   *   *

Jennet was late for work that morning, something only Miles Beckwith seemed to notice. The session was lively that day, for Dr. Durrell had picked one of Jennet's favorite topics: the use of weaponry in the York Tapestry. Somewhat to her surprise, the fragile-looking, elderly professor from Stirling, who looked as though a strong wind would topple him, had similar bloodthirsty interests. Jennet was sorry Preston was still in London; she wished he could have seen her holding her own in a debate over swords, lances, and crossbows. The compliments she received from the austere Dr. MacGregor capped a wonderful morning.

"Nicely done, Miss Walker," said Dr. MacGregor as the tapestry team strolled to the cafeteria. "I especially appreciated your noticing those bowmen in panel twenty; your young eyes caught some details there I missed. And, I must say, your note-taking during these meetings has been quite useful. Yes, quite, quite useful. I've been planning a short article on the tapestry's weaponry, which I'll write once these meetings end in September. I can't bear to work away from my computer, you see. Perhaps we could discuss this before then. You have an excellent grasp of the subject."

The food, as usual, was dreadful, but Jennet thoroughly relished watching the wrinkled, liver-spotted hands of Dr. MacGregor illustrating methods of using lances. The butter knife she chose for her weapon was not obviously lethal, but the professors on either side of the Scotswoman began scooting their chairs aside.

Walking back to the dormitory late that afternoon, Jennet found herself in an exceptionally good mood. The chronicle and the tapestry studies were exciting, she and Matthew seemed to be going well, even Olaf's sudden appearance in their investigation was welcome. Jennet had been concerned about keeping information to themselves. She still wasn't sure what the police—especially the dubious Dennistoun—

would think of all these developments, but simply telling another person was comforting to her. Perhaps Olaf could come up with some new ideas.

After dinner, she and Matthew went into the kitchen to help Olaf with the dishes. His news was only moderately encouraging.

"I asked Douglas if he remembered the name of that nursing home. All he knew was that it was Green-something. Green Meadows, Green Gables, Green Valley, something like that. I haven't had a chance to find a directory for Stirling." He scowled fiercely at a greasy pan.

"I'll check at the museum," Jennet promised. "They'll certainly have better sources than you two have at your digs. In fact, I had lunch today with a woman from Stirling." She recounted her triumphant day to her friends. Matthew was intrigued and began asking questions about the differences in late Roman and Norman crossbows. Soon they were at the table, sketching bows.

"Hey," Olaf complained, "are you two going to help or not?"

"Sorry," said Matthew, but he didn't sound at all apologetic.

The trio made quick work of the dishes and soon joined their colleagues in the living room. Everything was so peaceful, it seemed impossible to imagine the group as a hotbed of suspicion. The only noise came from Douglas, who was arguing with his brother over something technical. Kenneth, however, was more subdued than usual, which caused Jennet to wonder if he was missing Carleen.

She didn't have much work that evening, so she offered to help Leslie with some of Dr. Durrell's other papers. This, she imagined, was the height of charity, because she found the English girl stuffy and the work hideously dull. She told herself she was doing it for the professor, though she did feel sympathetic to Leslie's obvious tiredness. Her eyes were carefully made-up, but no amount of mascara could hide their redness.

"I haven't been sleeping well lately," Leslie admitted. "Thank you for helping out with this mess."

"No problem," Jennet said. "I've been so busy with the stuff from the museum that you've probably had to do more than your fair share of the everyday garbage."

They worked in companionable silence for a couple of hours. As was often the case, Amy Barclay was the first to prepare for bed. Jennet reflected that she looked worse than Leslie. Her petite face was pale and pinched, and the circles under her eyes were dark purplish smudges. Jennet knew the St. Oswald's crew hoped to break into the last suspected niche soon; she hoped Amy wasn't killing herself in an effort to make up for Lewis's recent absence. She didn't think Roger would let her be so foolish.

As it was, everybody suddenly seemed sleepy all at once. Notebooks and papers were shelved as they all followed Amy upstairs. As Jennet climbed into bed, she silently prayed that nobody—not even a real ghost of a medieval archbishop—would interrupt the night and spoil what had been a splendid day.

Either somebody was listening to her wishes or Gerard had the night off. The cheerful feeling she'd had the day before was still with her, and the ensuing debate at the museum buoyed it up even more. After a good-natured spar with Dr. MacGregor, she decided to treat the elderly woman to lunch at a nearby Chinese restaurant. The food was only vaguely Oriental, but Dr. MacGregor professed to loving it.

During lunch, Jennet recalled that her companion was from Stirling. She wondered how many nursing homes there were in that city, and decided to chance asking the professor if she recognized the name.

"Dr. MacGregor, Lewis Hunter's mother is ill and in a nursing home in Stirling. He's gone up to visit her, and some of us thought we might send flowers. The trouble is, we can't remember the name of the place. We think it was Green Meadows, or something like that."

"No, no, it must be Green Valley View. In fact, I have a friend there. Would you like the address?" She rummaged in her purse and located her address book. Jennet jotted down the address and the phone number, which they could use to verify Lewis's story.

Somewhat to Jennet's dismay, Dr. MacGregor was a punctual woman, unlike many of her fellow professors. At a quarter to one, she announced it was time to go back to work. Jennet knew perfectly well that most of the medievalists wouldn't straggle in until one-thirty, but she also knew better than to argue.

After they returned to the museum, Jennet went to copy that morning's notes on the director's Xerox machine. She was loading more paper when she heard Preston screaming from the director's office. *The Shark is back: look out, little fish!* she thought. However, Preston appeared to be in the middle of a trans-Atlantic yell.

"Yes, that is my credit card number. I've already entered it twice! What's the matter with your computers? What's that? Oh, the call is going through? Great." There was a lengthy pause. "Hello? Hello? Jo-jo? This is Mr. Samuel. Is Lillian there? She's in San Diego? Well, what the hell is she doing in San Diego? Damn, she's visiting her cousin, I bet. Listen, Jo-jo, I want you to do something very important for me. Very, very important. Get a pencil and paper. I want you to check . . ."

At that moment, the director mercifully closed the door. Jennet finished loading the paper tray and continued copying. As the machine hummed, she wondered what Preston wanted so badly that required a call to his housekeeper. He certainly sounded in a vile temper. No matter; she wasn't going to let him upset her good spirits. Preston, she concluded, would perk up when he heard what the tapestry team, including its faithful amanuensis, had done during his absence.

Her mentor, however, was in an abstracted mood all afternoon. He hardly took part in the discussion, and instead of returning to the dorm with Jennet and Miles, he disappeared with Dr. Durrell. She consigned Samuel Preston to the nether regions of hell, and went to tell Matthew and Olaf about Green Valley View Nursing Home.

Olaf smacked a huge fist into the palm of his hand. "Let's gather our change and ring the home from the telephone at the campus gate."

"Good idea," Matthew agreed. He stuck his head into the kitchen, where Pete was preparing a fruit salad. "Pete, we have a phone call to make, so we may be a little late for dinner, okay?" They left without listening for his reply.

They hurried down to the gate, and Olaf soon had the nursing supervisor on the line. "We're inquiring about Mrs. Hunter. We're friends of her son, Lewis. Yes, could you tell us how she is? I see. Has Lewis Hunter been there? Thank you so much." He replaced the receiver and turned to his friends.

"Well? Well?" asked Jennet. "What did they say?"

"They aren't permitted to release information about patients. She merely said 'Mrs. Lewis's condition remains the same.' "

Matthew asked, "Has Lewis seen her?"

Olaf nodded somberly. "He was there yesterday, but she wasn't sure if he came today. It looks as though his story is true. He does have a sick mum, and he did his filial duty."

"So where does that leave us?" Matthew said. "Maybe we could find out some more about that mysterious trou-

ble Roger had at his last place of employment. Maybe we
could . . .''

Jennet didn't want to start contemplating alternative
routes of inquiry, or whatever the police called such speculation. "A pox on Gerard! Maybe we could have dinner,
and worry about this some other time.''

Her companions stared at her in amazement. Finally Matthew spoke. "Okay, Jennet, if that's what you want to do.''
His tone clearly showed he was offended.

Olaf also sounded miffed. "We were only trying to
help.'' His accent thickened slightly, as it did when he was
upset.

"Oh, c'mon,'' she said, as she linked arms with them. "I
don't mean that we should permanently abandon everything
we've done. It's just that I've had a terrific day, and I do not
intend to let this stupid business ruin it for me. Also, I'm
starving.''

Olaf gave Matthew a look that could only be interpreted
as "Women!'' and Matt responded with the appropriate
agonized expression.

"Okay, boss,'' he said. "We've done our bit for today,
anyway. We can always think about it tomorrow.''

"What's this, Scarlett O'Hara in blue jeans?'' Olaf joked.

"He's right,'' Jennet said. "Besides, Dr. Durrell doesn't
expect Gerard to do anything before the next niche is
opened. Unless we find any more mysterious paintings or
have more ghostly visitations, things should stay quiet until
then. So let's eat!''

The next few days passed quietly, as Jennet predicted.
She found herself working at the abbey chronicle in nearly
every spare moment, concentrating on the accounts of the
abbey's early years. The unnamed chronicler for that segment was one of the original monks from Dijon, a mere
youth during the early period, who composed the work

nearly fifty years later. It offered an example of continuity that historians would gladly kill for. Unfortunately, the subsequent chroniclers were far more typical of medieval writers. Jennet, specializing in the Anglo-Norman era, was primarily interested in the earliest account, and relished the author's sometimes cynical tone. In particular, she searched for references to Archbishop Gerard, whose twelfth-century life was far more pleasant a subject to study than twentieth-century, head-bashing imitations.

One evening, she was curled in a corner of the couch, scribbling notes on her photocopy of the chronicle, when Matthew plopped down by her side. He looked tired. She told him so.

"I'm not surprised. Mary Lou has me and Pete working overtime. Thank God Carleen comes back tomorrow so we can spread the load more evenly. I'm exhausted. Tell me something soothing. Like what are you reading, anything good?"

"Mmm-hmm. My monk has some interesting things to say about Gerard."

"They couldn't possibly be more outrageous than that account in—who was it?—Hugh of Flavigny? Worshiping the pig in the lavatories and all." He popped open a bottle of beer and took a healthy swig.

"No, nothing like that. But I'm getting quite a conflicting picture. Look, Matt, on the one side you have Hugh and his sort, accusing Gerard of sorcery, although he was never brought to trial."

Roger looked up from the table, unable to stay out of the discussion. "Of course not. They accused him at Henry's court, and he was one of Henry's staunchest supporters."

"Right. But there still were plenty of rumors. He read Hebrew, owned a psalter, read Firmicus, and therefore knew at least a little about astrology. His brother was an admitted homosexual who died a horrible death and was refused Christian burial. A regular nutcase, right?''

Matthew nodded solemnly. ''Right.''

Jennet whacked the chronicle. ''But our friendly monk of St. Oswald praises him to the skies—he's wise, he's kind, he's generous!''

''Why shouldn't the monks love him? He was their patron,'' said Olaf from across the room.

''True,'' said Jennet. ''But if Gerard is such a depraved character, what's he doing running around patronizing monasteries?''

Olaf shrugged, and returned to his potsherds. ''I haven't a good answer for you.''

''Remember,'' Jennet added, ''we also have that letter of Gerard to St. Anselm of Canterbury in which he complains about his canons and their riotous ways, entertaining ladies in their neighbors' homes. Exactly one year after that letter, he brought the monks from Dijon to start St. Oswald's. Does that sound like a demon-worshiping fiend, or a reformer attempting to establish clerical celibacy?''

Matthew drained his beer. ''You've got something there. Anything else?''

''His death is suspicious. Hugh the Chanter wrote that on May 21, 1108, he was bothered by a slight illness and was resting in an orchard near his home so he could smell the spring flowers.''

Amy remarked, ''All the necromancers I know just love smelling flowers.'' Her husband shushed her.

Jennet said, ''Gerard ordered his attendants to leave him and take their meal. When they returned they found him dead, 'a book of curious arts' on a pillow by his side.''

''Weird,'' Matthew said. ''That book could have been the Firmicus, or even the psalter, to an uneducated eye. That book, I suppose, and the earlier rumors about necromancy no doubt led to his initial burial under the front porch.''

"Exactly my thinking," said Jennet. "But it's not easy to reconcile those images."

Matthew began squeezing his exercise ball. "Where could he have found a copy of Firmicus? That's what puzzles me."

"I've looked into that, too," said Jennet. "Before he was appointed to York, Gerard was bishop of Hereford. His immediate predecessor at Hereford was a brilliant man, Robert of Lorraine. He was an astronomer, an abacist, an excellent mathematician, who trained in the cathedral schools of France. We know he introduced various mathematical texts at Hereford; maybe the Firmicus was a copy of one of those."

Roger applauded. "That's a fine bit of deduction. You should write it up."

Jennet looked surprised. "You know, I hadn't even thought that far. I've been too busy plugging along."

Matthew beamed approval. "Publish or perish! And for now, I must sleep or I'll perish! Here's to Carleen's speedy return."

Carleen did return the next morning, and she regaled Matthew and Pete with stories about her meeting with the famous Burkes-Power. She assured them that she'd mentioned their names, always keeping her fellow Romanists in mind. They both snorted in disbelief, but Carleen insisted she would never forget them, not even in the presence of academic royalty.

As she watched them talking, Jennet thought that she had never seen Carleen so vivacious; the tall girl's face glowed with more than just her hard-earned tan as she described the coin collections she'd seen. Jennet wasn't the only one with her eyes on Carleen. For once Kenneth was not paying devout attention to his excavation notes. He looked as though he wanted to burst out into one of Olaf's sentimental ballads. The tableau, however, soon went from Nelson Eddy and Jeanette MacDonald to the Three Stooges, as Douglas whipped his twin's elbow out from under his chin. To Douglas' disappointment, Kenneth saved himself from falling face down into his teacup, but Douglas did win a furious glare. He smiled beatifically in response.

"Quit moonin' and hand me the red notebook, if ye please."

Kenneth refrained from throwing it at his brother, but he shoved it across the table with such force it scattered some other notes.

Jennet chuckled along with the others, but soon found herself wondering again: *How can any of these people be a thief?* She glanced around the room. Carleen was still holding forth on the treasures she had seen, with Matthew and Pete listening attentively. Olaf and the MacNucators, having stopped their minor tiff, were scribbling away on their notes. Lewis, who had returned from Stirling, was catching up on the progress the Barclays had made in his absence. His face was drawn and intense, yet he had insisted on returning to work immediately. His mother, he told everyone, had stabilized and her condition was no longer critical. He had seen no reason to stay, especially since they were so close to the third niche.

The Barclays shuffled papers back and forth with almost telepathic skill. From time to time their fingers brushed together, bringing forth quiet smiles on Roger's face and broad grins on Amy's. Miles Beckwith and Samuel Preston sat on the couch, quietly leafing through academic journals. Rounding out the group was Leslie Stafford, sitting alone, as usual. She still didn't fit in well, but she had taken on a number of onerous tasks for Dr. Durrell since the discovery of the York Tapestry. Jennet appreciated the effort the English girl was making, even if she thought Leslie was rather pretentious.

The trouble was, she didn't want any of them to be the culprit, for she had come to like or admire all of them. Not for the first time, she wished the whole problem would miraculously vanish—leaving the stolen treasure behind, of course. There had been other recent appearances by the ghost of Archbishop Gerard throughout northern England, but those began to taper off as the public latched onto new fascinations, such as a fortune-telling sheep or the latest rumors about the royal family. In any event, Jennet was convinced that these ghosts had nothing to do with the one she and Pete had encountered.

She sighed audibly, which caused several male heads to turn in her direction, then tried to finish the outline she was preparing for the next day's session with the tapestry team. It was hopeless, she concluded, to keep chewing over the same old problem on her own. She decided to leave it until tomorrow's lunch date with Matthew and Olaf. Olaf was investigating the circumstances behind Roger's dismissal from his last job. Jennet's good mood of several days ago had quickly evaporated. As the St. Oswald's team drew closer to the third and final niche, her apprehension increased. Dr. Durrell's blithe comments about Gerard's not acting until he knew what was in the last niche haunted her.

We may be safe now, she thought, *but what happens after that niche is opened?*

Just as the morning session ended, Miles stopped her before she could hurry over to the restaurant. "I say, Jennet, could we meet for lunch today? I know I'm tired of those fossilized sandwiches, and there's a decent cafe near Clarence Street." His face fell as he read hers. "Don't tell me—you already have an engagement."

"I'm so sorry, Miles! Could we try for Friday? I'm really

not Miss Social Butterfly, you just keep catching me on bad days.''

Still, he didn't seem too upset. "Friday it is. And I'll hold you to it.'' He shook a long finger at her and waited until she jotted it in her appointment book. "See you in an hour.''

She dashed off to the restaurant and found Matthew already there. He had met an American tourist in the bar, and was catching up on the latest baseball standings. He soon joined her at the table, muttering arcane curses on the collective heads of the Kansas City Royals. He glanced around the restaurant.

"Speaking of curses," he said, "where's our erstwhile companion in detection?''

"Be nice," Jennet said. "He's trying to help.''

Matthew affected innocence. "Of course he is! Of course he is! So where is he? He can't help if he's not here.''

"Maybe he's having trouble calling that friend who works at Roger's old university. Let's just order our meals and wait for him.''

They didn't have long to wait. Olaf barged in the door, bellowing Norwegian obscenities with such vehemence that it put Matthew's earlier comments to shame. His volume was worthy of one of Douglas' rages.

Before the owner could throw him out, Jennet tugged him toward their booth. "Calm down! What on earth is the matter?''

There were tears in Olaf's eyes. "Some bastard stole my car!''

+ + + + + + + + + + + + + + + +

XII

OLAF ORDERED A stiff gin and tonic. He swirled the ice with such vehemence, Jennet was positive the swizzle stick would snap.

"I don't have much use for a car right now, not with the dig so close to the dormitory. Still, I check on it every few days, start the engine, drive it around. That's what I was going to do this morning—and it was gone!" The stick snapped. Olaf didn't even notice the pieces floating in his glass.

Matthew made sympathetic noises. "Once I bought an expensive stereo system for my car. It got stolen three days after it was installed. Where did you have it parked?"

"I hired a space in a lot just outside the city walls. Unfortunately, I didn't pick one with security guards. Damn! I'll probably never see it again. It had some of my favorite cassette tapes in the boot, too."

"Did you report the loss?" Jennet asked.

"Of course I did! The poor machine's no doubt in pieces by now. Bastard. If I could get my hands on whoever stole it, he'd be in pieces." He heaved an enormous sigh. "Well, what's for lunch?"

They ordered. While they waited for the food, Olaf told them he finally contacted an old college friend who was now on the staff of Marsden University.

"She isn't sure of the details because she was on leave

that term, nor was she in the history department, but she was fairly certain that another professor had filed criminal charges against Roger. The charges were dropped when Roger was given the ax. And that's all she knows, but she said she'd ask around to find out what those charges were.''

Jennet frowned. "That must have been why Inspector Dennistoun wanted to question Roger in private, and it explains Roger's earlier comments about some encounter with the police. I must admit, I can't imagine what kind of crime Roger could have committed. He certainly doesn't look like a crook. He looks, well, so ordinary. Salt-of-the-earth type.''

"So how many real criminals have you met?" asked Matthew.

"One, possibly two or three. A girl I went to high school with was arrested for shoplifting several times; I have a cousin hooked on crack; and I'm convinced her boyfriend not only uses the stuff but pushes it, too. He's revolting.''

"I don't mean that there's a criminal type; I was thinking of Roger's face when Dennistoun dragged him away. He looked like righteousness incarnate.''

"And Amy watched him as if he were St. George going to face the dragon. All pure and shining,'' Olaf added.

Matthew was staring into his beer. Jennet poked him in the ribs. "Hey, are you with us, or is there a fly in your brew?''

"Huh? No, no. I heard you. Roger looked holier-than-thou. I was thinking about your former high-school chum, the shoplifter. Do you remember that weird little episode of shoplifting just before the treasure disappeared?''

"How could I forget it? I was public enemy number one for a while,'' said Jennet. "What about it?''

"Have you given any thought to it lately?'' asked Matthew.

"No,'' she said. "There have been a few other things going on, you know.''

Olaf jumped in, his accent thickening with excitement. "Do you t'ink the one who stole those t'ings stole my car?"

Matthew shook his head. "No, I'm sure England has its own share of car thieves. But don't you find it strange that we had those incidents and everything's been quiet since then? No more missing cassette players. Compulsive shoplifters don't just suddenly stop snitching goodies. So what happened?"

"It was a setup," Jennet said slowly. "A setup to make me, the new kid in town, look like a bad guy. But the police weren't impressed, because they haven't really fussed about it. Though Dennistoun keeps looking at me like a vampire out for a midnight snack."

"It's your neck," Olaf said. "You have a lovely neck. 'Lovely to look at, delightful to gnaw . . .' "

"Ahem. As I was saying," Matthew interrupted. "You're right, Jennet. It must have been a setup to make you look like the prime suspect when the treasure was stolen. Unfortunately for Gerard, the police weren't very convinced. I still think Gerard tried to frame you one other time."

"When he tried to break into the Durrells's to steal the chalice? It could be. And even though he didn't steal the chalice, Gerard has made me look like one of those hysterical housewives having visions of archbishops. It doesn't do much for my character, seeing ghosts in the night."

The food arrived. Matthew suspiciously sniffed his plate. He had proclaimed himself on a quest to find the best pizza in England. So far, he had had a hard time finding pizzas that qualified as edible. He tasted, shook his dark head gloomily. "They'd better stick to roast beef and Yorkshire pudding."

Olaf ignored him. "So that explains why Gerard chanced nipping the chalice while you were at the Durrells's that night. Now here's something I don't understand: why did Gerard bother with Pete?''

Jennet told Olaf how they had spotted Pete returning from the Romanists' trailer late at night in an obviously agitated mood. ''Maybe Matthew and I weren't the only ones to see him. If Pete is doing something even remotely naughty at night, don't you think Gerard would want to capitalize on that and turn suspicion on Pete?''

''Especially since the police aren't very interested in Jennet, and Pete has a criminal record back home for possession of pot,'' Matthew pointed out.

''You have a point,'' said Olaf. ''So where does that leave us? Roger and Pete have had previous tangles with the forces of law and order; Kenneth's copies of the St. Oswald paintings have mysteriously disappeared, possibly on Carleen's recent trip to London; Lewis has also been out of town, visiting his mum, so he could have taken those paintings along. That leaves Douglas and Amy, and we can assume that they'd be in on it if either Kenneth or Roger are. Whew. Is that everybody?''

''Is this really mozzarella?'' Matthew pushed the plate aside in disgust. He returned to more serious matters. ''Amy and Roger do seem devoted to each other, but I wouldn't be too certain that Kenneth and Douglas are partners in crime, even if they are twins. But you work with them, so maybe you know them better.''

''They fight, but Douglas drives anyone mad. Especially me. Still, the way they work together is 'no-canny a'va,' to quote Douglas. Uncanny, that is. They can go at a problem from two completely different directions and get to the same answer at the same time. I usually can't tell their work apart, though Kenneth produces more than Douglas. And they both need money.''

''Who doesn't?'' Matthew groaned. ''Except you, and possibly Lewis. Doesn't being stinking rich bother you?''

"No," Olaf said blithely. "But you're wrong about Lewis; at least, I think you are. I happened to see one of those reports he keeps getting from those investment firms—I wasn't snooping, it was an accident. I thought it was one of mine. Anyway, that particular portfolio is in serious trouble. Of course, he does seem to have his money spread around, judging from the variety of banks that write to him."

"So Lewis can join the ranks of the undeserving poor. You forgot Leslie, the former scion of the nobility," said Jennet.

"Ugh," said Olaf. "Miss Hoity-toity. We heard quite a bit about the famous Stafford family before you joined our merry band. Pete eventually told her to shut up, and I don't think she's spoken to him since. There's one thing in her favor, you know: she's a modernist. How would she know what to do with medieval art treasures?"

Jennet suddenly had a ghastly thought. She also had a mouthful of prime rib. She motioned frantically, and hastily chewed. Her companions stared at her. Finally, she could speak. "What if she found an ally, somebody who knew plenty about the Middle Ages?"

"Oh, no," Matthew said, "I don't want to start juggling suspects. Next you'll propose Pete in cahoots with Amy and Carleen with Preston. Oh, no. No, no. You don't mean Preston, do you? I know some people don't get along with their Ph.D. advisors, but do you really think . . . ?"

"Not Preston," said Jennet. "But what about Miles Beckwith? We don't know anything about him; he's the only one of the tapestry team besides Preston living at the dorm; he certainly is an expert."

Olaf said, "But Miles wasn't anywhere near St. Oswald's when the treasure was discovered! Or was he? You know, that just might bear looking into. We have no idea if he knew Leslie—or anyone else in our merry band—before this. She could have told him about the treasure and they could have plotted the theft together.''

"He certainly showed up quickly after they found the tapestry. Was it merely eager professional interest or a desire to 'return to the scene of the crime,' as they call it? Is he particularly friendly with Leslie?'' asked Matthew.

"I don't think he's particularly friendly with anybody," said Jennet. "He treats everybody with devastating politeness, with the possible exception of certain professors on the tapestry team." She tore a French roll to shreds in frustration. "This is getting too complicated. To think I hoped this lunch would settle some questions! It's only made things worse."

Matthew rubbed his stomach. "I don't think this *lunch* will settle, but it will get worse if I don't take some antacid. Well, at least we've muddied the waters once again. Let's wait until that third niche is opened and see if Gerard strikes again.''

"Assuming he waits that long," Olaf said darkly.

Although Jennet was concerned about her sudden suspicions of Miles, she tried not to let it show during their days together at the museum. In fact, she was even looking forward to their lunch date on Friday. For that matter, the entire dormitory seemed to be at a fever pitch. The Romanists had made several good finds early in the week: some pewter vessels and fragments of a jet bracelet. On Wednesday, Kenneth literally danced in the living room after announcing that a Swiss tourist liked his paintings and had bought seven of them. But the St. Oswald's crew was the most excited.

"Everything's going so well for everyone. We should have a celebration," said Amy. "Let's do something really grand, like throw a big bash."

"When? After we open it?" asked Lewis. "Or before?

How about before? If it's empty, we'll be too disappointed to party.''

"Wonderful idea!'' said Dr. Durrell, who had joined them for dinner that Wednesday, while his wife visited a friend. "How about Saturday night? At the rate we're going, the big day should be next Monday. That will leave us Sunday to recuperate from our celebratory debauch. We want to look bright and chipper for the ladies and gentlemen of the press.''

"What's this about the press?'' asked Dr. Preston.

Dr. Durrell looked sheepish. "I admit I made a big mistake in keeping secret the discovery of the first niche. We had such splendid success with the second one, I'm hoping that luck will continue. So I've invited the press once more. They're not much of a nuisance, are they?''

"No,'' grinned Amy. "I love seeing myself on the telly, with AMY BARCLAY, ARCHAEOLOGIST, underneath.''

"Of course, we'll look damn silly if it's empty,'' said Lewis, thoughtfully rubbing his chin.

"Who cares?'' said the professor. "We've already made one of the discoveries of the century. If those monks packed away any more for us, why, it will be frosting on the cake. That reminds me. I'm expecting to get that poor remaining chalice back on Saturday afternoon. I'll bring it to the museum on Monday. With any luck, we'll have more to bring!''

The professor chortled, but Jennet, whose ears began pricking as soon as he mentioned the word 'chalice,' felt uneasy once again. What was the old man trying? Obviously, he wanted to broadcast the news that the chalice would be back, and unguarded, at the same time as the third niche was due for opening. Did he hope to force Gerard's hand? She wished she had extra work to do so she would have a reason to spend the weekend at the Durrells', not to

protect the phony chalice or even to unveil the phony archbishop, but to protect that tubby maniac!

While she was thinking, everyone else began making lists
for the party. Olaf and Douglas volunteered to provide
music—live and taped, Carleen offered to get paper plates
and plastic utensils, and Matthew and Pete planned to buy
the beer. Lewis said he would make a wine punch, and the
others started a menu. Shoving her nervousness aside, Jennet suggested steak *picado* and flan as her contributions.
"Does anybody know where I can get chilies in this city?
Can I get chilies in this city? In this country?"

"I see it as my personal responsibility to save the honor
of the kingdom, at least in the culinary sense, to guide you
to some chilies. We do know how to cook in England,"
said Miles.

"Not pizzas," muttered Matthew.

"Seriously, Jennet, shall we go chili shopping after lunch
on Friday? I'd like to pick up some things for my concoction, and I know a gourmet food store." Miles's tone was
quite relaxed, unlike his usual reserve.

"I'm not sure, Miles—what about the afternoon session?" Jennet began, but Dr. Durrell stepped in.

"Bother the afternoon session! I'm cancelling it! After
all, I have things to prepare myself!"

Jennet decided she didn't like the sound of that.

Lunch with Miles was a curious affair. On the other hand,
she enjoyed his company as always. He was witty, and they
had much in common, especially in their academic backgrounds. On the other hand, she found herself wondering,
first, if he was somehow associated with Gerard, and second, if he was simply acting like a gentleman, or if he was
gay. After all, her last few dates—especially that one with
Douglas—had produced sexual tension of various kinds.

But Miles just chatted away cheerfully, just as he would have in dining with elderly Dr. MacGregor or Dr. Durrell. Jennet didn't know if she should feel relieved or insulted. She decided to feel relieved. It was easier.

Indeed, Miles had a charming way about him she never noticed before. Perhaps he held it back except in more private settings. After lunch, they wandered through the store together, laughing over some of the more exotic offerings. Jennet was therefore completely thrown off guard when he suddenly turned to her in the check-out line and said, "I say, Jennet, can I tell you something in the strictest confidence?"

It took her a moment to recover. She watched his face, which had changed from relaxed to tense in an instant. Then it somehow changed again, becoming unreadable. She realized she had delayed her answer too long. "Yes, of course you can," she said quietly.

He hastily looked back at the produce section. "I have, er, I have a deep and abiding passion for, for raspberries. They're outrageously expensive, but I must have some. Will you wait here a moment?" He ran away to find them.

When he returned, he changed the subject entirely. *Whatever he meant to say, it wasn't about raspberries*, she thought. It irritated her the rest of the day.

Saturday began with a special session of the St. Oswald's crew. They stopped after only a few hours because they were so close to the niche. Roger wanted to break in right away, then seal it up again for the television cameras. Lewis and Dr. Durrell vetoed that plan.

Roger groaned. "I'm going to spend the whole weekend wondering what's in there."

"No, you're not," Amy said. "We're going to dance the night away. You won't have a chance to think about secret niches."

The dormitory had never looked cleaner or more festive.

Kenneth supervised the decorations with his artist's eye, producing colorful posters in record speed. The kitchen was jammed with people cooking and banging elbows. Upstairs, Olaf and Douglas were alternating between arguments and songs. The Durrells provided a Dobos torte—courtesy of their fine cook, Matilda—and a punch bowl. Pete and Matthew filled trash cans with ice and beer, though Roger requested that his be kept at room temperature. Leslie brought sodas and seltzer water for those avoiding liquor, though there weren't many. Mary-Lou Henley and Archie Graham arrived at seven with boxes from the nearby Indian restaurant.

When everyone was there, Dr. Durrell stood on a chair, with Lewis holding his arm to steady him. He looked around with satisfaction and announced, "*Nunc bibendum est!* Or, for those of you who don't know Latin, let's party!"

And party they did. The tape Olaf and Douglas had prepared was a well-balanced mixture that included everything from folk to rock to light opera. None of it was particularly raucous, which no doubt pleased the older guests. The two musicians promised live entertainment later in the evening. For the moment, everyone headed for the table, which was loaded with goodies. Jennet had wondered if the party would split into small segments: Romanists, medievalists, professors, students. Fortunately, a good deal of mixing was going on, though Kenneth seemed glued to Carleen's side. Preston had overcome whatever had been bothering him since his return from London, and he was hamming it up in great style. A few members of the tapestry team, including Dr. MacGregor and the bombastic Dr. Bertel, intently listened to Olaf explaining the progress of the Viking dig. Leslie was chatting with Miles about London theater, and the Barclays were discussing vacation spots in Scotland with Archie Graham. Mary-Lou Henley endeared herself to Kenneth when she admired his posters and asked to see more of his work. He rushed upstairs for his portraits and instantly drew a crowd of prospective customers. Matthew and Pete, war-gamers since their teens, were pumping Jennet and Lewis for details of the Battle of Tinchebray so they could devise a game and cash in on the tapestry's popularity.

"I don't know much about war games, but don't you need quite a lot of material for them? To make the game more interesting?" asked Lewis.

"You got plenty with this battle," Pete said. He was drinking hard already, and Jennet wondered how long he'd stay conscious. "You got castles under sh-s-siege, allies and mercenaries, bowmen, cavalry, infantry. Even hand-to-hand melee, which I know from you medievalist types was pretty rare, but it'd be fun for the players. It'd be a helluva game."

"We'll make a bundle," Matthew said. "Jennet, Lewis, you can be our special advisors. We'll give you each five percent."

Lewis's eyes widened slightly. "You're serious about this! Turning a historical battle into a game for kids?"

"Well, not kids. Usually these games are too complex for anyone under fourteen," Matthew explained. "But they sell like hotcakes."

"How fascinating! We will have to discuss this further."

Miles had left Leslie and joined them. "If you're done picking Jennet's brain, I'd like to ask her for this dance."

While Matthew and Pete were devising war games, a few couples had ventured out onto the living room floor, including the Barclays, the Durrells, Kenneth and Carleen, and Olaf and Dr. MacGregor, who danced quite smoothly for her years. Matthew appeared somewhat taken aback by Miles's request, but Jennet was glad he didn't make any stupid, macho, proprietary remarks. She wouldn't have expected it of him. The stupidity started soon after.

While Jennet was dancing with Miles, she noticed Douglas and Olaf elbowing each other on the sidelines. Miles saw it also. He remarked, "They look like your American football quarterbacks, each wanting the coach to put him in for the next play. Are you the coach, Jennet?"

She groaned. Miles held her a little more tightly, but still in a gentlemanly manner. "I'm not the coach," she said, "I'm the defense. Or possibly the goal line. Oh, no, this song is ending."

Her two admirers practically raced to get to her side. Miles, who was around five nine, gazed up at them and murmured, "Hut, hut, hike!" as he stepped aside.

"Jennet, may I have the honor of this dance?"

"Jennet, me love, would ye go dancing with me?"

The requests came simultaneously, as did the glares the two men gave each other. They turned to her. "Well?" they chorused.

She glanced desperately around the room. Matthew, perched on the edge of the couch, gave her a cheery wave. Clearly, he was leaving it up to her. She suddenly saw an escape route. Dr. Preston was just heading toward the makeshift bar. She grabbed his sleeve.

"Dr. P., aren't you forgetting you promised me this dance?"

Whatever else one could say about Samuel Preston, he never missed a cue. He took in the situation in an instant. "I'm getting senile. How could I forget a dance with my favorite grad student? Jennet, you look ravishing tonight. Promise you'll never tell Lillian about this!"

They moved onto the floor, leaving the would-be escorts behind. "Doesn't this merely postpone the fight until the next song?" asked Preston.

"No, just swing me by the table when the song ends."

He did, with utmost ease, and Jennet had scooped up pasta salad and chicken curry before the dancing duo could approach. "I think I've had enough for now, fellows," she said. "Maybe later?"

They looked at each other and shrugged. "Let's get the music," said Olaf.

"Aye."

Though Olaf and Douglas often quarreled about work and the object of their affections, there was no denying they made terrific music together. The big Orcadian did most of the vocals. Douglas played an outstanding guitar, and Olaf played what looked like a baby accordion. It was hexagonal, with tiny buttons that seemed far too small for Olaf's great hands. Mary-Lou teased him about it. "What happened, Olaf? Did you leave your accordion out in the rain overnight?"

"It isn't an accordion. It is an Anglo-concertina. It was invented by Sir Charles Wheatstone almost a century before the accordion."

"Take notes, students," yelled Archie Graham. "Dr. Guthfrith will administer an examination at the end of the party."

"I also play the accordion, the melodeon, the piano, and the guitar," said Olaf.

"Don't forget the mouth organ," snickered Douglas.

"Please! We are speaking of music!"

"Quit speakin' and start singing."

They began with a bouncy number about a man who meets seven hundred elves in the woods, only to find them just as terrified of him as he was of them. Next came a few Scottish ballads, which Jennet suspected were included to curry favor with their boss, Archie Graham. Olaf then played a solo guitar for a Russian folk song, and the audience was eating out of his hand. He returned to the concertina for the next number. The song was a beautifully sad saga of an old mother and her fisherman son. Jennet had heard of the tradition in fishing villages of knitting sweaters in patterns which helped identify drowned bodies. Olaf rendered the custom into a poignant number.

"Lovely, lovely," called Betsy Durrell when he finished. "How long ago was that written?"

"Just a few years back," said Olaf. "John Kirkpatrick of Brass Monkey wrote it. It certainly sounds like you'd find it in the *Journals of the Folklore Society*, doesn't it?"

"Enough of these folksie tunes! How about some rock 'n' roll?" Roger shouted.

Olaf and Douglas obliged him with "Sympathy for the Devil," with Douglas hamming it up as Mick Jagger. The upbeat tempo spurred Matthew into getting his guitar from his room. He clearly wasn't in their class, but did a respectable job on a half-dozen rock classics. However, he refused to sing a note. "Couldn't carry a tune to save my life," he announced.

They were arguing over chording, when an overnight delivery man interrupted the party. He had a package for Preston, but was clearly interested in the festivities. "Hey, can I stop by later? I get off at one o'clock."

Preston pounced on the package and shoved him out the door. "Closed party. No one admitted without a master's degree."

A faint voice called out, "I have a Ph.D. in nineteenth-century English literature . . ." but Preston was already vaulting up the stairs with his prize.

Dr. Durrell scratched his head. "What on earth was that about?" No one had a good answer. When Preston returned a few minutes later, he had left the package in his room and was in a horrible temper. When Betsy Durrell timidly inquired, "Is it bad news?" he whirled on her as though he intended to bite. He recovered in time.

"In a way, yes. I'll discuss it with you and Edwin tomorrow." And he said no more about it, but poured a rum and coke.

It was almost midnight. A few of the older guests had left, but Olaf was accompanying himself on the piano, singing Cole Porter and Irving Berlin. He genuinely liked all kinds of music, and the ballads on the earlier cassette tape reflected his taste, not just an attempt to cater to the desires of the older professors.

The remaining guests were clustered in groups of twos or threes, talking quietly. Carleen, whether spurred by the party atmosphere or by Harvey Wallbangers, had abandoned her reserve and was sitting in Kenneth's lap. Kenneth had not been drinking, but he appeared intoxicated with love. Lewis, Mary-Lou, Archie, and Dr. Durrell were discussing Monday's meeting with the media so the Viking and Roman digs in York could get some free publicity, courtesy of the St. Oswald's crew. Jennet was enjoying the romantic mood that Olaf was providing, though she was sure he didn't appreciate her enjoying it snuggled next to Matthew.

As she looked around the room, she decided the party was a grand success. Everyone was having a good time, with the possible exception of Samuel Preston. *What could have arrived by special delivery that could upset the Shark?* It couldn't have been anything too serious, such as Lillian's having an accident or getting sick. In fact, his face showed more anger and disappointment than sadness. *Oh, well, when Sammy wants us to know, he'll tell us. Loudly.*

All of a sudden, the lights in the living room went out. Those in the kitchen remained on, providing a dim glow. "What the hell?" asked several people at once.

"I'll check the circuit breaker," said Lewis.

He moved to the hallway, but his path was blocked by a figure clad entirely in white, a miter perched crookedly on his head. His face was ghostly white, but not shiny as Jennet remembered. He brandished his staff and bellowed,

"Who dares disturb the sleep of the holy archbishop Gerard?"

Lewis stepped backward hastily, while Leslie, Amy, and Dr. Bertel let out piercing shrieks. Everyone else jostled about in confusion. Drinks spilled and glasses broke. Matthew grabbed Jennet's hand and asked, "Same Gerard?"

"No," she replied firmly, "In fact, I think it's—"

Her remark was cut off as Pete, in a drunken rage, charged past everyone and attempted to tackle the "ghost." Gerard stepped aside at the last moment, and Pete crashed to the ground. The phony archbishop could contain himself no longer. He broke into peals of laughter and leaned against the wall for support.

Jennet finished. "—It's Douglas."

Lewis and Roger turned lights back on. Kenneth dashed over to his twin—pushing away Pete, who was still trying to get at Douglas—and screamed, "Ye daft old sod! What the hell are ye trying to do? Scare us half to death?"

Douglas's face was covered in white greasepaint. He wiped away his tears of laughter and smudged it. "Aye. That's what I planned to do. I thought we'd invited every one but the proper guest of honor. So I decided to have Gerard come. I rigged the costume yesterday and used a timer to kill the lights for the right moment. Och, I just wish I had pictures of your silly faces!" He howled again.

Pete was struggling to stand. "Then this was all a joke? Was it a joke the other night, too, when I got attacked? When the Durrells were burglarized? Your idea of fun, MacNucator, is not mine."

Douglas looked offended. "That wasna me. I had nowt to do with it. I swear it."

Roger Barclay stared at him. "How can we be sure of that, Douglas? This isn't a matter for fun and games. We have no way of proving you weren't the same 'ghost' that attacked Pete and Jennet, and now you come barging in with a robe and a miter. What else are we supposed to think?''

For once, the burly Scot could think of nothing to say. He began wiping his face with tissues. Surprisingly, Olaf came to his defense. "I believe him. He's always up to stupid pranks, and this is just another one. I can't see him attacking people in the night. That's not enough audience for our Dougie.''

"Thanks. I think," said Douglas.

"Besides," Jennet added, "I would swear that the Gerard I saw was wearing a mask, maybe a ceramic one, and not just greasepaint. What do you think, Pete?''

Pete, perhaps embarrassed by his display, had disappeared into the kitchen. He returned when Jennet called him, carrying a cup of coffee. He gulped it down, then said, "I guess you're right. I seem to remember the lights shining on the face in a funny way. Man, don't do that again. You're lucky I didn't come at you with a knife.''

"I won't, laddie," said Douglas, politely ignoring the fact that Pete was probably too drunk to slice butter, let alone a moving target.

Some of the others were obviously not convinced by Douglas's declarations of innocence, but Dr. Durrell put an immediate end to idle speculation.

"Let's drop the matter right now. Douglas, it was rather an unfortunate choice of subject. Try to restrain your enthusiasm for mischief in the future." He patted his wife's arm. "And now, I think we could all do with some more refreshments. Some tea, perhaps?''

"I'd love some tea," said Lewis. "And I've made some more punch for those who want it.''

Mary-Lou tried on Douglas's cardboard miter. "Y'all do know how to throw a memorable party." She quoted the

befuddled king from *Start the Revolution Without Me*:
" 'I thought it was a costume ball!' "

After the excitement of Douglas's prank, the party dwin-
dled down to something resembling a late-night kaffee-
klatsch, with the guests sneaking extra helpings of dessert—
the torte was long gone—and drinking everything from
Swedish lagers to punch to caffeine-loaded stimulants. Jennet was puzzled to see Pete drinking coffee as if he had to
drive home on the freeway. She wondered if the sight of
Douglas-as-Gerard had haunted him so much he felt he had
to sober up in a hurry. She had a cup of tea herself.

The guests who did not stay at the dorm left by one-
thirty. Miles claimed he wanted another cup of tea, but
everyone else began to stumble upstairs. Leslie said with a
ladylike yawn, "Let's all go to bed. That's certainly enough
excitement for one night."

As they soon discovered, she was dead wrong.

Someone was hammering in Jennet's dream. It was Kenneth, nailing up pictures of St. Oswald. The pictures were
attractive, but made no sense: St. Oswald with an Anglo
concertina, St. Oswald eating Dobos torte, St. Oswald with
a baseball bat, hitting fly balls to Archbishop Gerard.

She woke up briefly, and rolled over. She fell asleep
instantly, but to her annoyance the hammering went on.
Bang, bang, bang. She wished it would stop. It was very
irritating.

It took her a moment to realize that the banging was not
part of a dream, that she was awake and had a slight hangover. The clock's malevolent blue digits glowed: 4:15 A.M.
The noise, she eventually figured out, was coming from the
door. Someone kept tapping on it.

"I'm going to kill whoever's out there," she muttered.
The first weapon that came to her hand was her hair
dryer. It was vaguely pistol-shaped, but Jennet intended to

wield it as a club. She gripped it firmly, then threw the door open in the middle of a *tap-tap-tap*.

She was forever grateful that her reflexes were good enough to keep the dryer from crashing down on the latest midnight intruder. Betsy Durrell stared at her in dismay. Matthew and Olaf stood a few feet behind the professor's wife.

"Mrs. Durrell! What's going on?" she stammered.

Betsy Durrell had lived through air raids and depressions, and Jennet always regarded her as possessing an exterior as seemingly fragile as Wedgewood, but with a core of steel. It was shocking to see her twisting her purse straps in agitation, her face haggard and drawn. She whispered hoarsely, "Could I sit down first, dear? It's a complicated story."

"Yes, of course, come in," Jennet said. She suddenly realized she was still clutching the hair dryer. She dropped it on her desk while Matthew and Olaf guided the elderly woman to the chair.

She looked up at the two men in some confusion. "Edwin had a message he wanted me to give to Jennet. But I'm not sure if he meant it for her ears alone."

Jennet quickly said, "I know that Matthew and Olaf can be trusted, Mrs. D. Could you tell us what has happened? Is the Professor alright?"

"He's in hospital, but the doctors say he'll be fine. Oh, where to begin this?"

Jennet's worries quadrupled at the mention of hospitals. "Is it his heart?" she asked.

"He's under observation now, but they think there may be some damage. Look, I'm telling this all wrong. His message was to tell you exactly what happened tonight, so I must try to do that properly." Matthew vanished, to return with a glass of water, which Mrs. Durrell sipped gratefully.

"We went straight to bed after the party. I am a light sleeper and often wake up at night. About an hour and a half ago, I woke when I heard the French windows being opened. Foolishly, I roused Edwin. If only I'd let him sleep! Then that thief could have taken that cursed chalice, and Edwin would be fine!''

Matthew broke in, ''Someone took the last chalice?''

Mrs. Durrell shook her head. ''He didn't take it. Edwin leaped out of bed'' (Jennet had trouble imagining the professor 'leaping.') ''and ran into the dining room. I followed him, screaming for help. There was a man or possibly a tall woman, dressed in those horrible robes and a bishop's hat, standing by the fireplace. I think you were right, Jennet, he seemed to be wearing some kind of ceramic mask, like a harlequin or the Phantom of the Opera. He was examining the chalice but suddenly threw it right at Edwin. He must have felt it was his only chance to create a diversion so he could escape. It caught him on the side of the head and knocked him to the ground. While I ran to Edwin, the thief vanished out the windows. Edwin was just barely conscious. He said, 'Tell Jennet what happened. Tell her what he did.'

''Matilda rang the hospital and the police. I came here as soon as I could leave Edwin. I knocked and knocked, and finally these young men answered. Do you have some idea of why he wanted to tell you about the attempted theft?''

Jennet assumed it had to do with the professor's phony-chalice plan. Mrs. Durrell, she decided, had more than enough to worry about right now. She didn't need to be told that her husband had idiotically, deliberately baited a trap for the thief. She shook her head and hoped she sounded convincing. ''No, I'm afraid I'm just as confused as you. I have had some discussions with him over the last time the thief tried to steal the chalice. Perhaps he meant that.''

Matthew tugged thoughtfully on his chin as she spoke; he also knew about the phony chalice. Olaf, who was still uninformed, patted Mrs. Durrell on the hand. ''I'm sure he had reasons, and I'm sure he'll be glad to know you carried out his request. Would you like us to take you home?''

''No, no, that's not needed. I've a cab waiting in the street to take me back to the hospital.'' She rose, with Olaf's help. ''I'm sorry to wake you with such awful news, my dear, but Edwin seemed to think it was important to tell you.''

''I don't mind, honestly, and I do hope he's better soon,'' said Jennet.

Betsy stopped at the doorway. ''There was one other strange thing which I didn't learn until I was preparing to leave the hospital. After the ambulance came for Edwin, the police were searching for clues with Matilda. They found an unconscious man in the street next to our house. They didn't know if he was some drunk, a victim, or the thief himself. He wasn't wearing any robes or such things. The doctors were busy with him, but the police would like me to take a look at him later.'' She sighed. ''I just want to see Edwin, not some bum from the gutter.''

Then men helped her down the stairs and they all escorted her to the taxi. ''Try to rest, Mrs. Durrell,'' said Matthew. ''The professor won't like it if you tire yourself out.''

The taxi sped off, leaving the trio on the front porch of the dorm.

''Well!'' exclaimed Olaf. ''What in hell do you suppose that was all about?''

Matthew and Jennet exchanged glances. They had a damn good idea. It was time to let Olaf know, to gather as many allies as possible. Jennet broke the silence. ''Gerard's struck once tonight, and my guess is that he's at it again. Right now.''

Olaf may not have had all the information they did, but he could guess Jennet's meaning. ''The third niche?''

''The third niche,'' she replied.

+ + + + + + + + + + + + + + + + + +

XIII

OLAF BUNCHED HIS hands into fists. "Then let us go down to the church and murder the thieving son of a bitch!"

Matthew grabbed his arm. "Wait a minute, wait a minute! We don't know who it is or how many there are! Why don't we rouse the dorm first? We can take a head count and then go to St. Oswald's. Anybody not snoozing in bed is automatically a suspect. And there's safety in numbers."

Jennet was still pondering the story Mrs. Durrell had told her. There must be something there, or else why would the professor want her to know so quickly? Was it to prevent a break-in at the church? It suddenly occurred to her that Olaf and Matthew were proposing a vigilante raid. "Hey, fellows, don't you think we should let the police know first? Gerard can be dangerous."

They gazed at her with injured pride. "If the whole dorm comes, we can take on any ghostly archbishop," said Olaf.

Matthew added, "Besides, maybe everything's quiet. Would you want to call the cops out for nothing? We can check and see if the niche is undisturbed. If all is well, we'll peacefully head for home. Okay?"

Jennet wasn't entirely happy about the idea. She did want to see if any of her colleagues were out in the early morning hours, though, so she joined Matthew and Olaf in pounding on doors. Jennet had taken the women's floor, and found neither Leslie nor Carleen in their beds, which were both neatly made, complete with hospital corners and straightened pillows. She hoped Carleen was sleeping with Kenneth, not out hurling chalices at elderly professors.

Douglas was there also, bellowing curses in fine form at being roused by Olaf. But once he grasped the situation, he thumped on doors with the rest of them. Dr. Preston, Jennet knew was customarily useless before ten in the morning, but when he heard of Dr. Durrell's injury, he looked as alert and bloodthirsty as Olaf.

To their surprise, the dorm was practically empty. The Barclays' bed was rumpled, but vacant. Miles Beckwith's bed looked untouched. Kenneth's bed definitely looked slept in—or at least used for some purpose—but his window onto the fire escape was wide open, though the night air was cold. Pete Sharp's and Lewis Hunter's rooms were locked, but Douglas picked the locks with astonishing speed. "Dinna ask where I learned that," he muttered. Those rooms, like Miles's, were neat and orderly.

The remaining five dormmates gathered in the living room. Jennet explained the situation as succinctly as she could. "We're only guessing, but we think the thief could be breaking into the third niche right now. It would make sense, since Dr. Durrell plans to open it on Monday. If the thief wanted to chance it, he'd have to do it tonight or Sunday night." She saw the first thin light of dawn through the window. "I guess it's Sunday already. We can either go to the police with our suspicions, which may be unfounded, or we can check out the church ourselves, as Matthew and Olaf have suggested, and see if we can locate our missing colleagues. Shall we put it to a vote?"

Judging from Preston's and Douglas's angry faces, there was no need. They were united not only in their passion for the past, but in their desire to avenge the first theft and prevent further loss. Douglas spoke for them all: "We

should go to the church, and quickly. I canna believe that
my brother is responsible for this, but I mislike the feeling
in me wame.'' He struck his stomach with his fist. ''The
last time I felt this queer, Kenneth and I were seven, an'
living in separate homes, miles apart. Kenneth had been in
a car accident and was pinned under a lorry for nearly three
hours. I ken sommat is wrong, badly wrong.''

''How do you know that you wouldn't feel just as strange
if he were out there robbing the church and beating up old
men?'' asked Olaf.

Douglas looked daggers at his colleague. ''He's my twin,
that's why!''

Jennet intervened: ''Look, Olaf, this is not the time to
argue about psychic contacts between twins. We don't know
where the hell anybody's gone, and at the moment the ab-
sentees outnumber those present, eight to five. If they're all
in this together, don't you think it's rather dumb of us to go
charging into the church?''

Matthew emerged from the kitchen with a paper in his
hand. ''This explains where two have gone. It's a note from
Lewis; it was stuck on the fridge. He says before he went to
bed, he called that nursing home and they asked him to
come as fast as he could. His mother won't last long. He
says Leslie's come with him to help, but she'll try to come
back Sunday night. And we know that excuse is legit—his
mother really is in that nursing home.''

Most of the crowd appeared relieved; at least two mysterious disappearances were solved. For some reason, Dr.
Preston looked disappointed. Jennet had no time to think
this over, however, for the gang was busily donning sweaters and jackets.

Although Jennet continued to fret over their decision and
Douglas was uncharacteristically silent, Matthew and Olaf
were in a jaunty mood as they marched down the street like
a posse. Olaf tried singing the ''Ballad of Brave Sir Robin''

from "Monty Python and the Holy Grail," but Preston told him to shut up. Wild speculations flew about the culprit's—or culprits'—identity.

"It's the Barclays," Matthew guessed. "They know the church better than anybody else, Roger's been in police trouble before, and Amy's an art historian. She'd know more about the individual pieces and their values that anyone else."

"I like Jennet's idea from the other day: it's Leslie, teamed with Miles for his expertise in the Middle Ages," said Olaf, still humming. "Leslie was with the St. Oswald's team from the first discovery, but she'd need outside help. Miles steals the goods, while Leslie innocently accompanies Lewis."

Douglas shook his head gloomily at their proposals. His brother's absence disturbed him more than he would admit. "I hope you're right. I hope it's anybody but my idiot brother, who is probably off cavorting with Carleen right now. I hope. What about Pete, who claimed the ghostly bishop clubbed him?"

"Archbishop," Jennet corrected automatically.

Matthew zipped his warm-up jacket and removed the green exercise ball from the pocket. He tossed it absent-mindedly as he spoke. "I haven't mentioned it to Mary-Lou, but we think Pete's been up to something at our dig."

"*Your* dig?" said Douglas. "But you haven't reported anything missing from your dig."

"I don't mean anything's been stolen. But a few weeks ago, Jennet and I spotted Pete sneaking out of the trailer in the wee smalls. He could have been there the night Gerard landed him in the rose bushes."

Olaf was thoughtful, the pale light of dawn giving his blond hair a rosy tint. "Wonder what he was doing?"

Matthew was describing a nefarious scheme involving everybody at once, including all the elderly guests from the party and the express-mail messenger, when they turned the corner and saw the bulky Georgian building that was the Church of St. Oswald. Olaf suddenly let out a bellow. "My car! My car!"

Olaf's stolen white Volvo was parked in front of the church.

Oblivious to his friends' whispered demands for quiet, he rushed to the car like a man finding a long-lost love. He prowled around it, searching for signs of damage, then knelt down by the plates.

"Look at that! He's changed the number by painting the eights into threes. You'd never know the difference unless you looked closely, so any policeman checking for *my* number would think this was another chap's car."

"Well, Olaf," said Dr. Preston, "I'd say this indicates we're not too late to stop whoever's inside the church. Unless it's mere coincidence that your car thief parks in front of churches."

Matthew asked, "Olaf, do you have the keys? Maybe there are clues inside."

The big Orcadian had been murmuring "Poor baby" to the car, but Matthew's suggestion made him fumble in his pockets. He opened the trunk, which revealed two unlabeled, locked suitcases.

"Anybody recognize these?" asked Matthew. No one did, though Douglas swore they didn't belong to Kenneth. They had all stowed their suitcases or backpacks in closets after they arrived at the dorm. It was easier and neater to keep belongings in drawers or closets.

"I could rip them open," Douglas offered.

Olaf snarled, "Form a queue!"

"Aren't you forgetting something?" Jennet said with exasperation. "Whoever owns those suitcases is down under that church, chipping away at the walls. Shall we wait here for Gerard to come out or shall we go in there and meet him?"

"Let's go," said Matthew.

The main gate to the church was locked. Matthew, the most athletic of the group, and Olaf, the tallest, studied the wall for the easiest means to scale it.

"It won't be too hard to climb, though I wouldn't like to try it carrying a treasure chest," said Matthew.

"The thief undoubtedly has a key," said Olaf.

Suddenly Dr. Preston began turning out his pockets on the sidewalk. A bag of jalapeño jelly beans, a pocket calculator, crumpled three-by-five cards, assorted coins, and other odds and ends cascaded to the ground. He reached down, grabbed a key from the pile of junk, and waved it excitedly.

"Edwin gave it to me when I got here, in case I wanted to use his office. I forgot all about it until now."

He opened the lock and shoved the gate aside with typical dramatic flair. "After you, valiant comrades." He shoved the junk back into his pocket.

Jennet would forever remember their entry into the church as a combination of the Marx brothers and "The Twilight Zone." The church door was unlocked; someone was inside, sure enough. She feverently hoped they were interrupting the vicar or some staff member, but the building was empty. A dim light shone near the canvas partitions which covered the opening to the lower level. The sound of metal tools against stone echoed from below.

They were all trying to be as quiet as possible, but five people stumbling in the dark couldn't avoid making noise. Jennet had been trailing behind Matthew, wondering what their plan of attack would be. For that matter, she wondered if they had a plan of attack. The whole idea suddenly seemed idiotic. They should have gone straight to the police. Who knew what kind of arsenal the thief could throw at them?

Throw at them. That brought back the image of Gerard hurling the phony chalice at the defenseless professor. They had all assumed Gerard did that to buy time to escape, but

surely a healthy young man or woman could outrun two
senior citizens. Why did he throw the chalice—the very
object of the theft—instead of running for it?

Jennet suddenly realized why: Gerard had thrown it because he had recognized it as a modern imitation. And out
of the entire dorm, just two people were specialists in art
history and therefore capable of spotting the replacement in
an instant. Other pieces of the puzzle fell into place.

Her fury caused her to forget her earlier caution. She
pushed to the front of the vigilantes and shouted, "We
know you're in there, Lewis, so come on out. We outnumber you." *At least I hope we do*, she thought. *I don't know
who else is down there.*

Her outburst brought surprised gasps from her colleagues, including a muffled curse from Dr. Preston. Matthew whispered, "Lewis? But what about that letter and
his mom?"

The chipping stopped and they heard Lewis laugh. "I was
afraid someone might think to check here. I should have realized it would be a clever girl like you, Jennet. I'm not
comping up, though, just yet. Why don't you come down?"

Jennet began to move toward the stairs, but Matthew and
Olaf pulled her back. "Let go of me," she said. She was
confident that while Gerard was a thief, he was not a mur-
derer. They compromised, and scuttled down the stairs in a
pack. There was barely enough room for them all to get a
glimpse of the site.

Lewis was working by torchlight. In fact, he had resumed
his patient chipping while they jostled each other on the
stairs. They soon saw the reason for his calm air: Leslie,
elegantly clad in a leather skirt and beige silk blouse,
perched on a stone slab with a revolver in her hand. A
second gun rested beside her. Jennet was not so certain that
Leslie would refrain from using them. She remembered her
stories of the Staffords's shooting box in Scotland.

"Hello, everyone," Leslie said quietly. Like Lewis, she wore a paper filter over her face to protect her from the dust and mold. The bright blue mask clashed with her clothes.

"Good thing I brought you, my pet," Lewis said. "This damned job is taking longer than I expected."

"You can't hope to get away with it, Lewis," said Jennet. "We know all about it." *Unless Leslie shoots us all, of course.*

"Of course we can, Jennet," said Lewis. "Your arrival merely makes life more complicated in some ways, but less complicated in others. I've already had to adjust my original plans after certain—ah, difficulties—last night. You see, I had hoped to take whatever's in here on my way north and to return after visiting my mum."

"In *my* car," said Olaf angrily.

"Yes, your car. It's been waiting for us in a car park all week. Rental cars leave paper trails, and there are limits to what one can carry on our noted rail system." *Chip-chip-chip.*

Matthew thought fast. "When you visited your mother the last time, you used the professor's van and not the train. Because you were bringing the treasure to Scotland?"

"Got it in one, Matthew. Of course, you came as close as anyone to finding it that night when you were prowling around. It was pure chance that I knew you were going treasure hunting. I overheard you mention it to Jennet on the quad that afternoon. You'd be surprised at how well voices carry."

"And after that, you knew it wasn't safe in the dorm, so you moved it . . . to its original site?" guessed Jennet.

"Oh, well done! I'm almost sorry I tried to frame you for the theft earlier. As it turned out, the police didn't go for the bait, but that didn't matter once we found Gerard's bones. All those newspaper reports of ghosts gave me a plenty of chances. I'd planned to leave the costume here so everyone would think Gerard stole it, protecting the abbey's treasures. Yes, I've had rather a jolly time pretending to be an archbishop." He loosened another stone and carefully removed it.

"Jolly time?" said Preston. "Attacking Jennet and Pete, throwing that chalice at Dr. Durrell?"

Lewis frowned as he worked. "Yes, that chalice was a bit of a bother. If I'd known the old man had replaced it with a forgery, I'd never have wasted time trying to steal it. I'd probably be on the road by now. Yes, that was a critical delay for a number of reasons. Of course, we very nearly didn't get off the campus—we were spotted by the lovebirds, who were up late disporting themselves."

"Do you mean Carleen and Kenneth?" Matthew asked in a low voice.

"Yes, love's young dream," said Leslie from her perch. "It was almost funny. They came vaulting down the fire escape, half-dressed."

Douglas balled his hands into fists. "Wha' hae ye done with my brother?" He looked ready to pounce. Leslie kept a careful eye on him.

"Relax, Dougie, we tied, gagged and locked them in the workshed behind the dormitory. They didn't anticipate that I was armed."

"Neither did we," murmured Oluf regretfully.

"Careless of you," said Lewis. "But I assure you they're hale and hearty and probably extremely furious. That's when it became obvious that we'd have to be on our merry way, after stopping at the Durrells' and the church. Damn this mortar! Jennet, remind the professor to pay close attention to the composition of the fill in this area."

Lewis, even while detailing his criminal accomplishments, was still a scholar. Jennet decided to try another tack. "Why, Lewis, why? You're part of one of the most

important discoveries of the century. It shouldn't be too
hard to get tenure after this. And I hear you've written an
excellent monograph; you're a good scholar . . .''

At this remark, Dr. Preston thundered in Jennet's left ear.
"Good scholar, my ass! He's not only a thief, he's a pla-
giarist!''

If at all possible, that stunned the crowd even more than
finding out who Gerard was. Few things raise the wrath of
academics more than the theft of another's work. Even
Lewis was impressed enough to stop moving stone. "May
I inquire how you discovered that?'' he asked politely, as if
in a classroom.

Preston's face was flushed with anger. "You may. Your
monograph seemed familiar to me, but I couldn't place it at
first. I knew it wasn't published, or I'd have seen it listed in
catalogs. Finally I remembered I'd read a paper with the
same topic almost thirty years ago, when *I* was a lowly
assistant professor at the University of Cincinnati. The author was a young English girl, a student with a great deal of
promise. She was married to an American, but I heard some
years later there was some trouble and she returned to England. I never heard what happened to her, but I kept a copy
of the paper in my files, which was sent to me last night.''

"She was my cousin," said Lewis. "She abandoned history for greener pastures, as I shall do now. Unfortunately,
she was killed in a car wreck. My aunt gave me all her academic papers, and I decided it was too good not to publish.''

"Under your name, eh?'' said Douglas. "Ye thievin'
shiftless scoundrel!'' He took another step down the stairs,
but Leslie trained the gun on him.

"Don't try it,'' she said. "Lewis, how much longer?
They'll be getting ready for Sunday services in a few hours.''

"I know, I know. I'm almost there. I thought Roger had
made more progress yesterday. Where are my valiant co-
workers, anyway?''

Matthew said, "They've gone for the police. Why don't you give up, Lewis? I'm sure if you gave back the treasure that something could be worked out. Dr. Durrell is a reasonable man."

Lewis laughed. "You're not a bad liar, Jonas, but I know that the Barclays would be the last couple in the world to run to the police, no matter what the circumstances. I can't give up, however. My finances—or rather the lack of them— are such that I've often contemplated disappearing from sight in the last year. The discovery of the treasure provided a means to escape my creditors and remain in academics. I know how to dispose of it properly; do you recall the thefts of the thirteenth-century ivories from Chichester and the illuminated manuscripts from Senlis? Some friends of mine were responsible for the theft, though I accomplished the marketing. That's how I met Leslie, who was getting rid of some family heirlooms without letting the family know. However, thanks to certain events of the evening and your untimely arrival—uh!" He grunted as he removed another stone. "We shall indeed disappear, and the treasure will help us get a new start. You know, I rather enjoy seeing it stay out of the creditors' fists."

This callous explanation of the theft of priceless historical relics infuriated the crowd on the stairs, but they could only watch helplessly. Leslie, with a hunter's wariness, kept her eyes on them as Lewis broke through the wall. He gingerly removed a wood and metal casket, around two feet square. He put it in a packing case, wiped his hands on his pants with satisfaction. "I think it's time to leave your pleasant company. Perhaps, if I have a chance, I will write you and let you know what was inside. Sadly, we are pressed for time. Leslie, could you escort them upstairs?"

"With pleasure." Jennet could hear the triumph in Leslie's voice. All these weeks, she had struggled to understand their medieval and classical jargon and put up with rude comments about her own field of study. Now her expertise with small firearms was all that stood between the vigilantes and the loss of yet another treasure from the past. Jennet felt more frustrated than ever. They'd come so close to saving it!

"What are your plans now, Lewis? You can't hope to get far. We'll have the police after you in no time," said Preston.

"That's what I meant by the situation getting more complicated. It would have been so nice to just pop off with the find, then return after visiting my poor old mum, as horrified as the rest of you at the latest ghastly crime. But a clever man prepares for all possibilities: we knew the time might come when we'd have to cut and run, and we're ready, even to the extent of having our cases packed."

"Aye, we saw them," growled Douglas.

"We're wasting time," said Leslie, who was growing impatient with her partner's braggadocio. She herded them to front of the church. She began to follow Lewis to the western entrance when Olaf rushed her, roaring, "She's bluffing!" But she wasn't. Retaining her poise, she quickly shot Olaf in the foot, the sharp retort echoing through the empty church. He collapsed in a heap as a dark stain spread over his boot. He shrieked once, then fainted. Leslie smiled nastily, as if she relished the opportunity to take on the rest of them; Lewis looked on with distaste.

"How annoying," he remarked. "That will draw unnecessary attention, but it should convince you that we *are* serious."

Jennet noticed Matthew had slipped from her side during the confrontation and moved to the outside of the group. She prayed he wouldn't try anything stupid, not after what just happened to Olaf. "I wish we had time to tie them up," Leslie said. "Do you think they'll stay put?"

"Of course. I'll lock them in. The windows are too high

for them to climb out, and there aren't any telephones in here," Lewis replied.

They watched unhappily as Lewis and Leslie headed toward the western door. Leslie walked backward for part of the way, then decided that she had put enough distance between them for safety. She turned to help Lewis with the door. In that instant, Matthew's hand flashed from his pocket. His body twisted like a blur, something whizzed through the air, and Leslie fell like a stone, dropping her weapons.

"A beanball!" crowed Dr. Preston.

Lewis, stunned by the loss of his protection, hurried to escape the rampaging crowd of historians now bearing down on him. He had enough of a lead that he still might have squeezed outside ahead of them, but he stopped just short of the door. "The archbishop!" he gasped, "The archbishop!" His eyes were wide and frightened.

Douglas led the mob and reached Lewis first. The older man had recovered from whatever momentarily startled him and was again trying to open the door. Douglas tackled him, knocking him to the ground, still clutching the crate. Jennet, meanwhile, dove for the guns beside the groaning Leslie. Matthew picked up his exercise ball, which had bounced into a corner after ricocheting off Leslie's head. He looked curiously thoughtful.

Preston was too overweight to arrive in time for the capture, so he roared, "Be careful of the casket!"

Police sirens wailed in the distance, and there were shouts from the churchyard.

Douglas shook Lewis by the shirt. "Let me gi'him what he deserves, before they take him away." Preston persuaded Douglas to wait for the authorities, but Lewis seemed not to notice any of the chaos around him. The thief had a haunted expression, and kept staring at a spot on the wall where the morning sun sparkled.

The sirens sounded closer; car doors slammed. The door suddenly burst open, and a crowd of constables looked around in considerable surprise. Jennet, squatting beside the unconscious Olaf, reflected that it must seem like the last act of *Hamlet*, with bodies strewn everywhere.

"Ere naow, wot's going on?" asked one.

Everyone tried to explain at once, but the bobbies wouldn't have any of it. "Is a Miss Walker here?" asked a second.

Jennet rushed forward. "That's me. Did Dr. Durrell send you?" she asked.

"No, miss. Inspector Dennistoun dispatched me and P.C. Dooley, after receiving information from a Mr. Miles Beckwith, who is in hospital. He asked us to check out this church, see if anything queer was happening. We would have come in sooner, but we noticed a car with altered plates which matched the description of one stolen earlier this week, and we felt we should report that first. Then we heard a gunshot, so we called for additional support."

Matron Yeatman believed in keeping a firm rein on her hospital ward. She preferred things quiet and running like clockwork. She certainly did not approve of the enormous boisterous party heading down the hall to room 351. However, the police inspector had convinced the patients' doctors that it would be a kindness to the injured men if they could hear the whole story. And what a story it was! All about treasures and ghosts and guns and, very likely, spies and drugs.

The young nurse's aides were all atwitter, especially when the burly redheaded man began winking at them. Matron Yeatman had already disposed of a horde of reporters that morning. Now she shooed the aides away on meaningless errands. She intended to see that these visitors—goodness, how many were there?—would not upset her patients. "I shall come with you," she announced. "You must not overstimulate these men."

One of the group—an older, heavy-set man—laughed loudly. "Overstimulate them? After what happened last night and early this morning, what on earth could we innocents do to overstimulate them? Short of smuggling some celebratory champagne into their room, I mean."

Matron sniffed. One expected such high jinks from the young, but this was a man her own age, another of these noted professors. He should set a better example. She began checking the visitors for bulky bags which could contain contraband. A short girl with wavy brown hair carried a cardboard box. Matron stopped her. "You there! There isn't anything to drink that box, is there?"

The girl smiled. "Nobody knows what's in this box. If there is anything to drink, I suspect it's dreadfully rancid by now. After all, it's at least four hundred years old."

At that, the group began laughing again and clapping each other on the backs. Matron didn't know if the girl was joking or not, so she ignored the comment and pulled up a chair in the hallway. "You have fifteen minutes."

The room held four beds, which were all occupied. Miles Beckwith, his head wrapped in bandages and his left eye resembling a technicolor extravaganza, rested in the first. Dr. Durrell, looking pale but cheerful, sat up in the second, with Betsy at his side, Olaf, his right foot heavily wrapped, reclined in the third. The last bed contained a middle-aged man who was pretending to read a novel while he eavesdropped on his neighbors.

The crowd squeezed into the room, pulling up spare chairs. Everybody began to talk at once, causing Dr. Durrell to wave his hand and implore, "Order! Order, please! I've seen better behavior in kindergarten students! Someone should speak for the group and explain just what has happened, or else Miles and I shall perish from curiosity. Inspector Dennistoun was rather close-mouthed earlier. Jennet, somehow I feel you should do the honors.''

The murmurs of approval that met this suggestion made Jennet feel warm all over. She edged her chair closer to the professor's bed, tucked the box safely on the floor. "I think we all want to know how you and Olaf and Miles are feeling. That's more important than anything else."

"Tut!" he snorted. "It would take more than a rampaging archbishop to keep me down for long!" Betsy shushed him and patted his hand.

"Speak for yourself, Professor," said Miles. "I feel as if the worst hangover I ever had were doubled. And I didn't even get drunk at the party!"

Olaf grimaced, his moustache twitching. "I'm merely eternally grateful that Leslie aimed low and used a small-caliber gun. The surgeon says my ankle will get better, but maybe it will twinge the next time I think about acting like a hero."

"Och, if it's any consolation tae ye, Olaf, I was just about tae jump the schemin' bitch but ye moved first. I thought she was bluffing, too." Douglas's comments produced a hint of a smile under Olaf's whiskers.

Miles thumped this mattress impatiently. "Come, Jennet, don't keep us in suspense any longer. Give us the details! Dennistoun gave a rather fragmented account."

"I think we all need to join the pieces together for this to make sense. First of all, you do know that Lewis Hunter was responsible for the crimes, and Leslie was his assistant. He admitted to us that he had acted as a fence for black-market art finds before—the Chichester and the Senlis thefts. As I understand it, Lewis invested that money, which did well until recently. He was in a desperate situation, so he was forced to foul his own well. After the professor hired me, he decided to steal the treasure and made a half-hearted try at framing me for it. He knew Leslie's family was also broke, so he asked her for help.''

Dr. Durrell sadly shook his head. ''I thought I was doing her a favor by keeping her on even though she really wasn't qualified for the job. And this news about Lewis! I think the shock of realizing he was the criminal hit harder than the chalice did.''

''So you guessed who it was even with that mask?'' asked Olaf.

''Oh yes,'' said Dr. Durrell. ''I had suspected him before, and when Samuel told me he thought Lewis' latest work was plagiarized, I feared the worst. Still, seeing him with that chalice . . .''

''What's all this about the chalice?'' Olaf asked in exasperation. ''And just how did Jennet know it was Lewis? We'd found that note saying he was visiting his mother, so I'd crossed him off the list of suspects.''

''You remember that Dr. Durrell still had one of the four original chalices from the treasure; he showed it to us the night of that party,'' Jennet said. ''He decided to draw the thief's attention by saying he'd sent the chalice to an expert for examination, then announcing that it was back in his house. Lewis couldn't resist the chance to complete the set. After all, he knew it was easy to break into their house.''

''You old fool,'' said Betsy Durrell fondly.

''In fact, it was an imitation chalice. That was how the professor knew Lewis was disguised as Archbishop Gerard only Lewis and Amy were trained in medieval art history and familiar enough with the St. Oswald's treasure to recognize a fake in an instant. When Mrs. D explained what happened at their house, the figure she described was 'a man or a tall woman'. Amy isn't much taller than I am, and would make a petite archbishop. Roger is a fine archaeologist, but his specialty is hagiography. It probably wouldn't take him long to sniff out a fake, but I doubt he could do it in a dim room under intense pressure. It had to be Lewis."

The Barclays were resting together on the spare bed. "I'm glad you had some faith in us," said Roger. "I'm afraid there were times we doubted you."

Jennet was willing to let all that pass. She replied, "We suspected you for a long time, too, so I guess we're even."

"I certainly suspected you two last night when we found your empty bed," said Olaf. "Where were you?"

Amy ducked her head into her husband's shoulder. "We were here, in the emergency room," she mumbled.

"Amy's been feeling poorly these past few weeks," said Roger. "Last night, we were afraid she was coming down with some intestinal flu. Instead, the lab report says she's pregnant!"

This announcement brought fresh cheers from everyone. Jennet smiled to see Amy, whose exterior was as tough as nails, blushing a brilliant red.

"Just don't name him Gerard," said Matthew.

"How about Oswald?" Miles suggested. "St. Oswald's been on our side all along."

"Ozzie Barclay? Over my dead body!" said Amy, sounding more like her feisty self.

"We weren't the only ones to suspect you two," said Olaf. "Dennistoun dragged Roger off that evening, and Lewis made some remarks about your bad relations with the police when we tried to bluff him into thinking you had gone for help."

"Oh, that," said Amy. "It's old business."

"They're our friends, love, they're entitled to know," said Roger. "One of the professors at the university was harassing Amy. He went a little too far one day, and so did I. I beat him up. I felt he deserved it. We went through charges and countercharges and dropped charges. Eventually, I was fired, and the old bugger 'resigned.' That's that.

Old business, as Amy says. It did interest Dennistoun, though.''

Jennet had trouble believing that the even-keeled Roger, with his breezy, care-free manner, could ever be driven to assault. Yet when she saw how devoted he was to Amy, she knew just how strong his feelings were. She was glad for the two of them.

Pete had been sitting some distance away from the rest of the group, smiling, but not contributing anything. Roger's explanation made him clear his throat uncomfortably.

''I guess it's true confessions time. I wish I could say I was out having a pregnancy test, too, like Gerard's miserable brother Peter. Unfortunately, I wasn't. It's hard for me to explain, but I understand a little of what Lewis has been going through with money troubles. I've been in up beyond my ears lately, and I stole some money from the excavation's account.''

Matthew's face fell as he heard his colleague confess. Carleen, who had not been on good terms with Pete lately, thumped the nightstand with her hand. ''All this time I've been thinking such horrible things about you, and all you did was raid the petty cash? You dummy! Why didn't you borrow some from me or Matt or even Mary-Lou? We would have helped you out!''

Pete's face flushed, but whether the cause was embarrassment or pleasure at Carleen's sudden support was not obvious. ''I already borrowed from Matt this summer, and I didn't think I knew you well enough. I really tried not to think of this as stealing, but as a kind of borrowing. You see, I've paid it all back. My trouble was fixing the computer records to cover up what I did. I'm better at word processing than I am at the spreadsheet programs. It took me four or five late night trips to finish.''

''Jennet and I saw you one night,'' said Matthew, ''and

Lewis must have known you were doing something fishy, so he ambushed you another evening.''

"Didn't he just!'' Pete said, with feeling. "I was scared— er—to death. I didn't mention that he kept whispering to me, 'I know what you've done, I know what you've done,' while I was tangled in that blasted rose bush.''

"I fear Lewis had a bit of a cruel streak in him,'' said Dr. Durrell. "Taunting you, casting suspicion on Jennet, frightening everyone with that absurd costume. I never would have guessed it from working with him.''

"Well, I know better now. That road is not for me. I intend to confess the whole thing to Mary-Lou this week. She may have my head for it, but at least I'll be clean.'' Pete's voice was firm, but his slouch showed how unhappy he felt.

Carleen rose from her chair beside Kenneth and walked over to her fellow Romanist. "Pete Sharp, you're a damn good scholar and a better archaeologist than me and Matthew together. Mary-Lou won't toss you out because of this; she'd better not, or she'll have to contend with me!'' Everyone knew the reality of the situation: as a lowly grad student, Carleen had no chance of influencing her academic superiors' decisions. Still, Pete clearly appreciated the support. He gave her a big hug.

Matthew surveyed the room. "That accounts for Pete and the Barclays. We know where Lewis and Leslie were. You're another missing person, Miles. You had some sort of run-in with our friend, the scepter-bashing archbishop?''

Miles gingerly patted his bandaged head. Jennet had the feeling that the unassuming Professor Beckwith had been waiting for his moment to preen his heroic feathers and that he would make the most of it.

"Professor Durrell told me about the phony chalice last week. I told him he was mad to try such a scheme—''

"Hear! Hear!'' "Damn right!'' Jennet and Matthew said.

"But he insisted it was too late to do anything, unless I cared to watch the house for them after he announced that the chalice was back. To be honest, I didn't much like the idea, being rather overly fond of my warm bed and having heard about 'Gerard's' violent tendencies. I knew Jennet had heard about the chalice, and I almost told her that I was now an 'insider,' but at the last moment I decided to keep that a secret. I also assumed I'd do better in an outright confrontation with the blackguard than the professor would."

He gestured toward the older man's bed, squinted with his swollen eye. "Wrestling, alas, is not my forte. I had settled down in their garden with a lawn chair and a blanket. It wasn't very long before he showed up. I jumped him as he was trying the French windows, but he fought very well. The next thing I knew, there were policemen everywhere, and I was taken to hospital. I was very woozy then, but I remember trying to tell them to alert Dennistoun to check the church."

"To think of those puir bobbies, busy noting Olaf's stolen car, when all the while there was real thievery inside the church," laughed Douglas.

"I'll have you know that's a valuable car," Olaf said indignantly.

Kenneth routinely ignored the fights between his twin and Olaf. He paid no attention to this one, and remarked, "Carleen and I missed out on everything. We heard Lewis and Leslie sneaking off and tried to stop them. Instead, Leslie herded us into the shed like a pair of sheep. I feel a proper fool."

"You aren't the only one," Olaf said with feeling. "I was flat on my back at the end. I still don't know how Leslie wound up on the ground or why Lewis started wailing about archbishops."

Preston slapped Matthew on the shoulder. "Prettiest

beanball I've seen in ages! Didn't you say you once were scouted by the pros, Matt? Well, what baseball has lost, history has gained."

Matthew grinned. "I never had a really super fastball, but I had damn good control."

"You hit her?" asked Pete.

"Plunked her."

"That sill doesn't explain why Lewis hesitated at the door," Preston continued. "Was he having some vision of Gerard taking revenge on him or what? I was afraid he was going to slip by us until that happened."

"I think I know what it was," Jennet said slowly. "You remember that the dawn light was filtering through the church windows. If you stand just where Lewis was, right in front of the door, it makes a weird effect. It looks like a figure with a pointy hat."

"A miter?" asked Matthew.

"If you'd been up all night and were suddenly on the run, it could look like that. Another long thin beam of light next to the 'figure' might resemble a staff, if your nerves were stretched tight as Lewis's. I could see it was just the sunlight shining into the portal. Who knows what Lewis saw?"

"Who indeed?" said Dr. Durrell. "It would be nice to think that Gerard would approve of what we are doing. After all, he was a noted reformer in his old age. I imagine he'd oppose theft with the same vigor he applied to clerical celibacy. And I'm sure he wouldn't like having crimes committed in his name. Ah, me! But, as Jennet said, it was probably just a trick of the light."

Douglas had a strange glint in his eye. His brother saw it and kicked the redhead in the shins. "Don't even think of it. Don't you dare try it."

Douglas feigned innocence. "Why are you kicking me, you big ogre?"

"Because we all know how much you love those idiotic

tabloids. If you run to the press and start blabbing about
Archbishop Gerard personally intervening on our behalf to
save the treasures of the Abbey of St. Oswald, I'll squash
you.''

"And I'll help," added Matthew.

"Don't leave me out," said Olaf. "I've still got one
good foot."

"The lot o' ye are nae fun at all," complained Douglas.
"It would make such a lovely tale."

Preston was enjoying the altercation, but decided to add
some comments of his own: "I suspect it would make a
lovely mess of your future credibility as a scholar. Presti-
gious universities don't like having their names associated
with people who believe in ghosts."

That quieted Douglas faster than any threats of violence.
He still muttered, "Nae fun at all," under his breath, but
was a serious archaeologist despite his reckless ways.

"I have a question for you, Kenneth," said Jennet, who
was anxious to turn the discussion away from real or imaginary ghosts of Gerard. "We found those copies you painted
of the St. Oswald's miniatures. For a while, we had you and
Carleen at the top of our list of suspects. We assumed you
were making forgeries and she was taking them to London.
Your absence last night didn't help, either."

Kenneth looked both shocked and pleased at the same
time. "Jennet! Did you really suspect me? You mustn't
have looked at those paintings very closely. They're decent
copies, but terrible forgeries. It was the Professor's idea that
I make them."

Betsy Durrell suddenly sat up straighter. She glared at her
husband, who was complacently enjoying every moment.
"Edwin, if this is another plot of yours, I'll, I'll, well, I
don't know what I'll do, but it will be something good."

The elderly scholar patted her hand reassuringly. "I'm
innocent this time, my dear. I had Kenneth paint them from

the photographs, and I sent them to those art historians in Hexham.''

Jennet and Matthew and Olaf stared at each other. ''If you only knew,'' said Matthew, ''how much worry those pictures caused us!''

Jennet said, ''I think we suspected everybody at one point or another. Tracking down Lewis's mother and finding out that he actually had visited her added credibility to his side.''

''He said he took the treasure to Scotland on his last trip. I wonder what he did with it,'' Matthew mused.

''I can't resist that cue,'' said a voice from the doorway. All heads turned to see Inspector Dennistoun in the doorway. He looked more relaxed than they had ever seen him, but Jennet still had an uneasy feeling about him. She wondered if some of his teeth really were longer than the others.

''Sergeant Corbett suggested that we try the Staffords' hunting lodge in Scotland. I came over as soon as the officers reported the results of the search; they've recovered the treasure and it appears to be intact.''

This news resulted in such wild celebrating that Matron Yeatman rushed in and demanded silence. No one took any notice of her, not even the man in the fourth bed, who was cheering as loudly as any of the historians.

Inspector Dennistoun squeezed through the crowd to Dr. Durrell's bed. He shook the old man's hand and remarked to the group as a whole, ''I apologize for any inconveniences our investigation may have caused you. We're thankful it's all come to a successful resolution. We'll be getting back to you about the transfer of the goods later today.'' He nodded briskly and walked out.

Olaf folded his arms across his chest in annoyance. ''I like that! We did all the thinking, all the work, nearly got killed saving the box in the last niche, and *he's* thankful for the successful resolution just because they searched that hunting lodge.''

"Now, now," said Pete. "Weren't the police right outside the church this morning? They would have stopped Lewis in time. Give them some credit."

"Huh!" said Amy. "They were only there because Miles tipped them off."

Dr. Durrell thoughtfully pressed his fingers together. "We've all had so much to tell, I don't suppose any of you ever did get to open that last box, did you?" He sounded wistful.

Jennet reached down for the box on the floor. "No, Professor, we didn't open it. We thought you should have the honor." She placed the box on the bed.

Tears came to the professor's eyes. "You shouldn't have. This is most unprofessional. Oh my! Well, shall we peek at it, as long as you've brought it all this way? But then you must take it right over to the museum. Don't delay!"

The room fell silent as he opened the cardboard box and removed the casket. He carefully unlatched the hook and raised the lid. He burst out laughing.

"What is it? What is it?" thundered Preston, who was trapped behind the husky twins.

Dr. Durrell wiped his eyes with his bedsheet. "This really has been a most extraordinary dig. We've found those splendid treasures and that magnificent tapestry. What else could those frantic monks have packed away in those secret niches while awaiting the arrival of Henry VIII's brutal forces?" He turned the casket so the group could look inside. It contained grayish and yellowish cloths, most of which were in shreds.

"They packed their nicest priestly vestments, of course. Along with some sixteenth-century moths, I'm afraid."

The next few days were busy. The group was interviewed by both police and reporters; Miles, Olaf, and Dr. Durrell came home from the hospital; museum officials carefully installed the recovered St. Oswald's treasure in their vaults. Everyone was in resounding good spirits, though Jennet had the feeling that Matthew had something on his mind. Pete, on the other hand, had enough energy and enthusiasm for three men. He emerged from an evening's session with Mary-Lou Henley with his job and his confidence intact. He would say nothing about the confrontation except that Dr. Henley admitted doing "stupid things" in her own youth and that she was very understanding.

While Dr. Durrell recuperated at home, Jennet worked with Roger and Amy on the final excavation notes and with Dr. Preston on the tapestry team's proceedings. The Barclays were very anxious to do as much as possible to save the professor any extra work.

But what Jennet passionately wanted was to play with the pieces of the abbey chronicle concerning Gerard. Now, after the turmoil of the theft and its resolutions, the twelfth-century prelate occupied her mind in every spare moment. Unfortunately, due to the loss of Lewis and Leslie and the weakened condition of Dr. Durrell, there was more work than ever for Jennet. She resolved to make some time for her study of Gerard and stayed up late one night, poring over the chronicle, Hugh the Chanter, Hugh of Flavigny, and William of Malmesbury. Matthew and Olaf sat up with her. The big blonde was yawning, but he kept flipping the pages of a thick volume on medieval Icelandic settlements.

Matthew tapped his finger on the photographs of the panels in the York Tapestry depicting Gerard and Henry I. "Roger is right, Jennet. You've got a potential monograph here, or at least a decent-sized article. I don't suppose there's enough to build a dissertation around, though."

"I've had my dissertation topic planned for months, and not even St. Oswald could get me to change it. But I'm not denying that I could do something to reconcile those conflicting images of Gerard, the wily chancellor, the aged reformer, the lustful youth, the Hebraic scholar, the mysterious necromancer. Why couldn't he have been all those things? It's not impossible. So much of what we know is colored by our sources. Hugh of Flavigny hated England and all things in it, so he naturally wrote the most appalling account. Hugh the Chanter, the York canon, supported Gerard because he was his archbishop and therefore remained quiet about the rumors, yet even he had to report Gerard's sudden death and his subsequent burial. Then we have the St. Oswald chronicler, who praised his patron to the skies and most likely took part in his reburial beneath the abbey. It's fascinating.''

Matthew thumbed through Dr. Durrell's copy of Dobson's *The Jews of Medieval York* which Jennet had borrowed for information on Gerard's psalter. "A complex character, our Gerard. Worldly, scholarly, mysterious, religious, a chancellor and a prelate both. You'll have fun writing this up, Jennet. Let me know if there's anything I can do to help.''

"Keep Sammy off my back. He seems to think I'll have this thing done *and* my diss by the end of the summer. And if you can help me track down and translate Firmicus Maternus, I'd be eternally grateful. I don't know much about ancient astrology.''

"Sure.'' He rose, stretched, glanced at Olaf who continued reading placidly. Olaf's foot, encased in a plaster cast after corrective surgery, was propped on pillows. "I'm for bed,'' Matthew said.

"Good night,'' Jennet replied. "I'll be up soon, I expect.''

Olaf waved as Matthew left the room. Jennet continued working for another half hour. As soon as she piled her Xeroxes into a neat stack, Olaf tossed his book aside.

"I was afraid you'd be at that all night and that I'd fall

asleep," he said. "Would you mind going for a walk? I'd like to talk with you."

"A walk?" she said. "Are you sure? It's getting late, and you're on crutches. Couldn't we talk in here?"

"It's not the same. Too many folk about, even if they're all tucked in their beds. The atmosphere's not right. Take a sweater if you think you'll be cold, and don't fret over my crutches. I don't expect this to take long, one way or the other." His voice sounded odd on the last sentence.

Jennet wondered what he had in mind, but she wasn't particularly exhausted that evening, so she grabbed her sweater without complaining and accompanied Olaf into the cool night air. It was dark on the campus; the moon, which was nearly full, dominated the heavens. Jennet breathed deeply. She suddenly felt sorry for all the people who were in bed already; what a lovely night they were missing!

Olaf clumped along on his aluminum crutches. "Do you mind walking up the quad and back?"

"No, not at all. It's gorgeous out here."

Olaf began humming "Isn't It Romantic?" but stopped abruptly and didn't say a word until they reached the quad. He led the way to one of the benches; curiously, it was the same one she and Matthew rested on when the old watchman surprised them. That brought a grin to her face. Olaf noticed it.

"What are you smiling about?" he asked.

"Just happy, I guess," she answered: Olaf would be offended if she told him what she was really thinking about. She *was* feeling happy, though, so she wasn't hiding everything from him. "What did you want to talk about, Olaf?"

"You," he said quietly. "I can't get you out of my mind, Jennet, or my heart. Are you really in love with Matthew? I've got to know."

"Olaf—" she began.

"No, wait, don't answer that yet." He bent over and kissed her thoroughly. Now she understood why he didn't want to stay in the dorm. The moonlight and the night air gave an added wallop to a devastatingly passionate embrace. Jennet found herself abstractedly noticing two things: Olaf's mustache tickled and her pulse was pounding.

He withdrew and looked at her face. "Are you going to tell me you didn't enjoy that?"

"No. I'd be lying if I said that. I'm fond of you, Olaf, and you're a damned sexy man, but there's more to love than heavy breathing."

"I know that, I know that. I just had to try it." He engulfed her hand with one of his own. "I can't tell you how I truly feel, Jennet, short of stealing words from Porter and Gershwin and Hammerstein. Are you sure of how you feel for Matthew?"

"As sure as I can be about anything. It's not earthshaking, my relationship with Matthew, and that's what makes it different from any I've ever had before. We fit together comfortably. Our goals and interests and backgrounds mesh. What we have is solid. It might not sound exciting or be the kind of thing you could write songs about, but it feels right." She didn't have the heart to tell Olaf that one of the things that made him attractive to her—his blatant romanticism—was the principal difference between him and Matthew. Singing corny songs could add spice to certain occasions, such as moonlit nights, but living your life by them was too much. Jennet knew Matthew's practical nature wasn't as well-ingrained as her own. He could be flighty and quirky at times. She also knew, however, that their principles matched at heart. She hoped Olaf found stability some day, or met someone who would either instill it in him or love him without it.

"What if I asked you to marry me?" He interrupted her reverie.

"Marry you?" she echoed. "Olaf, I haven't even talked about marriage with Matthew yet! I guess we'll see what happens once we get back to the States. It's possible, but we have to talk more. I'm afraid Matthew is more reticent than you are."

"All right," he said sadly. "I told you this wouldn't take long, one way or the other. Let's head back to the dorm. But I'm warning you—if I don't get an announcement within six months, I'm flying out to California to try again."

"I hope that won't be necessary," she said, taking his hand. "You're a good friend, Olaf, and I don't want to lose that. I won't forget you."

He sucked in his breath. "I know I won't forget you."

The following morning, Jennet came downstairs to breakfast to find everyone there except Olaf. She sat next to Matthew, who was eating an enormous pile of salami and eggs. Pete sat on the kitchen counter, legs swinging, watching Matthew unconcernedly eat. Pete wasn't the only one acting strangely. When Jennet entered the kitchen, Douglas began hovering around her, asking her how she was, did she sleep well, and a host of other polite inquiries. Then he began messing with her breakfast.

"Are you sure ye wouldna like some sugar for that grapefruit? They can be deadly sour sometimes, bitter as a broken heart." He shoved the sugar bowl at her.

"No, thank you, Douglas. I like them plain."

"Some honey for your tea, my sweet? Honey as sweet as you, as sweet as a woman in love?"

She grabbed the newspaper from Kenneth. "Douglas, go away. I can fix my own breakfast."

"Aye, she can fix her own. But whose breakfast will she be fixing in future?" Douglas's eyes twinkled, and Jennet began to suspect that Olaf had done some talking before his chat with her last night. Pete kept watching like a spectator at a tennis match, glancing from Douglas to Matthew and back again. Dr. Preston crackled his newspaper imperiously and disappeared behind it in an effort to tune out the boisterous Scot.

"Shut up, Douglas," snapped Amy, who was investigating how awful decaffeinated tea could be. "I'm not in the mood for your games this morning, and I bet nobody else is, either."

"But soft! Here comes the conquering hero!" Douglas threw the kitchen door open for Olaf, whose clanking crutches could be heard at some distance. "Well, laddie, how did it go? Or shall I guess for ye?"

Olaf looked glum but not heart-broken. He glared nastily at Douglas. "What do you think? She turned me down."

Douglas clasped his heart theatrically. "Och, puir boy! What a hard-hearted woman! First she spurns me, then you! Ah, Matthew, ye'd best beware her clutches!"

Matthew grunted noncommittally and sipped his cola. Preston peeked around his paper, curiosity aroused. Jennet made a rude face at Douglas. She didn't appreciate his dragging into the open what she thought was a private matter. But then, that was Douglas's nature. She hoped neither Olaf or Matthew would be offended.

"Wait, wait," said Carleen. "Is something going on that I've missed?"

"I'll explain it to ye, seeing as you're practically one of the family," said Douglas, affectionately patting her hand. "Olaf here has asked Jennet to marry him, and she's said nay. She doesna want me, either, so that leaves Matt here."

Pete began chuckling from his perch on the counter. Matthew calmly finished his eggs and seemed to ignore the boisterous dialogue around him. He put the dirty dish in the sink.

"This is turning out to be quite an interesting morning!" Pete declared. "Especially in the light of what Matthew discussed with me last night. You said you might need prompting—shall I help?''

"No, thanks," said Matthew. "I can do it myself." He sat back down next to Jennet. "I don't admit to having any great flair with words, Jennet, but I've been meaning to ask you something as soon as all the problems at St. Oswald's were solved.''

Jennet realized this was not the time to get squirted with grapefruit juice. She pushed the bowl aside, tried to ignore the multitude in the room who were hanging on every word, then figured, so what? They were her friends.

"What is it?" She was glad her voice didn't squeak.

"Will you marry me?" He looked as casual as ever, sitting on the vinyl-covered chair, elbows resting on the greasy kitchen table. But his eyes were extraordinarily bright. Funny, she'd never noticed just how beautiful they were before.

It was strange to hear the same words from Matthew's lips that Olaf had uttered less than twelve hours ago. Yet Olaf's proposal, given under a starry sky and following a breathless kiss, didn't shake her insides to Jell-O the way Matthew's did, given in the presence of nine other people in a kitchen with dirty linoleum.

She realized everyone was waiting for her to answer.

"Sure," she gulped. The word sounded funny, but the feeling was oh-so-right.

The Barclays cheered, as did Miles and Kenneth and Carleen. Pete kept crowing, "I knew ya could do it!" and Dr. Preston began rummaging in the refrigerator for leftover champagne from the party. Unfortunately, they had drunk it all celebrating the return of the treasure.

Jennet hardly had eyes for anyone or anything but Matthew (as he did for her), but she was sensitive enough to know this must be very painful for Olaf. Yet when she looked over at the big Orcadian, he was trading jibes with Douglas again, as always.

"Well, Dougie, Roger has Amy, your brother has Carleen, Matthew has Jennet, but it's not a total loss."

"Oh, and how might that be, Olaf? She turned down a penniless Scot and a filthy rich Orcadian, but accepted the middle-class American. We lost, my friend, in case ye hadna noticed."

Olaf clapped Douglas on the back. "We've still got each other, sweetheart."

Jennet, however, was not paying attention to them any longer. She was discovering that one doesn't need moonlit nights for certain breathless encounters.

About the Author

Laura Frankos is a California native who has lived in the Los Angeles area for over twenty years. She attended UCLA, where she majored in history. She began by concentrating in medieval English history but eventually wound up passing her Ph.D. exam in Roman history in 1983. Her dissertation has been put on hold by the subsequent arrival of three daughters and by the writing of this novel, which she found more fun and profitable than researching fourth-century Imperial policy. Her hobbies include reading, music, chasing after small children, playing simulation baseball and following the Angels, UCLA Bruins, 49ers and Lakers. She is happily married to science-fiction writer Harry Turtledove; their children are Alison, Rachel, and Rebecca. She is now at work on another novel.